D1483066

Delta-v

Delta-v

DANIEL SUAREZ

DUTTON

DUTTON

An imprint of Penguin Random House LLC
penguinrandomhouse.com

Copyright © 2019 by Daniel Suarez

LIBRARY OF CONGRESS CATALOGING-IN-PUBLICATION DATA
Names: Suarez, Daniel, 1964– author.
Title: Delta-v / Daniel Suarez.
Description: New York: Dutton, an imprint of Penguin Random House LLC, [2019]
Identifiers: LCCN 2018045342| ISBN 9781524742416 (hardback) |
ISBN 9781524742423 (ebook)
Subjects: | BISAC: FICTION / Technological. | FICTION / Science Fiction /
Adventure. | GSAFD: Science fiction.
Classification: LCC PS3619.U327 D45 2019 | DDC 813/.6—dc23
LC record available at https://lccn.loc.gov/2018045342

Printed in the United States of America
10 9 8 7 6 5 4 3 2 1

In memory of Carl Sagan

You can't cross a chasm in two small jumps.

—David Lloyd George

Delta-v

Prologue

James Tighe exploded from the surface of a cave pool and gasped for air as he yanked off his rebreather mask. For several moments he alternated between coughs and deep breaths while his helmet-mounted LED lights illuminated the silted water around him. Beyond this island of light lay endless darkness.

As the confusion and hammering heartbeat of his hypoxia receded, daggers of decompression sickness stabbed into Tighe's joints.

But the pain kept him conscious.

He'd been forced to shortcut several decompression stops from lack of air and waited several moments until it became clear he was going to survive. Still wincing from joint pain, he finally looked up to examine his surroundings.

The helmet lights shined on a sheer brown limestone wall a few meters ahead. Behind, he heard distant, echoing shouts—then screams. Tighe turned to illuminate a rocky shoreline 10 meters away. It looked different from when he'd departed eight hours earlier. Clouds of dust lingered in the air, and newly fragmented limestone boulders the size of houses were strewn across the upward-sloping cavern floor beyond.

The sheer scale of the Gebiya Chamber was difficult to grasp. Nearly a kilometer long, its arched ceiling was lost in darkness 200 meters overhead. If it weren't for the lack of starlight, Tighe could almost convince himself he was outside, instead of deep underground in one of the largest limestone caverns in the world.

On the distant upslope he spotted several tiny lights gathered roughly where Camp 3 had been. The terrain had changed. Another, brighter light suddenly appeared, closer at hand, as it scrambled over boulders, heading toward him.

Tighe shouted. "Chris!" His voice echoed. "Chris, are you here?"

The bobbing light answered, "Here, J.T.!"

Tighe finned toward the shore. As he crawled through the shallows, Danish cave diver Christen Lykke waded in and extended a gloved hand to help Tighe up onto the rocky ledge. They both wore dry suits and rebreather packs.

Tighe could see the stone bank was wet for several meters upslope. Waves had evidently lashed the shoreline. He removed his fins and stood in his dive boots. "How bad is it?"

Lykke looked stricken. "The camp's buried. Sam is trapped, and four others missing. The aftershocks keep coming."

Another agonized scream sounded in the distance.

"I don't think Sam's going to make it. Most of our medical supplies were lost." Lykke stared at the water. "Where is Richard?"

Tighe turned to face the pool as well. He struggled to keep his composure. "Richard's gone."

Lykke knelt and ran his hands through his hair, grappling with his own emotions. "I tried to reach you." He looked up. "My reserve bottles were buried, J.T. I couldn't descend—"

Tighe gripped Lykke's shoulder and knelt beside him. "There was nothing you could have done, Chris. Nothing." Tighe turned toward the sound of distant screams. "Let's focus on helping the others."

Lykke nodded grimly.

Tighe moved upslope in the boulder field. "Where's Yuen?"

Lykke followed. "Searching for survivors."

A moment later, Tighe rounded a massive boulder to find Chang Fu Yuen, the expedition leader, clawing at rock fragments. Chang's muddy orange caving suit and white helmet were spattered with blood. He looked up at Tighe. "Help me with this!"

Tighe and Lykke started removing stones.

Tighe asked, "Who are we digging for?"

"Pell and Nakamura. They were filming somewhere down here."

"Have you heard them?"

Chang shook his head.

Tighe examined the rock field. "If they're under this, they're probably dead, Yu."

"They could be in a gap."

"Are you certain you saw them here?"

Chang stopped, then looked around, apparently unsure. The area of the collapse was vast. As they stood there, occasional rocks fell from the darkness above and tumbled downhill.

"Have you made contact with the surface yet?"

Chang shook his head again. "The phone line is cut."

"We need to reestablish communications with base camp. How many survivors are there at Camp 3?"

Chang was pacing around, examining the now-unfamiliar ground. "Pell was standing right—"

Tighe gripped Chang by the shoulders. "How many survivors do we have at Camp 3?"

Lykke answered for him. "Six. Seven with Sam."

"There's too much rockfall here." Tighe turned toward the distant lights. "We need to evacuate the rest of the expedition back to Camp 2. The phone link to the surface might still be intact there."

Chang said, "We can't leave. Cobbett is trapped."

Lykke said blankly, "He will not survive."

Chang glared. "You are not a doctor, Christen."

"Half his body is crushed. You don't have to be a doctor to—"

Tighe stepped between them but spoke to Chang. "You and I can stay with Sam. Everyone else should retreat."

Chang started clawing at the rocks again. "We stay together."

"Look around you." Tighe stared up into the darkness. "These karst chambers are inherently unstable. If this ceiling comes down the entire team will be buried."

Suddenly a rumbling sound deeper than he could hear reverberated in Tighe's chest.

Lykke dropped to his knees and pressed against the face of the nearby boulder. "Aftershock!"

Distant screams echoed as Chang and Tighe took cover alongside Lykke. Suddenly the solid rock all around Tighe began to undulate and shift violently, cracking as it did so. A nearby *boom* stunned Tighe, and the stone floor tossed him a meter in the air. He landed hard as dozens of boulders and rocks hurtled over and past his headlamps, bounding down into the cave pool, where they impacted the sloshing water, hurling 10-ton waves against the far wall.

The tremor dwindled and finally stopped. Huge rocks continued to rain down for several moments afterward, the earsplitting *boom* of their impacts followed by scores of secondary impacts.

Tighe got to his feet and grabbed Chang, pulling him upslope. "You need to order the others to safety."

Lykke followed.

Chang looked back to where Pell and Nakamura had disappeared.

"They're gone! Help the survivors."

The sound of rushing water rose within the massive chamber, echoing against distant walls. All three of them halted, listening. The sound suddenly swelled to a roar emanating from the upper end of the chamber.

Lykke staggered back, a look of horror on his face. "The river."

Tighe said, "It's changed course."

Chang shouted over the increasing roar of water. "We cannot head back now!"

"But we can't stay either!"

Lykke looked to them both. "What do we do?"

Tighe continued toward the lights. "We free Sam, take what supplies we can, and then we climb."

Chang grabbed Tighe's shoulder. "Climb where?"

Tighe pointed up. "There are half a dozen unexplored passages in the ceiling—tributaries of the original riverbed. One of them could lead us back toward the entrance."

"If we do that, the rescue party will not know where to search for us."

"No one can mount a rescue under these conditions. We need to rescue ourselves." Tighe switched off his headlamps. "Conserve batteries. Every other person goes dark. We'll need every minute of light to find a new route back."

Chang stared.

"Lead us, Yu."

After a moment Chang nodded and moved toward the lights. "Follow me."

CHAPTER 1

Baliceaux

ONE MONTH LATER—NOVEMBER 6, 2032

James Tighe moved through a crowd of well-dressed party guests, following a path lit by tiki torches. Uniformed servants patrolled with trays of crab and caviar on brioche or pickled oysters with cucumber.

Attractive people stood chatting all around him, drinks in hand, laughing. Tighe was older by a decade at least. Across the cove more people danced to algorave music beneath a moonlit Caribbean sky someone thought was improved by laser lights. The acrid aroma of sativa wafted past. Black dresses with spaghetti straps; tailored jackets with dress shirts; handmade chronometers on every man's wrist. Tighe felt like an alien.

Snatches of conversations came to him as he passed.

"Tarantula cheese."

"How on Earth do they make it?"

"Founded a blockchain nonprofit."

"What's their exit plan?"

A beautiful young woman exhaled from a jeweled vape pen and eyed him as he walked past.

Tighe's good looks had always eased his way. Blessed with a gymnast's physique and boyish charm, he'd been able to avoid the more serious consequences of his bad life choices. And tonight, clothed in a bespoke jacket, slacks, and dress shirt, he projected an image of casual wealth.

Which was a lie, of course.

Thirty-seven years old, and Tighe didn't own a respectable outfit. This one had been tailored for him on his arrival to the island. The jacket draped perfectly off his shoulders. The shirt fabric was soft as liquid.

In this disguise Tighe surveyed the social terrain. Several hundred guests of various ethnicities, with straight white teeth, clear complexions, and the laid-back stance of people whose futures were assured.

They seemed to accept him as one of their own. Other guests nodded in recognition as he passed.

A man tapped his arm. "Are you James Teeg?"

Tighe nodded. "It's pronounced 'Tie.' Call me J.T."

Another man shook his hand. "J.T.! Brilliant, mate!"

A pat on the back. "Well done, Yank."

A Gen Alpha woman in a formfitting minidress shouted, "Oh! My! God!" She produced a phone quicker than a gunslinger. In moments she was doing a duck face next to him as her phone flashed a selfie. Smile gone for a quick inspection. "One more." An instant laugh and this time a raised eyebrow and quizzical smile next to his nonplussed face. *Flash.* "Got it." She walked off without another word, head down and thumbing her screen.

Tighe recalled the Kayapo tribesmen of Brazil. They hated to be photographed. He felt a sudden kinship with them as he feared for his social media soul—then remembered he didn't have one.

Somebody pressed a cold Red Stripe into Tighe's hand. "Cheers, mate!"

Nearby guests all raised their glasses and beer bottles. One of them was an actor Tighe recognized from American television. The path ahead was filled with fashion models, entrepreneurs, artists, and pundits. And here Tighe was among them, soaking up his fifteen minutes of Internet fame. Brought in from the edge, he felt more like an outsider than ever before.

Just then a hissing sound rose, drowning out the dance music. A shout went up from the crowd. Fingers pointed skyward. The hiss soon resolved into a whoosh of jet motors.

Tighe followed the collective gaze upward to see a lone figure on high, backlit by whirling laser lights—a rider on a jet board carving through the night sky. The noise grew deafening as the pilot controlled the craft like a surfer, banking and arcing above the center of the party. Jet wash tangled palm fronds and kicked up skirts as the audience roared approval. The helmeted rider in a white jumpsuit passed above them, arms held up in triumph, urging their applause—his outfit emblazoned with a stylized logo of the name "Joyce" down its entire length.

The crowd went mad, cheering as the rider sailed off northward, the jet roar receding toward the Great House on the far side of the island. The algorave dance music returned along with excited chatter.

A woman nearby: "Holy shit! Was that really Nathan?"

"Look . . ." A man held up his phone to show proof of what they'd all just seen.

Nathan Joyce. Their billionaire host.

Tighe felt relieved to no longer be a focus of attention. Instead people around him breathlessly recounted what had just happened—playing phone video to one another of Joyce's overflight.

"Send me that!"

"I'm uploading it."

Why am I here? That was the question that kept repeating in Tighe's head. Nathan Joyce's invitation hadn't said much.

"Mr. Tighe?"

Tighe turned to see a dignified Filipino man in a white jacket and black tie—who had pronounced his last name correctly. Tighe nodded.

"Mr. Joyce has just arrived from Mustique, sir, and wishes a word with you in private, if it's convenient."

Convenient? That was funny. Tighe had been flown halfway around the world to be here. Convenience had nothing to do with it. "Sure."

"Follow me, please."

Tighe put his beer down and fell in behind the butler as they made their way through the party crowd. Before long the two of them boarded a waiting autonomous golf cart that promptly whirred down the island's main path— headed toward the Great House half a mile away.

All Tighe knew about Nathan Joyce was what the Internet told him—lots of manicured fluff pieces rising to the top of the SEO stack with the actual news buried sixteen pages deep. Admired and despised in equal measure, often by the same people, Joyce preached the gospel of risk—and his faith was ascendant worldwide.

Joyce had risen from middle-class obscurity to become a billionaire at a young age, first in cryptocurrencies and then when one after another of his tech startups (none of which Tighe had heard of or understood) were bought out by tech giants.

Now in his late thirties, Joyce had controlling interests in dozens of closely held enterprises in new media, real estate, biotech, aerospace, and renewable energy. He often made headlines by announcing grandiose, impractical business schemes. It was hard to pin down Joyce's net worth, but estimates ranged from a few into the tens of billions of dollars.

Baliceaux Island shed some light on Joyce's modus operandi. For centuries this place had been an undeveloped 320-acre speck in the Grenadines. Its rugged topography made development too costly for resorts and vacation buyers, but Joyce saw what others did not: the elevation necessary to cope with the rising seas of climate change.

Now with beachfront celebrity mansions up in the Exumas routinely flooding, Baliceaux had gone on to become one of the most valuable private residences on Earth. Even if the sea rose 5 meters, the party would still go on here.

The autonomous golf cart rolled to a stop beneath a grass-roof portico at the entrance to the Great House.

The Filipino butler dismounted. "This way, please."

He led Tighe through a carven wood doorway, past dour, suited security men. The décor was rustic tropical, the rooms chilled and dehumidified into a climate approximating summer in Norway. It was surprisingly serene inside, given the enormous open-air discothèque not far off.

After guiding Tighe down the main hallway, the butler opened twin doors and ushered him into a sprawling, well-appointed study filled with mementos and antiques from around the world—scrimshaw, sextants, a large brass telescope on a pedestal, models of sailing ships, racing aircraft, rockets, framed ancient maps, and shelf after shelf of books.

It would have been a soothing refuge, except for the presence of a 120-inch, 8K flat-screen television on the wall above the fireplace—on which Tighe's dirt-smeared face appeared in crystal-clear video, larger than life, filmed in POV from someone else's helmet-cam.

A lone figure sat on the sofa watching the video. Even from behind, Tighe recognized the tousled brown hair and broad shoulders of Nathan Joyce, still wearing his white flight suit.

The study doors closed behind Tighe.

On-screen Tighe shouted into the camera, *"We can't stay here!"* The bass rumble of cracking rock shook the study with the aid of impressive speakers.

A man shouted off camera. The helmet-cam turned to look—revealing a caver in an orange trog suit and light-bedecked helmet, clinging to a rock wall as it broke apart around him. A rope trailed from the man's harness back along the rock face.

A voice. *"Let go, John! The roof is collapsing! Let go!"*

Nearby, Tighe unclipped his own rope line and then without hesitation leaped across the gap, over darkness, and grabbed the other caver—pulling him roughly from the rock face, even though the man didn't want to let go. Moments after they swung back on the rope line, the entire cliff face and a large section of the ceiling fell away with a deafening roar. The camera captured Tighe and the caver clinging to each other, a human pendulum swinging over the void.

Tighe clipped in to the caver's harness and then looked up at the camera. *"Bring us up, Lars."*

The image froze.

The counter on the bottom right of the screen indicated the video had more than thirty-two million views.

Joyce spoke without turning. "Hell of a risk to take, to save a man you barely knew."

Tighe shifted uncomfortably. "He was carrying batteries we needed."

Joyce paused a moment to process this. "I see." He stood and turned to face Tighe. "You were trapped in the Tian Xing cave system for four days after the quake."

Tighe remained silent as Joyce walked around the sofa to meet him.

"Four days. Ropes and communications cut. Carrying wounded, few supplies, constant aftershocks, collapsed passages, flooding. No immediate hope of rescue."

Tighe still said nothing.

"Yet you brought ten out of sixteen to the surface alive—and you weren't even the expedition lead."

"I didn't have a choice."

"Oh, I disagree. You made nothing *but* choices—life-and-death choices under intense constraints." Joyce studied Tighe. "This is the only clip that's made it to the Internet, but there's over two hundred hours more from the expedition helmet-cams. I've watched every minute."

Tighe narrowed his eyes. Had Joyce really gotten hold of the expedition video? Not even Tighe had seen it.

"Organizational psychologists will be studying the footage for years. You could make a solid career on the team dynamics speaking circuit."

"Is *that* why you invited me here?"

Joyce laughed again. "God no. What a waste that would be." He extended his hand. "I'm Nathan Joyce."

Tighe paused, then shook his host's hand. "Everyone calls me J.T."

"J.T." Joyce was tall and lean, with an intense gaze as he gripped Tighe's hand firmly. A smile in the corner of his eyes. "Thanks for coming all this way. I think you'll be interested in what we're up to."

Tighe heard a chair creak in the corner and suddenly noticed another man seated at a round table there—South Asian, in his sixties, with a trim gray beard and expensive-looking glasses. The man wore a jacket with slacks but was nowhere near as fashionable as the poolside party guests.

"This is Nobel Prize–winning economist Sankar Korrapati. Sankar, this is J.T., the cave diver I was telling you about."

The academic approached and vigorously shook Tighe's hand.

Tighe felt out of his league. "I don't know anything about economics, but it's an honor."

"Mr. Tighe. The honor is mine. You are most daring."

There was no reasonable reply to that so Tighe simply nodded.

Joyce offered the sofa. "Have a seat. Can we get you anything to drink?"

"No. I'm fine, thanks." Tighe sat warily. Something was up. He just didn't know what.

The professor retrieved a small remote from a nearby credenza and clicked it. The TV winked off and instead a hologram glowed into existence above the coffee table. It consisted of 3D words in bold white letters:

What is money?

Tighe was momentarily startled. He'd never seen an open-air holographic display in person.

Joyce noticed his reaction. "Pretty cool, eh? *Software-defined light.* I was an angel investor in the firm that pioneered it."

Tighe gazed at the words: *What is money?* Their meaning started to sink in. He couldn't help but think this looked like the beginning of the world's most elaborate time-share pitch. "Mr. Joyce—"

"Nathan, please."

"Uh, Nathan, I appreciate the invitation—"

"But why are you here? I'll explain, but first, I'd like you to listen to a talk Sankar has been delivering in certain circles." On Tighe's attempt to speak he added, "Indulge me." Joyce turned to the professor. "Doctor, if you will."

"Of course." Korrapati moved alongside the glowing hologram and stared intently. "Can you tell me from where money comes, Mr. Tighe?"

Tighe looked from the professor to Joyce and back again. Apparently they were doing this. "I . . . I guess it comes from a mint."

"To be clear: by 'money,' I do not mean the physical instruments—the paper and the coins—but the unit of value that money represents. How does a given unit of money come into existence?"

Tighe was about to answer when he realized with surprise that he did not know.

"Do not be embarrassed. Many MBAs do not know either."

The holographic words morphed into a US one-dollar bill.

"The reality is that only 5 percent of all money is created by governments in the form of cash in circulation."

The holographic dollar shrank to a minuscule size against a backdrop of scrolling database records.

"The remaining 95 percent of money is created by commercial banks whenever they extend credit to a borrower."

Tighe looked at Joyce quizzically. Joyce nodded for him to pay attention.

The hologram now transformed into a house with a "Sold" sign on the front lawn.

"For example, when a new mortgage is originated, that money does not come out of a bank vault. Instead, the money is *created* as a result of the loan. The bank supplies it to the borrower as a bank credit, with the borrower promising to repay the principal plus interest at a future date. This new debt is registered with a federal reserve or a central bank to the commercial bank's account, allowing it to now loan out more money based on a multiple of that new loan—usually at a ratio of ten or more to one. So the more money the bank lends, the more it has *available* to lend."

Tighe frowned. "Hold on. How can that be?"

"Because in the modern world money does not represent value, Mr. Tighe—money represents *debt*. And the more debt that is created in the world, the more money there is."

Tighe looked again at Joyce.

Joyce gestured for Korrapati to continue.

"To be clear, it is very important that banks get back this virtual money they loan out—and with interest—or the bank will become insolvent. However, as long as loans keep getting repaid, a bank can continue creating new money in the form of credit."

The hologram now depicted a bar graph with the arrow traveling rightward and ever upward.

"And so it continues, with new money being created all the time as more and more people, companies, and state and local governments borrow. But this system has a weakness . . ."

Another line appeared on the graph. It was labeled *Payments Due* and began well above and not far behind the rising debt line—chasing it uphill.

"Banks lend only the *principal*. However, loans must be repaid *plus interest*—and with long-term loans like mortgages, the total interest payments far exceed the principal itself. Unless the overall money supply keeps growing, there will never be enough money to pay back all the loans plus interest.

"This is why we see 'growth' as the central mantra of finance. Why consumers are urged to ever-greater consumption, why prices continue to rise—because new debt must feed ever-growing interest requirements.

"Most shocking to the layman is the fact that repaying debt *destroys* money. If most debts were paid off, far from helping the economy, it would increasingly paralyze it. No debt would mean there was no money."

The hologram morphed into a line of people in tattered clothes waiting before a soup kitchen.

"Recall the Great Depression, Mr. Tighe. Between 1929 and 1933 the overall US money supply was reduced by nearly a third. As bad loans were written off, there was less money overall to meet interest obligations, resulting in a cascade of failure."

The hologram now dissolved to show cartoon bank buildings toppling like dominoes.

"The Great Depression wasn't a case of too much debt. It was a case of too *little* debt."

Tighe raised his eyebrows, bewildered.

The virtual graph returned as the debt line resumed its upward trajectory.

"Debt powers modern economies, which is why it is constantly growing. The greater the debt, the larger the money supply, the more economic activity—but also the more interest that needs to be repaid to keep the system running."

Korrapati looked grim. "So at the very time that climate change threatens to destroy human civilization, our economic system compels us to pursue ever-greater business growth—which will eventually become impossible."

The holographic line of repayments finally overtook the debt line—and suddenly both lines plunged straight down.

"My financial model predicts that on its present course this unsustainable debt bubble will pop within the next decade, collapsing the entire global economy—with the potential for world conflict, mass starvation, and possibly the end of modern civilization as we know it."

Tighe was speechless.

"However, there *is* a place where near-infinite expansion can occur—is, in fact, *already* occurring. Where our current debt-based financial system can expand for millions of years uninterrupted." Korrapati pointed upward. "Space."

Korrapati clicked on the remote, and the holographic display dissolved.

"Commercial exploitation of our solar system can expand the human economy beyond Earth to address the accumulated debt in our economic system, massively increasing the total amount of raw materials and energy without increasing carbon emissions or hastening climate change. It is the only sure way to avoid imminent, global economic collapse."

Tighe sat numbly for several moments, but then he looked up at an expectant Korrapati. "Let me get this straight: you're saying humanity must expand into space—not for the sake of science or exploration, but to stop the banks from going broke?"

"To preserve civilization."

"Wouldn't it be easier to just redesign money?"

"Redesigning the financial system is more challenging than you might think—especially with winners in the current economic system prepared to use all their power to preserve the status quo. And cryptocurrencies have their own energy- and climate change–related drawbacks."

Joyce cleared his throat.

Tighe turned to look at the billionaire.

"I have two words for you, J.T.: *asteroid mining.*"

"Asteroid mining."

"I've examined Dr. Korrapati's financial model. So have my fellow investors. We're convinced that unless something changes, our portfolios could be worthless within a decade."

"Look, I'm not sure why you brought me here, but I think there's been some sort of mistake." Tighe stood. "I'm not an investor."

"There was no mistake, J.T. I've launched an asteroid-mining company, and we're looking to crew our first manned expedition. I'd like you to sign on."

Tighe slowly sat back down.

"Asteroid mining will be a dangerous business. A job for the adventurous." Joyce gestured to the television screen. "I've seen what you're capable of. We'll pay all training expenses, and there's a signing bonus—yours to keep even if you don't make the final cut."

"You're sending people to mine asteroids?"

"Yes."

"*In space.*"

"Correct."

"Aren't there already companies doing that with robots?"

"There are several in the preparation stages. Their tech is still unproven. We think that, despite the significant added costs, sending humans along with robots will give us a competitive edge—chiefly, the ability to iterate new designs on-site to accelerate innovation. As Dr. Korrapati demonstrated, time is a factor."

Tighe pondered this. "Right. I see a couple problems . . ." Tighe peeled them off on his fingers: "One, I know nothing about asteroids, and two, I know nothing about mining."

"I'm aware of that. This new industry is so speculative nobody's sure how difficult it's going to be. We have some idea, of course, but there are likely to be many surprises. For that reason, the primary qualification for our crews will be the ability to think creatively during a crisis—something you have amply demonstrated."

Tighe pointed at the dark television screen. "You think I wasn't afraid back in Tian Xing? I was scared shitless."

"But you remained focused and took effective action. We want people who thrive on the unexpected."

Tighe laughed ruefully. "People 'who thrive on the unexpected'? I can barely cope with the *expected*. You'll find that out soon enough. Look, my personal life is a mess. I wouldn't pass a *credit check* much less a psych test. I'm not what you'd call a responsible person."

Joyce studied Tighe. "I don't want responsible people—I want *reliable* people."

"What on Earth makes you think I'm reliable?"

"Because every caver we spoke with says they'd trust their life to you."

Tighe was surprised Joyce had done so much research on him.

"It's a sad fact that some individuals don't function well in everyday life but *excel* under extreme circumstances. I think you're one of those individuals."

Tighe began to shake his head, until he thought more about it.

Joyce persisted: " 'Responsible' people avoid unnecessary risks, but you regularly risk your life just to go someplace no one ever has. If you were a *responsible* person, J.T., we wouldn't be talking. But then, if I was a responsible person, I wouldn't be rich."

Tighe met Joyce's intense gaze.

"Why do you do it?"

"Do what?"

"Cave diving is one of the most dangerous activities there is. It requires courage, technical skill, intelligence, physical endurance. Yet you do it at your own financial expense and beyond hope of rescue. Why?"

Described like that it sounded crazy even to Tighe. "It's hard to explain."

"Try me."

Tighe searched for words. "When I dive an unexplored cave, it's not a thrill. It's almost the opposite. I feel *in focus*. It's a heightened reality—like how you might feel if a tiger walked into this room right now; you'd be 100 percent in the present. The past and the future would cease to exist."

Joyce considered Tighe's words. "The Buddhist monks in Kopan call that *mindfulness*—a meditative practice that's difficult even for the enlightened to achieve."

"My good friend Richard Oberhaus, he said cave diving stripped away the impedimenta of life. Maybe that's the same thing as meditation. I wouldn't know."

"The 'impedimenta of life.' I like that." Joyce nodded appreciatively. "Well, if it's 'heightened reality' you seek, I can deliver like no one else—and for what it's worth, I can also pay you, not to mention providing a workplace with one hell of a view. . . ." With that, Joyce made a gesture, and a brilliant hologram of the Milky Way expanded in midair between them.

The lights dimmed, making the stars more vibrant.

The entire Milky Way glowed before Tighe, as though he was already floating out in space. Across from him stood the man who wanted to send him there.

However, Tighe wasn't going to let himself be distracted by high-tech parlor tricks. "You really think humans make sense for asteroid mining?"

"If humanity is ever going to become a spacefaring species, we actually need to *go* to space—and not just to visit. That means establishing commerce there. Robots will help us, but they're not the end goal. We need to expand human *presence* in our solar system—that's the only way we get exponential growth."

Tighe considered this. "Why start with asteroids? Why not the Moon?"

"Geopolitical and legal complications. Think about it: the Moon is heralded throughout history in human culture—in song, in poetry, in literature. No one is going to have an easy time setting up a mining industry on its surface. My advisers think it's going to require years of legal wrangling before commercial Moon mining can profitably commence."

Joyce dissolved the galaxy hologram with a wave of his hand. "Plus, certain near-Earth asteroids contain hundreds of millions of tons of water, iron, nitrogen, and ammonia. And can be reached with *less* energy than it takes to reach our own Moon. More to the point: some of those same asteroids present a deadly threat to humanity should they ever strike the Earth. Which means no one's likely to sue to preserve them."

"So you bring their resources where?"

"Most of the value of asteroid resources is in their trajectory—above Earth's gravity well, and that's where they should remain. It's there, in cislunar space, that I plan to establish orbiting power-generation facilities, carbon-intensive industry, and an off-world commodity exchange—the beginning of an entire cislunar economy that could usher in the near-infinite growth that Dr. Korrapati described, even while alleviating climate change."

Tighe looked around to realize that Dr. Korrapati had at some point discreetly made his exit. They were now alone.

"Mined resources could be returned from near-Earth asteroids to a lunar distant retrograde orbit at a *lower* delta-v than it would take to lift the same mass from our own Moon's surface."

Tighe interjected. "Delta-v? I don't know what that is."

"The Greek letter *delta* is a standard notation in mathematics for a change in value. Delta-v describes a change in velocity. All celestial objects are in motion—which means you either need to accelerate or decelerate to reach them. The higher the delta-v, the greater the energy—and the greater the expense. When it comes to commerce in space, J.T., delta-v means the difference between profitability and loss. In other words: delta-v means *everything*."

Tighe could scarcely believe he was beginning to consider this offer. "Mr. Joyce—"

"Nathan."

"Nathan, it took me *years* to learn how to dive caves down to 200 meters. I don't know *anything* about space—my lack of knowledge could get other people killed."

Joyce moved close to Tighe. "Our crews will be thoroughly trained. Your technical expertise in breathing mixtures and atmospheric pressure puts you ahead of most candidates—even ahead of many of the ex-astronauts."

Tighe tried to think of more objections. Going into space had never even occurred to him—it was a child's daydream. But the earthquake in Tian Xing had shaken apart every other aspect of his life. Why not his future, too? And yet, he suspected it was only a matter of time until they discovered he was not all they thought him to be.

Or what Richard Oberhaus believed Tighe to be.

After several more moments Tighe looked up. "You mentioned a signing bonus."

"Twenty-five thousand US dollars—assuming you pass a basic physical. The money is yours to keep even if you don't graduate from the training program. We pay all travel and lodging expenses."

"How long is the training program?"

"Initial candidate selection lasts ninety days. Those selected will begin six months of rigorous training, followed by two weeks' training in low Earth orbit. If I'm not mistaken, you have no expeditions lined up at the moment."

Low Earth orbit. Tighe pondered other questions. "And if I change my mind?"

"You can keep the signing bonus. I consider it a cheap form of insurance against poor candidates. Better—and less costly—to discover them here on Earth." Joyce sat on the arm of the sofa. "So what do you say, J.T.? If you're really an explorer, this is the ultimate expedition."

Tighe looked toward the darkened television screen. "The helmet-cam video from Tian Xing—I'd like a copy."

"Of course. If anyone has a right to it, it's you."

Tighe took a deep breath. "I won't pretend to know anything about business or space, but I've never turned down a challenging expedition. Count me in."

Joyce smiled and shook Tighe's hand. "You made the right choice. My people will stop by your bungalow with the paperwork tomorrow. In the meantime, go have fun tonight." Joyce clapped him on the back and escorted him toward the office doors.

The odd encounter was ending the moment Joyce had gotten what he wanted. The double doors opened, and the white-jacketed butler was standing there waiting.

As Tighe exited, he noticed a strikingly attractive woman around his age with long black hair standing to the side of the doorway. A white-jacketed female butler stood alongside her. The woman studied Tighe with a penetrating gaze. He nodded, but she turned away to focus on Joyce, exchanging greetings.

Tighe guessed she must be some supermodel or celebrity. Such was Joyce's life.

Tighe looked back as he followed the butler down the hall. Before the study doors closed, he noticed the woman glance back toward him as well.

CHAPTER 2

The Billionaire Whisperer

The United States Senate Appropriations Subcommittee on Commerce, Justice, Science, and Related Agencies held its hearings in a high-ceilinged wood-and-marble-lined chamber in the Dirksen Senate Office Building in Washington, DC. At the head of the room was a raised semicircular wood-paneled desk sporting an array of nineteen leather chairs overlooking a long wooden table with a microphone. This table was backed by a modest gallery for reporters and government aides, while an aging digital camera was mounted like a heavy machine gun on a tripod aimed directly at those slated to give testimony.

Today its target was Erika Lisowski.

Three US senators sat, seemingly at random, among the nineteen chairs on the dais—except for the committee chairman, who sat at the very center. A gruff-looking man in his seventies, he rearranged papers and spoke into his microphone without looking up.

"Welcome, Ms. Lisowski. Would you please introduce yourself to the committee."

"Yes, I am Erika Lisowski, PhD, program executive for emerging space at NASA headquarters here in Washington."

"Ms. Lisowski, all of your testimony today will be made part of the hearing record. Let us proceed."

The chairman donned reading glasses and studied a document in his hand. "As we examine the proposed NASA budget for fiscal year 2033, it's our continued goal to eliminate waste and duplication in NASA programs, while preserving American interests in space and US national security." He looked up. "Perhaps you can explain to us your role as program executive for . . ." He lost the thread.

"Program executive for emerging space. Of course. I've been tasked with conducting ongoing economic analysis of emerging private space companies—what's been termed 'NewSpace'—with an eye toward encouraging industry to invest in cislunar enterprise."

"Cislunar? What is that?"

"It's the region of space just beyond Earth's atmosphere reaching out to a point about 65,000 kilometers past the Moon. You might consider it the local celestial neighborhood."

"And what sort of 'enterprise' are you encouraging there?"

"A sustainable and growing space-based economy, which could create a more cost-effective framework to aid future NASA missions."

"This space economy would be administered under the auspices of the United States?"

She hesitated. "Not specifically, Senator, although the US will no doubt play a major role. Any space economy would intersect with Earth-based international economic systems—like the one developing in Luxembourg. The traditional doctrinal term for this is 'entanglement'—that is, creating a marketplace open to all that gives the community of nations a vested interest in its success."

The younger senator off to the side leaned toward his microphone. "You said 'new' space. How is that different from 'old' space?"

"*NewSpace* is an unofficial term used to describe private space entrepreneurs that are commerce focused rather than government focused."

The chairman asked, "Certainly the companies you engage with must be beholden in some degree to the US national interest."

"No more so than commercial entities in Silicon Valley or Wall Street."

"Then I find it difficult to see how this effort helps preserve American dominance in space."

"Senator, I think we must acknowledge that absolute American dominance of outer space no longer exists. Launch technologies are rapidly advancing worldwide, and the number of national and commercial space participants is expanding drastically. As of 2031, the total number of operational satellites orbiting Earth is 14,312, of which only 1,004 belong to the United States. The vast majority of the remainder belong to private industry."

The chairman was reading as he spoke. "Most of those companies are based in the US or its allies, correct?"

"At the moment, yes."

"Then why, Ms. Lisowski, do we need a whole department at NASA to promote the private space industry? It sounds like it's doing just fine on its own."

"My role is not to 'promote' the private space industry but to encourage economic investment in technologies and capabilities that will boost NASA's scientific and exploratory missions at a savings to the US taxpayer. If we are to reach other worlds—"

"Forgive me, but I'm not sure I share your faith that creating a marketplace 'open to all' in outer space will achieve geopolitical stability there. How do we know, Ms. Lisowski, that some foreign space company isn't a front for placing a rival nation's weapons in orbit?"

She considered his stern look. Lisowski knew the senator had formerly been an executive at a defense contractor, and prior to that had been an air force general. "I am not a defense analyst, Senator, but due to the velocities involved, literally everything in orbit is potentially a weapon. An errant bolt dropped by an astronaut during repairs could destroy an entire satellite. For this reason no nation would win *any* conflict in low Earth orbit. The wreckage from even modest hostilities would likely impact other satellites, creating clouds of lethal debris, which in turn would hit still more satellites. This could ultimately result in what's been called the *Kessler syndrome*—where the area above Earth's atmosphere becomes blanketed by debris that denies access to outer space to all of humanity for generations."

"So is it your belief, then, that America should not assert its primacy in space?"

"What I'm saying, Senator, is that every single nation on Earth has a legitimate, vested interest in space, and developing international commerce there provides the greatest chance for a stable, peaceful future. The US should be a leader in that effort, but if we are not, other sovereign states will take up this role."

The chairman and the other senators took notes. The female senator spoke briefly to an aide. In a moment the chairman looked up. "Let's turn on the screen, please."

A screen lowered, and a projector glowed from somewhere in the back. Suddenly an image appeared.

"Here's a photo from an article in the June 2028 issue of *Rolling Stone* magazine. . . ."

The image showed several people gathered at what Lisowski immediately recognized as the Davos conference in Switzerland under the headline "The NewSpace Titans." The photo showed a dozen luminaries holding drinks and talking against a backdrop of alpine scenery. It looked like an opulent affair. She recognized the image because she was in it—near the center. A red dot appeared on the face of the man standing next to her.

"The general public is fascinated by private space companies and the people behind them. Can you tell me who this is?"

"That is Nathan Joyce, Senator."

"And who is Nathan Joyce?"

"He's a tech billionaire and angel investor in NewSpace companies, CEO of both Catalyst Corporation and Asterisk Holdings."

A dot appeared on the other side of her, highlighting the face of another man, this one of South Asian extraction. "And can you tell us who this person is?"

"Dr. Sankar Korrapati, an economist."

"A *Nobel Prize-winning* economist. 'Dr. Doom,' I think some call him."

A gentle chuckle spread through the gallery.

The dot then focused on Lisowski's forehead—like a sniper's mark. "And this person?"

"That's me, Senator."

"The article says that you introduced Dr. Korrapati to Mr. Joyce at Davos— that they've been thick as thieves ever since. Is that why they call you the Billionaire Whisperer, Ms. Lisowski?"

She considered the photo for a moment. "This article is clickbait. It was a purely random encounter. We were standing next to each other, and I made perfunctory introductions."

"How did you know Dr. Korrapati?"

"I'd seen his acceptance speech in Stockholm."

"So you attended *both* the Nobel Prize ceremony and the Davos conference?"

"I was invited to the Nobel ceremony, yes."

"By whom?"

Lisowski hesitated. "The queen of Sweden."

"The queen of Sweden? Well, you're quite the jet-setter for a government bureaucrat."

"Senator, in order to engage with NewSpace leaders, I need to be present in their world. These are not frugal people, and they do not enjoy coming to Washington—if they can help it."

More chuckles from the gallery.

She pointed at the screen. "They do business in exotic locales, and that is where I must meet them."

"That's quite a job you have. And what has resulted from these 'meetings'?"

"Over the last eight years NASA has initiated multibillion-dollar public-private partnerships in cislunar space, freeing up almost half of our budget for deep space projects—including the recent Moon landings. We've encouraged orbital industries like fiber-optic printing, pharmaceutical and metallurgic research, space tourism, nanosats, and commercial logistics for the Lunar Gateway, which, as a result, is now in a near rectilinear halo orbit around the Moon. We were able to facilitate those deals by speaking the language of entrepreneurs."

"What do you think commercial competition for outer space looks like, from a global perspective?"

"Again, I would not frame outer space as a competition. We should view the establishment of a common market there as a goal of all humankind."

"Not all nations share the same belief system as the United States, Ms. Lisowski. What do Chinese entrepreneurs, for example, bring to this 'common goal' of expanding into space?"

"The Chinese government exerts close control over their space startups, and as a result they move conservatively—avoiding major risks. Thus, no manned commercial launch systems as of yet."

"And Russian space entrepreneurs?"

Lisowski considered the question. "I don't think we'll be seeing any private-sector space investment that the Kremlin doesn't want—and right now they've got domestic budgetary problems that China has not solved for them."

"What about European, Japanese, and Indian space startups?"

"The ESA continues to invest in unmanned probes, but Europe's manned commercial space sector isn't well developed. Japanese companies are developing amazing industrial robotics for use in space. India and New Zealand are doing commercial satellite launches, LEO, GEO, but I think their commercially oriented systems in deep space are a ways off."

"So no *manned* commercial space systems overseas yet?"

She nodded. "The only individuals with the resources and the will to truly pursue commercial manned spaceflight right now are US or US-based entrepreneurs."

"And among the US-based billionaires with the resources—what's your assessment of their individual goals?"

Now everyone in the hearing room was listening intently—especially the only, and otherwise bored, journalist in attendance.

Lisowski took a sip of water from a glass on the table. She realized this was going to be tricky. A NASA employee couldn't very well ignore questions at a Senate hearing, but she also had several confidentiality agreements to consider. "I'm not a psychologist, Senator."

"You've gone native with these billionaires, so to speak, at great cost to the taxpayer. I expect you to have some insights on what drives them. Jack Macy, for example."

"Mars. Macy is focused on humanity colonizing Mars—becoming a multiplanet species. Everything he does supports his proposed mission to Mars. Even his lunar aspirations are mostly as a staging area for Mars. He'd already have sent a ship to Mars if it weren't for political resistance."

"What about the others?"

"George Burkett's quieter, more calculating, but he's been investing billions in space for decades. He's focused on heavy-lift rockets, rocket reusability, but also building commercial logistics systems in cislunar space to support his Moon-mining aspirations. As the richest man in the world, Burkett's got the money to pull it off—but he's taking the slow-but-steady approach."

"And Halser?"

"Raymond Halser, hotel tycoon. Delivered on space tourism when he built the Hotel LEO from his inflatable hab units in the ISS's old orbit. However, the strategic investments we made in his inflatable hab technology paid off when we built NASA's Lunar Gateway. Similar habs are also slated to be components of NASA's Deep Space Transport. Of all the billionaires, Halser is the only one currently making a significant profit in space."

"What about that British fella, Morten?"

"Sir Thomas Morten. His company's technology is suborbital—making it more of a tourist ride than a serious space vehicle. I wouldn't say that's in the same league as the other NewSpace Titans."

"And your Davos friend—the one with that party island?"

"Nathan Joyce. He's not a traditional aerospace investor, true, but I believe he intends to make significant investments in the NewSpace sector over the next decade."

"It's hard to take him seriously when he's mounting Kickstarter campaigns to finance a manned asteroid-mining operation. Sounds a lot like selling the Brooklyn Bridge to me."

Staff and folks in the gallery chuckled.

Lisowski shifted in her seat. "NASA likes to encourage risk-takers and dreamers in private industry whenever we can, and hopefully we can coordinate their activity to the benefit of all." She leaned in to the microphone. "But I wouldn't underestimate Nathan Joyce, Senator. He's more serious than most people realize."

CHAPTER 3

Settling Accounts

DECEMBER 13, 2032

N athan Joyce stood on a tarmac in an orange flight suit, helmet under one arm, and smiled into the camera. *"It's time humanity stopped flirting with manned deep space exploration and actually got busy doing it—which is why I founded Catalyst Corporation, with the goal of sending a group of exceptional people on a mission to mine a near-Earth asteroid. In fact, I'm willing to match all the funds raised by this Kickstarter campaign to make that happen . . ."*

Archival video footage played of an oblong asteroid moving against the background of Earth. *"We all remember when the asteroid Apophis missed Earth by just 20,000 miles back in 2029. That showed the threat asteroids pose for humanity. However, these same asteroids also contain the raw materials we need to establish new, space-based industries."*

The video cut to a close-up of Joyce. *"Your contribution can help launch the space age we've all dreamed about. Pledge now at the two-hundred-dollar level, and you'll receive this commemorative Catalyst Corporation hoodie with the—"*

James Tighe clicked the video off and lowered his phone. He couldn't help but wonder what he'd gotten himself into. An extended publicity stunt, apparently.

And yet, part of that publicity stunt included Joyce purchasing eighteen seats on Burkett's and Macy's commercial launch systems—ostensibly for "in-orbit training." That meant eighteen people were definitely going into space on Joyce's dime. Tighe hoped to be one of those people.

He moved through Orlando International Airport among sunburned tourists and checked the instructions again on his phone. Tighe then followed signs for a shuttle to the "general aviation" terminal. This was a smaller, nicer facility with shorter security lines. In just a few minutes he arrived at his gate and checked the time—half past nine in the evening.

He was early, and there was a phone call he had to make that he couldn't put off any longer. Stepping to the side in the flow of other business travelers, Tighe scrolled through the contacts on his phone, then hesitated a moment before tapping the name.

The line rang a couple of times and then picked up, with the sound of children in the background. *"Wow, Jim. Is it really you?"* A Wisconsin singsong accent was evident in the voice.

"Yeah, hi, Ted."

"Merry Christmas. I hope everything's okay."

"Everything's fine. Merry Christmas to you, too."

"You're not stuck in some foreign country?"

Tighe had to admit it was a valid concern. "No. I know it's been a while since I've been in touch."

"So did that documentary thing ever work out, or ..."

"That's partly why I'm calling."

Kids shouted again in the background. An aside: *"Quiet, please. Daddy's on the phone!"* Then he was back. *"I'd ask where you've been all this time, but I'm sure it would take an hour. Where are you, anyways?"*

"I'm here in the States. Orlando."

"You there to dive those limestone caves? What are they called? Cetotes?"

"Cenotes. No, I'm catching a flight out this evening. How are Jill and the kids?"

"Oh, you know. We're all fine. Jill's practice is growing. We went to the Caribbean, all of us, last year. Mom, too. One of those Disney cruises."

"Yeah?"

"It was really something. I posted the pictures on Facebook. I don't know if you saw them."

Tighe didn't have a Facebook account.

"The buffets! Let me tell ya, we just about ate ourselves to death."

Tighe could already feel the vortex threatening to suck him in. "My mom went? I'm surprised."

"*Oh yeah. She even let Jill pay, if you can believe it. To be with the grandkids.*"

Tighe glanced at the time on the flight listings. "So listen, Ted. I want to wire you some money—partial repayment for what I owe."

There was momentary silence on the other end. Then: "*Really?*"

"I know it's been a while."

"*Well . . . yeah. I . . . To be frank I wasn't thinking—partial payment. So . . . how much would that be, then?*"

"Twenty thousand. I have the account number you gave me back when you—"

"*The 9360 account?*"

Tighe looked at the contact listing on his phone. "Right. Bank of the West."

"*That's the one. Twenty thousand! Really? An early Christmas present. And you'll wire it today?*"

Tighe's thumb hovered over his banking app—then clicked "Send." "I just sent it. You should receive it in the next few minutes."

"*Well, that's a surprise, Jim.*" Then he backed off. "*Not . . . I'm not saying—and it's not the whole amount—especially when you factor in interest. You remember the interest.*"

"Fourteen percent."

"*I think that's right.*"

"It is right."

"*Well, that's really great. I'll work out the balance and send your new total.*" There was shuffling on the other end. "*What's your email address these days?*"

Tighe glanced at the clock on the gate listing. "Same, but I don't check it much."

"*Facebook account or . . .*"

"Like I said, I'm headed out of the country—in fact, I've got to race to catch my flight."

"*So, is this phone number—?*"

"I'll be unreachable for the next ninety days at least. Just send it to my old email address. I'll get it."

"*Three months. Wow, where are you off to now?*"

"Just another expedition."

"Okay. Be safe. But hey!"

Tighe almost hung up anyway. But then he lifted the phone to his face again. "Yeah, Ted."

"You should call your mother. It's Christmas, and she hasn't heard from you in a while. You're still her son. She goes on about it."

"She doesn't really want me to call. She wants to tell people that I don't call."

"But you don't call."

"I don't know what it would accomplish."

"We're family. It doesn't need to accomplish anything."

"Look, I've got to catch this flight. Tell my mother I said hi. And best to Jill, too."

"Okay, Jim, if you—"

Tighe hung up and pocketed the phone. He headed toward his gate. In the darkness beyond the tall windows, the nose cone of an unmarked white Boeing 787 loomed—a plane destined for Joyce only knew where.

Just one passenger stood in line ahead of Tighe at check-in, a slim, sharply dressed Asian woman in her thirties. Tighe glanced down at his own faded jeans and T-shirt and wondered if he should have made a better impression. The instructions said clothing would be provided at the destination.

Then it was his turn. He stepped up to a young man in a Joyce Airlines polo shirt at the check-in podium. Nearby, two suited men with earpieces watched Tighe closely. There were several more people—older men and women—in business casual clothes milling about in the waiting area. They kept their eyes on him, too.

The clerk nodded. "Good evening." He gestured to an iris scanner on the desk. "Please look into the eyepiece with your right eye."

Joyce's people had scanned Tighe's iris and taken blood and fingerprint samples during the contract signing back on Baliceaux. While that had given him pause, the signing bonus helped it go down smoother.

Tighe lowered his head to the scanner.

The clerk watched the display until it chimed, at which point he gestured for Tighe to board the aircraft.

Tighe continued down the jet bridge and was met at the aircraft door by a middle-aged woman, also in Joyce Airlines attire.

She glanced at a handheld tablet computer before smiling. "Mr. Tighe, good evening."

"Good evening."

"Please follow me."

Tighe followed her through the galley section. He noticed the first-class cabin to the left was sealed off by a closed bulkhead door. She brought him past a gauntlet of several more men and women wearing khakis and polo shirts, all of them carrying computer tablets and studying him as he passed.

While she brought him down the nearest of the plane's two aisles, Tighe glanced at who he presumed were other candidates, all spaced rows apart. The plane was barely a quarter full. Each candidate looked physically fit and in their mid-thirties to mid-forties. In fact, the youngest people on the aircraft seemed to be the staff. The candidates were ethnically diverse, with every skin color and continent of origin in evidence. Likewise, the group seemed evenly split between men and women. It was like a charter flight to a middle-aged Olympic village.

His escort brought him to an unoccupied row, then gestured. "You're in 21A."

It should have been a window seat, except for one detail. He looked up and down the cabin. "No windows." The plane appeared to be a converted air freighter.

She studied him. "Does the lack of windows cause you anxiety?"

Something about the way she said it put Tighe on alert. "No. Not at all."

"Very well." She nodded and gestured for him to sit. "Please refrain from speaking with your fellow travelers. It will be a long flight. There will be meal service but no in-flight entertainment, no Internet connection, and no phone service. Hopefully you've brought something to keep you occupied. The lavatories are behind you, but again, please refrain from speaking with anyone. Do you have any questions?"

Tighe dropped his bag on the seat next to him. He shook his head. "No. Thanks."

She departed.

Tighe looked around again and exchanged glances with several other candidates who were doing the same. A South Asian man grimaced as if to say, *Pretty strange, eh?*

Tighe turned forward again and couldn't help but notice that tinted surveillance camera domes dotted the center of the ceiling at intervals. He decided to give all the outward appearances of patience.

Eventually the flight staff took their seats, and a voice came in over the speakers to announce their imminent departure and that all passengers had to fasten their seat belts. It felt oddly liberating not to get the obligatory safety speech.

He took a deep breath as the jet's engines spun up. He had no idea where they were going.

After a half hour or so sitting quietly in flight, Tighe looked over at his bag. He dug through the pockets and produced a small plastic case containing a microSD chip. The case bore the printed label "Tian Xing Exp. Vid." Joyce's staff had given it to him. Four terabytes of XHD video—more than two hundred hours in all. He tapped the case nervously with his finger. He'd intended to watch the video over the past weeks, but perhaps he was more traumatized than he thought. Somehow he hadn't found the time. Yet, he needed to see it, and right now he had nothing but time on his hands.

He slipped on wireless earphones and carefully took the tiny chip out of the container, inserting it into a socket in his phone. A moment later he was navigating thumbnails of video clips.

There were hundreds of numeric file names without any discernible pattern. The file dates didn't help either, since they'd all been copied at the same time a couple of weeks ago. He peered at the thumbnail image for each one and tried to guess what the file might contain.

Finally, he just sorted them in ascending order by file name, then clicked the first one, an image that appeared to show people surrounding an orange glow.

His phone screen filled with a view of the Tian Xing caving team, mostly men, standing around a campfire in relatively clean orange troglodyte suits, sans helmets, raising large brown bottles of local Chinese beer. Tighe stood arm in arm with Richard Oberhaus, his fifty-something mentor.

It was bittersweet seeing those smiling faces.

Most of the expedition members weren't cave divers like Tighe, Richard Oberhaus, and Christen Lykke. The other thirteen members were there to establish base camps and rig ropes to descend a thousand meters over kilometers of uneven limestone chambers and passages, all to reach the place where Tighe, Oberhaus, and Lykke could *begin* their dive—to push forward the map of Tian Xing to places unknown, beyond the 200-meter-deep flooded passages that blocked their way.

The camera now focused on Chang Fu Yuen, a handsome and successful thirty-something businessman from Beijing who had financed the entire expedition as part of his effort to increase Chinese interest in caving, and to prove that China's karst regions contained the largest and deepest caves in the world.

Chang raised his beer bottle in a toast, speaking in English. *"Here's to the best team of* guilos *I could assemble."*

Everyone laughed uproariously at this inside joke. *Guilo* was a mildly derogatory Cantonese term for white people; roughly translated it meant "ghost man." Chang was referring to overheard comments by his rural countrymen about the cavers. Laughing at the term defused the tension. The fact was, caving was only just becoming accepted by Chinese society at large—as something not entirely insane. Chang wanted to change that, and the team he had assembled included several local up-and-coming cavers, eager to gain experience from veteran cavers from around the world.

But before everyone could raise their bottles, Chang waved them aside. *"Not the real toast. The real toast is this . . ."* He raised his bottle again. *"To caves that go long and that go deep. To caves that go, and to the people that go with them."*

Everyone shouted, "Hear! Hear!" and clanked bottles.

Tighe closed the video.

Chang wound up surviving the expedition—although Tighe knew they would never speak again.

There were hundreds of video files.

Tighe decided to scroll way down the list and noticed a thumbnail that looked dirty brown. He clicked on it.

The video opened with the camera heaving as the wearer panted for breath. It was a view of the ground as it shook and stone cracked. The roar was deafening. Memory of it raised Tighe's pulse.

Caves were never entirely stable. So being in a cave during an earthquake was *hell*. With darkness all around and huge boulders falling, the helmet-cam whirred and blurred, indicating panic.

But then the tremor subsided. There was rubble and dust everywhere. Someone—male or female—was screaming unintelligibly in the background.

The wearer of the camera seemed to come to a decision and started pulling at a pile of shattered rock with gloved hands, grunting with the effort. After a while, the rescuer uncovered a still-illuminated LED lamp and pulled more frantically to uncover a body brown with mud and dust. The helmet on the body was crushed sideways, the face difficult to see.

The camera moved in as the rescuer removed a glove and checked for a pulse on the neck.

The wearer of the helmet-cam cursed in Mandarin.

Tighe stopped the video. He put the phone aside for several minutes. But after a while, the need to see what he was searching for was too strong. Tighe picked up the phone and scrolled even further in the file list, clicking a random file.

The video opened on several bloodied and exhausted-looking cavers standing near a chasm several meters across. Lights shined down revealing a 100-meter drop. The helmet cam turned upward again and then pushed through the crowd.

Tighe recognized his own voice, as the wearer of the camera, shouting, "Share light whenever possible. We need to get to Camp 4 before we go dark. Keep moving!"

A nearby voice—Chang's—said, "What happened to trying for Camp 2?"

"We no longer have time to rebelay. Bolt climbing will take way too long."

"There's almost nothing at Camp 4."

"We'll be closer to the surface."

"What does that matter? Camp 4 is a dead end. The rising water could trap us."

Tighe's helmet-cam turned to face Chang. "There's the HeyPhone."

"Richard's old magnetic induction radio? How do we know anyone's listening? Or that the thing even works?"

"Because he tested it. Richard always had backups. We can put our faith in Richard."

Tighe stopped the video. He noticed that the files from his helmet-cam shared a three-digit suffix—possibly the camera number. He filtered out the files from other helmet-cams and now saw a much shorter listing.

He clicked somewhere in the middle of the list.

The video opened on the calm, leathery face of Richard Oberhaus, his gray hair meticulously trimmed. There was laughing and music somewhere in the background. The helmet-cam did indeed belong to Tighe. He recalled this moment. Oberhaus was cleaning a Riegl laser scanning rig as some sort of Zen exercise at the edge of one of the underground camps. There were no campfires underground, only LEDs, chem lights, and candles.

In his late fifties, Oberhaus was exceptionally fit. An osteopathic surgeon from Hanover, Germany, he was partially retired with two adult children, and yet, instead of golfing, he was one of the most respected and courageous cave divers in the world. He'd taught Tighe everything he knew.

Oberhaus glanced up at the camera and with his slight German accent said, "There is a small party?"

Tighe heard his own voice. "Lei brought a few spliffs down, if you can believe it. They're sparking up. You want to join us?"

Oberhaus lowered the Riegl and looked at him sternly. "There comes a time, J.T., when you realize you're the oldest one at the party."

Tighe's camera held Oberhaus's gaze.

Oberhaus eventually looked back down and kept cleaning the Riegl.

Tighe closed the video. He sat for several minutes in his airplane seat. Oberhaus's words reverberated in his head. Should he continue searching for this clip? Would he even be able to watch it?

After a long while he picked up the phone again and scrolled down, clicking another video.

The screen opened on an underwater passage perhaps 30 meters high and 20 wide. The water was clear as air while the camera followed 5 meters behind Oberhaus, who wore a Viking dry suit, with dual Se7en series rebreathers, one on his back and another on his chest for emergencies. Oberhaus was piloting an electric diver propulsion vehicle—or DPV—which was a motorized submersible scooter that a diver held on to to move along at a speed of 1 meter per second. Strapped beneath it were eight bottles of "working gas"—heliox, a helium-oxygen mixture, for use at depth. With a range of 30 kilometers, the DPVs made impossible traverses of long, deep sumps possible.

This was the clip Tighe was looking for—viewed from his own helmet-cam.

The target that day was a sump called Turkey Leg in Tian Xing.

Tighe was kitted out just like Oberhaus, piloting his own DPV, and glancing behind him he confirmed that Christen Lykke, the third diver, was following as well.

Beams of light from the aquaflash lamps on their helmets revealed house-sized boulders jumbled below them. They still had the squared edges of relatively recent limestone breaks—from the last hundred thousand years or so.

Suddenly the passage turned 90 degrees downward and Oberhaus came to a halt over the void. He shined a bright lamp down, but it dissolved into the depths.

Over the radio link, Tighe heard Oberhaus's calm voice. *"Careful of the line, J.T. . . ."* Their full face masks allowed them to speak over radios while underwater—making it much easier for teams to work together.

Tighe's helmet-cam glanced at the dive computer on his wrist. It showed they were at 32 meters' depth and breathing 30 percent nitrox—a mix of nitrogen and oxygen intended to stave off *rapture of the deep* (the layman's term for nitrogen narcosis), a false euphoria that could blunt a diver's awareness and lead to death.

Under Oberhaus's mentorship, Tighe had learned the critical role that pressure played in the human body's ability to metabolize various gases. Even with a modern rebreather system that maintained safe partial pressure of oxygen, Oberhaus had taught Tighe to always know what his gas mix was, and why—because machines could fail.

In the helmet-cam the three divers convened above the deep hole of Turkey Leg sump—apparently named by someone who was not Chinese.

Oberhaus's voice came over the radio link. *"This is where we leave you, Christen."*

Lykke's voice. *"Sicher zurückkehren.* Safe journey to you both."

In Tighe's helmet-cam, Oberhaus turned downward, following an existing guide rope and comms line run by the previous diving expedition. Tighe accelerated his DPV, motor whirring as he fell in behind and above Oberhaus. At 40 meters' depth they passed a decompression station, with its cluster of a dozen reserve gas bottles tied off on the line for use on their way back up.

Tighe paused the video and took a calming breath. He then fast-forwarded, searching for something he knew was coming. As he did so, Oberhaus's on-screen form continued to descend, finally pausing at a depth of 57 meters to confirm their dive computers had switched them to heliox-14—a mix of 86 percent helium and 14 percent oxygen.

Generally, the greater the portion of helium a diver could function with, the more clear-headed they'd be at depth. But the problem with breathing a lot of helium was its thermal conductivity—twenty times that of normal air; a diver lost body heat *much* faster while breathing helium. Tighe watched the screen as he and Oberhaus partially inflated their dry suits with argon gas to insulate them.

Soon they were descending again. Down to 70 meters. Then 80 meters. Still following the old rope line, they reached 90 meters' depth.

Tighe stopped fast-forwarding. The video resumed normal playback.

He wasn't sure he remembered the event correctly. But the moment he heard the sound in his earphones, it spiked his adrenaline all over again.

A rumble deeper than anything he'd ever heard.

The shock wave passed through them in the water and was picked up by his comm microphone.

They both came to a stop. Breathing this much helium, Oberhaus sounded like a munchkin as he said, *"What is that?"*

They floated, swaying with the unpredictable movements of the water around them in the middle of the shaft. Somehow they were being shoved around, as if by a current.

Oberhaus and Tighe exchanged searching looks through their face masks. Then there was a piercing *crack* somewhere. They both knew what it was.

Oberhaus motioned with a gloved hand and squeaked, *"Collapse! Get beneath that overhang."*

The water was still rolling them around. Tighe's helmet-cam looked back as Oberhaus guided his DPV beneath an overhang of rock. His own helium voice replied, *"I think it's an earthquake!"*

More booming and cracks came to their ears through the water, and they were getting closer.

"One leads to the other. Get to cover!"

Before they made it to the shelter of the overhang, Tighe's view turned upward to see a collection of massive boulders dropping from above, bouncing off one another and both walls as they came, and trailing along with them finer rocks and sediment.

His munchkin voice shouted, "*Rockfall!*"

Tighe's helmet-cam looked to see Oberhaus reach the cover of the overhang as car-sized and larger boulders rained down from above, booming as they sank.

One large rock tore Tighe's DPV from his grip and nearly dragged him down by his tether before it snapped.

Tighe's helmet-cam showed him swimming the last stretch through a rain of massive boulders, their suction clawing at him. When he got to the safety of the overhang, Oberhaus hauled him in.

"*Against the wall!*"

Looking down at the continued shower of debris, Tighe realized his DPV was gone for good—its headlamps extinguished. Then he spotted the reflective flag of their decompression station, falling along with it.

Oberhaus's helium voice: "*Our deco gas. The collapse swept it away.*"

Tighe's helmet-cam looked toward Oberhaus, then went to check his dive computer.

A gloved hand came into view, grabbing Tighe's wrist.

"*Your current supply is not the issue. We cannot breathe heliox all the way up to 30 meters.*"

"*I'll try to contact Christen. He can bring his DPV down to us.*" A pause, and then Tighe's voice speaking via their wired phone line. "*Christen! Christen, do you copy?*"

No answer.

Oberhaus tried to hail Lykke as well—unaware of what Tighe sitting here in the present now knew: all their comm lines had been severed. Lykke had retreated when the sump entrance collapsed, nearly sucking him down with it.

Oberhaus finally gave up on the comm link. "*We must abort the dive. There will be aftershocks.*" He turned to Tighe. "*We need to change to a 30 percent nitrox mixture for decompression starting at 40 meters, then compressed air to 21 meters, then pure oxygen from 9 meters until the surface.*"

Oberhaus checked his own dive computer. "*Without that deco station, there's not enough gas for the two of us, James.*"

Tighe's helmet-cam looked up to Oberhaus. "*We can make it work.*"

Oberhaus tapped at his dive computer, calm as always, while he made adjustments. When next he spoke, his voice was no longer tinny with helium. It was his normal baritone. "*Yes, we can make it work. But not for both of us. One of us is not going to make it back this time.*"

In the moment, Tighe hadn't noticed the change in Oberhaus's voice. But now, watching the video, he could see that Oberhaus had already made his decision. Already thought it through. In turning down his helium, he had already killed himself—and done so in order for Tighe to hear what he was saying, to hear his mentor's voice.

Tighe, still unaware, said, "*You go, Richard. I'll stay.*" Tighe saw his hands begin to unsling air bottles.

Again the gloved hand on his wrist. "*We must be rational about this, James.*"

Tighe tried to press an air bottle into Oberhaus's hand.

Oberhaus pushed it away. "*I have lived twenty-two years longer than you. My children are grown. You have so much of life ahead of you.*"

Tighe's helmet cam shook vigorously, side to side. His voice, still squeaking from helium: "*You said it yourself: you have a wife and children.*"

"*And you should have a chance for the same.*"

"*I refuse to go.*"

Oberhaus was unslinging all his oxygen and nitrox canisters. "*There is no gas to spare discussing this. Leave now and you may have enough to survive decompression. You are in better physical shape than me, James. You've always been better able to withstand nitrogen narcosis than I. Between the two of us, you stand the better chance of making it.*"

Tighe's helmet-cam remained focused on Oberhaus's face.

"*I will not remain conscious for much longer. Go.*"

Sitting in the airplane seat watching the video, Tighe was gripped by grief. Staring into the face of the man who'd been a father to him. Those calm eyes, reassuring him.

"*We do not have the luxury of a long good-bye. Say good-bye to me, James.*"

Tighe heard his voice squeak, *"Good-bye."* His gloved hand accepted the gas canisters. He then embraced Oberhaus.

Oberhaus's voice, weaker now. *"Go!"*

Tighe grabbed the controls of Oberhaus's DPV and accelerated away, and upward.

After a few moments, Tighe's helmet-cam turned back to see Oberhaus's aquaflash lights illuminating him. Oberhaus nodded as he receded into the gloom, and then the lights went out. Oberhaus had extinguished them purposely—so that Tighe could not look back.

In his airplane seat, Tighe surreptitiously wiped tears from his face. He turned off the video with trembling hands and nursed his private grief.

CHAPTER 4

Ascension

fter nearly ten hours in the air, James Tighe exited the windowless Boeing 787 into daylight, shielding his eyes against a blustery wind. Outside it was cloudy but still warm.

He followed the other candidates down an old-fashioned aircraft gangway as they gazed at their surroundings. They'd arrived at a small airport terminal on a rocky coastline. There was nonetheless a broad tarmac and a long runway. Several gray military cargo planes with RAF and US markings stood in a line some ways off, but smaller civilian craft were closer at hand.

The terrain was austere, almost alien, with volcanic cinder cones of reddish grit devoid of plant life. The summit of the nearest one was studded with antennas and microwave transmitters. A few kilometers away a mountain rose a thousand meters, covered in greenery and partially masked in clouds. The lowlands around the airport consisted of fanned-out lava flows scattered with tufts of hardy green plants.

Tighe followed the other candidates, crossing the tarmac in a silent single-file line, headed toward a distant terminal building. Male and female security personnel in gray fatigues and red berets motioned for them to keep moving. The runway was quiet. No other aircraft had arrived or departed since they landed.

As the line of candidates approached the small terminal building, Tighe noticed above the doorway a blue-and-red-striped sign with a bird silhouette that read: "Welcome to Ascension Island Base." Nearby letters stenciled onto a cinder-block wall proclaimed this to be Wideawake Field.

Several dozen candidates crowded around the entrance to the terminal while a woman in a polo shirt and cap—emblazoned with the compass-like logo of a company named Polestar—motioned for them to gather around.

She spoke with a British accent as she shouted above the wind. "Welcome to Ascension Island. You are in the South Atlantic. This island is a British territory and this airfield part of the air bridge between Saint Helena and the Falkland Islands. We will be escorting you through customs. Afterward, you will board buses for the drive to our private training facility. There you will receive further instructions. Form up, please, and have your passports at the ready."

After waiting in line for more than an hour, with the light waning to early afternoon, Tighe reached the front of the line and stepped up to a woman and two men, all wearing Polestar polo shirts and holding computer tablets.

The woman held out her hand without looking up. "Passport, please."

Tighe complied.

"Mr. James Tighe." She looked up from his photo. "Is that correct?"

Tighe nodded.

One of the men held an iris scanner up to Tighe's face. The moment it beeped approval the woman handed Tighe's passport to the other man, who motioned for Tighe to follow.

After getting Tighe's passport stamped by a weary-looking British official in an olive-drab shirt and peaked hat, the Polestar rep led Tighe toward a line of three unmarked blue electric buses, where another female rep was waiting. She marked Tighe off on a digital list and pointed him toward the second bus. "We'll be leaving shortly."

Tighe nodded and climbed the steps. He found an aisle seat halfway down the length of the bus and spotted more surveillance camera domes on the ceiling as he sat down. Apparently management was observing them here, too.

Soon the bus was full, and a Polestar rep stood at the front. "We will now be departing for Devil's Ashpit Camp."

Murmurs and a few chuckles spread through the bus.

"We call it DAC for short. If you are lucky, DAC will be your home for the next three months. There, you will undergo a battery of physical and psychological tests to determine your suitability for further training with our commercial space client, Catalyst Corporation. It's a short drive—just 15 kilometers—but we'll be gaining 1,200 meters' altitude on switchback roads. So hopefully none of you get carsick."

There was a smattering of laughter among the passengers. Spirits were high.

Moments later they were under way. The buses seemed to be headed toward the big green mountain in the distance, which was rounded and more lush than anything else in sight.

After traversing volcanic lowlands for several kilometers and passing no other automobile traffic, the electric buses began climbing narrow switch-backs. As they gained altitude, the landscape became simultaneously more austere and yet in some ways greener—with sparse grasses sprinkled across stark scoria slopes of black volcanic grit. Gazing out across the Atlantic, which stretched to the horizon in all directions like hammered steel, Tighe got the full measure of their isolation.

Up ahead a newly constructed checkpoint blocked the road, with razor wire perimeter fencing stretching out in both directions. Behind it stood a facility with twin massive white antenna dishes aimed straight upward and dozens of modern prefab buildings spread around them. Signage at the entrance gate warned: "Restricted Area. Authorized Personnel Only."

As the buses passed through the checkpoint, Tighe noticed it was manned by serious-looking security guards in gray camouflage military fatigues, with red berets and sidearms on their belts.

The buses continued down a smooth blacktop road past metal barracks buildings before entering a central parking lot in front of a large single-story concrete structure. Here, a dozen camp staff with computer tablets and an equal number of security personnel stood near folding tables.

Tighe's bus halted with a hiss. The doors opened, and a male Polestar employee entered.

"Welcome to DAC. Let me remind you that from this point onward your candidate selection contract is in force. All your activities at this facility are subject to surveillance. Please exit the bus and wait for your name to be called."

Tighe stood in the bus aisle with the other candidates and eventually descended the steps, where he was halted by two security guards. One raised a handheld iris scanner to Tighe's eye, checking the display as it beeped.

"Name."

"James Tighe."

Meanwhile the other guard swept a scanning wand over him and his bag. "Hold out your right hand."

Tighe did so.

One guard locked a flexible green plastic bracelet around Tighe's wrist. "This tracking bracelet must be worn at all times. Tampering with it will result in dismissal from the program. Understood?"

Tighe nodded.

They motioned for him to proceed, and Tighe joined the other candidates—at least a couple hundred of them—milling around the coffee urns in the parking lot. More were still exiting the buses.

Tighe moved about the crowd, examining his surroundings.

The camp looked military in nature—orderly, austere. Metal poles topped with camera domes stood at each corner of the parking lot and on nearby buildings. Cameras were everywhere, in fact.

It occurred to Tighe that this whole place might be an elaborate *Survivor*-like reality TV show—with contestants vying for a chance to go into low Earth orbit. Joyce did own new media companies, after all, and it sounded like something he'd be capable of. Tighe began to regret not reading every single page of the contract he'd signed.

Near the edge of the parking lot stood a woman in a worn hooded sweatshirt, jeans, and boots, sipping a coffee. Her black hair was tied back in a ponytail, but Tighe recognized her immediately. He'd first seen her back on Baliceaux, in a cocktail dress, hair down, when she'd met with Nathan Joyce in the billionaire's study, just after Tighe left.

The woman's penetrating eyes suddenly turned toward him. She apparently recognized him, too, because she nodded slightly.

The PA sounded. "*Rabindra Bhaduri, report to Building A, Door 3. Rabindra Bhaduri, report to Building A, Door 3.*"

Tighe moved through the crowd toward her.

She continued to sip her coffee as he approached.

In a moment he came face-to-face with her. "Back on Baliceaux I thought you were Joyce's SO. My mistake."

She replied, deadpan, "I'm not the SO type."

"I gather you did something extraordinary to wind up here."

"Not really. I'm a mountain climber. Nathan funds all my expeditions."

"Yeah? Where have you climbed?"

She looked him up and down. "So I'm supposed to impress you now, is that it? Name some peaks I summited?"

"Just sizing up the competition."

"You're the cave diver. Joyce told me about you. Tough break, that quake in Tian Xing."

"Yes. It was."

The voice on the PA called out. *"James Teeg, report to Building A, Door 2. James Teeg, report to Building A, Door 2."*

Tighe gritted his teeth. "It's pronounced 'Tie.' "

"I know." Her eyes motioned toward the building. "You're up, J.T."

Without looking back, Tighe headed toward a doorway marked with a large numeral 2 in the central building.

Though the building looked old, the door and its hardware were new. Tighe entered into a wide room with half a dozen candidates undergoing what looked like enhanced security screening—except that the screeners wore lab coats.

A Latina staffer motioned for Tighe to come forward. "Remove your shoes and place them on the counter, please. Then step into the 3D scanner."

Tighe slipped off his trainers and stepped into a booth, where he was surrounded by scanning devices.

"Arms extended at your sides."

Tighe did as instructed.

"Don't move."

Electric motors purred as the scanning heads revolved around him for thirty seconds. Then they stopped.

"Step out of the scanner and proceed to the next station, please."

In his stocking feet Tighe moved up to a black woman who proceeded to take his blood pressure. To either side of Tighe, candidates were having blood drawn, their reflexes tested, their teeth inspected, and their eyes examined.

Suddenly a man's voice grew loud off to Tighe's right—the accent British.

"Disqualified? Fuck's sake, what for?"

Tighe turned to see a diminutive Caucasian technician facing a lean black man in a tan T-shirt and jeans.

"You exceed the height requirement by 4 centimeters, sir." The technician pointed to a screen displaying the man's 3D scanned image. "I don't know how you got this far in the process, but you're too tall. This should have been caught in the physical. Before you even boarded the plane."

"Height's that important, is it?"

"Yes. Both weight and height, sir."

"And am I a biffa?"

"A what?"

"Am I overweight?"

"No, sir."

"Right then . . ." Holding his shoes, the man looked around the crowded room. "Where can I sit?"

"You can put your shoes on outside, sir."

"I'm not planning on putting my bloody shoes back on."

"Sir, you must leave. You cannot continue in the candidate selection program. You're too tall."

A couple of security staff began moving toward them from the back wall.

"I'm just lookin' for a chair. Can I get one, please?"

Tighe looked around with just about everyone else. No chairs in sight.

"Not in here, sir."

"Lovely . . ." Ignoring the approaching guards, the man dropped his shoes to the floor, then stood on one leg. With a *riiipp* he pulled apart his other pant leg at the seam, where it was evidently held together by Velcro. This revealed that his calf was a black carbon fiber prosthetic. Hopping in place, he said, "This'll only take a sec . . ."

Taken aback, the security guards—and now everyone in the room—watched in fascination as the man hopped up and down, adjusting the height of his prosthetic lower leg. In a few moments he was finished—and he then performed the same process on his other prosthetic leg.

The guards and the technician exchanged surprised looks.

The man closed the Velcro seams on both legs and stood up straight, somewhat shorter now, but otherwise perfectly stable. He nodded to the technician. "All right, Joe Bloggs, measure me again."

Stunned, the technician looked down at his tablet, flipping from screen to screen.

The man clapped. "Time's wasting, sunshine."

The technician lifted a hand scanner, pulling the trigger to take another measurement.

"Satisfied?"

The technician nodded as he read the display. "Yes. You now satisfy the height requirement, Mr. Morra."

Everyone in the room—including Tighe—broke out in raucous applause and hoots. Even the security guards joined in.

Morra waved them off. "All right, all right. Settle down."

Tighe found himself still chuckling several moments later as his blood sample was taken. He cleared the rest of the physical without incident.

He and the other candidates were then separated, with Tighe directed to a small interview room where he was told to stare into a camera lens while he was asked a series of bizarre questions by a man in a lab coat.

"Do you enjoy sex with animals, Mr. Tighe?"

"What? No."

"Do you not enjoy the sex you have with animals?"

"I don't have sex with animals."

"But if you did, would you enjoy it?"

"What the hell is your problem?"

The strange interview lasted another twenty minutes, and afterward, Tighe was escorted into a room where a man in a Polestar-branded polo shirt sat at a folding table with stacks of documents to either side. The man motioned for Tighe to sit in a folding chair across from him, then slid a document and a pen toward Tighe.

"What's this?"

"This is a rider to the candidate selection contract you signed back in the States."

Tighe read the heading: "Indemnity for Accidental Death or Dismemberment."

The company man spoke in the soothing tones of an undertaker. "An unfortunate necessity. This selection program needs to be physically rigorous. As a result, certain activities here run the risk of serious injury or death."

"Why wasn't I shown this when I signed the other documents?"

"Out of context this document can seem unduly alarming."

"Meaning I'd be more likely to put it in front of a lawyer. Which I can't do here." Tighe read from paragraph one, "'Candidate hereby acknowledges the company selection program may bring about permanent impairment or death.'" Tighe looked up. "And if I don't sign this?"

"You'll be dropped from the selection program and flown back to Orlando on the next flight out of Wideawake."

"Hmph." Tighe flipped to the next page. "How'd the airport get that name, anyway?"

The company man stared.

"You don't know."

"It was built by the Americans during World War II. The noise of thousands of nesting birds kept the GIs awake at night." He spread his hands. "Wideawake Field."

Tighe was busy reading. The rider basically said that if he was killed or maimed in the course of his selection or training (with fatalities euphemized as a "Type A Mishap"), he would be covered by a standard insurance clause but otherwise prevented from bringing suit against the company. Likewise, all disputes would go into binding arbitration. As he read through the arbitration details and maximum payout amounts, Tighe realized this would be the first time he had ever had life insurance.

Tighe sighed. "What the hell." He signed his name and dated the rider, adding his mother's name and address as the insurance beneficiary.

The company man nodded. "At this point I've been instructed to remind you of the confidentiality clause in your candidate selection and training contract."

"So go ahead."

"You are not to share with any outside person or organization anything you learn or experience during candidate selection, up to and including the fact that you undertook this candidate selection program. You will take steps to actively maintain the confidentiality of such information, and you will immediately alert the company upon learning of any breach of this agreement, either intentional or accidental, committed by yourself or by another."

The company man added Tighe's signed rider to his pile. "Do you understand the terms of the confidentiality clause you have already signed and of which I have just reminded you?"

Tighe waited for several seconds before replying. "Yeah, I understand."

"I've also been instructed to remind you of the special terms of the company's sexual harassment policy."

Tighe was bemused. "Such as?"

"Article 17, subsection B: selection candidates accept that in the course of this program they will lack personal privacy. Likewise, they will be working in close proximity to other candidates—either male, female, or transgender—under conditions that may require nonsexual physical contact. Candidates may also be exposed to the nudity of other candidates and/or the sexual activity of other candidates, of any sexual orientation. However, under no circumstances will any selection candidate be required or expected to engage in sexual activity themselves or be required or expected to tolerate unwanted intimate sexual contact or sexual harassment." The company man stared at Tighe. "Do you understand the special terms of the sexual harassment policy you have already signed and of which I have just reminded you?"

"Now I do."

"Do you have any questions?"

Tighe thought hard for several seconds. "Why aren't there any young people here?"

"You're hardly old, Mr. Tighe."

"I'm thirty-seven. Everyone I've seen out there is in their midthirties to early forties. Why no one younger?"

"There *is* one candidate in his twenties."

"That doesn't answer my question."

After a few moments the company man said, "Cosmic rays. Older people are less susceptible to cumulative radiation exposure. Most of you will die of old age before you develop more serious cancers."

"Then why the twenty-something?"

"He's from a region with below-average life expectancy."

"Charming."

"Any other questions?"

"Nope."

"You may exit through that door." The company man pointed behind him.

Tighe pushed through the doorway and into a tiled corridor. A uniformed staff member directed him to a set of double doors, opening one for him.

Tighe entered a tiled room where trainees, male and female, were sitting on stools to have their heads shaved by camp staff. Piles of multicolored hair were being push-broomed into the corner.

Tighe sat at the first open chair, and after he was draped in an apron, his head was buzz-cut for the first time in many years. He hoped it would all grow back.

Afterward, he was directed to the next room, where he joined a queue of trainees, male and female, that snaked down a corridor lined with square openings. Through these, he could see camp staff passing folded clothing and other items to trainees.

Just then Tighe noticed the lean black man with prosthetic legs step up behind him. He nodded. "Good to see you made it, Morra."

Morra laughed. "These wankers won't get rid of me that easily." He held out his hand. "What are you called?"

"James Tighe. J.T.'s fine." They shook hands.

"J.T., Dave Morra, British Army Royal Engineers."

"A soldier?"

"*Ex*-soldier. More of a builder really. I did what I had to, to get an engineering degree."

By then they'd come to the first window, where staff members passed them both half a dozen sets of folded dark-blue jumpsuits.

Tighe leaned down. "I usually take a medium."

The staff member said, "You're all mediums. Part of the selection process. There's Velcro straps for minor adjustments."

Tighe looked up the line and realized that the trainees were indeed largely the same height. Different builds, but no one was dramatically taller or shorter than anyone else.

Soon the trainees were all piled high with gear as they entered a room lined with benches.

A thick-necked camp coordinator walked among them handing out numbered plastic bags, shouting with an American accent. "Strip off all personal clothing—including socks and underwear—and place them in the storage bags provided. Place all jewelry or other valuables in the small security bag. The contents will be returned to you upon departure. If you are found with any personal, unassigned items in your possession beyond this point, you will be dismissed from the program."

There were thirty or so people in the bench-lined room, half of them women and half men. Several raised their hands.

The coordinator pointed at a blond woman. "What don't you understand?"

She gestured to the others. "We're supposed to strip down right here in front of each other?"

"You should already know this." The coordinator turned and shouted for everyone to hear. "Listen up, people. There is no privacy at this facility. You will not have privacy in outer space either. If you're shy, drop from the program. Otherwise, get naked, put all your personal items in the storage bag, and suit up in your utility dress: jumpsuit and boots."

After a moment's pause, several trainees started peeling off their shirts and dropping their pants—possibly thinking about their ticket to space. The others did the same. The blonde who asked the question finally shrugged and started disrobing, too.

Morra didn't seem affected in the slightest. As he pulled off his shirt, Tighe noticed burn scars and shrapnel marks on the man's sinewy frame, as well as a florid tattoo of flames issuing from a round vessel above a banner bearing the word "Ubique."

Looking around confirmed that everyone was in excellent physical shape, yet they all bore scars and tattoos that made it apparent how much life experience was assembled here. Everyone seemed to be taking the lack of privacy in stride.

Soon the trainees were all dressed in blue jumpsuits, carrying the rest of their issued supplies in a duffel. Each jumpsuit had a reflective white number on it. Tighe's number was 363. Morra's was 173.

The coordinator marched them out, and moments later they were walking on a blacktop road between metal barracks. Staff members motioned for them to enter a building marked with a large number 4, and once inside, they saw lines of Spartan bunk beds with lockers between—ten to either side. Forty cots in all.

The coordinator shouted, "Grab a bunk, and stow your shit!"

The group surged forward, but not as fast as Morra, who bypassed the nearest bunks and headed to the middle of the barracks. Tighe decided an ex-soldier like Morra would know where to bed down, and he headed toward the middle, too.

Morra gestured to the lower cot just past his own. "That's a good one there."

Tighe tossed his duffel bag onto the cot before anyone else could claim it and then opened the locker to start stowing his gear. "Why'd you go for the middle of the barracks?"

"When they come in before dawn banging trash cans, you'll thank me."

Tighe spoke softly. "You think this place is legit?"

"Whadju mean?"

"I mean, are we sure this isn't just some reality TV show instead of an asteroid-miner selection program?"

Morra was stowing his gear as well. "I read through the contract. There's no grant of telly rights."

"What about the 'no privacy' clause? Everyone getting naked?"

Morra laughed. "You have a skeptical mind, J.T. I like that." Morra pointed at the ceiling. "I did notice the cameras."

"Yeah." They both gazed up at surveillance domes in the barracks ceiling. "In the parking lot, the bus, and the aircraft, too."

A South Asian man with a few nicks on his newly bald head nodded to the bunk above Tighe. "May I?"

Tighe gestured. "All yours."

The man carefully placed his duffel up top and extended his hand. "Rabindra Bhaduri. Geologist. My friends call me Rabby."

Tighe shook his hand. "Hey, Rabby. James Tighe. J.T.'s fine." He pointed. "That's Dave Morra."

He and Morra shook hands as a Caucasian man tentatively pointed to the bunk above Morra. "That one open?"

It was the last open bunk in the place. Morra nodded.

The man tossed his duffel and extended his hand. "Looks like we're bunk-mates. Jamie Parks."

Morra shook hands and gestured to the others. "I'm Dave. That's J.T., and that's Rabby."

"Hey, guys."

Rabby turned to Tighe. "I overheard you say this might be a reality TV show."

"Just a theory."

Parks frowned. "TV show?"

"Maybe. Doesn't mean there's not a trip to space in it. At least for the winners."

They all looked up at the surveillance domes on the ceiling.

Morra said, "I reckon we'll find out soon enough."

CHAPTER 5

The Devil's Ashpit

By early evening, the candidates sat grouped by barracks at long tables in the central mess hall. Tighe counted twenty-two tables in all—which meant around 440 candidates. Given that Catalyst Corporation had purchased passage into orbit for only eighteen trainees, Tighe's prospects for getting into space were starting to look less sunny than Joyce had led him to believe.

The mess hall buzzed with hundreds of conversations. Now that the candidates were all gathered in one place, Tighe finally got the measure of his competition. It was an ethnically diverse crowd, seemingly a fifty-fifty split between men and women—which suggested the company was looking for an even mix. All the shaved heads gave him first-impression blindness, which was probably the point.

Food was already being served, cafeteria style, so Morra, Tighe, Bhaduri, and Parks grabbed plastic trays and got in line, glancing around all the while.

Morra asked, "Know anyone here?"

Tighe searched for the woman from Baliceaux but didn't spot her. Then again, her head would now be shaved, just like his own, making her difficult to recognize. "No. You?"

Morra shook his head. "I was hoping to see some mates from the service."

"Did Joyce recruit you there?"

"Who's Joyce?"

Tighe was taken aback. "Nathan Joyce—the billionaire. The reason we're here."

"Oh. Right. No, some gents came to see me at the QEH in Birmingham.

They said a man like me could get work out in space—that it was dangerous but high paying. And that's exactly what I was looking for."

Parks leaned forward. "J.T., you know Nathan Joyce?"

"I wouldn't say I know him, but I spoke to him at Baliceaux."

Parks nodded. "I've been meaning to get there."

"Rabby, who recruited you?"

Bhaduri seemed surprised to be in the conversation. "I was approached at a geology conference."

The food turned out to be standard institutional fare—dishes of indistinct meat in a substrate of gravy, starches, and mushy vegetables. Juices and water to drink. They found seats at their barracks table and dug in. Tighe had had much worse food on expeditions, and at least he wasn't damp, cold, or dirty while he ate it.

Morra looked up. "So this Joyce guy—I reckon he approached you for a reason."

"I'm a cave diver. I explore submerged cave systems."

"Like with robots?"

"No, in person. Technical diving down to 200 meters."

Bhaduri leaned forward. "That sounds dangerous."

Parks nodded. "I've done some diving myself."

Morra gave Parks the side-eye but turned his attention to Bhaduri. "Rabby, you said you're a geologist, but I'm guessing that's not the only reason you're here."

Bhaduri finished chewing. "I placed third at the World Peace Marathon in Dhaka last year."

"Bangladesh."

He nodded. "And I once led an opposition political party, for which I lost my professorship and was imprisoned."

Parks's eyes widened. "Really?"

"Eight men in one cell—which we did not leave for four years."

The group winced.

"I was told that the company is interested in my ability to cope with confinement in close quarters—as well as my geological expertise."

"I'll bet." Tighe wondered whether he could endure what Bhaduri already had, much less come back for more.

Morra looked to Tighe. "Still think this is a put-on, J.T.?"

Tighe looked across the table at Parks. "How'd you wind up here, Jamie?"

"Serial entrepreneur. Radical disruptor. I founded Watsoi. Primrest. Gooshvol." He searched their faces for some sign of recognition.

The others exchanged looks and shrugged.

"Those were vertical-market, Internet 4.0 plays. Now I'm looking to branch out into NewSpace. I've always admired Nathan Joyce and realized that direct experience in space would give me an advantage when courting NewSpace investors. You know, book some flight time."

Morra paused. "Wait. Did you *pay* to be here?"

Parks turned to them each in turn. "I didn't 'pay.' I *invested*. This is an investment."

"Oh, Christ." Morra pushed away his empty tray.

Parks looked annoyed. "You think your skills are more relevant than mine, Dave? This is the *commercial* space industry."

"I'd wager my skills are more relevant to asteroid mining. I was a combat engineer."

"Well, a cislunar economy is going to require businesspeople. Most of the actual mining will be done by robots."

Morra laughed ruefully. "God, the space lawyers'll be coming next."

Bhaduri asked, "Does anyone else here have children?"

Parks and Tighe shook their heads.

Morra nodded. "Two daughters." He took a breath. "No visitation rights, though."

Tighe looked up from his mashed potatoes.

"I had some anger issues over the loss of my legs. Helping other vets finally helped me, but working in space is my chance to help my girls."

A sharp whistle suddenly brought the din of conversation to a halt. A thick-necked camp coordinator shouted, "Listen up!"

A quartet of serious-looking individuals, one in security fatigues, the others in business attire, walked to the head of the mess hall. The lead one, a stern man with graying blond hair and sharp features, picked up a microphone and turned to address the room.

He spoke with a clipped Nordic accent. "Welcome. My name is Robert

Jensen, supervising director of Devil's Ashpit Camp." He studied the faces. "You may not be aware that this camp has special significance in the history of space travel. It was originally built by NASA back in 1965 as a tracking station for the Apollo Moon missions. The name derives not from the area's resemblance to hell but a nearby geological formation." Jensen paused.

"However, it was here—at *this* site—where Neil Armstrong's words from the Moon were first received and then relayed to NASA Mission Control in Houston, where those words made history. So in a sense, we are here on sacred ground to spacefarers. Ground that was abandoned in 1999 due to budget cuts. However, we have rebuilt it. Improved it, and made it ready to serve a twenty-first-century Age of Exploration. Now it is time to get down to business— because that is what space exploration must become: a business."

Jensen turned to the other three individuals standing nearby. "These are my colleagues . . ." He pointed to an exceptionally fit man in a tracksuit, sporting spiked black hair. "Physical training director Aleron Dastous."

The man nodded.

"Psychological director Dr. Angela Bruno."

Bruno was a diminutive Caucasian woman in her fifties or early sixties with a shock of long gray hair. She did not acknowledge the introduction.

Jensen then pointed to a hulking individual in security fatigues and a red beret. "Camp security director Makar Yegorov."

Yegorov glowered.

Jensen then took to pacing the head of the room, microphone in hand. "Ask yourself: why are you here? Why *you* and not someone else?" He let the question sink in. "The answer is because you are abnormal in some way. We have sequenced each of your genomes from the blood samples you provided and have determined that—as expected—a disproportionate number of you share what's known as the 'wanderlust gene,' DRD4-7R. This gene is highly correlated with a desire for novel experiences. Many of the world's greatest explorers, adventurers, and entrepreneurs have this gene. Its prevalence in this room is an interesting statistic, but it is just that—a statistic. What we will do over the next several months is to test *you*, the individual, to determine who here is truly ready to undertake our client's expedition.

"Lone wolves—no matter how talented—will not succeed here. You will be judged not only by your own actions but also by the company you keep. Think always: who would make a good crewmate? Your ability to successfully balance cooperation with competition will be closely watched."

Jensen pointed. "You may have noticed the camera domes and microphones. Get used to them." In answer to the murmurs of concern: "Yes, you will be observed while you are showering. Yes, while you are shitting. If you think what you're signing up for involves privacy, let me disabuse you of such notions now. We need to determine whether you have the physical and psychological traits necessary to work in close quarters with other people for extended periods of time in an environment of hardship and deadly danger—but which also offers unparalleled opportunity to expand the frontiers of human experience. If you have a problem with lack of privacy, save us both a great deal of time and expense. Leave now."

Jensen paused.

To Tighe's surprise, two candidates at different tables did indeed get to their feet, and camp staff ushered them away—presumably to be dismissed.

Jensen surveyed the trainees as he paced. "Not only will you not have privacy from us, you will not have privacy from each other. There are no separate men's and women's showering or restroom facilities in this camp. Neither are there modesty partitions in restrooms or bathing facilities. You will bunk together, shower together, shit together. Do we have any more departures?"

No one stirred. "Good. Good." He moved back to the head of the mess hall. "Over the course of this selection program we will winnow down the number of candidates to a core of highly qualified individuals who will continue on to technical and operations training in Antarctica—in preparation for a position working under contract for our client, Catalyst Corporation, whose commercial operations will be conducted outside the atmosphere of the Earth, in the very hazardous environment of deep space."

A cheer of enthusiasm went up among the crowd. Then applause.

Tighe joined in, realizing that these folks were indeed members of his special tribe—adventurers. He and Morra exchanged appraising nods.

Jensen allowed their enthusiasm for several moments before motioning for silence. "I am glad you are excited by this prospect." He began pacing again. "But be warned—candidates can be dismissed for any or no reason. Completion of the training program does not guarantee the offer of a company contract—although successful completion does provide a payment of fifty thousand US dollars."

Jensen held up his hand to stave off any more applause. "This is not a theater. There will be no more clapping. We have work to do here and precious little time in which to do it." He turned. "Dastous."

The physical training director stepped forward, grabbing the microphone. He spoke with a French accent. "Good evening. No doubt you all consider yourself to be in peak physical condition. No matter, over the next several months we will find the limit of your physical endurance, and I promise you that the process will not be pleasant."

Dastous studied his charges. "No one will succeed in this program unless they can not only meet the most stringent fitness of which the human body is capable, but also prove that they can voluntarily push through the agony of that limit to complete physical collapse."

The trainees exchanged concerned glances.

At that, Dastous handed the microphone to Dr. Bruno. Unhurried, she silently assessed the audience for several moments before raising the microphone to her mouth.

"It is true. My staff will be observing your every interaction over the next several months—both with our own eyes as well as thousands of algorithmic eyes—analyzing your social interactions, facial expressions, micro-expressions, thermal signature, body language, mental state. In short: everything. It's important that you do not think of us as your adversary. For those among you who will really be going into space . . ." She paused for effect. ". . . and I assure you, that is a tiny minority of those assembled here . . . I am in some ways your most important friend. It's up to my team to ensure that you are not confined in a spacecraft for months on end, in tight quarters, with someone who is irrational, ill-tempered, unstable, sociopathic, selfish, overtalkative, aggressive—or worse. If we do our job well, not only your work but your very lives become better. Please bear this in mind as we probe you for emotional or behavioral weaknesses. We do so out of deep compassion for the challenges you will face."

She then turned the mic over to security chief Yegorov, a bald-headed bull of a soldier, who spoke English with a thick Russian accent. "There is private space race on in this world. Billions being spent by five main competitors, each with own strategy for commercializing space, and each in warious stages of technical and operational readiness."

Yegorov walked among the tables, staring down everyone who locked eyes with him. "This means is likely one or more of you is corporate spy—or will be recruited as one. This is why facility is in lockdown. Why all devices have been confiscated. You will not be permitted to speak with outsiders even when you leave camp on drills. And know if you fail confidentiality terms of your contract, we will sue to reclaim all payments made to you, and seek substantial damages. Secrecy will be critical to maintaining competitive edge of client company. My people will be watching, but unlike Dr. Bruno, I am not compassionate. I live to punish thieves and liars."

Jensen then collected the microphone from Yegorov. "Thank you, Makar." He looked over the candidates. "You have all the information you need for now. Although you may still be on different sleep schedules, I advise you to return to your barracks and get some rest. You will be awakened at five a.m. to begin the selection program."

Groans spread through the audience as the trainees stood from the benches.

"I assure you, the early wake-up will be the least of what you will face in the next few months."

CHAPTER 6

Aliens

Tighe jolted awake at the sound of a female voice on the PA system. "*Five a.m. Wake up. Five a.m. Wake up.*"

The barracks lights came on, with the bunk above blocking most of the glare.

Two coordinators in gray sweatpants and hooded sweatshirts entered banging on trash cans. "Get dressed, people! Get dressed! Sweats, caps, and trainers! PT gear! Wake up, wake up!"

Tighe rose and saw Morra pulling on his legs. The other candidates were rifling through lockers and getting dressed. Tighe always kept his gear well organized, so he was dressed and ready to go before most of the others.

"Pick up the pace, J.T."

Tighe turned to see Morra, already dressed and heading toward the exit. Tighe raced to catch up.

Within minutes, they were all outside in the chill morning air. A brilliant field of predawn stars stretched overhead—the Milky Way arcing vividly toward the horizon.

The lead coordinator shouted, "Listen up!"

A sound similar to a hopping pogo stick approached, and the group turned to see a headless robotic dog jogging down the blacktop toward them on four dexterous peg feet. The robo-dog had a "face" of sensors at the front of its body, and a swirling orange orb flashing on its back. A glowing number 4 was emblazoned on both flanks. It stopped in front of the group.

"This is Spot! See Spot run!"

The robo-dog suddenly took off at a trot down the road, headed toward the camp gate.

"Follow Spot. Keep pace with Spot, or you will be dismissed from the candidate selection program! Go! Go! Go!"

With that the squad of candidates took off after the robo-dog, closing the distance. Tighe found himself in the middle of the pack, while Morra kept slightly ahead. To either side Tighe saw the shadowy forms of other candidate groups following the flashing lights of their own robo-dogs.

The camp gates opened silently and Tighe's group followed Spot out across an austere landscape. This close to dawn no Moon was visible, but the stars themselves provided sufficient light.

In addition to the pogo sound of Spot up ahead, Tighe could hear the footfalls of scores of the runners around him. Silhouettes of rounded mountain peaks loomed ahead and to the right. The landscape was beautiful and still.

Suddenly, surprised exclamations rose among the lead runners.

Moments later Tighe's foot crushed something in the road with a disturbing crunch-squish sound. "What the . . ." He glanced back but could only see the candidates behind him dodging around something.

Morra tapped him and pointed down at the road. "Crabs."

Tighe squinted, and sure enough, dozens of small crabs seemed to be scuttling across the asphalt in the darkness—even though the road was thousands of feet up and miles from the ocean.

"Freaking land crabs?"

"Must be gettin' us ready for alien encounters."

The candidates around them laughed.

Tighe tried to sidestep the crabs, but they were all over the road, with runners ahead blocking his view. Eventually he just had to accept squishing the occasional crustacean.

Before long, Spot's flashing light led the candidates off onto a dirt road, across a stony slope dotted with light brush, headed toward the island's largest mountain, which was covered with actual trees.

As they ran, Tighe fell into the sort of absent physicality he sometimes experienced when ascending a long pitch in the blackness of a cave, away from any stone wall. In such situations, he often extinguished his helmet light and rose in sensory deprivation—his entire world just the pressure of the rope, his harness, and his hands in the darkness.

The robo-dog soon brought them over the crest of the hill, which over-looked DAC, and then down the far side.

Despite the morning chill, Tighe was soaked in sweat by the time they crested a second rise and began taking a switchback path toward the sea. This was followed by a run along the coast, an ancient lava flow that broke off like peanut brittle at the water's edge.

The Sun had still not crested the horizon by the time Tighe followed the robo-dog back into the DAC via a side gate. Uniformed guards watched the candidates stumble in, soaked in sweat. Tighe estimated they'd been running for roughly an hour and that they'd covered about 12 kilometers.

Spot guided them back to the mess hall, where another barracks of runners was gathering their breath and mopping sweat off their faces. The moment Spot reached the mess hall, its flashing light turned off, and a uniformed co-ordinator bellowed, "Barracks 4! Half hour for chow! Get inside!"

Over breakfast most of the trainees were too exhausted to do more than eat and drink. Morra looked up at Tighe and nodded as he spooned oatmeal into his mouth. Tighe sat across from him and did likewise.

Bhaduri sat down next to them and looked around. "Have you seen Mr. Parks?"

Morra answered, "Just eat, Rabby."

Afterward they formed up again outside—but this time not in barracks groups. Instead, they were called out by candidate number and re-sorted ac-cording to some unknown calculus.

Tighe found himself among a group of twenty new candidates—half men, half women—and brought to something resembling a construction site, with a barren concrete pad and modular construction materials stacked on work-tables nearby.

A female coordinator called out, "Ascans, gather round!"

Someone muttered, "Ascans?"

"That's right! Asteroid-mining candidates—ascans! Now, gather round!"

They did so.

"You're to work together as a team, building the shelter detailed on this printed schematic." The coordinator held up a document. "You will be as-sessed on both speed and adherence to the printed spec. Camp staff will not answer questions or provide additional information." She offered the schematic to the nearest candidate, a Japanese American woman with elaborate tattoos visible along her neck and wrists. "Get busy!"

Tighe glanced around. There were half a dozen other groups at nearby construction sites of their own, also being briefed by a coordinator. He spotted Morra, and also the woman he'd seen from Baliceaux, both in different groups. The entire work area was ringed by metal poles holding surveillance cameras.

The Japanese American woman flipped through the pages of the document. "We should divide this work."

A man with a Scottish accent said, "Anyone here wi' construction experience?"

Two other men raised their hands.

"Take charge then, lads."

The Japanese American woman cast a look his way and showed the cartoonish diagrams on the document. "This is basically an IKEA assembly guide."

"Na offense, but I don't think we should be takin' instructions from you jus' because they handed you the document."

"I'm an industrial chemist. I think I can figure out a—"

"Yer bum's oot the windae! Chemistry's not construction."

One of the other men said, "This isn't a man-woman thing."

A nearby woman answered, "No one *said* it was a man-woman thing."

Tighe glanced up at the camera domes. He whistled loudly. "Hey!"

Everyone looked his way. "See those cameras?" He pointed out the surveillance domes. "The shrinks are scoring our ability to work together—not our debating skills." Tighe pointed at the Japanese American woman. "What's your name?"

"Amy Tsukada."

"Amy, I'm fine with you being in charge. Maybe you guys who know construction can counsel her as we go. I'm happy to just be a grunt."

The others exchanged looks, then nodded.

One of the men started examining the pile of materials. "These parts all have numbers on them. Amy, start calling out the inventory list in the order it's needed, and we'll get it organized."

More group members moved into action. Soon they'd lined up and counted all the parts and tools, comparing them with the printed list.

Tsukada slapped the paper. "We're missing parts. A socket wrench, six 20-millimeter nuts, a door hinge, a 2-meter I beam, and a 20-millimeter bolt for the joist hanger."

The Scottish man held up some parts. "We've got an extra door handle and a wee bag of bolts."

The construction guys searched to see if anything had fallen behind the panels or beams.

Tighe gazed across the work area to see that some groups had already started construction. I beams were rising on foundations. The field contained a couple hundred workers in blue jumpsuits and caps while camp staff observed from the sidelines.

A fair-skinned woman with zinc oxide protecting the bridge of her nose approached from a neighboring group. A wool cap gave her the look of a snowboarder. She smiled at Tighe as she approached. "You guys missing any parts?" She had a barely detectable accent and like everyone else smelled of sweat.

Tighe nodded. "Yeah, we are." He tried to ignore the fact that she was physically attractive, and turned to his group. "Hey, guys! They're missing parts, too."

The woman in the cap looked around the field. "You're the second group I've talked to. The instructors are screwing with us."

He guessed she was Scandinavian.

She deftly climbed onto a nearby worktable and stood, cupping her hands over her mouth. "Hey, everybody! Listen up!"

Her voice wasn't loud enough to get the entire field's attention.

Tighe whistled as loudly as he could. The entire field of candidates stopped and looked up.

She cast a slight smile down at Tighe and then shouted, "Raise your hand if your group is missing parts or has extras!"

Hands in every group went up.

"This is by design! The true purpose of this exercise is most likely to see how we cope with frustrating difficulties! This is how we'll cope. . . ." She pointed at the ground. "Bring me a list of all the parts you are missing and also bring me all the extra parts you have. We'll sort this out in short order."

The entire field of candidates talked among themselves before getting busy making their lists.

Tighe offered his hand as the woman moved to descend from the table, but instead she hopped down to the ground beside him, alighting with the dexterity of a gymnast.

She tsk-tsked. "Sneaky of them to sabotage us."

"I'd say it's just the beginning." He extended his hand. "James Tighe. Call me J.T."

"J.T., Eike Dahl."

"Eike." She had a natural beauty and easygoing confidence. "I can't quite place your accent."

The edges of her mouth turned up. "From Bergen. Have you ever been?"

"Norway." Tighe nodded. "Yeah, I had a diver friend who brought me through there years ago. The fjords are beautiful."

She grabbed his arm as her eyes came alive. "You should try the wing-suit flying. Stryn is fantastic."

Looking down at her hand on his forearm, Tighe was starting to think he was going to like the Devil's Ashpit.

Hours later Tighe ran an obstacle course for the third time as an Australian stunt woman named Cassie Elwyn screamed into his ear from inches away while she kept pace on the sidelines. She was freckled and fierce. "Move, ya cunt-ass blodger! You call *this* hard yakka?"

They had all run the course separately at first but were then randomly assigned to another candidate, with the instruction to coach that person into improving their initial course time by 5 percent. Afterward, the coachee became the coach.

Tighe had the poor luck of clocking an excellent time on his first run, and Elwyn had her work cut out for her. Tighe started climbing the rope wall.

"Move yar arse! This is a piece a piss!"

By the time they had lunch at eleven a.m., Tighe already felt they should be having dinner. It was hard to believe the better part of the day was still ahead.

After lunch they were brought to classrooms to watch a film on the physical rigors of spaceflight. It gave him a chance to digest and rest his muscles.

Afterward, they were told to change into swimsuits and brought to an indoor pool facility where they were timed on 100-meter, then 250-meter freestyle in an assembly-line format. Immediately afterward, they were instructed to swim twenty solo laps—a kilometer in total.

As Tighe stepped up to the starting block, awaiting his start, he looked over to see the dark-haired mountain climber he'd seen in the parking lot and back in Baliceaux—although she, too, was now bald. She was second in line in the neighboring row and wore a one-piece bathing suit. Her lean body was impressively fit, unadorned by tattoos, and with a scar from a serious injury running under her right suit strap.

She soon stepped up onto the starting block beside him.

He called over to her. "I didn't catch your name, by the way."

She affixed her swim goggles. "If you're still here in a month, I'll tell you."

A whistle and a shout from the coordinator. "Go!"

They both dove into the pool and started their kilometer swim. Her words fired Tighe up, and he soon outpaced her.

CHAPTER 7

Rue de Marche

Twenty-seven-year-old Lukas Rochat sat at a window table in the Café de Trullue, on Krautmaart across from the Hôtel de la Chambre des Députés—the Chamber of Deputies—in the heart of Luxembourg City, capital of the Grand Duchy of Luxembourg. Though smaller than the US state of Rhode Island, on a per capita basis Luxembourg was the richest nation in the European Union. Precisely *why* wasn't common knowledge, but despite the city's medieval charm, its success had a great deal to do with spaceflight.

Like the other attorneys and political staffers conversing all around him, Rochat was nattily dressed. This morning he'd worn his three-button gray mohair Prada suit with a blue silk necktie and orange pocket square. It would help him stand out, and he would need all the help he could get to be noticed this morning.

Rochat nursed a caffè Americano as he divided his attention between watching people exiting the Victorian-era chamber across the street and glancing at his phone to view photos of American limited-edition athletic shoes on an auction website. The kicks on-screen right now were signed by the Chinese rapper Smoov-OB and boasted a striking crimson and white colorway, with silk laces, gold eyelets, and gold aglets. He thought of two outfits they would perfectly complement, and, more important, no one else in Luxembourg City would have them. They'd make him unique.

The online auction commenced but the price instantly surpassed Rochat's bid of 851 dollars, soaring past 6,000 dollars in the couple seconds it took him to close the browser tab with a sigh of disgust.

Story of my life. Outpaced and outspent.

Rochat glanced across the street and spotted the person he was waiting for—Athelme Gagneux, Ministry of the Economy deputy director of space affairs.

Rochat called out, "Miretta, *je dois courir!*"

A young Turkish woman nodded to him and moved to a hundred-year-old espresso machine encased in artfully pounded copper. She poured espresso into a to-go cup, quickly adding steamed milk, then raced over to him with a payment terminal.

Rochat waved his phone over the device.

She grabbed his elbow as he tried to leave. "*Merde!* The charge was declined, Lukas."

"Shhh." He dug in his pocket for a ten-euro note and quickly passed it to her.

"Let me get your change."

"No time. *Merci!*" With that he abandoned his own coffee and grabbed the to-go cup. Rochat exited the Café Trullue and fast-walked in pursuit of his prey, who was already headed down the Krautmaart. Rochat navigated through a crowd of bureaucrats, lobbyists, and staffers.

Outsiders tended to perceive Luxembourg as the world capital for collectible postage stamps, but in fact, it had long been a center for the private space industry. Back in 1985 a consortium of Luxembourg bankers known as the Société Européenne des Satellites (European Society of Satellites)—now known simply as SES—made bold investments in what was then an unproven industry: communications satellites. Those investments paid off handsomely, and by the dawn of the twenty-first century, Luxembourg was receiving two billion dollars a year in royalties alone from global comsat firms.

So when commercial Moon- and asteroid-mining startups began forming at the turn of the millennium, the grand duchy doubled down on investments in space. To lure this new industry to its borders, in 2017 the Luxembourg parliament passed the world's most progressive commercial space legislation—known simply as the Space Law—which guaranteed space-mining companies headquartered in Luxembourg the legal right to profit from resources extracted from celestial bodies. This meant space revenue could flow through

Luxembourg's banks—and, thus, EU banks, and from there, the world. It was, in fact, Luxembourg's express goal to make itself the most space-commerce-friendly sovereign state on Earth.

As he walked, Rochat knew that the people in these streets were helping to chart the future of space commerce. Rochat was convinced this would be the biggest single industry in human history—that it would make the Internet look like a toy. If now was not the time to risk all and put out his own shingle, then when?

That's what he'd told Sheila, the mother of his two-year-old son back in Vevey. She was legal counsel for a major food company, and their life was secure in Switzerland—but boring. Now was the time to strike out on his own. To make his mark. He'd clerked for a year at Pritzer & Wallace, one of the leading space-law firms with an office in Geneva. But LC was where the real action was. All the best space lawyers were setting up shop or hiring on with space startups here. Opportunity was everywhere.

Rochat knew he had to make his move now or be left behind. *Again.*

The balding, pear-shaped deputy director of space affairs was apparently not in a hurry, but he was also unfortunately talking on his phone as he walked.

Damn. Rochat couldn't very well interrupt Gagneux's phone call. He kept pace several people behind. No personal security detail, thank goodness. Not for a middle-level bureaucrat.

Then Gagneux hung up, and Rochat made his move as the man slipped the phone into his coat pocket.

"Good morning, Deputy Director."

Gagneux glanced up with a neutral expression at first, but not recognizing Rochat, he turned away. "I am late for a meeting."

"I won't delay you." Rochat handed over the coffee. "A caffè caramel, as you like it."

This didn't have the desired effect. "You think spying on my coffee preferences is the right approach?"

"I'm in the Trullue every morning and noticed you were too rushed today to go inside."

"Early hearings." He eyed the coffee. "I cannot accept that."

Rochat dug into his coat and held up a completed gift declaration form.

"Lukas Rochat, Sirius Legal Services. I am registered with the Ministry of the Economy. I'll submit the paperwork. Surely, no one will begrudge you coffee during a meeting."

"That's only if I agree this is a meeting." The deputy director eyed the coffee and finally accepted it. "Speak fast, Mr. Rochat."

"I'm following up for a client—Lunargistics, LLC." Rochat produced a sheaf of papers a hundred pages thick from his dispatch case. "I submitted their 37-B Space Operations Permit application five months ago, and—"

The bureaucrat cast a bemused expression Rochat's way. "Lunargistics?"

"Yes, sir. I know they're not a big player—for the present. They're a cislunar logistics services firm, proposing to support operations of lunar mining companies. Market cap of just over fifty million euros, but on the strength of an approved SOP they'll have a second funding round. I've been trying to get word about what's delayed their application so they—"

"Don't sack you?"

Rochat paused. "In short, yes, sir."

"Brevity is a blessing in business, son. Remember that. This Sirius Legal Services you work for, I've never heard of them."

"We recently opened an office here in Luxembourg City."

"We?"

Rochat cleared his throat. "Me. I started the firm six months ago. Lunargistics is my first client. I just need to get them an answer on the status of their permit application."

"You should have done some time in the bigger space-law firms. Made connections before hanging out your own shingle."

"I was an associate at Pritzer & Wallace in Geneva for a year, Deputy Director. I've still got friends there, but nobody could tell me what's holding up this permit application—otherwise, I would not have bothered you."

The deputy director looked to him with a bit more interest. "If I call David Wallace, he won't tell me you were sacked?"

"No, Deputy Director. I was on a career track, but I left to—"

"Start your own firm. They must still be angry with you."

"They'll give me a good reference. Wallace is firm but fair."

"Hmm. Young people—always starting companies." He sipped his coffee again. "Next time mention you were at P&W from the outset. It means you're not a *complete* moron." He glanced over at the sheaf of papers in Rochat's hand. "You say your client is Lunargistics, LLC?"

Relieved, he said, "Yes, Deputy Director. You can have this copy. If I could get a response in writing—anything I can bring back to my client to state what's delayed the application."

Gagneux waved off the documents. "I don't need a copy, Counselor."

Rochat's hope sank. He offered the forms again. "Just to make sure you look up the correct firm. The application number is right here." He pointed.

"I don't need to look up the status of your client's application—because I already *know* why it's been delayed."

"You know . . . already?" Rochat paused momentarily in midstep. His client was barely a blip in the multibillion-dollar commercial space services industry. The fact that the deputy director knew their name off the top of his head was *not* a good sign.

Rochat raced to catch up alongside Gagneux again. "I . . . may I ask what then is the reason for the delay, Deputy Director?"

The bureaucrat stopped and eyed the young attorney as he sipped his coffee. "If you are going to succeed in this business, son, remember that clients are a reflection of you. You need to do your due diligence."

Due diligence was a luxury Rochat did not currently enjoy, but he nodded. "There's a problem with Lunargistics?"

"Your 'tiny' client, Counselor, is not so tiny. Lunargistics has financial ties to a much larger organization, one that hired a dozen young attorneys—like yourself—to submit space permit applications for seemingly separate startup companies. However, our research revealed common links to shell companies in the Cayman Islands and Dubai, interlocking boards, and shared bank accounts."

Shit. Rochat felt the ground crumbling beneath him.

"Lunargistics' permit application has been flagged, along with the others, and sidelined pending further review. The Ministry of the Economy takes a dim view of misrepresentation. The entities behind this could be engaging in stock fraud or money laundering—with no intention to develop space industry. That could hurt the duchy's reputation as a transparent and legal marketplace. Space is a very big place in which to launder money, and we want no part of that. Do you understand?"

"Yes, of course, Deputy Director." Rochat was still trying to process the news. The question that kept coming back to him was, *Why me?* But then, this sort of thing happened during booms. That didn't make the news any less bad.

"So the parent entity was larger than they revealed?"

"Capitalized in the *billions*. Privately held. The individual investors unknown."

Rochat was dumbfounded, but then a thought occurred to him: *The parent companies were capitalized in the billions.*

"Deputy Director, I appreciate you informing me. Would it be possible for me to see the other company applications—so that I can cancel my contract for cause?"

The bureaucrat sighed, but he seemed to have taken pity on Rochat. Or perhaps he really did need the coffee. "Contact my office. Ask for Maurice. Tell him you are Lunargistics' attorney of record. You can request a copy of the ministry's findings report by filing a Form 914. It is public information—however, the filing is not free."

"Yes." He winced. "Do you know how much it is?"

"In the hundreds, I imagine. Ask Maurice." They had reached the deputy director's door. The man raised his cup. "Thank you for the coffee, Counselor. Let's hope you learn something from this first mistake."

"Thank *you*, Deputy Director. I will do just that, sir. I'll phone Maurice." Rochat produced his business card. "In case you ever need to contact me."

The deputy director wrinkled his nose as he looked at the card. It showed the words "Sirius Legal Services" with a silver rocket plume powering the *S* skyward. "This isn't Silicon Valley, Counselor. Get yourself an adult business card." The deputy director entered the building.

"Yes, sir. Thank you again, Deputy Director."

Rochat stood for several moments in the medieval cobblestone street. So his insignificant first client was bigger than he thought. *Valued in the billions.*

He might have a chance to turn this around yet.

CHAPTER 8

Potlatch

D uring the Cold War, the International Astronautical Congress—or IAC—had been one of the few forums where East and West could meet to discuss issues of the space race. Now the IAC was where everyone met to discuss everything about space.

As an emcee worked the conference audience, Erika Lisowski stood just offstage and focused on her phone screen, studying questions for the panel she was about to moderate. She noticed the edge of her phone quivering slightly and willed it to stop. Public speaking didn't frighten her. Neither did the aerospace heavyweights who would sit on her panel. Instead, what worried Lisowski was that she was about to cross a line beyond which there might be no return.

There was no doubt that her panel would make news. No one had ever managed to get all six Space Titans on one stage before. It promised to be a good show, and as a result the audience was already beyond standing room. Her panel would also be simulcast live to the Internet. Millions were expected to tune in.

The trick would be getting the Titans to go beyond their carefully crafted PR-speak and into a bare-knuckle discussion about development of space. To have the debate that really needed to take place in public.

However, Lisowski had an ace up her sleeve—one that she hoped would come through for her when it really counted.

Five out of six of the Titans already stood impatiently nearby.

George Burkett had arrived with an entourage of assistants and suited security men wearing earpieces. Diminutive and slim, Burkett kept his head not just bald but polished. His intense demeanor was belied by a tendency to wear checkered shirts, jeans, and sneakers. Worth north of three hundred billion dollars, Burkett had become the richest man in the world by creating the world's largest Internet logistics and cloud computing company.

Raymond Halser stood next to Burkett. In his seventies, with a prodigious belly, big hands, thick-framed eyeglasses, and Asimov-like muttonchop sideburns, Halser kept sighing and checking his enormous watch.

Next to him stood tanned, bearded British entrepreneur Thomas Morten in a gray plaid jacket—and Jack Macy, Burkett's direct rival in the reusable rocket race. Macy wore a tailored suit, but without a tie. He had his own security detail and assistant entourage.

Asteroid-mining robotics entrepreneur Alan Goff rounded out the group, appearing generic enough to be mistaken for part of Macy's security detail.

Stagehands worked to get the Titans miked up.

Burkett frowned. "Weren't we supposed to be onstage by now, Erika? I have a tight schedule."

Lisowski checked her watch—a timepiece hand-built by her grandfather, an aerospace engineer. It was one minute after they were scheduled to begin— but just then she heard a familiar voice.

"Lighten up, George. A true showman knows to let the audience wait."

Everyone turned to see Nathan Joyce approaching, sipping on one of his own brands of nootropic energy drinks. He was dressed in a Clash concert T-shirt and ripped jeans. Joyce stood several inches taller than the others and had a casual swagger that immediately irritated the shit out of everyone.

Lisowski clamped back a relieved smile. "Nathan's here. Wonderful. We can begin."

The stagehands quickly miked up Joyce as Lisowski signaled the emcee, then placed her hands together. "Gentlemen, if you are ready . . ."

Suddenly there was a swell of applause, and Lisowski motioned for her guests to follow her onstage. Their emergence prompted even more rapturous applause, as the Titans waved to the assembled aerospace investors, executives, government officials, and academics. These six individuals could make humanity's dreams come true—or so the room appeared to believe. Phone cameras flashed as people recorded this historic scene.

It took another minute to calm the room down and get the billionaires seated in their Danish-modern armchairs. Lisowski motioned for silence and eventually brought the room under control.

"I want to thank the International Astronautical Federation as well as NASA and ESA for making this exceptional panel possible. My name is Erika Lisowski, NASA program executive for emerging space. In that role, I've had the opportunity to get to know the world's leaders in commercial space exploration, my esteemed guests today."

Lisowski introduced each of the billionaires in turn, to varying levels of ovation—with Burkett and Macy garnering the lion's share, as expected.

Joyce—whose recent crowdfunding scheme for asteroid mining was generally seen as undignified—received just a smattering of applause.

Introductions over, Lisowski took a deep breath and turned to her panel. "First question: George Burkett, back in 2017 astrophysicist Stephen Hawking warned that unless our species found a way to colonize another planet in the next century, humanity faced the real threat of extinction. He said, and I quote, 'With climate change, overdue asteroid strikes, epidemics, and population growth, our own planet is increasingly precarious.' In light of Dr. Hawking's statement, do you feel there is sufficient urgency about investment in space exploration?"

If Burkett was irked by the question, he didn't show it. Of all the billionaires here, Burkett had been investing in private space exploration for nearly three decades. He had a reputation as a methodical investor—which stood in stark contrast to Macy, who was already fidgeting in his chair, clearly itching to speak.

The audience chuckled at this.

Burkett ignored them as he pondered the question for several more moments. Finally he said, "Space exploration, more than just about any other investment I can think of, requires adherence to reason. No amount of passion gets you to space—physics and economics are what get you there." He paused for applause. "We will only be able to make deep space viable for humanity when the math makes sense, and at the moment, we're still working that problem."

Macy fidgeted some more.

Lisowski turned to him. "Jack, you seem eager to respond to that."

He gasped melodramatically to more laughter. "Yes. I don't think there's anywhere near enough urgency."

That earned even more applause.

"I share Dr. Hawking's goal to make humanity a multiplanet species. It's why I'm all in when it comes to industries that will either help us colonize Mars or buy us the time to do so—by addressing climate change through electric cars and solar power, for example."

Burkett calmly responded, "You've invested a fraction of what I have, Jack, and although you were first, Starion's reusable launch systems are now more reliable and more cost-effective. Which means they'll lift more payloads into space. Slow and steady wins the race."

"I'm glad that we're competing, George. The more the merrier, I say."

The audience applauded once more.

Lisowski piped in, "That brings up a good point; there are now dozens of smaller space-launch startups in several countries. Jack, if satellite launch services become a low-margin business and Zenith's profit margins slide, does that make your self-imposed goal of colonizing Mars more difficult? You're already a decade behind your original timeline."

The audience oohed at the challenge implied in Lisowski's question.

"Not at all, Erika. If launch costs go down, my plan to settle Mars is more attainable, not less. Those reduced launch costs have complicated the situation far more for NASA and their SLS"—he pointed at Lisowski—"which is why I still have a chance to beat you guys there."

The audience laughed and applauded.

Joyce shook his head. "What is it with you and colonizing Mars, Jack? It makes no damn sense."

The audience was shocked into silence.

Macy actually turned his seat to glare at Joyce.

Joyce held up his hands. "Don't get me wrong. Your innovations in reusable rockets helped launch this entire commercial space race. We're all grateful, but that doesn't mean we should colonize Mars."

Macy replied immediately. "Stephen Hawking seemed to feel it was a worthy goal. I share his concern that humanity must become a multiplanet species or risk extinction."

Joyce casually crossed his legs. "Now, why would you act like I don't know that? I didn't say we shouldn't expand into the solar system. I asked you why you're so fixated on Mars—*in particular.*"

Macy looked impatient. "Because Mars is close by, has a vast supply of resources, and it's the most Earth-like destination. Nathan, I'm glad you're on this stage with us, but everyone else here has been investing in commercial space for over a decade. Some of us for three decades. You've made a hodge-podge of very recent, modest investments—and one very optimistic fund-raising video."

The audience laughed.

"That might get you on this stage, but it doesn't make you an expert."

Joyce waved it off. "I understand if you don't want to talk about it—"

"I've 'talked about it' all over the world. It's not a secret why I want humanity to colonize Mars."

"I think there are better options."

The audience murmured.

Macy actually turned to Burkett, who for once just shook his head.

Halser leaned in. "What in the blazes are you on about, Nathan?"

Morten also frowned in confusion.

Joyce swiveled in his chair. "Why wouldn't we build colony stations near Earth instead of settling Mars? In cislunar space. O'Neill cylinders or—"

Macy turned on Lisowski. "Erika, can we move on from this? Twenty-mile-long colony ships are a century or more in our future. The theme of this year's conference is 'What's Next,' not 'What's Next Century'—we should be talking about what's happening in commercial space exploration."

Joyce leaned forward. "Who says space colonies are a century in the future?"

"We eventually *will* have space colonies, Nathan, but Mars—"

Burkett interjected, "And the Moon."

Macy nodded. "And, yes, the Moon, will provide humanity the resources we need to expand into space. We can't just start out building 20-mile-long constructs in the vacuum of space. We need to begin on another planetary body."

Lisowski asked, "Does that include asteroid mining, Jack?"

"No. Why would we go vast distances seeking tiny, isolated rocks that contain barely anything, only to expend lots of delta-v to get the material back to where we need it?"

Goff now leaned in. "No offense, Jack, but that's not an accurate representation of the asteroid-mining business model. The return delta-v's on NEA resources are—"

Macy shook his head. "Alan, you can't obtain the tonnage of material that we can from Mars. The surface area of Mars is equal in size to all the continents of Earth."

Halser said, "Sounds like you're going to need lots of inflatable habitats."

The audience laughed.

Macy chuckled, too. "Yes, we will, Ray."

Halser turned to the audience. "See why I'm in the inflatable habitat business? No matter who wins . . ."

The audience laughed again, breaking the tension.

Joyce still focused on Macy. "Colonizing Mars is madness."

The audience groaned.

Joyce looked out at the audience. "You heard me. I'm not a member of the Church of Mars."

Macy now looked truly annoyed.

Joyce continued. "Sure, we need to *visit* Mars—and *do research* on Mars—but colonizing Mars is a trap." He turned to Macy. "Jack, what do you propose to do about the fact that Mars only has a third of Earth's gravity? How are you gonna change that?"

"We don't know that that's a significant problem."

"We have some idea. The human body evolved over millions of years to function in one Earth gravity. Astronauts suffer health issues from just a few months in microgravity." He peeled off the problems on his fingers. "Bone and muscle loss, eye damage—to say nothing of the viability of pregnancy in a low-gravity environment. You're willing to send people all the way to Mars before we find out if that's a problem? Why not build a station in cislunar space that can rotate to simulate various levels of gravity long-term before we send people to colonize Mars? Oh, but then, I guess if you did that, you'd be halfway to building a space colony, wouldn't you?"

Burkett turned to Lisowski. "Will we be having any new questions from you, Erika?"

Lisowski nodded. "We will move on—but I imagine Jack wants to address Nathan's gravity objection first." Lisowski looked out at the audience questioningly. "Right? Is everyone interested in hearing Jack's answer?"

The audience applauded their encouragement.

Macy sighed. "One-third gravity isn't the same as microgravity, Nathan, and it will make construction of habitats and greenhouses that much easier."

"Well, let's talk about those greenhouses. What are you going to do for food?"

"We've already proven that Martian soil can support plant growth, and the carbon dioxide–rich atmosphere of Mars will make plants flourish."

"Not without nitrogen it won't, and nitrogen is pretty damn scarce on Mars."

Macy projected calm. "It can be baked out of surface regolith, and it's 2 percent of the Martian atmosphere."

"Extracting it will require energy—and solar panels have half the efficiency on the Martian surface that they do here on Earth. Plus, you'll need nitrogen for more than just the crops, Jack. In a closed-loop habitat you'll need about 110 kilograms of nitrogen per person for chemical processes in the human body. Add another 540 kilograms per person of nitrogen to provide atmospheric pressure and as a fire retardant. That totals about 650 kilograms per colonist just for life support, and some of that nitrogen would need to be replenished on a regular basis."

"That's not impossible."

"But it is a challenge. Even if you can maintain a livable atmosphere in your habs, whatever crops you grow with that Martian soil would poison any colonists who ate them."

Macy shook his head.

"See, Jack, this is why I get irritated with you about colonizing Mars. You know as well as I do that the Martian surface is covered in perchlorates—salts that are classified as industrial waste here on Earth. They're great for making rocket fuel but highly toxic to human beings. They overwhelm the thyroid gland, blocking the ability to absorb iodine—which the body uses to produce a hormone that regulates human metabolism and mental function, and which is also vital for prenatal and postnatal development. Perchlorates *cover* the surface of Mars—including any dust you'd carry into the habitats."

Macy waved it away. "It can be dealt with, Nathan."

"Perchlorates are so toxic that here in California the legal limit is one part per billion by mass." Joyce looked out at the audience. "Anyone care to guess what the concentration is in Martian regolith? Anyone? It's *six million* parts per billion. The entire planet makes a toxic Superfund site look like a children's day care."

The audience murmured in response.

Macy looked annoyed. "There are microbes we can bring that could consume the perchlorates. It can be handled."

"I'll bet planetary scientists and astrobiologists will be less than thrilled by your plan—especially since it will ruin any chance to determine if indigenous microbial life exists on Mars, which could answer for us the question of whether life in the universe is rare or exceptionally common."

"It could be done in consultation with—"

"And what about the hexavalent chromium also present in Martian soil? That's a potent carcinogen."

Macy jabbed a finger at Joyce. "If it was up to people like you, humanity would never have gone to the Moon."

The audience roared in applause.

Unfazed, Joyce stayed focused on Macy. "You and George keep saying that we should settle the Moon and Mars. And I agree that we should *go to* those places, do science there, visit—but we shouldn't colonize them."

Some members of the audience booed.

Burkett turned his calm eyes toward Joyce. "Nathan, you're suggesting it makes more sense to venture into the absolute vacuum of space—a desert so complete that it makes the Sahara look like the Garden of Eden—and to there build, *from scratch*, what? A fully enclosed, completely sustainable habitat that will also shield its occupants from solar and cosmic radiation and meteor strikes? How can you seriously suggest that that is an easier task than settling either the Moon or Mars?"

"Because it's the *whole fucking point of going into space!*"

A hush fell over the auditorium.

Joyce waded into that silence. "If we want to have any future as a species, then we must learn how to build *our* biome—the one for which we evolved— out in the harsh vacuum of space. By learning how to create our ideal environment with our own hands and our own minds, we can even begin to understand how Earth's ecosystem functions—and in doing so we will not only secure humanity's future but we may learn how to fix Earth's climate as well."

A moment of stunned silence was soon filled with applause.

Burkett shook his head. "That sounds great on a stage, Nathan, but now actually execute it. The difference between you and us is that you're all talk."

Macy nodded. "Everything you described will happen centuries from now."

Joyce nodded back. "It *will* be centuries if it's up to you two."

Some of the crowd shouted, others booed, some clapped. Others broke out into individual debates.

Joyce shouted over them. "We shouldn't just accept that we're destined to live on whatever planets have been dealt us. If you solve the problems of living on Mars, then you've only solved the Mars problem, but if we learn to build habitats in open space, then we have solved the entire future of the human race. We can harvest materials"—he pointed to Goff—"from asteroids, for example."

Goff nodded. "I agree."

"And bring those materials into a lunar distant retrograde orbit to build massive, lavish, amazing structures, spun to use centrifugal force as artificial gravity, designed for people, instead of consigning future generations to an inhumane purgatory on the Moon or Mars."

Burkett crossed his legs impatiently. "There's zero operational experience with centrifugal spacecraft systems of even modest size. And you want to *start out* building gigantic ones."

"Why *haven't* we pursued centrifugal force to simulate gravity in spaceship designs? Konstantin Tsiolkovsky wrote about it way back at the turn of the nineteenth century. We *know* we need to do it if we want to stay in space long-term. Then why the hell aren't we making it a priority? Instead, everybody's rushing to be the first one to plant a flag on something."

Macy jabbed his finger at Joyce. "What happens, Nathan, when your prototype O'Neill cylinder breaks apart, killing everyone, or when it leaks, or its completely enclosed biome goes sour?"

"Okay, Jack, what happens when *your* Mars or Moon enclosed biome goes sour? The only difference between what I'm suggesting and your plan is that I want to *also* have normal gravity and to put our built environment reasonably close to Earth—while you put yours so far away it can only be reached during a once-every-two-year orbital window. Any habitat we build off Earth will have to be an enclosed system. Mars will be no different. It'll just be much farther away and much more difficult to live in."

"We can terraform Mars."

"Now look who's talking about centuries. That will take millennia."

Lisowski waved her hands. "Let's get this discussion back on track."

Burkett and Macy spoke in unison. "Please, Erika."

Burkett added, "For god's sake, start moderating."

Joyce focused on Macy again. "Jack, if you're so concerned about the danger of an asteroid hitting Earth and the 'need to be a multiplanet species,' then you should want humans on more than two planets—we should have a constellation of colony ships in orbit around the Sun. The more people and resources we have in space, the better the chance we'll have of protecting Earth—detecting and deflecting a dangerous asteroid. A colony on the surface of Mars won't help stop an asteroid strike on the Earth."

Morten—who hadn't yet said a word—leaned forward. "Nathan is right about one thing: every strategy in the effort to commercialize space travel should be tried. There's no reason to rule out the plans of anyone up here."

There was a smattering of applause.

Burkett snorted. "Of course you don't want to rule out anything, Tom; you run a parabolic carnival ride."

Morten visibly reined his temper in. "Vestal is making space available to more people than you are, George."

"You're making 67 miles high *briefly* available to more people than we are. Congratulations."

Goff spoke across Halser and Morten. "I agree with Nathan that asteroid mining makes more fiscal sense than colonizing the Moon or Mars."

Even Burkett was now visibly irritated. "Alan, the Moon is close enough to Earth for robotic mining via telepresence. You can't remotely control asteroid-mining robots. The signal delays are too great."

Goff hesitated before he pushed back against the richest man on Earth. "That's why we have autonomous systems."

Macy scoffed. "And what happens when something goes wrong? Your mission is a total loss."

Joyce piped in, "I agree with Jack on that point."

Macy rolled his eyes. "I don't *care* if you agree with me, Nathan."

Joyce turned to Goff. "And if we send autonomous robots, humanity won't be mining anything—you'll be mining it, Alan. I say human beings can beat you to the solar system. In fact, I'm going to challenge all of you to a race right here on this stage—John Henry style."

The audience hooted.

He turned to Burkett and Macy. "And while you're getting sued over mining rights to the Moon and Mars, I'll beat every one of you to market—because I'm going to send humans to the asteroids. And I'm not going to wait. I'm going all in on space, too, Jack."

The crowd applauded again, though it was followed by excited, confused chatter.

Macy shook his head as he muttered, "You're such a publicity whore . . ."

Burkett nodded. "He's turning this into an infomercial about himself, Erika, and I don't want any part of it."

The crowd was descending into chaotic discussion.

Joyce laughed. "Deep space is a potlatch, George, don't you know that by now? And I bet I'm willing to burn more money than you to get there."

"That would be a surprise. Your biggest investment so far is a party island." Burkett removed his microphone.

The crowd groaned in disappointment.

Macy shook his head. "I'm not going to be a prop in Joyce's infomercial, Erika." He, too, removed his microphone and headed toward the wings, to even more audience groans and boos—although it was hard to say whether they were booing Burkett and Macy, or Joyce's grandstanding.

The audience immediately began a raucous discussion as journalists tried to push past the line of security at the edge of the stage, shouting.

"Mr. Joyce! What do you mean you're all in on space?"

"Mr. Joyce, do you really think it's foolish for humanity to colonize Mars?"

Goff, Morten, and Halser stood up. Halser removed his microphone and walked past Lisowski. "Nice work, Nathan. You asshole. This could have been a boost to the entire industry. We don't need to compete like this with each other. We should be cooperating."

Morten's microphone was still live as he asked Lisowski, "Is this really over already?"

Lisowski switched off his mic and nodded. "It looks like it, Sir Thomas. I apologize."

Goff passed Lisowski, also shaking his head. "That was quite the disaster, Erika."

Joyce approached Lisowski, holding out his wireless mic and transmitter— but as she reached for them, he deliberately dropped them onto the stage. The impact thundered over the speakers. His eyes smiled at her as he walked past, patting her shoulder before heading offstage in the opposite direction to the other billionaires.

Lisowski watched Joyce go, then looked out at the audience and the cameras. She imagined the tens of millions of people who would see this worldwide. Maybe hundreds of millions in evening news clips. Based on the furious debates under way in the audience around her, the clash of the Space Titans would no doubt go viral.

In short: it had gone perfectly.

CHAPTER 9

Self-Selection

JANUARY 19, 2033

Electric motors wailed as James Tighe focused on a glowing dot in the middle of a computer screen. He wore a flight suit, helmet, and oxygen mask as he manipulated a joystick to keep the dot in the center of a white circle. This simple task was made difficult by 6.3 g's of acceleration.

The electric motors rose in pitch, and the g-forces increased. His field of vision narrowed, requiring a supreme act of will just to hold his head upright.

Eight point five g's. Eight point seven.

He blinked rapidly.

Nine point two g's.

His vision constricted like a camera iris—and he suddenly found himself swatting away blowflies in a swamp somewhere in Tennessee. It didn't seem at all strange that he was here. He just was.

But then he wasn't. The swamp was replaced by a persistent, annoying beeping sound. Finally Tighe focused on a blinking yellow button and recalled that he was supposed to press it when he regained consciousness.

It all came back to him: he wasn't in a swamp. He was inside a centrifuge testing facility on Ascension Island in the middle of the South Atlantic. Tighe tapped the button and the sound stopped. The centrifuge was no longer moving.

A voice in his headset said, *"What is your candidate number?"*

"Ascan 3-6-3."

"Ascan 3-6-3, are you ready to go again?"

He took a deep breath. "Gimme a second."

"Do you want to stop?"

Tighe caught his breath. "No. No, I'm good."

"Launching evolution five in three, two, one ..."

The electric motors wound up—and the g-forces increased once more, smashing him into the seat as the glowing dot returned.

Tighe exited a Polestar bus onto the sunny tarmac of Wideawake Field. Still unsteady on his feet, he leaned to one side. Marcel Cortez, a Spanish salvage diver, grabbed his arm and spoke in accented English. "You are okay, J.T.?"

"I'm fine. Just gonna sit down a sec."

Cortez walked on as Tighe sat on a nearby pallet containing bags of concrete. A dozen other candidates milled around in their blue jumpsuits. They'd been told to prepare for a parabolic flight. The idea was to ride an aircraft through a series of steep climbs and dives to mimic the free fall of spaceflight. NASA astronauts had dubbed such training flights "vomit comets" because invariably participants got sick—and that was probably just the sort of weakness the company was checking for.

Tighe took in the sun and a light tropical breeze to help him recover from the centrifuge and listened to the other candidates chatting excitedly. They were clearly looking forward to free fall.

A young man with dark black skin was sitting next to Tighe on the pallet. Tighe had seen him around. In his early twenties, the guy was jotting down notes on a small pad of paper. No one else seemed interested in the young man, nor he in anyone else.

Tighe leaned toward him. "You looking forward to trying out free fall?"

The young man looked up from his notepad.

Tighe nodded toward the others. "The parabolic flight, I mean."

The young man answered with a thick Nigerian accent. "Anything way go up, dem no born am well, 'e must come down." He then went back to writing.

Tighe stared. "Pidgin? Really?"

The kid cast a wary glance Tighe's way. "Comot! Dem send you?"

"We both know you can speak English—otherwise, you wouldn't be here. If you don't want to talk, fine."

The young man paused his writing.

"It's just that I'd heard the company wasn't interested in young people. And yet, they made an exception for you. I'm curious why you're here."

The young man tapped the stub of pencil on his notepad, then looked up. He spoke in accented English. "Because my *oga* said I must come."

"Your 'oga'—what's an oga?"

"Oga is a patron. He provides protection. In exchange, you obey. Everyone in Lagos has an oga—all except the e-lite."

"So why'd your oga send you here?"

"Because of Mr. Joyce. He caused problems for me with the government."

"Why would Joyce do that?"

"Because I stole his satellite."

Tighe couldn't help but laugh.

"You find that funny?"

"Sorry, it's just that I'll bet Joyce was impressed."

"I did not do it to impress Mr. Joyce. I have brothers and sisters in Aje-gunle. A mother. I could not refuse my oga. Ransoming satellites pays the bosses too well."

"Where'd you learn to hijack satellites?"

"A satellite is just a computer in the sky. When I was small, I found electrical components in the dumps of Mushin and Ijora. I took apart things—to see how they worked." The young man waved his arm across the sky. "There are many new satellites—the cube sats have poor security. I used them for my education."

"You taught *yourself*?"

"I taught myself how to learn."

Tighe recalled skipping school as a boy and felt a twinge of guilt. "How'd Joyce find you?"

"He paid the ransom—plus a fee for my name."

"So your oga sold you out?"

The kid nodded grimly. "I worry about my brothers and sisters. I must do well here."

"So you didn't come here because you *want* to get into space."

He contemplated this. "As a boy, I dreamed of space, but now I know there will be ogas there as well."

Tighe noticed the young man was lean and bore scars on his neck. Life had apparently been tough for him. Tighe extended his hand. "I'm James Tighe. Call me J.T."

The kid hesitated but then cautiously extended his hand. "J.T." They shook firmly. He placed a hand on his chest. "My name is Adedayo Adisa. People call me Ade."

"Good to meet you, Ade."

There was an awkward silence.

Adisa gestured to the pad in his hand. "I am writing to my brothers and sisters in AJ City."

"You know you won't be able to mail that, right?"

He nodded. "I know. But it helps me. I learned so much while explaining things to them."

"Have you ever been outside of Nigeria before, Ade?"

Adisa shook his head. "I have never been outside of Lagos." But then he brightened. "I had always wondered what it was like to fly. Now I know."

A coordinator spoke over a PA system. "*Five minutes to departure. Last call for bathrooms.*"

Adisa stood. "I should prepare."

Tighe nodded and watched as Adisa and a few other candidates moved toward the nearby hangar complex escorted by a coordinator and security detail.

A clean-shaven Asian man with close-cropped black hair leaned against the cement pallet near Tighe. Most candidates had let their hair grow and some were sporting short beards. Not this guy.

The man gestured toward Adisa and spoke with a slight Chinese accent. "What do you think of the boy?"

Tighe shrugged. "Seems smart."

"He knows more about orbital mechanics than me."

"What do you do?"

"I am an astronaut—although I suppose you Americans would call me a *taikonaut.*"

"Chinese space program."

He nodded.

"What are you doing *here*? It's not like Joyce is really launching an asteroid mission."

"No, but there will be training in low Earth orbit—at least for those who make the cut."

Tighe and the man exchanged appraising looks. "So you haven't been in space yet?"

The man shook his head.

"You'd stand a better chance of getting there in a real space program."

"I agree, but the CNSA is no longer an option for me." The taikonaut looked after Adisa, who was now out of sight. "Imagine having a mind like that. How many Liu Hui's and Qin Jiushao's must be walking this Earth, thwarted by the circumstances of their birth?"

Tighe looked after Adisa as well. "So you spoke with Ade?"

"Several times. In Mandarin."

"Huh."

He looked at Tighe. "You are the cave diver. J.T., is it?"

"That's right." Tighe extended his hand.

"Jin Hua Han."

"Pleasure."

The sound of jet engines approached, and soon the company's windowless 787 rolled past on the runway. Tighe stood, and they both watched it as the others cheered.

Tighe said, "You ready to go for a ride, Han?"

"Always."

JANUARY 22, 2033

Tighe's calloused hands joined a dozen others as he and his teammates hoisted a tar-soaked log over their heads, carrying it as though they were a knot of ants, laboring up the slope of a cinder cone. Trampled black and red soil bogged down their feet as they struggled toward the 100-meter summit. Different teams beyond their field of view approached from different compass points on the cone's slope in a competition apparently designed to sap their strength—and after a while, the will to live.

Now on their fourth out of ten logs, Tighe and his teammates were soaked in sweat, which had also combined with volcanic dirt to smear them all Mars red. The mud and sweat made it even more difficult to hold on to the log. Each laborious step upslope made Tighe's muscles burn. Adding to their misery was the occasional gust of cold wind that blinded them with grit.

A voice behind Tighe hissed through pain, "There are no logs in space. Why the fuck are we doing this?" The voice belonged to Eric Reyes, an ex–US Air Force test pilot who hadn't been able to find civilian work due to the spread of autonomous aircraft. Reyes was a pro at bitching. His bitching had a cadence you could heave to, and it was better than focusing on muscle pain.

"I'd like to take this log and jam it up Joyce's ass!"

Five weeks into the selection process and physical training director Dastous had made good on his promise to test the candidates' physical limits. The misery was as advertised. Already a quarter of the applicants were gone. Tighe's competition was slowly dwindling.

As he strained, Tighe glanced over to see another candidate nearby, staring at them with arms folded. Like all the other candidates', her hair was short, and she was attractive, but in a tomboyish way, with auburn hair. More important—she wasn't smeared with mud. Instead just a light dusting of volcanic grit covered her knees.

"Guys! Why are you doing it like that?"

Tighe's entire group stopped and with unconcealed annoyance turned to look at her.

She motioned with her hands. "*Roll it* up the hill. We did two at a time. Everyone else is already finished."

Tighe's group exchanged horrified looks.

After a moment Tighe started laughing.

The woman walked past. "Don't you have an engineer among you?"

Reyes cursed. "Goddamnit!" He paced away. "Goddamnit to fuck!"

Jogging back to DAC after the exercise was finished, Tighe caught up to the woman. "Hey!"

She turned around. He and his team were easy to recognize, since they were the only ones coated in mud.

"Thanks for the help back there. We'd still be on the hill otherwise."

She chuckled. "I felt bad for you. It's easy to get groupthink—especially when you're tired."

"You and I are both in Barracks 4, aren't we?"

"Yeah, I'm on the far end."

"You an engineer?"

"Geologist. You're that cave diver who got caught in the earthquake, aren't you? I saw the video. That must have been hell."

Tighe nodded.

She extended her hand. "Nicole Clarke."

A short while later Tighe, Morra, Reyes, and Clarke walked into the shower at Barracks 4. The room was filled with two dozen men and women. As Tighe moved past, other candidates were chatting, laughing, or just holding their heads under the showerheads in exhaustion, letting the hot water blast their scalps. Rivulets of the island's volcanic dirt swirled down the drains.

They passed Rachel Gardner, an Irish foreign war correspondent. Clarke stopped to chat, while the men moved on.

Morra whispered to Tighe, "You ever have a wank before you come in here?"

"Whenever possible. Makes it simpler."

They got under the first showerheads that became available.

Tighe nodded to the man next to him, Katsuka Akira, an around-the-world solo sailor, who was knotted with muscle. Katsuka nodded back as he continued a conversation about hypothermia with Elizabeth Josephson, a British former ESA astronaut and flight surgeon. Even fully clothed Josephson would have turned Tighe's head.

He turned to face the wall. "Goddamnit, I'm thinking about sex *all the time.*"

Morra scrubbed his tattooed arms with soap. "One of the challenges of space travel, I reckon. I imagine that's partly what they're testing."

JANUARY 24, 2033

Walking back from mess hall duty one evening, Tighe noticed Eike Dahl speaking with the dark-haired woman from Baliceaux. The two of them parted ways before Tighe arrived, and Dahl smiled as she spotted him.

"Mr. J.T."

"Hey, Eike. Glad you're still here." He was, too. He hadn't seen her in a week. He gestured. "You know that woman?"

"Don't you recognize her?"

"We met before—at Joyce's private island—but I don't know her name."

Dahl laughed. She had a mischievous smile. "J.T., that's Isabel Abarca—the Argentinian mountaineer. Don't tell me you've never heard of her? She's a legend."

He shrugged. "What can I say? My subscription to *Mountaineering Weekly* must have lapsed."

"Ha ha." She swatted his arm playfully.

She always touched him. He didn't mind at all.

"She's a trauma surgeon from Buenos Aires, but she's become one of the most famous mountain climbers in the world—one of the few who's climbed all of the eight-thousanders; Kangchenjunga, both Gasherbrums, Annapurna, Dhaulagiri, Lhotse, Everest, and the rest. And she did them all without supplementary oxygen."

Tighe narrowed his eyes. "No way."

"Like I said, she's famous. The only other woman in history to do that was Gerlinde Kaltenbrunner. But Isabel also made the first successful winter climb of K2."

Dahl stopped short and moved close in to Tighe's chest. His heart raced as her face grew near. "And get this, James: Isabel's father disappeared on the south face of K2 when she was a young girl. But four years ago, she led an expedition to find his remains."

"Did she?"

Dahl nodded. "Found her father's body half buried in snow at 6,000 meters—frozen about the same age *she* is now. And you know what she did?"

He shook his head.

"She left his body there—but claimed his ice ax. Then climbed to the summit with it. She now carries it on every climb."

"No shit."

She nodded. "Since then, the press calls her the Ice Queen."

Tighe bristled. "What the hell do they know?"

She studied Tighe. "So you don't think what she did was coldhearted?"

"I think she wanted to know him."

Dahl didn't step back. She remained close.

"Fair warning, Eike: if you don't move back, I'm going to kiss you."

That mischievous smile again. "You don't scare me."

He brushed his lips against hers, and in an instant they were locked in a passionate embrace. Tighe's blood felt like it was on fire.

"My bunk is close by."

He laughed lightly as he kissed her neck. "Really? Right in the barracks?"

She breathed rapidly. "We are all adults here. Come…" She took his hand, and he did not resist.

JANUARY 27, 2033

Tighe and Jin Han stood with six other candidates in an unfurnished concrete room sealed by a steel pressure door. Each of the four walls had a pair of keypads and small computer screens set 2 meters apart.

A coordinator's voice spoke over an intercom. *"The keypads on each wall are linked. Move to the first one available."*

The candidates spread out to claim a keypad. Tighe noticed Jin was on the far wall and tapped a guy to Jin's right. "Mind if we trade?"

The guy shrugged and took up the remaining slot on the next wall.

Tighe looked to Jin as he took position.

Jin nodded to him.

The intercom voice said, *"When a number appears on your screen, relay it to your partner, who must correctly enter the code on their own keypad. If entered correctly, a new number will appear on their screen, and the procedure will reverse. Repeat this procedure thirty times to complete the exercise."*

A woman behind Tighe said, "That doesn't sound so hard."

Suddenly a series of eight numbers appeared on Tighe's screen. He glanced to Jin. "Han, here's the number: one-six-four-eight-one …"

As Tighe called out the numbers, Jin tapped them into his keypad. However, other candidates were calling out their own numbers all around them in the echoing chamber.

"What was that last digit?"

"A six. Six!" As people shouted louder, it became necessary to outshout them. And then the other shoe that Tighe knew would drop did.

Cold water suddenly issued from vents near the floor, washing across their feet and quickly rising above their ankles.

"Fuck, that's cold!"

"What's the number?"

"Hurry up!"

The candidates started shouting and keying in numbers more urgently with every inch the water rose. Tighe tried to block out the other voices.

Jin shouted, "Four-three-four-six . . ."

The cold water was already up to Tighe's knees. From experience he knew that the cold would shock his system—make him breathe faster—and that, in turn, could increase the sense of panic. He ignored the cold and focused instead on entering numbers.

Someone said, "The water will stop before the ceiling. They're just trying to freak us out."

Tighe did not listen to the musings behind him. Instead, he and Jin operated with mechanical precision, calling out and entering numbers. Back and forth.

Quite soon the water covered the keyboard—and then the computer screen. The movements of other candidates made waves that increased the difficulty of deciphering the numbers glowing on-screen.

Focus on the task. Nothing else matters.

Jin called out, "Seven-seven-two-three-four . . ."

As the next code appeared on his screen, Tighe called out, "Jin, put your fingers on the top corner buttons. That way you can enter the numbers by touch."

Jin nodded and positioned his hand. Tighe started calling out the new code.

After several more cycles the water came up to their chins, and he and Jin were swimming to be able to breathe. Others all around them were splashing and shouting. It was descending into anarchy.

Still the water rose.

Jin called out, "J.T.! Take a breath and dive!"

Tighe nodded, and they both dove. Once they were at their keyboards, Tighe looked to Jin, who held up four fingers. Tighe nodded and tapped in four while Jin continued to relay numbers to him with his fingers. Without having to compete with all the shouting on the surface, this new method was actually easier.

Once the code was entered, they both pushed off toward the surface to gulp for air. As they did so, they heard the screams of terrified candidates mixed with the voices of others who were still calling out numbers.

Tighe and Jin dove again and repeated their number hand signals as feet kicked and thrashed around them. By the time they pushed toward the surface again, only a few inches of air remained before the water completely filled the room.

One voice shrieked in panic, "Let me out! Let me out!"

Jin looked resolute with his cheek pressed against the ceiling. He called to Tighe. "Take a deep breath! On three, we go down for the duration!"

Tighe nodded.

At the count of three, they both dove. The relative silence beneath the water was calming. They immediately began flashing numbers to each other with their fingers.

Tighe had no idea how many more numbers they needed to enter. All around him swimmers thrashed aimlessly; he heard muted, bubbling shouts and hands pounding on a steel door.

But Jin stared calmly at Tighe, holding up different numbers of fingers. Tighe keyed them in, read the new number, then started flashing numbers of his own to Jin.

Soon the urgency of his need for air began to intrude on Tighe's concentration. He willed it away. Knowledge of his need for air would not help. Only entering the numbers would solve that problem, and so he continued. Two more times they exchanged numbers, and Tighe could see that Jin was struggling—but coping.

They both continued, and suddenly the word "Complete" appeared on Tighe's display. Powerful pumps whirred somewhere in the walls, and water started being sucked through the baseboards. Tighe looked up at the surface just now reappearing, and he pushed off from the floor.

He, Jin, and the rest of the candidates burst to the surface gasping for air. Even as they thrashed, the water fell another meter, and then another. Within seconds they all lay tangled and soaking on the concrete floor, watery coughs and vomiting interspersed with gasps for breath.

Tighe and Jin rose to look at the screens around the room. Only theirs had the word "Complete" displayed.

They clapped each other on their sopping shoulders.

Later, as the group warmed up outside under foil emergency blankets, Tighe and Jin sat silently together in the sun. They did not need to speak.

JANUARY 29, 2033

Tighe sat inside a hyperbaric chamber. Across from him sat ex-cosmonaut Sevastian Yakovlev. A wooden block puzzle was placed on a table between them. Other candidates sat to either side, each with wooden puzzles of their own. As they worked cooperatively to assemble their puzzles, vents in the ceiling hissed.

Yakovlev was sweating and fidgety. He tugged at his collar. "Air is close, yes?" He squinted. "Is this how you say in American—close?"

Tighe nodded. "They've increased the carbon dioxide levels. I'd say 4 percent."

"You know this?"

"After fifteen years of technical diving, if there's one thing I know, it's air. Point zero four percent CO_2 is normal, but most people can deal with 2 or 3 percent. At 4 percent most people get uncomfortable. Six percent and people start passing out. Ten percent is lethal."

Yakovlev shifted in his seat, wiping sweat away with his sleeve.

"Feel that unease—like you're strangling?"

"Da."

"Our brains use carbon dioxide levels in the blood as an alarm signal. The more carbon dioxide, the more the alarm. If we were breathing pure nitrogen, we'd suffocate in complete calm. Wouldn't even feel it."

"Fascinating." Yakovlev did not look fascinated.

Tighe motioned to the puzzle. "You need to keep placing pieces, Yak."

"Ah." Yakovlev focused back on the wooden puzzle. "This does not affect you, J.T.?"

"I try not to focus on it. Didn't you go through this training at Roscosmos?"

"I hated it then, too." Yakovlev was slowly placing pieces now.

Tighe tried to change the subject. "Morra told me you've been to space four times."

"*Da.* I spent a year on the ISS."

"He also said you reached your career radiation limit."

"After l sievert, I was forced to retire."

"If you don't mind my asking, why would the company take you on as a candidate if you're already maxed out on rads?"

"This is private space industry. Rad limits are different. Besides, I have three ex-wives to support on my pension." Yakovlev scratched his neck and face. "This puzzle—it would be difficult in normal air. In here, it is impossible."

Tighe had to agree.

Next to them Adedayo Adisa sat working on his puzzle alone. His cross-table partner, Anselmi Rinne, a Finnish cross-country skier, struggled to stay awake and might as well have been asleep for all the help he was providing.

However, Tighe noticed that Adisa's puzzle was nonetheless nearly finished. "The air doesn't seem to be affecting you, Ade."

Adisa glanced up. "This puzzle, it has a flaw."

Tighe and Yakovlev exchanged looks.

"What flaw?"

Adisa held up two wooden pieces. "The designer, he is lazy. If you touch two puzzle pieces on their ends, then turn them perpendicular, you can lower the pair onto alternating corners. They will always fit." He looked up, having successfully added another pair of pieces.

Yakovlev sighed. "This is his brain starved for oxygen."

Tighe followed those instructions, and it worked like a charm. "I'll be damned."

FEBRUARY 3, 2033

Tighe floated in a wet suit with a dozen other candidates, in the waters off the eastern coast of Ascension Island. They clung to a rope line strung between orange buoys and in turn linked to rope lines that descended to marked depth measurements.

A coordinator sat in a nearby Zodiac fast boat, shouting instructions. The candidates all shivered, despite their wet suits.

"Grab one of the dive lines! When you hear the whistle, dive to the 10-meter mark. Remain at depth as long as you can, then return to the surface. You will be scored in the order you surface—first one up fails. Falling unconscious or failing to surface under your own power also means you fail the exercise."

Rescue divers in rebreather gear treaded water nearby.

Tighe swam for one of the vertical lines and in doing so crossed paths with Isabel Abarca.

"You're still here." She grabbed the dive rope beside his, and they both treaded water. Her once long hair was now short black with a few streaks of gray.

"Don't bother telling me—I already know your name. They say you're a mountaineering legend."

"*Cualquiera*, I don't say that."

"What I can't figure out is why you're here."

"For the same reason you are: to get to space."

"You must know Joyce's asteroid-mining scheme is bullshit."

She nodded. "What's that got to do with getting into orbit?"

"So you lend your name to his publicity stunt. Is that it?"

"Haven't you?"

The coordinator just then blew his whistle. After exchanging another glance, Abarca and Tighe took a deep breath and dove under the water.

Holding the rope, Tighe pulled himself downward past the 5-meter marker and then stopped at the 10-meter line. Above he could see the coordinator boats and the buoys. The ocean below extended into darkness. Although they were just half a kilometer offshore, the bottom had dropped off alarmingly fast. Large and small fish swam on the periphery. Tighe could only make out blurs without a diving mask.

He turned to see the blurry outlines of other candidates extending to the distance in a line. Abarca floated calmly next to him.

He let his mind wander as they stared at each other. Before long his lungs began to burn. Thirty seconds later a couple of candidates down the line started racing for the surface.

Tighe looked back at Abarca and could tell she was looking right at him. She folded her arms and drummed her fingers.

Tighe let the burning in his lungs continue. Several more candidates broke for the surface. His need for air was starting to become intense.

But Abarca still didn't move.

Tighe knew his own body. At this depth, he didn't have too much longer until he'd start to black out.

The rest of the other candidates suddenly started clawing for the surface. Bubbles raced upward, and the rescue divers moved toward one motionless subject.

Tighe looked toward Abarca again. Her eyes were still on him. They were the last two candidates underwater.

Screw it.

His lungs screaming, Tighe swam for the sunlight. He broke the surface and sucked for air, grabbing the buoy line.

Several people around him were coughing and gasping for breath.

Tighe looked down and saw the rescue divers move toward Abarca—but she waved them away. They circled her like sharks. She looked upward.

Another voice nearby: "Christ, is she still down there?"

In a few moments, Abarca swam toward the surface, and as she emerged she took a deep, controlled breath.

The coordinator blew the whistle. "All candidates accounted for!"

Abarca didn't look particularly affected by the exercise. She noticed Tighe's look. "This sea level air is like a meal to me."

CHAPTER 10

Puzzle Pieces

Lukas Rochat fobbed in through security and crossed the atrium lobby of his Flexspace building. Here he leased an officette on daily terms for his law practice. Located on rue Edward Steichen, just a couple of blocks off Space Row, every square meter was exorbitant, but you had to spend money to make money.

Six months ago he had a suite with a temp legal assistant. Twenty-first-century agile business practices now allowed him to fail slowly, instead of all at once. With every week that his bank balance dwindled, he was tempted to downsize further. Soon he figured he'd be renting a spot to stand in.

As Rochat walked the common areas on the way to the elevator, it amazed him how the place was crawling with hopeful young people—aerospace engineers and marketing folks from all over the EU, Asia, and the US tapping at laptops and tablets, discussing NewSpace startup ideas in a dozen languages around the coffee kiosk. He'd initially viewed these youthful entrepreneurs as potential clients, but pro bono work had been a waste of time. That first batch of entrepreneurs was long gone, along with the hours he'd put into them.

However, Rochat did not give up. He networked constantly for new business—attending meet-ups and "launch" parties (for companies that were launching their first payload into space). None of his carousing had yielded paying clients.

Rochat tried to recall how excited he was when he first arrived in Luxembourg City. The entrepreneurial atmosphere here was so unlike the staid business scene in Switzerland. But lately he'd noticed that the faces kept changing as he remained. Either everyone else was failing and giving up faster, or they were succeeding and moving up. Either way, he was doing something wrong. It depressed him.

While he was taking the elevator to the third floor, Rochat's phone rang for the fifth time in the last hour. He checked the caller's number and weighed the chances of it being a bill collector. He decided the likelihood was 100 percent. The incoming call went to his voice mail. Collection calls sapped his confidence. They were a reminder that his lack of success was long-standing.

Rochat checked for mail at his floor's reception desk. The friendly young woman who'd been there the day before had been replaced by a surly young man who looked down his nose as he handed over a stack of mail marked "Second Notice" and "In Collections."

"Oh, and there's this . . ." The young man handed over a heavy brown package the size and weight of a law book.

Rochat perked up. It was marked from the Ministry of the Economy—Office of Space Affairs. "Hello . . ." He hefted it as he retreated to his officette.

The package weighed a kilo at least. The ministry seemed impervious to the irony of a twenty-first-century space agency shipping around paper files.

Rochat waved his key fob over his office door lock and entered the tiny windowless cell. There was barely space for the half-sized desk, chair, and filing cabinet. Gazing on his officette depressed him all over again. He took one more glance at the overdue bills and tossed them onto the desk, then headed out cradling the package under his arm.

There was a quiet café a couple of blocks away on the rue Dr. Nicolas Clasen. As he walked in the winter chill, Rochat inspected the package. Hopefully it was worth the three hundred euros in processing fees it had cost him, which was sorely missed at the moment. He needed business leads.

Rochat's phone rang again, and he went through the effort to power it down. He didn't want any reminders of his failures just now. After all, the only reason this package had been sent to him was because he'd managed to convince the Ministry of the Economy's deputy director of space affairs to help him out. That showed moxie, didn't it? That was the sort of thing winners did.

He was in a better mood by the time he entered the quiet café. Just a few blocks off Space Row, most of the office buildings nearby had their own automated coffee kiosks. Yet, the café's proprietor stubbornly refused to fail. For that reason alone Rochat was happy to patronize the place. He sat at a table in the rear, away from the window, and ordered an Americano.

Only then did he place the package on the table and pull the zip seal. He slid the package contents onto the marble tabletop. Before him was a thick stack of Space Operations Permit applications processed by the Grand Duchy of Luxembourg's Ministry of the Economy Space Affairs Division. These were the filings that the deputy director had told him were linked to his own client, Lunargistics, LLC.

Rochat spread them out across the table, dozens of applications, each twenty or thirty pages thick—printed on both sides. Same as the forms he'd been hired by Lunargistics, LLC to complete and shepherd through the application process. He glanced through the signature blocks at the names of the space attorneys who'd filed them. None looked familiar. Nor their firms. No doubt they would say the same of him.

Form 37-B was designed to give the grand duchy a clear idea of what commercial space activity the applicant proposed to engage in—for example, Moon mining, microgravity pharmaceutical research, fiber-optic printing, or whatever. Applicants had to delve deep into the details of their financing, expertise in the industry, and also detailed specifications for any spacecraft or equipment they intended to use, operating budgets, pro forma profit and loss statements—basically their entire business plan.

The difference between this and a normal business plan was that the grand duchy wouldn't invest. They'd merely act as the Earth sovereign nation through which any space-earned revenue would flow. For this, Luxembourg expected a small cut, and in order to ensure their nascent private space industry wasn't tarnished by fraudulent investment schemes, the ministers examined applicants carefully.

Lunargistics, Rochat's only client, was most likely a fraud. However, its parent company might be real enough to require space-law services.

He took out his computer tablet and snapped photos of the first page of each application. Each of these was financially linked to his own client in some way. He was surprised there were so many—thirty-three applications in all. Poring through the filings, he found they encompassed cislunar businesses in personnel training, avionics design, spacecraft maintenance, and logistics for a NASA/ESA Moon base, as well as for Moon-mining companies that had yet to commence operations. Most of the revenue projections on these applications were optimistic at best.

Among the applications, he also noticed an internal Ministry of the Economy report listing shell companies linked to these thirty-three firms. The shell companies were incorporated in places like Dubai, Panama City, and the Cayman Islands, but the report went on to link those shell companies to venture capital firms managing tens of billions of dollars—some of them sovereign funds in the Middle East and Asia.

He flipped back to the applications.

That's when he noticed that several of the firms had *already* commenced construction of spacecraft in low Earth orbit. He leafed through pages of documents showing launch dates from Kourou in French Guiana, Sriharikota in India, and Cape Canaveral in the US, payload manifests, and flight permits—all of which had already been approved in other legal jurisdictions.

Thirteen of the companies had actually sent equipment into space. At least according to all this documentation. That didn't match the behavior of a money-laundering operation.

As he spread the documents out, Rochat realized that those thirteen companies had collectively spent *billions* of dollars lifting several hundred tons of construction materials and equipment into geostationary and lunar distant retrograde orbits. In front of him was a substantial percentage of last year's commercial launches. These entities already had half a dozen unmanned private spacecraft orbiting the Moon. The other twenty firms appeared to have contracts with one another providing security, training, staffing, design, construction, communications, logistics—the list went on. Some of these firms had launch-services contracts with Burkett's and Macy's firms. Another with Halser's company.

These were huge bets to make on a Moon-mining industry that had not yet even commenced. Of course, Rochat was aware that big bets were being made—it was part of the reason he'd come to LC—but what he hadn't known was just how much of it was interconnected.

Rochat contemplated this. Why would these linked companies spend so much money launching and building spacecraft in lunar orbit when they didn't even have their commercial space enterprise permits approved yet?

Were they so convinced the industry would be huge that they didn't want to miss out on first-mover advantage? Is that why they did everything they could to spread the launches out across so many companies—to make it appear like it was a smaller individual bet than it was?

As he paged through the forms again, Rochat stopped at the design specification for one of the spacecraft. There was an accompanying schematic. It looked a lot like the gantry cranes used in construction around Luxembourg City, with sparse composite box trusses running for a hundred meters or so and an inflatable habitat on one end. The company's business application indicated they planned to serve as a hub for storage of Moon-mined aluminum—although the spacecraft's suitability for that purpose didn't seem immediately obvious. There were only two docking ports and lots of girders—on which to mount what? Shipping containers? Material hoppers? Fuel tanks?

The companies apparently used telepresence construction robots to do most of the modular orbital assembly. It was safer and cheaper than having humans do the construction, and one of the other companies had designed the robotic construction equipment.

He flipped through several applications and folded one open on the design illustration for another company's spacecraft.

This looked similar to the first. A long truss of exposed girders. A flat-bottomed, inflatable habitat module on one end.

Rochat opened the first application and looked at the two ships side by side. They were damn near identical—which wasn't surprising, considering that the ministry's forensic accountants had determined the companies were actually owned by the same investors. No doubt they'd used the same aerospace subcontractors for both designs.

He pored through more filings, looking for companies planning to operate a spacecraft in lunar orbit.

Locating one, he folded the page back and placed that illustration alongside the first two.

Similar in theme, this spacecraft was longer—a girder truss nearly 200 meters in length with five methalox rocket engines purchased from Burkett's Starion Aerospace. There were spherical inflatable fuel tanks on one end and a circular inflatable habitat built by Halser's company on the other.

The startup was proposing orbital transfer services—which explained the rocket engines. It was intended to move hundreds of tons of mined resources into different cislunar orbits.

But five rocket engines? Each of them had a vacuum thrust of more than 400,000 pounds. That was a lot of delta-v.

Just beneath that application was yet another spacecraft—this one with a large solar panel array at one end of a long box truss and a four-slot docking collar at the other.

As he studied the illustration, he noticed the other spacecraft designs had identical composite trusses. Rochat laid them alongside one another and saw the spacecraft with the engines and the other with the solar panels were both vertically oriented, while the other two were horizontal.

An odd thought occurred to him, and Rochat started sorting through the couple dozen other applications, searching for any more spacecraft designs. After paging through them all, he discovered one more girder truss design—this one remarkably like the first four. He slid it next to the others, rearranging them in several configurations.

Until one layout fit just right.

He stopped short as his pulse began to race.

On the café table in front of him was a single large spacecraft—he was convinced of it. It had a vertical truss with rocket engines on one end, a circular hab in the center, and a solar array on the other end, with three spokes radiating from its center, all three ending in identical inflatable habitat modules. The spokes joined at the central habitat module on the vertical truss.

After a minute spent staring he suddenly remembered to breathe.

This was a *gravity ship*—clearly intended to spin to create centrifugal force; in effect, artificial gravity. The habitat modules at the end of each spoke were designed with flat bottoms. That had seemed unusual to him since they were supposed to be microgravity habs, like Ray Halser's Hotel LEO. However, if they were rotating to mimic gravitational force, the flat bottoms made perfect sense. And each of the spokes was identical.

Someone had designed and launched the world's first artificial-gravity ship and concealed that fact from everyone on Earth by doing it in pieces—hiding the activity through dozens of shell companies.

And no one knew. Possibly not even the Ministry of the Economy Division of Space Affairs. If they had known, they never would have sent him this. This information was potentially priceless.

Rochat glanced up at the other patrons of the coffee shop. He raised his tablet computer and snapped a photo of the carefully arranged pages that revealed a single spacecraft—then jumbled the documents again to conceal his discovery from other patrons. No telling who worked where in this neighborhood.

Rochat then examined the photo on his tablet screen. It was definitely a single ship. The design was clear. But why the big engines? If it was intended to be a space station settled in a stable lunar orbit—like NASA's Gateway—then what were the engines for? Especially such large ones?

The answer that popped into Rochat's head shocked him all over again.

It's not meant to orbit the Moon. It's going somewhere.

He lowered his tablet. All the materials to construct it were already up in space. The ship itself might already be built, or well on its way to being built. That's why they placed it in lunar DRO—because no telescope on Earth would be able to resolve an object that small at a distance of 384,000 kilometers. But surely its thermal signature would be noticed by NASA or the US Department of Defense. Wouldn't it? Or would everyone assume these vessels were there to join in the coming Moon-mining industry? Nonetheless, in a lunar DRO the assembled ship would be sitting at the very top of Earth's gravity well—capable of heading just about anywhere.

Somebody was secretly launching a manned commercial deep space mission—the first one in history.

What do I do with this information?

Rochat's mind buzzed with the possibilities. For the past year he'd scoured *Aviation Weekly* and *SpaceNews*. He'd subscribed (and more recently pirated access) to hideously expensive space-law journals, but he hadn't heard a whisper about any gravity ship orbiting the Moon. Lots of news about all the companies investing in cislunar services and mining support spacecraft—nothing about this mysterious vessel.

No one knew. Yet.

That meant he was in a privileged position. For once in his life, Lukas Rochat had gotten in before anyone else. Should he tell the industry press? The deputy director of space affairs?

What would that accomplish? It would tell potential clients and regulators that he couldn't be trusted with confidential information.

Leverage.

This was more than just information—he had figured out something no one else had. That should impress a client—as could his discretion with their secret. Therein was his leverage.

Rochat's course of action immediately became clear. He filtered the contacts on his phone to "Clients." The result was a single name—Lucrezia Bogdanić, vice president and legal counsel for Lunargistics, LLC. He clicked to create a new, encrypted message and then attached the photograph he'd just taken of the final spacecraft assembled from various company permit applications. He thumbed in the following text:

> If I figured it out, so will others. I can help you keep it secret.

After a moment's hesitation, Rochat tapped "Send," and the encrypted message was on its way.

Whoever was behind this had billions to spend developing and building a secret spaceship. Surely they could spare a tiny bit more to retain Sirius Legal Services.

CHAPTER 11

The Mindfucker

FEBRUARY 8, 2033

A voice spoke over the camp's PA system. *"Ascan 3-6-3. Ascan 3-6-3. Change into utilities and report to Dr. Bruno's office in Building A immediately."*

James Tighe looked up from a group problem-solving exercise.

The other candidates murmured.

Jin Han and Isabel Abarca exchanged knowing glances but said nothing. They knew what everyone knew: all candidates were eventually called to the psychological director's office for a one-on-one. Not all candidates returned.

With a nod to Jin and Abarca, Tighe headed back to barracks for a shower and a change of clothes.

Building A had been the original NASA building for Devil's Ashpit Tracking Station. Now it was used by camp administration. After waiting in an anteroom, Tighe was shown into an orderly office with a broad view of the grounds.

Dr. Angela Bruno sat not at her large desk in the corner but in one of two cushioned leather chairs arranged around a coffee table. Bruno was a diminutive woman with long gray hair. She wore a thick wool sweater and simple black plastic-frame eyeglasses. In her hands she held a computer tablet.

"James Tighe. Have a seat." She motioned to the empty chair as she read through notes on the tablet. "You prefer to be called J.T." She looked up. "Is there a reason you don't use your given name?"

Tighe sat. He shook his head. "J.T. carries farther in a cave."

She studied him for several moments. "If you wish to get into space, James, don't do that again."

"You mean bullshit you?"

"Yes."

He consciously willed himself not to bob his leg or fidget, and he looked her directly in the eye. This small woman terrified him. He wasn't certain why.

"I'm not here to counsel you or to help you work through your problems. I'm here to identify your problems—to drag them out into the light, so we can have a look at them. To see if they're fatal to a career in space."

"Understood."

"You have a criminal record, James. One that you did not disclose to us."

A flash of adrenaline swept over Tighe. "My juvenile record was expunged on my eighteenth birthday. So, no, I don't have a criminal record."

She spoke calmly, methodically. "Our client does not care about the juvenile records laws in Wisconsin. We will use all available data to make business decisions, and you should know that data, once gathered, never goes away—ever. Instead, it is bought and sold. Worldwide. You demonstrated antisocial tendencies as a youth. A fact you withheld from us."

Tighe took a deep breath. "I had some difficulties as a boy. I worked through them, and now I'm an adult."

"In grade school you were a model student, but as a teenager your classwork deteriorated. Even though you received individual tutoring and attended a well-regarded private school, your grades were terrible. You were frequently absent. Often disciplined. Your school counselors described you as 'highly intelligent but alienated.'"

"I graduated."

"Most likely a social promotion. I think they just wanted to get rid of you."

"There were family issues."

"Your stepbrother and stepsister, and your half brother, did well in school. There's no record of any domestic or substance abuse in your household. No legal or financial problems. The only police reports relate to your own trespassing offenses."

"You looked up old police reports?"

"We are not going to send people into space unless they are fully vetted."

"The trespassing was urban exploration—something I was involved in."

"Sneaking into industrial and civic infrastructure to explore."

Tighe nodded.

"What motivated you to visit places you weren't supposed to be?"

"Curiosity." He paused. "And a desire to stay away from home."

She made a few notes. "Let's talk about your biological father. He disappeared when you were five." She looked closely at Tighe. "And yet, your school grades and attendance remained solid at the time. Was his disappearance in any way related to your acting out later on?"

"I barely remember my father."

"Yet you travel with a photo of him. So he is important to you."

"You went through my personal things?"

"We're not your friend, James. Our client plans to spend billions of dollars to send a small group of people into space. Who they send will determine whether the company succeeds or fails. We will do whatever is necessary to make sure they send the right people. If you find my line of questioning invasive, you are free to drop out of selection at any time."

Tighe tried to calm himself. This wasn't a typical psychoanalysis session—like the many he'd experienced as a child. The company had done a serious background investigation of him. And they weren't trying to "cure" him.

"Why do you keep a photo of your father with you if you barely remember him?"

"I wanted to know him. I think I have fond memories, but I'm not sure. I could be conflating them with stories I've seen or heard elsewhere. That photo is all I have."

"And your stepfather?"

"He's fine. I never had a problem with Andrew."

"What do you think happened to your real father? Do you think he's dead? Or do you think he abandoned you and your mother?"

"I think he's dead. My father had a habit of taking long hiking trips alone."

"He was declared missing in Jasper National Park in the Canadian Rockies. His park permit indicated he intended to cover nearly 120 kilometers over rugged terrain. Solo."

"He was reckless. Look, I remember I missed him whenever he was gone, and I was happy to see him whenever he came back. My mother wasn't usually happy to see him, but I think they did have some good times."

"Do you think your mother recalls it that way?"

Tighe searched for words. "She struggled financially. I remember that."

"You were desperately poor, James." She glanced through her notes. "Your mother came from an abusive household. For much of your early childhood, you were on food assistance programs."

"I don't remember much about that time."

"You nonetheless performed well once you reached school age. You were reported to be a sociable and happy child according to Wisconsin Child Welfare Services reports."

Tighe narrowed his eyes. "You got ahold of child services records?"

"Tell me again why you don't think your father abandoned you."

"Why does it matter?"

"Because you said you barely remember him."

"What I do remember makes it likely he had an accident—alone in the woods somewhere—and died. He didn't seem unhappy, at least not around me. Do you have evidence otherwise?"

"Why didn't his disappearance affect you? Why did you disengage from your education only years later and not right away?"

Tighe stared out the windows to the camp beyond. But his mind was looking much farther.

Tighe is small—perhaps four or five years old—and wearing a stained blue parka as he follows his mother behind a big-box retail store, toward the dumpsters. They hold hands as they stagger across ice patches on the asphalt. His mother holds a garbage bag over one shoulder. She eyes the store's metal rear door and the surveillance camera above it, then turns to him. He can see her face, devoid of makeup.

Her brown eyes look into his, and she gives him a smile as she tugs the zipper on his coat tighter. "Honey, you stand there, and you look into that camera. Will you do that for Mommy?" She smiles at him. "Will you look into that camera for me?"

He nods.

With that, his mother moves over toward the recycling bins and opens the metal lid.

Tighe stares up at the security camera.

The security camera stares back. No one comes out to stop them.

He and his mother sleep in the back seat of their faded brown car with the rusted quarter panels. Tighe can still remember the mildew odor. It is summer, and the windows are open only a crack. The air is close. Nonetheless his mother holds him tightly, wrapping him in her arms, and it is too hot. He squirms, and she wakes.

"You can't sleep, honey? You need to sleep, sweetheart. You have school tomorrow." She kisses his forehead.

He turns to her silhouette in the dark. "Where is he?"

"It's just us now, sweetheart. You and me. We need to take care of each other."

Tighe is only slightly older, coming home to a garden apartment, letting himself in with his key. He hangs his school backpack on a chairback and goes to the kitchen. He finds a note from his mother. It tells him she will be back from work by six, and he goes to sit in front of the television.

Later, he hears rattling at the door, and he smiles as his mother enters. She's dressed in slacks and a polo shirt with a company name on it—Beris Industrial Supply. She smiles as she sees him, hugs him, and kisses him on the cheek. "How was your day, sweetheart?"

Tighe is eight and staring up at the big-jowled man who's come to meet him. He turns toward his mother, then back to the man—who wears a nice suit jacket and a dress shirt open at the neck. He wears polished black leather shoes like the successful men on TV and cologne that invades Tighe's nostrils.

His mother says, "Jimmy, this is Mr. Beris. What do we say?"

"Hello, Mr. Beris."

"Hello there, Jimmy. It's a pleasure to finally meet you." The man leans down, smiles, and extends his thick-fingered hand. "I've heard so much about you. Call me Andrew."

The man shakes Tighe's hand. The hand is soft, not like his father's was. "I'd like for us to be friends. Would that be okay?"

Tighe nods.

Tighe is older now—thirteen—and his mother glares at him as he sits in the back of a police car. He can see the police officer speaking with his mother and stepfather. His stepbrother and stepsister look on from the living room window.

His stepfather's company employs a lot of people in town. They let him off with a warning. But then, it's not the first time he's explored places he shouldn't. Broken into buildings. It's becoming a pattern.

His stepfather explains something to the police and shakes his head. Then all three adults look back at the patrol car. At Tighe. So do his stepsiblings. It occurs to Tighe that he is the only one of them whose last name is Tighe.

Later he stares at the ceiling of his own bedroom as he listens to his mother and stepfather argue about him. About what to do with him. He gazes around at his nicely furnished bedroom.

Tighe takes no comfort in things. Everything he cared about has vanished. Not even people are permanent. They all drift away—sometimes even when they're right in front of you.

Tighe sat, numb, as he realized a significant period of time had passed. Out the window, the light had faded toward evening. He looked to Dr. Bruno, who looked dispassionately back at him.

"Do you blame your mother for remarrying?"

Tighe shook his head. "Andrew was a good man. His children were kind to me. My mother had security for the first time in her life."

"You felt betrayed."

"I don't have a right to feel betrayed."

"Not about her remarrying—about her giving up on you."

Hearing it out loud for the first time hurt. A lot.

Dr. Bruno pressed. "That's the situation, isn't it? All of the advantages that she obtained for you and that you squandered. Your half brother and stepsiblings succeeding in her eyes."

Tighe struggled to keep it together. "I think she sees my father when she looks at me. And I think he caused her a lot of pain."

"Didn't you cause her a lot of pain? Didn't you disappear, too?"

Tighe felt a familiar guilt. "I tried. She saw the worst motivations in anything I did. I was just a confused kid. I wanted to get away from the constant disapproval. To escape. Who wants to stay around people who don't like who they are?"

Dr. Bruno looked through her notes. "Your recent signing bonus—you wired the majority of it to your stepsister's husband. If you're so estranged from your family, why did you do that?"

"Repaying a debt. Or part of one."

"Your stepsister and her husband have a net worth of over six million dollars."

Tighe turned to her in surprise.

"Were you not aware of that?"

"No."

"Within forty-eight hours of receiving the money, your brother-in-law transferred it into an account that he used to purchase sixteen thousand dollars' worth of sports memorabilia."

Tighe felt a familiar anger. Money had always eluded him. He knew it had to do with patience and owning things, but he just didn't seem to have the knack. "It was his money."

"You don't resent the fact that you needed it and he didn't?"

"I made my own bed, and now I have to lie in it."

"Your mother and stepfather provided the down payment for your siblings' first homes. They paid for their college educations as well—both undergraduate and graduate school, totaling several hundred thousand dollars."

Tighe looked warily at Dr. Bruno. "You're telling me this because you want me to be angry."

"I'm telling you this because it's true. Your family loaned you money at interest, while other family members were given substantial gifts."

Tighe took a calming breath. "What my siblings received wasn't a gift. It was an investment. My stepbrother and stepsister, my half brother, they did what was expected of them. It's what my mother and stepfather believe in.

Going to graduate school, becoming a lawyer, getting an MBA—these are worthwhile investments to them. Having children. A professional career."

"Are you not a worthy investment, James?"

Tighe sensed a trap, but at this point he was past caring. "I didn't invest my time in their world. Why should they invest their money in mine? I make no sense to them."

"Your diving mentor, Richard Oberhaus, would you say he understood you?"

Tighe felt crushing guilt again. It was several seconds before he could respond. "Yes."

"How were you able to make the decision you did—to let him die so that you could live?"

Tighe's emotions tightened his face several times, but he regained his composure by imagining Oberhaus's imperturbable face—and what he would have made of Dr. Bruno's line of questioning. "I would have laid down my life for him."

"Then why didn't you?"

"Because I trusted his judgment. And he was right—he would have died on the way to the surface. I nearly died myself, and Richard didn't have my resistance to nitrogen narcosis." Tighe struggled as tears formed in his eyes. "I wish I didn't disappoint him so often."

"Do you feel you disappointed him?"

"He often scolded me for not thinking about my future." Tighe wiped his face. "And then he gave me his."

"Do you know what complaints other candidates have about you?"

Tighe looked up in surprise at the sudden turn in questioning. He sat up. "No doubt you're about to tell me."

"I'd like you to guess."

"You want me to guess what other people don't like about me?"

"Yes."

"And how do you know?"

"We have microphones everywhere in the camp. Our algorithms hear everything. They're more sensitive than people think."

Christ. "I guess they say . . . I'm awful for celebrating when some candidates are dismissed from the program." He looked up at her. "For not being nicer."

She waited several moments. "The most common complaint about you is that you talk too much about caves."

Tighe nodded to himself. He laughed. "That's actually better than I thought."

"You may leave, James."

Tighe cast an alarmed look her way. "The island?"

She shook her head. "No. You may return to your barracks."

Tighe took a deep breath. "Thanks."

CHAPTER 12

Negotiation

Two weeks had passed since Lukas Rochat sent a photo of the secret spaceship to his client. He'd tried half a dozen times in the interim to elicit a response from his contact, Lucrezia Bogdanić, but the woman hadn't returned phone calls, texts, or emails. Rochat had been ghosted. The effect on his psyche was severe.

He was now paralyzed by self-doubt. Rochat kept replaying his actions over and over in his head at night. He hadn't slept more than a couple of hours at a stretch in weeks.

What had he been thinking sending that email?

Rochat had managed to take a priceless piece of business intelligence—one that perhaps he alone was aware of—and what did he do with it? He destroyed his only client relationship. And now, if he sold the information to the press, that same former client would know precisely where the leak originated, and they'd probably sue him to oblivion. They could keep him tied up in court until he was bankrupt. They might even go after his and his partner's savings, or their flat in Vevey.

What *should* he have done with his knowledge of the secret ship? He'd made the wrong choice, that much was clear—but what was the right decision? Why did everything Rochat touched turn to dust?

As days and then weeks of silence passed, Rochat took to dodging his domestic partner's concerned calls and texts. They both knew his legal practice was going under. She no doubt had seen the balances in his checking account and on his credit cards. She'd already moved money out of their common accounts. Now it was only a matter of time until he had to go back home to Switzerland with his tail between his legs to look for work. The thought of it killed him a bit inside.

So he kept striving.

He'd had to sell his collection of limited edition sneakers to retain his Flex-space office and tried not to notice the empty shelf space in his closet as he dressed in the morning.

He left his apartment in a state of almost Zen-like calm. Things couldn't get any worse, and so there was nothing to stress about. His every action today was working toward a better tomorrow. Hadn't one of his motivational books said that? Maybe. It sounded true.

Rochat boarded the bus along with other commuters and listened to an audiobook entitled *Always Be Closing*. It told him what any six-year-old an-gling for a birthday gift already knew, but it also kept the voice in his own head from screaming, *Loser!*

As he disembarked near his office, he buttoned his overcoat. The cold was bracing and demonstrated a profound truth: that the world wanted to kill him. He watched his breath stab out in plumes defiantly ahead of him. He was still here.

The thudding of a helicopter overpowered the sound of his audiobook, and suddenly a chopper passed low overhead. It descended toward the lawn next to Rochat's office building.

That was something he'd never seen before. He wasn't even sure helicop-ters were allowed to land there. Engine trouble?

He paused his audiobook and watched with curiosity as he continued walking. Soon he drew alongside the open stretch of lawn where a blue civilian helicopter noisily idled, grass buffeting in all directions. The frigid chopper wash cut through his coat. Rochat wrapped his scarf tighter around his face.

Then he noticed a man exit the chopper and frantically wave him over. Ro-chat glanced around to make certain the man wasn't signaling to someone else.

The man waved to him even more frantically. They couldn't talk at this distance over the engine noise.

Rochat left the sidewalk, and crouching a bit, as he'd seen people do in movies, he headed toward the helicopter. The man was perhaps sixty years old and wore a headset—possibly the pilot. As Rochat reached him, the man shouted, "*Connaissez-vous ce quartier?*"

Do you know this neighborhood?

Indeed Rochat did. He'd pounded the pavement for months stalking potential clients. He nodded, answering in English. "Sure. What company are you looking for?"

The pilot looked relieved and gestured to the passenger compartment. He answered in heavily accented English, "My boss can tell you," and reached for the door handle.

My boss. Rochat's heart raced. This was how it happened. He was ready to answer opportunity's knock and leaned into the chopper's passenger compartment as the door opened for him.

Two businessmen sat inside, both wearing excellent suits. The nearest one wore a fine Chopard chronometer—worth ten grand at least. Rochat also noticed a large coil of what looked to be velvet theater rope on the chopper deck between the men. It seemed odd, but the lead man gestured for Rochat to enter, pointing to his ear. "Close the door!"

Russian accent.

Rochat nodded and climbed into the passenger compartment, the pilot shut the door behind him, and it was suddenly much quieter. "You gentlemen are lost?"

The two Russians looked at each other. One nodded.

The other Russian thrust a handheld device into Rochat's temple, and an electrical jolt coursed through Rochat's entire body, a sensation that felt like someone hammering a railroad tie down the length of his spine. He fell forward onto the coil of soft red rope. Only the incredible pain still echoing in every nerve ending kept him conscious. Rochat finally found the wherewithal to groan but couldn't move. His muscles seemed frozen. He was unable even to form words.

Someone was zip-tying his hands behind his back. Another someone was lashing his feet together. Rochat was rolled over onto his back. His attackers stood over him.

Rochat felt the helicopter lurch upward, and through the windows barren winter tree branches and office buildings fell away. They were flying now—leaving.

After a few moments Rochat regained control of his muscles. He managed to grunt, "What . . . are you doing!"

The lead Russian put his knee hard into Rochat's chest, crushing the wind out of him.

Rochat struggled for air.

The man's beefy well-groomed face leaned down close as a hand groped through Rochat's inner coat pocket. The Russian pulled out the phone he found there, then passed it to his compatriot, who in turn passed it through a small opening in the chopper door.

Rochat's phone was gone. Fallen to the ground below. Bizarrely, the first thing that occurred to him was that he didn't have device insurance.

Judging from the clouds passing by, the chopper was moving fast now.

The Russian's knee eased up a bit, and Rochat sucked for breath. "Where are you taking me?"

"There is old saying: when you leap upon tiger's back, you cannot soon dismount. You know this saying?"

Rochat shook his head.

"Pity. It could have saved you."

The larger of the two men pulled Rochat onto his feet by his lapels, where Rochat hung from thick fists. Suddenly, bitterly cold wind rushed into the cabin as the door opened. Rochat struggled, but his hands were tied behind his back, and his feet were strapped together.

The Russian grinned into Rochat's face. "Good-bye, my friend."

Rochat craned his neck to see the open door. "No! Wait!"

The Russian hurled Rochat out of the helicopter.

Adrenaline made everything slow down—Rochat's vision constricted as fear encompassed him. He watched as the impossible happened. A forested landscape stretched out wide below him—the Luxembourg countryside in winter. It was like a postcard—one he plummeted toward at terminal velocity from a thousand feet in the air.

A primordial scream left his throat.

After sucking in air to scream several times more, Rochat finally realized that he should have reached the ground. He was no longer only falling, but alternately falling—*then rising*. Then falling again. He noticed a tight pull on his bound feet.

Rochat finally gathered the courage to look upward at the helicopter, still roaring above him.

A red bungee cord was wrapped around his ankles with some sort of professional strap clearly designed for that purpose.

His heart still hammering in his chest and snot running down his face, Rochat glanced back down to realize that the chopper was descending toward a gathering of several SUVs in what looked to be a construction site or a quarry. The light brown soil showed through snow where several acres of trees had been leveled, the ground dug away. Construction equipment sat idle nearby.

The helicopter continued to descend, and Rochat realized it was lowering him into the middle of a gathering of several more suited men. One of them filmed Rochat with a phone as he was lowered.

Rochat began to struggle as the ground came up faster than he would have liked. He tried to turn away but hit the ground hard on his shoulder and fell onto his side as more slack in the bungee cord played out on top of him. He found himself groaning in pain as he lay, still bound hand and foot, on muddy ground among several men who barked at one another in Russian, untying him.

With his hands and legs finally free, Rochat curled up into a fetal position and wept. He could feel wetness in his crotch where he'd soiled himself.

A man's voice shouted at him in English from close by. "Stand up!"

The rattle of the helicopter departed, fading away. It grew uncomfortably quiet.

Rough hands pulled Rochat up from the ground, dragging him in front of the man who was filming with the phone. Another powerful hand grabbed his jaw and focused Rochat's gaze on the lens.

A Russian-accented voice said, "You fuck with wrong people, my friend."

Rochat spoke between the fingers crushing his cheeks. "Yes! I'm sorry!"

"Go back to Vevey. And don't ever come back."

This news hit him hard despite the circumstances. Somehow things *had* actually managed to get worse.

The man sharply tapped Rochat's own temple for emphasis. "My friend, are you listening?"

"Yes. Yes, I'm listening."

"Do you understand?"

The hands let him go and he dropped hard to his knees before he regained control. Pain coursed through various parts of his body, but he couldn't keep his mind from the finality of this. It was a death of sorts.

Something heavy hit him in the stomach, nearly knocking the wind out of him. He wrapped his hands around it and saw it was a small black backpack.

"I tell them to kill you, but you are lucky. They do not wish to draw attention. But if you fuck up, they will listen to me." A hand smacked the backpack he clutched. "Go back to Switzerland, Lukas. Tell no one." A vicious-looking clasp knife opened next to his face. "Or I cut your tongue out." The hand grabbed his jaw again, turning his face toward the camera. "Speak into the lens. Tell them you understand."

Rochat felt thick fingers press like a vise against his cheeks. He could smell the man's overgenerous application of cologne. It acted like smelling salts—helping him wake up and smell the business opportunity.

Because he finally realized what was being transacted here was indeed business. They had not killed him. This was some sort of negotiation. Lessons from his business self-help books were all coming back to him.

The hand pushed him away, and he nearly fell over.

"Speak!"

Still on his knees, Rochat unzipped the backpack and looked inside at a dozen packs of fifty-euro notes. Maybe fifty grand in total.

Not a life-changing amount. Not for what he'd discovered. The thought of going home still deep in debt—just slightly less so—was galling. If business was about making tough decisions, then it was time to toughen up.

"Talk to the camera!" The knife came close again.

Rochat looked into the camera. "I don't want to go back to Switzerland."

The lead Russian leaned close to him. "What did you say?"

Rochat remained focused on the camera. "I won't tell anyone." He tossed the bag back to the Russian and looked into the lens. "But I can help you. My firm is small, but I can give you the personalized attention you need, unlike any of the big JFK Boulevard firms. I can move around the Division of Space Affairs without attracting attention. I can help keep—"

A hard object slammed into Rochat's stomach, and he doubled over in pain. Two Russian men started punching him, knocking him to the ground. Rochat covered his face with his arms as they started kicking him in the ribs and back. Rochat retched as his abdomen throbbed in pain. He sucked for air like a landed fish.

But Rochat started warding off the kicks and struggled back onto his feet even amid more punching. Blood dripping from his nose, he shouted at the camera lens. "You can't pay off everyone . . . and still expect it to remain a secret. The paperwork trail needs to be cleaned up . . . I can prevent the ministry from connecting the dots! I can obfuscate! I can help mask the project! They'd never suspect me! They think I'm a nobody!"

The punching and kicking suddenly stopped.

Rochat did not stop. Instead he stood up straight and shouted bloody-faced into the phone's camera lens. "More than anything, I can provide you first-class legal advice with the utmost discretion. I will dedicate myself to making certain your legal interests are protected and that your proprietary activities remain proprietary. You will not find any space lawyer in this entire town more dedicated to his clients. And none with my determination and work ethic. Please, give me a chance, and let me help you achieve your goals in space. Hire me."

Still winded, Rochat panted for breath, plumes of steam blowing away in the cold air as he wiped blood away from his swelling lips.

A phone rang nearby. One of the Russians answered it. The man passed it to the one who had been speaking to Rochat.

"*Da.*" The man listened. "*Da.*" Again he listened—looked up at Rochat for a moment, narrowed his eyes, and then said, "*Ya ponimayu.*" He hung up the phone and tossed it back to his colleague.

The man then walked up to Rochat, straightening the lapels on Rochat's muddy, bloodstained coat. "My client wishes to meet you." He clapped Rochat on the shoulder. "You had better be even more persuasive on that day, my friend."

With that the Russians walked off toward their vehicles. One of them tossed the rucksack of money at Rochat again, hitting him once more in the stomach and nearly knocking him over.

Rochat shouted, "When?"

"Just be ready."

Then they got into their obsolete combustion-engine vehicles and roared off, leaving Rochat in a dust cloud at the bottom of a construction pit with no phone and no clear idea which way led back to Luxembourg City.

CHAPTER 13

Filter

MARCH 7, 2033

The northeast coast of Ascension Island was barren, rock strewn, and buffeted by wind. James Tighe surveyed the Atlantic from a height of 150 meters. Below and just offshore was a steep-sided lump of rock stained white with bird droppings—Boatswain Bird Island.

The rock teemed with nesting frigate birds, petrels, boobies, and sooty terns that had taken refuge atop its remote cliffs. The birds all stood, beaks into a steady wind to prevent their feathers from ruffling. Hundreds more rode the winds above, making a racket.

Tighe turned inland to face Isabel Abarca. Beyond her stood five of the eighty-seven remaining asteroid-mining candidates—Atle Berggren, a Danish metallurgist and paraglide skier; Priya Chindarkar, an Indian roboticist and rock climber who'd worked for the Indian Space Research Organisation; Alyson Kelly, an Irish deep sea salvage diver; Grigol Lomidze, a Russian wildcatter; and Annetta Lazzari, a former member of the Italian navy's Gruppo Operativo Subacquei search and rescue unit.

They all stood on a stone ledge next to a cliff face. The sand-colored stone extended down to a scree field, which sloped away into the Atlantic. Waves crashed against the rocks below.

A company coordinator stood in their path. He was flanked by camp staff holding radios. Tighe and his fellow candidates all wore helmets, harnesses, and rock-climbing shoes.

The coordinator pointed to a series of narrow ledges and handholds running along the rock wall for a distance of 50 meters or so. "In this exercise you must traverse the cliff face to reach my colleagues on the far side. Whether you use the safety rope is up to you."

The candidates turned to spot two staffers standing on a similar stony outcrop beyond the cliff. Then all the candidates gazed down at the nearly 100-meter sheer drop onto a jumble of rocks.

Kelly spoke first. "Who wouldn't use the safety rope?"

The coordinator answered, "Candidates who want a much higher score in this exercise."

"A higher score—for being reckless?"

Berggren piped in, "That's outrageous."

Tighe studied the wall. "Atle's right. On an expedition you'd only free-climb in an emergency."

The coordinator was stone-faced. "This isn't an expedition. It's a test. What you decide to do is up to you."

Kelly spat on the ground. "And how many candidates will be dismissed as a result of this 'test'?"

Murmured agreement from the other candidates.

Standing at the edge of the cliff, Abarca said, "*Tómalo con soda*. This isn't that dangerous."

The others turned to her.

She pointed. "The cliff face leans slightly inland. Those handholds and ledges have been cleared of debris. They look solid."

"They *look* solid? Are you mad?"

Abarca said to Kelly, "If this was a rock climbing wall at the gym, would you really slip off that?"

"But *'tisn't* a wall at the gym, is it, Isabel? Fall from that without a rope and you'll die."

"If you think you'll fall, then use the rope."

"I'll use the rope—on you."

The others studied the traverse.

Berggren approached the coordinator. "Will low-scoring candidates be dismissed after this exercise?"

Kelly gestured to the group. "Notice they only brought six of us up here. They know if they tried this with a big group, there'd be a bloody mutiny."

Berggren called out, "We should all refuse—in protest."

Tighe noticed an octocopter drone hovering not far off the coast, watching them with a dozen camera eyes. He also noticed bodycams—no doubt with microphones—on the coordinators' shirtfronts.

The coordinator remained expressionless. "Either use the safety rope or don't. But refusal to traverse the cliff will result in immediate dismissal."

Kelly crossed her arms. "The rules of this exercise are illegal."

Berggren stepped between them. "If someone dies traversing without a rope, your employer will get sued blind. You'll be out of a job."

Tighe immediately thought of the Accidental Death and Dismemberment rider to their contract.

The coordinator seemed unmoved. "No one is forcing anyone to climb without a rope. It's your choice."

Kelly jabbed her finger in his face. "You're *penalizing* us for using the rope."

Berggren joined her. "Which makes it a de facto condition of employment."

The coordinator shrugged. "There's no guarantee of employment even if you climb without the rope."

Abarca called out, "We could already have been across by now."

Berggren frowned at her. "You're not seriously considering free-climbing this, Isabel?"

"Any expedition in deep space will be a lot more dangerous than this cliff." She looked at the others. "I'd rather go there with people able to cope with danger."

Kelly threw up her hands. "As if that asteroid expedition is really going to happen!"

Lomidze, the wildcatter, shook his head. "Alyson is right. I'm not willing to risk dying just for a chance to train in low Earth orbit."

Abarca rubbed volcanic dust between her palms. "I have no intention of dying. I want to go to space, and this traverse doesn't seem that difficult an obstacle. Not to me."

"Because you're a bloody mountain climber."

"This doesn't require skill—just nerve."

Berggren stepped in. "Isabel, don't do this. If everyone uses the safety rope, then it will render their scoring scheme moot. There's less than a week left. We all need to stick together."

Abarca's face remained impassive. "There aren't enough slots for us all. Right now, you and I are competing. And I intend to be selected for training."

"That's incredibly selfish. You know that, right?"

"I know that some people are suited for this and others are not."

"So you'll just do this arbitrary and dangerous thing to prove your obedience to the company?"

She got in his face. "It's not arbitrary. A willingness to face actual danger is a relevant filter."

Kelly groaned. "So it's a 'filter,' is it?"

Abarca pointed to the cliff. "Just keep one hand and one foot firmly placed at all times."

"If you fall without a rope, you'll *die*, Isabel."

"Then I'd better not fall."

Tighe had been studying the cliff face the entire time. "Isabel."

She and the others turned to him.

"How proficient do I need to be to safely cross this without a rope?"

"No proficiency at all. Like I said, if this traverse was five feet off the ground, no one here would give it a second thought."

Kelly shouted, "But it's not 5 feet off the ground!"

Tighe cinched his helmet and walked toward the edge.

Berggren intercepted him. "Not you, too, J.T. If anyone should call bullshit, I'd think it would be you."

"This doesn't look that dangerous."

Lazzari shook her head. "You're letting the company abuse you."

"And you're betraying the rest of us."

Chindarkar suddenly stepped forward.

Berggren groaned. "You, too, now? If we all stick together—"

Chindarkar tightened her helmet strap. "Isabel's right. This is a test of nerve, and if I ever want to go into deep space for real, then I need to prove to myself that I have courage—otherwise, I'm a danger to everyone else."

"Have you all gone mad?" Kelly searched their faces. "I, for one, refuse to go—safety rope or no." She pointed at the coordinator. "I'll take you bastards to court."

"That is your right." The coordinator looked to Berggren.

Berggren sighed. "I'll use the safety rope."

Then to Lazzari.

She nodded. "The rope, please."

Kelly threw up her hands. "Brilliant! For all your talk, you still give in."

The coordinator pointed last to Lomidze.

The Russian said, "I agree with Alyson. I refuse to participate."

"Suit yourself."

Berggren and Lazzari stood glumly as camp staff clipped safety ropes to their harnesses. The safety lines hung from bolts at the top of the cliff, where more coordinators gave the thumbs-up.

Without a rope Abarca moved to the edge of the cliff and extended her right foot onto a narrow ledge.

Several of the candidates sucked in their breath.

She looked ahead and then back at Tighe and Chindarkar. "Stay focused and you will make it. But if you have *any* doubts, use the rope."

Tighe and Chindarkar exchanged appraising looks, then watched Abarca edge forward and then step onto the next ledge, finding another handhold. She moved with a catlike grace and calm assurance.

Far below her a sooty tern glided along on the wind.

Chindarkar gestured for Tighe to go next.

"Thanks a lot." Tighe took several calming breaths and then stepped out onto the first narrow ledge, grabbing for the same handhold Abarca had. It was indeed solid. He glanced down and was rewarded with the sense of heightened reality he knew so well. Below him was death. Ahead was life. Nothing else mattered.

Tighe followed Abarca's steps along the cliff face as she carefully traversed from narrow ledge to narrow ledge. His every thought was on the present. Only once did he glance behind to offer reassurance as he saw Chindarkar prepare for her own first step. "You can trust the handholds, Priya."

"Good." She took a steadying breath—then stepped out. Her toe found the ledge, and she sighed in relief as she moved safely onto it.

Abarca shouted from several ledges ahead. "Keep your body tight to the wall! Remain focused!"

Back on the outcrop, camp staff led Berggren's rope line to the edge. Roped in, Berggren nonetheless looked nervous as he waited for Chindarkar to advance along the cliff face.

Tighe focused on the physical act of climbing. With each forward move and each successful reach, he felt his confidence increase. Viewed objectively, this was a simple exercise. The height was only an issue if he fell—and if he took care, he would not fall. Thus, the height was irrelevant.

Kelly and Lomidze watched, horrified, as the others went on without them.

Tighe stole a look ahead at Abarca planning her next move. She momentarily glanced back at him and flashed the first grin he'd ever seen from her. It made him grin, too. She was in her element.

Soon Abarca stepped onto the wide stone outcropping on the far side. Camp staff there made way for her, speaking into their radios.

"Ascan 2-4-7 secure."

She turned and gave Tighe the thumbs-up.

He refocused and crossed the remaining three ledges. Soon he, too, stepped across the gap and onto the rock outcropping.

"Ascan 3-6-3 secure."

Abarca smiled and to his surprise hugged him, slapping him on the back. "Way to go, J.T."

"You were right. It wasn't that hard."

Abarca turned to the remaining climbers. Chindarkar, Berggren, and Lazzari were making progress.

Chindarkar concentrated on her next move.

Tighe recognized the tense stance of Berggren on the rock face. He'd seen it before from reluctant cavers on a difficult pitch.

Chindarkar continued to make determined moves across the cliff face. Within a minute she closed the gap and stepped onto the outcropping alongside Abarca and Tighe.

The nearby coordinator spoke into his radio. "Ascan 4-1-2 secure."

Abarca grabbed her in a hug.

Chindarkar laughed. "I can't believe I just did a free-climb."

"You did great."

They all now watched Berggren move with extra care across the cliff face, occasionally swatting the safety rope out of his way. Coordinators at the summit were careful to reel in any slack. Lazzari often loomed behind him, clearly impatient with the slow pace.

Finally, Berggren pulled himself onto the rocky outcropping and came alongside Abarca, Tighe, and Chindarkar. Lazzari did so almost immediately afterward. They held on to their red safety ropes and looked behind them at the cliff face they'd just crossed.

Abarca observed, "I see neither of you fell."

Berggren said nothing. Lazzari stared at the cliff and just shook her head as she unclipped and walked away.

A voice came over the radio. *"Exercise complete."*

CHAPTER 14

Green Mountain

MARCH 14, 2033

James Tighe strolled across a manicured lawn surrounded on three sides by lush jungle, a mash-up of plants from around the world: ficus trees, Bermuda cedars, pandanus, stands of bamboo, banana trees, eucalyptus, Norfolk Island pines. There were also guava, jacaranda, mango, gorse, sedges, coffee plants—and those were just the plants Tighe recognized.

The western edge of the lawn opened to a broad view of Ascension Island from on high, with a brilliant sunset over the Atlantic. Behind him stood a well-maintained, whitewashed stone cottage with windows and doors framed in varnished wood. A sign at the farm entrance marked this as Green Mountain, part of a British garrison built in the 1840s, and the highest point on Ascension.

Strands of white lights hung in nearby trees. Forty newly minted asteroid-mining trainees spread out across the lawn in small groups, chatting, laughing, and dancing as classic hip-hop music played over speakers. The trainees wore new cobalt-blue utility jumpsuits with Polestar company patches on their arms and logos on their backs, along with the designation "Trainee" and their surnames stitched in gold thread on the front pocket.

They had finally graduated from a number to a name.

Tighe held six plastic flutes of champagne, stems between his fingers, as he sidestepped a small land crab that wielded a paper cocktail umbrella, apparently seized from an earlier human tormentor. He approached Abarca, Morra, Jin, Chindarkar, Adisa, Yakovlev, Clarke, and Dahl, standing near a low garden wall, and passed the flutes around. "Drink up. I don't think there'll be an open bar in Antarctica."

Clarke raised her glass in a toast. "To those who didn't make the cut."

Voices all around: "Hear! Hear!" They bumped plastic flutes together.

Yak added, "They have my thanks."

The others laughed, then drank.

Almost immediately Morra raised his glass again. "And here's to our reward: six months of darkness in the coldest place on Earth."

The group groaned and bumped flutes with considerably less enthusiasm. They drank again.

Clarke said, "On the bright side, our odds of getting into space are now almost fifty-fifty."

"We should enjoy the sun while we can." Morra pointed toward the sunset. "Look . . ."

The view beyond the edge of the lawn was gorgeous as the sun blazed reddish orange over the Atlantic.

Chindarkar said, "It's beautiful up here." Her gaze wandered to the surrounding trees. "I'm surprised how green it is. The terrain around the DAC looks like Mars."

Adisa moved alongside. "In the cottage there is a coffee table book. It says that Ascension was barren stone just four centuries ago—so desolate the sailors who discovered it did not come ashore."

Clarke nodded to herself. "That makes sense. The rock here is only a million years old, and it's a thousand kilometers from anywhere."

Adisa gestured to the trees. "The first British garrison seeded this mountain with plants from around their empire."

Jin Han seemed intrigued. "So they terraformed the island."

Yak said, "We must do the same in space, yes?"

"By 'we' you mean the Russians?" Eric Reyes, the former US Air Force test pilot, joined their group. He was holding a glass of bourbon and looked a bit glassy-eyed.

Yak nodded. "Da, Russians. Americans. Everyone."

Morra pointed. "Where'd you get a proper drink?"

"There's a real bar inside."

Morra headed off. "Be right back."

Reyes looked to Yak and then to Jin. "So how are we going to deal with this?"

Yak and Jin exchanged puzzled looks.

Jin replied, "Deal with what?"

"Authoritarian nations like China and Russia expanding into space."

The group groaned. "Whoa, whoa . . ."

Reyes held up his hand. "It's a fair question."

Yak glowered. "Russian Federation is democracy, Eric."

"Oh, right. You just happen to keep electing the same leader over and over."

"Better than leaders you have been coming up with."

"Is that right?"

Jin observed, "Perhaps you've had enough to drink, Eric."

"Why, because I'm willing to ask what everyone else won't?" Reyes approached Jin. "Do you guys plan on expanding authoritarianism into space?"

"Will you expand American imperialism into space?"

Tighe stepped between them. "Look, we're not here as nations. Catalyst is a private company. And tonight is a celebration. Let's not argue."

"It's a valid question, J.T. This is going to come up at some point. Let's not wait until we're up in space—let's have it out right here and now. These guys don't believe in human liberty or democracy."

Yak laughed. "Human liberty. Please . . ."

Dahl tugged on Reyes's arm. "C'mon, Eric. Don't ruin tonight."

"She is right." Jin looked calm as he said, "Besides, America is not a democracy—it is an oligarchy."

The group again shouted, "Whoa, whoa!"

Reyes wore an unnerving smile. "Fuck you."

Jin continued. "And oligarchy is an improvement because democracy is an inferior form of government."

The group grew quiet. Dahl turned to face Jin with a look of disappointment.

Reyes held out his hand. "There you go! Just beneath the surface."

Tighe narrowed his eyes. "Han, do you really believe that?"

Jin looked around. "Corporations are not democratic, and yet they rule every aspect of American life. If democracy is so important, why is this the case?"

Tighe sighed. "Because democracy is always a work in progress. That's why."

"Half of your countrymen live in poverty. Meanwhile, Chinese leadership has brought great prosperity to its people."

Morra returned to the group holding a glass of bourbon. "You think that prosperity would have happened without the West, Han? China just had cheaper labor."

Jin nodded. "So you admit, capitalism has no loyalty."

Morra took a sip of bourbon. "Are you really going to stand there and tell me China isn't capitalist?"

Adisa interjected. "Space does not belong to America."

Everyone turned to Adisa. It was an uncharacteristically blunt comment for the soft-spoken Nigerian.

Adisa looked to Jin. "And space does not belong to China." He looked to Yak. "Or Russia. Or any other nation." He gazed around the lawn. The entire party had turned quiet.

"I will tell you, when I was a small boy I dreamed of going to space. I read all I could find about it. I learned math. I learned software. I learned engineering. All because of a speech I once heard. It was made well before I was born—two years after Nigerian independence, at the height of the Cold War." Adisa seemed to realize all eyes were on him. "At a time when the world was close to nuclear annihilation, John F. Kennedy said these words: 'There is no strife, no prejudice, no national conflict in space as yet. Its hazards are hostile to us all. Its conquest deserves the best of all mankind, and its opportunity for peaceful cooperation may never come again.'"

The entire class of trainees stood in silence.

Adisa studied the faces of his colleagues. He raised his glass. "To peaceful cooperation."

The entire assembly raised their glasses. "Hear! Hear!"

CHAPTER 15

Parabolic Trajectory

Lukas Rochat exited Newark International Airport, Terminal B, rolling a carry-on suitcase behind him. Normally he'd be exhausted after a nine-hour flight from Frankfurt, but traveling business class was a different experience altogether. Aside from a touch of jet lag, he felt rested. The fact that a new client was paying for this trip made it stress-free. This was billable time.

He checked his phone for the location where his driver would meet him. He was in the right spot—Door 5.

This wasn't the first time Rochat had visited the States. However, it was the first time he'd traveled here on business. His new client was an American aerospace startup looking to set up an office in Luxembourg City. He'd met them at a space-law conference in Geneva. He wasn't out of debt yet, but his practice was definitely looking up.

Rochat spotted his name displayed on a tablet on the dashboard of an approaching black SUV.

He waved the vehicle down, and it double-parked across from him.

The driver, a large bearded man in a black suit, got out and came around to the curb. "Afternoon, sir."

Rochat passed his suitcase to the man. "Will we hit much traffic heading into Manhattan?"

"We'll be fine." Unlike most Americans, the man did not smile. Instead, he simply opened the passenger door and took charge of the luggage.

Rochat got in and used his phone to check email while the driver stowed his bag. In a moment they were under way, the driver bringing the electric SUV into the flow of terminal traffic.

Rochat checked news headlines on his phone as they drove but noticed the SUV pass by signs for New York as it drove onto a local aviation road.

Rochat leaned forward. "You missed the turn."

The driver stared darkly into the rearview mirror. "You were brought to the US for a reason, Mr. Rochat. I suggest you stop asking questions."

Rochat felt a bolt of fear cut through him. He leaned back in his seat.

The builders of the mysterious spacecraft. Rochat had been waiting for word from them. Here he'd thought that he was clever for bagging a new client. Apparently it was the same client—just under another name.

In a few moments the SUV came to a gate bristling with security guards. The driver showed credentials and the gate rose for them to pass. The SUV moved quickly toward an upscale terminal entrance and parked behind a Bentley sedan unloading passengers. The sign above the terminal read "Signature Flight Support."

The driver got out, retrieved Rochat's bag, and then opened the passenger door. "Follow me, Mr. Rochat."

"Yes. Yes, of course."

They left the SUV where it was.

Rochat moved quickly to keep up, gazing at the opulent décor as they entered a check-in area. Uniformed staff greeted them with smiles. However, Rochat's escort brought him through the check-in without stopping. Staff opened doors for them. No one asked for identification.

"Good afternoon, sir."

Rochat nodded. "Afternoon." It was a strange sensation. Some powerful force propelled him through all obstacles.

Moments later his escort brought him through an automatic door and out to the tarmac. Ahead of them was the most beautiful aircraft Rochat had ever laid eyes on—one he had only seen in aerospace magazine ads. It was a needle-shaped private business jet with the name "Aerion AS2" painted beneath its swept tailfin. The main wings were short, stubby things, but the fuselage was incredibly long. It had only eight passenger windows, and these occupied at most 20 percent of the length of the plane. The rest was taken up by nose cone, engines, wings, and tail. It was a supersonic business jet.

The cabin door opened as they approached. An attractive young blond woman in a dress and hairstyle reminiscent of the 1960s smiled at him. "Good afternoon, Mr. Rochat. Welcome aboard."

"Yes, I . . ." Rochat noticed his escort wheeling his suitcase to a hatch open in the side of the plane.

"They'll care for your luggage. Please come inside. We have a tight schedule."

Rochat climbed the steps. "Of course." He entered the passenger cabin to see a half dozen luxurious leather seats. Burled wood, carpet, and accent lights gave the compartment a soothing vibe.

The attendant showed him to a seat. "May I get you some refreshment before we depart?"

The sound of the hatch shutting outside reached him, and the engines immediately began to spool up.

"I . . . No, thank you."

She nodded and turned to head to the front of the plane.

He stopped her. "Excuse me, miss."

She pivoted, a pleasant smile on her face.

"Where are we going?"

"Approximately two and a half hours from here, sir." Another toothy smile. "Buckle up." With that she walked away, disappearing into the galley compartment.

Two and a half hours.

If he recalled the top speed of this aircraft correctly—Mach 1.5, nearly 1,800 kilometers per hour—where did that put him in two and a half hours? Imagining a map of the United States, Rochat realized it placed him anywhere in North America.

The engines surged higher, and soon they were taxiing toward the runway.

Although they left late in the afternoon, the supersonic jet chased the sun across the continent, heading due west. At this speed Rochat realized he would arrive about the same time he left—perhaps even earlier. Cruising at over 50,000 feet, Rochat could even see the curvature of the Earth.

Thankfully he'd had a chance to freshen up in the nicest aircraft bathroom he'd ever been in (replete with marble washstand), and curiosity made him have a light bite—an excellent salmon Niçoise salad made with mâche instead of frisée—served with skill by the cabin attendant.

However, despite jet lag, he couldn't sleep; they could land at any time, and he must be prepared. He had begun to accept the fact that this was going to be a forty-eight-hour workday.

A little over two hours later, the plane began to descend from the stratosphere. They soared low over a desert. He was somewhere in the southwestern US.

The attendant came in to ensure that his seat belt was fastened, and then he was left again to his own thoughts.

Who had built the secret spaceship? What was their intention with it? They clearly had immense wealth—but also desired secrecy. Was he in actual danger?

That last part seemed unlikely. If they wanted to disappear him, it wouldn't make sense to bring him to the US.

But then a disturbing thought occurred to him.

Unless they were the US government.

That last idea reverberated in his mind as the AS2 jet descended toward a pale, mountainous, and desolate landscape. Sagebrush and Joshua trees raced past below, but a long, modern airstrip soon appeared to receive them. The plane descended to a smooth, fast landing.

Rochat looked out the window. In the near distance scores of large, new commercial passenger jets were parked in a row, but not near any terminal. They were simply left on a tarmac in the desert, freshly painted with livery from every major world carrier. It was puzzling.

Soon the supersonic jet taxied toward a row of hangars, but instead of moving into one or waiting for a tug, the AS2 came up alongside a small control tower. A sign on the side of it read "Mojave Air and Space Port."

He was in Mojave, California. It was here that some of the most advanced aircraft in history had been built and tested. It was indeed starting to look like he'd stumbled across a US government black project. He tried to recall if Guantanamo prison was still in use.

The engines whined down, and the flight attendant entered the cabin. "We've arrived, Mr. Rochat."

Rochat descended the aircraft steps and walked out into a warm, dry breeze. It brought back memories of a holiday he'd taken in Spain—although he wasn't trembling in fear then. He noticed a serious-looking man in a dark suit and buzz-cut hair standing on the tarmac next to the entrance of a down-scale café. A faded sign announced it as "Voyager Restaurant." The man motioned for Rochat to approach.

As Rochat closed the distance, the suited man opened the door to the café and gestured for Rochat to continue inside. Rochat entered what looked to be a plain American coffee shop with ceiling fans, simple wooden furniture—and a huge map of the world on the wall, along with framed photos of jet fighter pilots, exotic test aircraft, rockets, and aerospace pioneers.

The café was sparsely occupied—just a trio who looked to be aerospace engineers in short-sleeve dress shirts, ties, and ID badges, and in a nearby corner what appeared to be a gray-haired rancher, replete with cowboy hat and leathery, sun-blasted skin. The man sipped a cup of coffee while interacting with a tablet computer.

The only other person in the place was a tanned man in his thirties, wearing absurd rose-colored sunglasses and a faded concert T-shirt for the Cure. His pronounced jaw and rugged good looks seemed vaguely familiar to Rochat. The man smiled and waved Rochat over.

Rochat approached warily. Whoever this was, it was hardly the person he was expecting to meet—and this was especially not the environment in which he expected to meet him.

"Have a seat." The man grinned confidently, revealing straight white teeth.

And that's when Rochat recognized him—despite the sunglasses. Sinking down into the booth on the far side of the table, Rochat fell into shock.

"What's wrong, Lukas? You look like you've seen a ghost."

"You're Nathan Joyce."

Joyce calmly put a ringed finger to his lips. "Shh. Trying to stay below the radar." He took a bite of a cheeseburger that was half finished and spoke with his mouth full. "Want something to eat?"

Rochat looked around the place. It was a dump. "No. No, thank you."

Joyce finished chewing, then shouted toward an elderly waitress reading a newspaper over by the cash register. "Helen! Get me a check, will ya?"

She nodded. "Sure, hon." And she started writing on a pad.

Rochat was still in shock. He was sitting across from famous billionaire

Nathan Joyce—one of the Space Titans. A man who'd invested billions in commercial space exploration. Only now did Rochat realize that this meant the secret spaceship had been built by Nathan Joyce himself. Rochat fell into stunned amazement once more.

"Best not to leave your mouth hanging open, Lukas. There's flies out here in the desert."

"Oh . . . sorry."

The waitress walked up with the check. "Nothing for your friend?"

Joyce grabbed the check. "No, thanks. We're just heading out." He passed her several twenties. "Keep it."

"Hey, thanks. You take care, now."

"You, too, darlin'." Joyce stood and slapped Rochat on his suited shoulder. "Let's take a walk, buddy. About time we had a chat."

Rochat, still bewildered, got up and followed Joyce—Nathan R. Joyce in the flesh—out the ringing front door of the café and into the warm desert air. In a moment Rochat caught up and they walked alongside a service road next to a rusted chain-link fence topped with razor wire. Behind the fence a line of wingless, sun-bleached jet fighter fuselages from the Cold War era languished in disorder, their rounded canopies as opaque as cataracts. Not far ahead, a squat rocket several stories tall stood in a tiny park as some sort of memorial. Signs reading "For Lease" were visible on most of the hangars and warehouses nearby.

"You know why I like this place, Lukas?"

Rochat shook his head.

"Because it reminds me—reminds me how risky it can be to play it safe." Joyce gestured to the dilapidated buildings around them. "A few years back this place was hopping. Space startups—like hot-rodder garages—each making their own 'spacecraft.'" This last word he bracketed in air quotes.

Rochat looked around. The neighborhood had an air of desolation about it.

"But they weren't spacecraft. They were carnival rides. Their builders thought too small."

Rochat had no idea what to say in response. He didn't even know if he could respond. He could barely breathe.

Joyce studied Rochat. "I hope you're not sore at me about that helicopter stunt. Damn Russians. Something got lost in the translation. You've got some balls on you, Lukas. I'll give you that."

"I am not easily deterred, Mr. Joyce."

"Good—and call me Nathan."

"Nathan." It felt odd being so familiar—but he remembered Americans were like this. They didn't stand on formalities. *Getting shit done* is what they'd say, and Rochat was definitely here to get shit done. "I meant what I said; I am very much willing to protect the confidentiality of your current endeavor."

"My 'endeavor.' You think we can keep that confidential? You figured it out all by yourself, and no offense, but you're not the sharpest utensil in the drawer. I can't imagine it's going to take the big boys long to do the same."

"How long must you maintain this secret?" Rochat realized he was way out of his depth. He barely had any idea what he was doing here, much less what the hell he was talking about. *Fake it 'til you make it* kept echoing in his head.

"Half a year. Maybe longer."

"And this . . . gravity ship, it is in lunar orbit already?"

"We are under attorney-client privilege, Counselor. Understood?"

"Of course, Mr.—Nathan. Everything you say to me I will hold in the utmost confidentiality."

"No notes about our meetings. Nothing with my name on it. You don't even whisper my name in your sleep. My people will tell you how to handle your billing."

"Absolutely." Rochat could barely contain his elation. If this was some sort of interview, he had apparently passed it. He was now working directly for Nathan R. Joyce. He could say good-bye to daily-rate office space. If his former colleagues knew, they'd ask *him* for a job. "I will follow your instructions to the letter."

"The 'gravity ship,' as you call it, is currently in a lunar distant retrograde orbit."

"Truly?" Rochat could barely keep the awe out of his voice. He laughed slightly.

Joyce put his arm on Rochat's shoulder. "Truly."

Normally reserved, Rochat didn't even mind the familiarity the American billionaire was presuming. The man had built the most advanced spacecraft in history—one that spun to create artificial gravity—and secreted it in orbit around the Moon. This conversation was quite possibly the most interesting one under way on Earth at the moment. Rochat could forgive Joyce his eccentricities.

"All the components have been brought together. It's in the final assembly stage."

"At what point will you inform the grand duchy's Ministry of the Economy and apply for human flight certification?"

Joyce grimaced. "Yeah, see, that's the thing, Lukas. I'm not a permit kind of guy."

Rochat furrowed his brow. "I don't understand. Surely you—"

"I need you to go back to Luxembourg City and file a blizzard of paperwork to keep the bureaucrats busy. Can you do that for me?"

This was a decision point. Every fiber in Rochat's being was telling him to agree out of pure desperation. However, it was time to advise his client. "Nathan, I realize you want to shortcut the process. However, if you wish to financially benefit from your endeavor, certain laws must be observed. Article 6 of the Outer Space Treaty states that activities of nongovernmental entities in space shall require authorization and continuing supervision by the appropriate state party to the treaty—which in this case is the Grand Duchy of Luxembourg. Moreover, the Registration Convention, UN Resolution 3235 of 1976, requires that all objects launched into outer space must be registered."

Joyce looked amused. "I received authorization, and they are registered."

"Not for their actual purpose and trajectory. Cislunar treaties are designed to minimize space debris and deconflict orbits. Assembling this spacecraft without notifying authorities of its actual location makes it a navigational hazard that could expose you to enormous criminal and financial liability."

"I have clearance; I'm just using my approved orbit for a larger spacecraft than I claimed, and which I assembled from other spacecraft in adjacent orbits—which I also legally obtained. So I have no spacecraft in unapproved orbits, Counselor."

"Even so, depending on what you intend to do in space, there are the COSPAR procedures for preventing biological contamination that must be observed. The UN's International Council for Science assigns a risk score for all missions, and if you intend to bring material back to Earth—"

"We will not be bringing material back to Earth."

"Nothing?"

"Nothing." Joyce chuckled. "Lukas, I appreciate you looking out for me, but we've got that all under control."

"Nathan, I do not understand why you filed paperwork with the Grand Duchy of Luxembourg at all, if you intended to ignore their regulations."

"Because *not* filing for space permits would have drawn attention. We needed those components cleared for flight, and that meant they needed to have a business purpose in space. We provided the boring description everyone expected. Everyone except you, Lukas."

Rochat was embarrassed how much the praise pleased him. "The Division of Space Affairs is investigating your shell companies. The truth will come out sooner or later."

"We need to make sure it's later. What I need you to do, Lukas, is make a complete and accurate filing of my spacecraft and its real purpose."

Rochat was now confused. "But I thought you said—"

"But file it as a *proposed* ship—like I've been saying in the news. Unbuilt. Unfunded. That way, everyone at the ministry and in the press will roll their eyes because no one believes a word I say. Which is exactly why I'm saying it."

"I am confused."

"Good. That's the point. File my plan with the ministry and keep filing revisions to keep them occupied."

"Well, I . . ." Was that ethical? Then again, why wouldn't Rochat want to have his name on something so historic? Surely that rated some consideration. "I can do that, yes." A thought occurred to him. "But creating such an application and filing for amendments—this will come at considerable cost. The filing fees alone could be half a million euros. And I'll need manpower."

"Don't worry about that. Hire the people you need. Develop your contacts at the Ministry of the Economy. Find out how much they know, what they're up to. Do you understand?"

Rochat nodded but said, "I should warn you that getting new permits approved once Luxembourg officials discover they've been deceived—well, that will be impossible. They'll invalidate every permit you have, since you're not pursuing what your permits claim." Rochat paused. "What is the ship meant for? Why the big engines? Why the artificial gravity? Those are features required for a long voyage. Where is your ship headed?"

Joyce stopped and turned to face Rochat. "Where do you think it's headed, Lukas?"

A sudden realization swept over Rochat, and he laughed. "*Mars*. You're going to Mars, aren't you?"

Joyce's genial expression morphed, and with alarming speed he grabbed the young lawyer by the suit lapels and threw him against the chain-link fence—pressing his intimidating face right up into Rochat's. "Goddamnit! Does everyone on this fucking planet have Mars fever? That's all I ever hear about is 'Mars, Mars, Mars!' Mars is a goddamned trap! It's a gravity well that will suck in mankind's future. At best it's a research location or an interesting vacation spot for your grandkids—but it's not a place for humanity to live. Never you goddamn mind where my ship is headed. All you need to do is keep the grand duchy and everyone else off my back for as long as possible. The longer you do that, the more money you'll make. And I do mean *a lot* of money, Lukas. Change-your-life money. Are we clear?" He released Rochat's lapels and backed away.

Rochat took a breath and straightened his coat. "Yes. Perfectly clear."

"I don't want to hear another goddamned word out of you about Mars. Understand?"

"Yes, sir."

Joyce extended his hand. "We in business, then?"

Surprised by the sudden shift, Rochat shook Joyce's hand firmly, looking him in the eye, just like the business books said.

Joyce maintained his grip on Rochat's hand. "I admire your ambition, Lukas. You remind me of myself at your age. Lots of unearned confidence."

"I will not let you down."

"As for the EU, the grand duchy, and the FAA—I'm not going to ask permission. Here on Earth you lawyers say that possession is nine-tenths of the law. Well, Lukas, in space I think possession is going to be more like 99.99999 percent of the law. Space is a goddamned frontier. What's the use of going to a frontier if it has rules?"

Joyce didn't let Rochat's hand go, but instead pulled him in close. "You'll be making lifelong enemies in the next few months."

"Enemies?"

"Enemies in government. At major aerospace companies. Especially among the other Titans."

That *all* sounded like an unmitigated disaster to his legal practice. Rochat felt weak in the knees.

"Don't worry. I'll make it worth your while. Personally, I find the respect of enemies to be sweeter than friendship. And certainly more honest—nobody ever lies about hating you."

Joyce let Rochat's hand go, and then he continued down the street. "Go back to Luxembourg, Lukas. My people will send you instructions on how we're to communicate."

Still reeling, Rochat nodded and walked away without daring to look back.

CHAPTER 16

Concordia Station

MAY 5, 2033

Klaxons wailed and LED strobes pierced the darkness as James Tighe bolted upright in his bed. Overhead lights rose to illuminate the circular radiation-shielded crew quarters he shared with Michael Harris, a bearded geologist from Spokane. Tighe shot a look across to Harris, who was sitting up in his own bed nearby.

A calm female voice said, *"Warning: imminent structural failure, Arm 2. Commencing emergency spin-down. Repeat: commencing emergency spin-down. Prepare for microgravity."*

The deafening alarms whooped.

Harris shouted over the din, "That's a new one!"

They both reached for biphasic crystal work glasses mounted on chargers in the built-in nightstand. Resembling high-end safety glasses, the devices served as a virtual window into the ship's systems. The crew had taken to calling them simply *crystals.*

Harris shouted, "Rosey, mute all alarms!"

The Klaxons became barely audible.

Tighe slipped his crystal on and an augmented-reality UI appeared before his eyes. It showed critical alarms projected over the 3D model of a spacecraft. The ship resembled a construction crane gone figure skating, spinning on its axis. It had three radial arms at its waist, and at the end of each was an inflatable flat-bottomed crew habitat—or *hab*—rotating at just under three rotations per minute to simulate one Earth gravity for the occupants. Tighe knew this generated considerable centrifugal load on the composite box trusses linking the habs to the ship's spine.

The female voice announced, *"Warning: asymmetrical thrust pattern detected. Spin-down aborted. Repeat: spin-down aborted."* Then almost immediately, *"Imminent structural failure, Arm 2 . . ."*

Harris looked up at the speakers. "What the hell is going on?"

"We need to stop our spin, and something's preventing it."

Tighe drilled into the 3D model and highlighted the source of the alarm: one of the ship's rotating radial arms. At the end of that arm was Hab 2, a 42-ton habitat occupied by four of his fellow crewmen: Nicole Clarke, Yating Yu, Robbie Allway, and Paul Hagopian. Tighe was stationed in Hab 1 with Harris, Dr. Elizabeth Josephson, and Chelsea Black, while the third hab was an unoccupied workshop known as the Fab Hab.

Black, one of their upstairs hab mates, spoke over the ship's comm link. *"Hab 2's comms are down. I can't raise them."*

Harris got to his feet. "We should suit up."

Tighe and Harris raced to their lockers and pulled on bright-blue flight suits. They flipped up the integral visor hood, zipping it closed at the throat, then grabbed emergency life support packs.

They clipped the hoses into the inputs and outputs of their suits, then activated oxygen.

Tighe checked his display. "Earth transmission delay is six minutes twenty-three seconds. We're on our own for the next thirteen minutes." He opened a long-distance channel. "Mission control, mission control, we have an imminent structural failure warning and an emergency spin-down abort. Please advise."

The sound of people moving in the quarters above could be heard through the polymer decking.

"Let's strap in."

Tighe and Harris both spun the wheel of the crew quarters pressure door and pulled it open. They raced out into the inflatable hab, which resembled the inside of a giant white propane tank. It was a squat circular tower 11 meters in diameter and 8.5 meters tall, its height divided into two levels by static-free decking. The hab walls were fashioned from a 50-centimeter-thick laminate of Kevlar, Nextel, Nomex, Viton, polyethylene foam, and insulation, designed to withstand the impact of micrometeorites.

The hab's upper level, where Josephson and Black's crew quarters were located, contained the ship's galley, medical bay, and living area, while the lower level held four crew workstations, a shower, a bathroom, and life support systems. The aluminum-walled, water-lined core contained the crew quarters and formed the center of the circular hab.

As they reached their workstations, Tighe and Harris strapped in to their seats. Josephson and Black slid down the gangway from the second-floor crew quarters and raced to their own workstations on the far side of the hab.

Black called out, "How's it looking?"

Harris answered, "Not great."

Tighe activated his workstation. The bridge of their spaceship wasn't at all like what he'd imagined from countless sci-fi movies and TV shows. Instead it consisted of Spartan office cubicles, the chairs bolted to the deck and equipped with seat belts and shoulder harnesses. There wasn't a control board, window, or porthole in sight. Lidar scanners at the corners of Tighe's otherwise empty work desk captured his hand gestures as he instantiated a virtual UI. Holograms of software-defined light flickered into existence in front of him.

The entirety of the ship's UI was virtual—projected onto Tighe's crystal and also onto the crystals of his crewmates. This eliminated the need to boost tons of display screens, dials, buttons, wiring, and switches into orbit—not to mention replacement parts. Instead, their spacecraft was equipped with dozens of extra pairs of lightweight, rad-hardened viewing crystals and a bank of redundant computer servers. Bridge virtualization made it possible to control the ship from just about anywhere on it, and it also gave mission controllers back on Earth the ability to remotely fix problems and to push improved versions of the ship's UI and OS out to the crew.

Harris's desk faced Tighe's, and they gazed in horror at a shared hallucination of their stricken ship—a detailed hologram of which floated between them, with rows of red alert codes scrolling to either side.

Harris tapped at a virtual console. "Lockout doors sealed. Emergency power systems on standby."

Tighe glanced at an emergency procedures checklist that appeared out of thin air to his left. "Life support set to—"

The ship's voice cut in. "*Spin-down abort overridden. Emergency spin-down commencing. Repeat: emergency spin-down commencing. Prepare for microgravity.*"

Tighe called across the hab, "Who overrode the abort?"

Something beyond the walls rumbled as dozens of CO_2 thrusters on the ship's radial arms fired to slow its spin. The hab shuddered, and a rocking motion began.

Suddenly dozens more critical alerts popped up on the displays. More alarms sounded. The hologram in front of Tighe grew intensely red as stress increased on Radial Arm 2.

The ship's voice said calmly, "*Warning: asymmetrical thrust pattern detected.*"

Harris called out, "Truss 2 is deforming!"

Tighe shouted, "Rosey, halt emergency spin-down!"

"*Two crew members required for override.*"

"Rosey, belay that order!" Josephson shouted back. "J.T., if we don't slow our spin, we'll break apart."

"The ship aborted the spin-down for a reason. We need to figure this out."

"There's no time."

Harris clicked through different CCTV monitors providing exterior views of the ship. "Broken gas lines. Arm 2 thrusters are off-line."

Tighe shouted, "If we fire thrusters on the other arms, Arm 2 might shear off."

"And if we *don't* fire thrusters it will tear off anyway."

Harris shook his head. "I officially have no idea what to do in this situation."

The hab shuddered once more as the lateral thrusters continued to fire.

Radial Arm 2 on the holographic model turned a deeper shade of red. A louder rumbling sound reached them through the superstructure. Harris and Tighe looked up at the ceiling. The creak and then groan of strained metal echoed somewhere above.

"That does not sound good."

Black's voice came through the ship channel again. "*Thirty-two more seconds . . .*"

Suddenly there was a loud *boom*, and then the floor jolted—the entire hab shook. Watching the 3D model, Tighe saw the girders of Radial Arm 2 bend, then break off from the ship. The arm spun off into space, and the rest of the ship began to wobble like a woozy top.

New and more urgent alarms began to shriek. Red lights flashed.

"Warning: structural failure. Warning: Hab 2 life support failure. Warning: ship off station. Warning: unstable spin state."

Josephson shouted, "Evacuate to the Central Hab!"

Harris sighed. "Hab 2 lost."

Tighe unclipped his harness and stood. "C'mon, Mike. Let's get to the airlock."

"Christ . . ." Harris leaned forward and rubbed his face. "I'm so fucking tired."

The lights suddenly dimmed, then went out—but the holographic displays remained. Emergency lights came on in the background. The sounds of twisting metal sounded all around them. Tighe and Harris watched in dismay as the rest of the ship's 3D model came apart—pieces sailing in different directions.

Harris threw up his hands dramatically. "Game over, man. Game over!"

The emergency lights turned off and the overhead lights came up. The virtual model of their ship was suddenly replaced by the dour face of mission control manager Gabriel Lacroix. His French accent was thicker than usual as he said, *"Mission failure. Ship lost with all hands. Ze cause?"* The holographic head loomed larger as he leaned forward. *"Yooman arror."*

Tighe sat back down. "Gabriel, would it be possible for us *yoomans* to catch a few winks before the hotwash?"

"It is called a 'hotwash' because we do it while the experience is still hot. In space you will not have the luxury of catching a 'few winks' if the ship is coming apart. That goes double for you, Harris."

"Yeah, yeah . . ."

Tighe and Harris carried trays of rehydrated rations across a small windowless dining hall. They joined a table with Abarca, Morra, Clarke, Chindarkar, and Amy Tsukada, a Japanese American from Seattle whom Tighe had met on his first day of candidate selection. Everyone wore blue utility jumpsuits.

Morra gazed down the table as Tighe sat down. "You destroy the ship again?"

Tighe picked up his fork. "It was more of a group effort this time."

Chindarkar pointed to Harris's tray. "What'd you get, Michael?"

"Turkey and noodles. Anyone's guess which is which."

"Wanna trade desserts?"

"For cobbler? Forget it."

Clarke leaned forward. "Amy, I like your ink."

"Oh, thanks." Tsukada sported large tattoos of Japanese calligraphy and anime characters on her neck and chest.

"Isabel says you're a chemist back in the world. What sort of work do you do?"

"I'm in carbonyl metallurgy."

She received blank looks.

"It's a process for refining metal."

Tighe said, "That can't be the only reason they chose you. You a BASE jumper or stunt pilot or something?"

"Nothing as exciting as that." Tsukada poked at her food. "It's just that I really *need* to get into space. To find some relief."

"Relief? From what?"

"From a noise I hear. I've heard it since I was a little girl. A constant, droning hum. In fact, that's what it's called, 'the Hum.' I hear it right now, and I hate it."

"The Hum." Abarca asked, "What is it . . . an ear disorder?"

"Doctors told my parents it was neurological—'spontaneous otoacoustic emissions.' They prescribed medications, but the Hum never went away. In fact, it's only gotten worse—especially in remote places like this."

Chindarkar looked horrified. "How awful."

Clarke pondered something. "I've read about this, but I've never met anyone who's actually heard the Hum." She turned to the others. "Free oscillation of the Earth's tectonic plates. It creates an ultralow-frequency resonance."

Tsukada nodded. "That's right."

"They aren't sure why some people can hear it—or feel it—but some people unfortunately do."

Tsukada added, "A few commit suicide. The rest suffer. But I have other plans." She pointed up.

Tighe said, "You think space will bring you relief."

"I distract myself with music whenever possible. But a few years ago, I suited up to go into a vacuum chamber at work, and the Hum disappeared."

Abarca said, "The vacuum."

"Right. For the first time in my life I heard silence. I want to hear it again. Space sounds like paradise to me."

JUNE 16, 2033

Mission control manager Gabriel Lacroix walked to the front of a darkened classroom. His forty asteroid-mining trainees filled out the seats. A hologram of the solar system instantiated in midair and zoomed in on Earth. The continents, oceans, and swirling clouds of Earth passed by, but the view continued into the vastness of space—until eventually a lonely rock resolved out in the void.

Lacroix said, "This is the reason we are all here. . . ."

The ash-colored chunk of rock continued to grow until the hologram filled the available floor space. It was an asteroid, shaped like a crude spinning top, with a pronounced ridge running around its equator. Its surface was littered with boulders, and there was one especially large boulder protruding near its north pole—like a fortress—that was alternately obscured and revealed as the hologram slowly rotated.

"Asteroid 162173 Ryugu." A label faded in as he said it. "Discovered in 1999, it is a rare C- *and* G-type near-Earth asteroid. Roughly 900 meters in diameter and 450 million tons in mass, it contains tens of millions of tons of nickel, iron, cobalt, nitrogen, ammonia, and water—worth an estimated 106 billion US dollars."

Whistles throughout the room.

"In 2018 the Japanese Aerospace Exploration Agency's Hayabusa2 probe visited Ryugu and remained for nearly a year. It obtained the detailed scans and images you see here, and it also gathered a sample of the asteroid's regolith, which it returned to Earth in 2020—dropping a capsule into the Australian desert."

Detailed photographs of black, almost coal-colored, dust materialized in front of the asteroid.

"This sample confirmed that Ryugu is composed of carbonaceous chondrite—which contains volatiles in the form of mineral hydrates, which can be readily transformed into water vapor."

Lacroix examined the faces of the trainees. "And water will be the single most valuable commodity in the early days of space exploration—creating air to breathe, fuel for rockets, and in sustaining human, animal, and plant life. However, Ryugu also contains other vital resources—ammonia, nitrogen, and metals. What makes these resources so valuable is their trajectory above Earth's gravity well. . . ."

The hologram panned away from Ryugu and zoomed in toward Earth once more. "Even with today's reusable launch systems, it currently costs seventeen hundred dollars per kilogram to lift a payload into low Earth orbit."

A holographic rocket barely climbed off the Earth.

"It costs over twice this amount to lift a kilo of payload to a geostationary transfer orbit—or GTO—36,000 kilometers above Earth."

The same rocket burned a tenth of the way to the Moon.

"That is because at present we need to bring all the fuel required for any space voyage up from Earth's surface. This is why placing anything into orbit around the Moon costs at least 6.6 million dollars per ton."

Lacroix looked out at the trainees. "Building truly useful structures in deep space—on the order of a million tons or more—from Earth-sourced materials would require investments of seven or eight trillion US dollars. And that is just to lift the materials. It does not include cost of R and D, design, and construction. Catalyst Corporation believes it can do better."

The hologram zoomed out to encompass the Earth, the Moon, and the tiny, labeled dot of Ryugu. "Due to its low gravity, mined resources from Ryugu, by contrast, could be returned to cislunar space for as little as a kilometer per second of delta-v. And in situ production can provide the fuel necessary."

An animation showed a robot tug departing Ryugu on a long, looping trajectory around the Sun, and then doing a brief burn before being captured in a Moon orbit years later.

"That is half the acceleration required to lift materials from the Moon's surface. By cost-effectively shipping millions of tons of resources from Ryugu into a lunar DRO, Catalyst Corporation aims to drastically reduce construction and refueling costs in cislunar space—in the process kick-starting a booming cislunar commodity exchange."

Lacroix examined his audience. "But how do we begin?"

The hologram then zoomed in toward the Moon and a 3D model of Catalyst Corporation's hypothetical mining ship in orbit there—its radial arms folded in preparation for a burn. The trainees had all grown familiar with the spacecraft in the training mock-up over the past month. The holographic ship fired its engines, sending it on a trajectory to intercept the passing asteroid Ryugu.

"Our training program has been predicated on the need for a crew of eight miners to depart from lunar orbit and rendezvous with Ryugu on its next close approach."

The hologram zoomed in to show the spacecraft arrive in the shadow of the asteroid.

"There, the crew will conduct robot-assisted mining operations for a period of approximately four years."

The assembled trainees murmured among themselves. Tighe looked to Morra sitting next to him. Their expressions said it all: *Four years?*

The hologram showed the Earth and Ryugu revolving around the Sun several times until they came into close proximity again.

"After which a relief crew will arrive from Earth and the original crew will return home, having mined 8,000 tons of resources—which is approximately one-third the entire mass that humanity has launched into space thus far. Those resources will have been sent back toward a lunar DRO via robotic tugs at regular intervals on slow low-delta-v trajectories—meaning that the crew will arrive back on Earth before most of their shipments show up in cislunar space."

Murmured discussions spread throughout the room.

Tighe had to admit it was a polished presentation, but how expensive were

computer graphics, after all? No doubt Joyce intended the video to hook investors. Having a crew of "trained" asteroid miners who believed in the mission
would no doubt come in handy during press conferences and investor road
shows. That didn't mean any of it would ever turn into an actual space
mission—much less a *four-year* mission in deep space.

Lacroix studied the faces of his audience. "I see many of you have concerns. Questions. But let us talk about how we will mine Ryugu. . . ."

The hologram zoomed close to the asteroid, rotating slowly along its ridge-
like equator. "All terrestrial methods are inadequate to the task of mining in
space." Lacroix pointed at the equatorial bulge. "Ryugu is more like a pile of
gravel in free fall than it is a solid object. Forceful methods at excavation would
result in scattering the material in microgravity. Even assuming you can gather
the regolith, how do you differentiate and refine the various useful materials in
microgravity?"

Lacroix gazed out at the trainees. "The answer is *optical mining*—utilizing
concentrated sunlight to harvest and process material."

The hologram panned to show four robotic spacecraft mounted on brackets
on the mining ship's spine. Each of the machines had twin parabolic reflectors
that dominated its profile like huge round ears.

"Over the next three months, with the aid of VR and AR simulators, you
will become proficient in the maintenance and support of the APIS optical
mining system."

The hologram dissolved to show an elevation of one such machine. The
scale indicated it was nearly 50 meters wide.

"The heart of the APIS system is the Honey Bee—a robotic craft originally
designed to autonomously identify, bag, and process small asteroids up to 10
meters in diameter. We intend to use it on boulders plucked from Ryugu's surface. To harvest those boulders, Catalyst Corporation plans to adapt NASA's
canceled Asteroid Redirect Mission hardware. . . ."

Another robotic hologram appeared next to the Honey Bee, and this new
machine looked like a three-legged spider, with 18-meter-long legs fashioned
out of metal triangles. Twin circular solar panels were attached to its smaller
hexagonal body.

"We're calling this the Asteroid Retrieval System—or ARS. In the low
gravity of Ryugu, the ARS can move boulders up to 10 meters in diameter

away from the surface and into a terminator orbit. There, the Honey Bees can bag them. . . ."

A holographic animation now showed cube sats scanning the asteroid's surface, highlighting a candidate boulder. An ARS robot launched from the mother ship, extending three long legs as it descended to the surface, eventually standing over the boulder. It then drilled into the rock with smaller, mandible-like arms, clamped down, and pushed off the asteroid, its legs curled around the boulder.

As the ARS rose above Ryugu's horizon, the Sun illuminated it, and the robot released its prize. A Honey Bee optical mining rig then rendezvoused with the floating boulder, expanding what looked like a large fumigation bag to enclose it. The bag cinched shut, and the Honey Bee then focused its twin solar collectors toward the Sun.

Lacroix looked out at the trainees. "Your job will be to help these robotic systems do their job. This will require a detailed understanding of their technical specifications and maintenance. Let us begin. . . ."

JULY 8, 2033

An axis trainer occupied one wall. This was a vertical framework of concentric rings mounted in gimbals. Set within the rings and secured at the waist and feet was a ruggedized space suit, burnt orange in color, ribbed with thick padding, and set with carbon fiber plates. The suit looked like a cross between a federal prison uniform and bomb disposal armor. The spherical helmet was especially odd; where a normal helmet had a visor, this one was instead an opaque shell. The entire surface of the helmet was studded with dozens of black nodules set in rows.

Tighe and the other trainees stood at ease, wearing white LCVGs (liquid cooling and ventilation garments) resembling long johns. The formfitting bodysuits were lined with water tubes to distribute heat, the nozzles for which emerged at the waistline.

An instructor with a South African accent paced the floor in front of them like a drill sergeant. "What you see before you is the Mark V Extravehicular Mobility Unit—or EMU. Also called a clam suit. . . ."

The instructor made a circular gesture, and two assistants swiveled the EMU on the axis trainer so its back now faced the trainees. The suit's primary life support pack was surrounded by a rectangular docking collar. One of the assistants opened the pack like a hatchway, revealing the suit's interior.

"In microgravity, you climb in and out of the EMU while it is docked to the side of the spacecraft. You then close and seal the hatch before undocking from the ship." He studied the faces of the trainees. "Can anyone tell me why this design is necessary for asteroid-mining operations?"

By now the trainees knew better than to raise their hands.

After a pause the instructor answered for them. "Because asteroid dust is an extreme biohazard. It must never get inside your ship. Asteroid regolith is five times finer than talcum powder, with particles as sharp as broken glass. If breathed in, they can enter your bloodstream directly—resulting in death. If taken into the lungs, they can penetrate deep enough to cause silicosis—stone grinder's disease—resulting in death. Regolith also sticks to and shorts out circuit boards and jams valves and seals—causing equipment failures that can also lead to death."

The instructor now had their full attention. "But asteroid regolith is just one of the dangers you will face during extravehicular activity—which you will hereafter refer to as EVA. . . ."

To Tighe's surprise one of the assistants put in earplugs and withdrew a semiautomatic pistol from a nearby box. He chambered a round while the other assistant pivoted the suit to face forward again.

The instructor barked, "Cover your ears!"

The trainees complied.

The assistant took aim at the suit and fired once at point-blank range. The bullet put a divot in the chest plate. Everyone uncovered their ears again, and the assistants rotated the suit once more to show that the round had not penetrated.

"The EMU's Kevlar-laminate armor is capable of stopping even high-caliber rifle rounds traveling 1,700 miles per hour. In deep space it might even protect you from a micrometeorite the size of a grain of sand traveling twenty times faster.

"Now let's talk about the biggest and most constant danger you will face while on EVA: ionizing radiation—galactic cosmic rays. . . ."

———

Three weeks later and Tighe had mastered every aspect of the Mark V EMU. He found the precise physical tasks required to prepare for a space walk similar to those for a cave dive. The clam suit's primary life support system was essentially a high-end rebreather, much like the Se7en series rebreathers he'd used for years. However, unlike with water-diving equipment, a space walker had to provide not just breathing gas but also atmospheric pressure across the entire body.

Space suits were pressurized to just a third of an atmosphere to prevent them from becoming a balloon that paralyzed the wearer. However, ambient air at such low pressure lacked sufficient oxygen to breathe, and for this reason pure oxygen was used.

Prior to any space walk, he'd need to prebreathe oxygen at normal pressure for a couple of hours to eliminate the nitrogen in his bloodstream—which would otherwise bubble out of his blood like a shaken-up soda can in the reduced-pressure environment and cause the bends.

Here, too, Tighe's diving expertise had direct application to his new profession, and he was soon able to coach fellow trainees.

The first time the instructors winched Tighe into the clam suit's hatchway, he removed his oxygen mask before wriggling into the suit's immobilizing embrace and poked his head up into the dark helmet. The clam suit hatch shut and sealed behind him with a hiss.

He felt like he'd stuck his head inside a stew pot. It was completely dark until glowing text appeared—an integrated crystal display. When he turned his head, the integrated crystal turned with him—although the helmet itself did not. No matter which way he turned his head, the crystal pane encompassed his entire field of vision.

On Earth the suit weighed 200 kilos, and he had to push down feelings of claustrophobia as he stared into the opaque helmet wall.

He heard a voice in his ear. *"Tighe, commence suit power-up."*

"Roger that." Tighe followed the steps of the suit's power-up procedure, tapping at virtual interfaces with his heavy arms. Soon he heard a whirring sound, followed by the suit pressure dropping. His ears popped as oxygen flowed down over his face. It was invigorating. Cooling water now also flowed through his LCVG, conveying the sensation that he'd just lowered himself into a pool of water.

His display crystal sprang to life, boot loaders scrolling past. Then suddenly the world opened up around him—as if he weren't wearing any helmet at all. Tighe glanced left, then right, and was stunned by the utter reality of the view.

"Holy shit . . ."

The helmet had simply disappeared.

The instructor shouted at Tighe from nearby. "The headgear you are wearing renders itself invisible to the wearer. The plenoptic apertures—those nodes arrayed outside the helmet—gather light fields from all around the helmet and the EMU's software stitches them together into a cohesive panorama. This technology gives you unprecedented situational awareness while on EVA." The instructor continued: "In the event of system failure, you access the legacy visor here. . . ." He lifted the opaque front faceplate like a shutter, revealing a clear visor beneath.

Tighe was barely listening to the instructor as he gazed around the room in wonder.

AUGUST 18, 2033

Tighe and Jin opened the Hab 1 airlock in the training mock-up and climbed up into Transfer Tunnel 1. Dressed in their lightweight blue pressure suits, they moved quickly, sealing the hatch behind them. Then they both looked up.

The 2-meter-wide tunnel rose 106 meters above them—the hatchway to the Central Hab barely visible. Electrical, data, and plumbing conduits ran to vanishing points along three sides, with composite ladder rungs rising on the fourth side.

Even after months of training in the mock-up, it still amazed Tighe that the company had gone to the effort of building a full-scale replica of their tenuous spaceship deep within the Antarctic ice—like a bug in amber.

As in the real design, the laminate-walled transfer tunnel had no atmosphere. However, here on Earth, gravity was in full force the entire length of the transfer tunnel; on the real spaceship, gravity would reduce proportionately as one "ascended" toward the Central Hab. Starting out at 1 g, you'd experience a half g at 50 meters, a quarter g at 75 meters, and so on.

Instead of an elevator, which would add significant mass and maintenance headaches, the crew ascended each of the ship's three radial tunnels by hooking their suit harnesses to carabiners on a steel cable. A twenty-volt planetary gear winch allowed them to traverse the tunnel in five minutes. Here on Earth, they were forbidden from using the ladder to speed things up—too dangerous.

Tighe and Jin clipped their harnesses into a braid of carabiners at the end of the cable, then used a virtual UI to activate the winch.

As they slowly rose from the Hab 1 airlock, Tighe said, "You ever do training like this at the CNSA?"

Jin shook his head. "No one has built a ship such as this."

"I'm surprised. Spinning a spaceship to create artificial gravity makes sense."

"Only if the radius of rotation is at least 200 meters. Otherwise, the Coriolis effect can sicken the occupants. Imagine gravity changing dramatically whenever you sit or stand up."

Tighe looked upward. "This tunnel isn't 200 meters."

Jin looked up as well. "A 106-meter radius could be endured with training, but launching a ship even this size into space would require tens of billions of dollars. Too expensive."

"It's a shame."

Jin nodded. "It is an interesting design. Perhaps one day our children will get the chance."

Tighe frowned. "But is it ethical to send children?"

Jin looked appalled until he saw Tighe grin. Then Jin laughed. "Very funny."

CHAPTER 17

First Light

SEPTEMBER 22, 2033

G abriel Lacroix gazed across the faces of his charges. "It has been a long winter for us all. However, the Earth-bound phase of your training has finally come to an end."

James Tighe and the other trainees stood at ease in dress blues in the dining hall. Lacroix and the entire training staff were gathered at the front of the room.

"Although just eighteen of you will be extended a contract to continue training in low Earth orbit, please know that were it economically feasible, Catalyst Corporation would send you all. Your work here has been outstanding, and those of you not selected today will receive preferential consideration for future expeditions."

Future expeditions. Tighe clenched his jaw. He knew these eighteen orbital training tickets were the only real thing about the program.

"Because this is an FAA-approved spaceflight-participant training program, all of you will receive civilian spaceflight certifications, qualifying you for employment with an increasing number of NewSpace startups. And of course, you will all receive your training completion bonus."

The trainees exchanged impatient looks.

"As I read the names of those selected for orbital training, I ask that you maintain the same spirit of camaraderie and professionalism you have demonstrated throughout this program."

The tension in the room was thick.

Lacroix glanced at a simple index card. "The following trainees have been selected to continue to low Earth orbit training . . ."

Everyone held their breath.

"Dr. Nalini Mishra."

Someone behind Tighe gasped in excitement.

"Dr. Dirk Geissler."

Another stifled gasp of joy.

As the names continued to be called out, Tighe began to detect a pattern.

"Dr. Yseult Sartre."

Ivy League geologist.

"Dr. Abidan Berkovich."

Ivy League astrophysicist.

Tighe wondered why he was surprised. The company had opted for the overachievers—the traditionally successful. It was the way of the world. He'd fallen for Joyce's pitch.

Lacroix continued to read off the names, but Tighe's only surprise was that Isabel Abarca and Jin Han were not among the eighteen selected. Both of them had world-class CVs and real-world experience. Sevastian Yakovlev may have been a veteran cosmonaut, but he was maxed out on radiation exposure. Adedayo Adisa was brilliant but a black hat hacker from the slums of Lagos. Nicole Clarke was basically an oil hunter. David Morra, an ex-soldier. Eike Dahl, an EMT. Chindarkar . . . well, Chindarkar also had an impressive résumé.

Soon Lacroix finished. Not a single one of Tighe's circle was chosen—and in a way, that made sense. No matter where he went, Tighe always seemed most at home among outsiders.

"Congratulations to those of you chosen, and for the rest of you"—he then held up what looked like a silver gift card—"you will receive, as a personal gift from Mr. Joyce, a travel voucher good for round-trip business-class airfare anywhere Joyce airlines flies."

Tighe noticed Jin staring at the floor in front of him, fists clenching and unclenching. Nearby, Tsukada was clearly trying to rein in tears—her rejection consigned her to suffering Tighe could only imagine.

Lacroix then announced, "Selected candidates please move to Barracks D."

The company staff applauded, and the selected trainees leaped for joy and hugged one another, laughing and shouting all around Tighe.

Tighe turned toward Morra—who appeared stunned by the sudden turn of events. "Well, that's nine months we're not getting back."

Across the room, Abarca nodded and shook Mishra's hand. It still mystified Tighe. Both surgeons—but Mishra was also a concert violinist. Why that would be useful in space was anyone's guess.

Eike Dahl stepped up to Tighe and noticed where he was looking. "Let's get out of here."

The next twenty-four hours in the barracks were like a wedding reception and a funeral booked at the same address. The music and laughter from Barracks D was hard to miss.

Morra sat in the corridor outside Barracks A. Tighe, Jin, and Abarca leaned against the wall nearby, sipping shots of tequila the company had issued them. Morra just kept shaking his head. "I did this for my daughters. To leave them something."

Tighe gripped Morra's shoulder. "We got some money. That's something."

Morra covered his head with his arms.

Tighe looked across the corridor at Jin, who was pacing, cursing between his teeth at intervals—looking more angry at himself than anything else.

The next morning forty hungover graduates left their training uniforms and equipment behind in the dorms and entered a coatroom. There, they donned insulated jumpsuits, parkas, face masks, gloves, and goggles.

Company staff escorted the entire group aboard a large cargo elevator. After the doors rolled closed, the car ascended through 200 meters of ancient ice. As the elevator boomed to a stop, the doors opened and a biting cold enveloped them.

They moved through a corrugated steel building whose interior was supported by steel beams to withstand powerful surface winds. They then passed through a thick door to stand on ice beneath a cloudless sky. Dawn filled the horizon with a reddish glow.

It was the first time in half a year that Tighe had seen sunlight. He, Morra, Abarca, and the others stood watching in silence for several moments before they were nudged along by company staff—joining the others as they marched, single file, toward a C-130 cargo aircraft that idled noisily on a nearby skiway.

After an eight-hour flight, the passengers bundled up and sleeping on the cargo deck, the C-130 landed in Christchurch, New Zealand. Everyone took off their parkas as the C-130 taxied for several minutes, and the plane finally came to a halt, the engines winding down.

The weary trainees stood, but a company staffer shouted, "If you are not among the eighteen chosen for orbital training, please remain seated. Orbital trainees, please check in at the cargo ramp. Orbital trainees only, please."

Tighe and Morra exchanged looks and sat back down. The "chosen ones" moved toward the rear of the aircraft. After several minutes getting changed into fresh blue jumpsuits emblazoned with the Catalyst Corporation logo, the orbital trainees were organized into three rows of six. Someone called out, "Smiles, people!"

A hydraulic motor whined and a beam of sunlight cut into the gloomy cargo bay as the ramp lowered onto the tarmac. Warm air flowed in. It was a bright spring day.

Tighe saw a phalanx of media, dozens of camera lenses aimed at the asteroid-mining trainees as they disembarked from the aircraft into what was apparently a press conference already under way. Nathan Joyce stood with a microphone, waving for his chosen ones to come on down, his voice booming over speakers. "Ladies and gentlemen, Catalyst Corporation's trained asteroid miners!"

The orbital trainees were met with a smattering of applause.

Someone tapped Tighe on the shoulder. He looked up to see a Catalyst staffer pointing the way toward an open side door in the fuselage.

"Please disembark this way. We have paperwork for you to sign."

Tighe, Morra, Jin, Abarca, Adisa, Chindarkar, and the others moved single file through the narrow cabin door and out onto the tarmac. The air was mild and the sky overhead was blue. The surrounding landscape was flat and green.

Adedayo flashed a bright smile. "It is good to be back on Earth."

Jin nodded toward Tsukada, who appeared to be in mourning. "Speak for yourself."

As they walked along the tarmac, a man in a suit and tie came alongside Tighe. "Mr. Tighe?"

Tighe nodded.

The man pushed a business card into Tighe's hand and spoke with a Kiwi accent. "Tim Hartig, Harbinger Aerospace. We're a NewSpace startup specializing in satellite maintenance and logistics."

"Okay . . ." Tighe took a look at the card.

Hartig gestured toward the distant press conference. "Tough break about Catalyst, but something tells me they're not heading out to the asteroids anytime soon. And if I'm not mistaken, you've just been flight certified at Nathan Joyce's expense."

"That's right."

"We'd like to discuss the possibility of you signing up with us. We're looking for highly qualified candidates, and we have competitive pay, good benefits, profit sharing."

Tighe noticed that other folks were speaking to Morra, Jin, Abarca, Yak. He listened as they continued toward the terminal.

CHAPTER 18

Legacy

Erika Lisowski guided her rental car, passing houses that looked unchanged from twenty years earlier. She parked along the narrow, curbless street and noticed several elderly men and women hugging good-bye as they got into their cars.

Her grandfather was still popular among NASA retirees. He had stories. Good stories—from the golden age of space. Her granddad had been in the control room when Armstrong landed on the Moon.

Lisowski grabbed a wrapped gift from the passenger seat and entered the ranch-style house into a crowd of family. She spotted her mother and father engaged in an argument in the kitchen—the same argument they usually had in any situation requiring their cooperation.

Her father spotted her and glanced at the clock. "Jeez, E, you missed dinner. I thought you were taking the morning flight."

She kissed him hello. "I told you I had a meeting on the West Coast."

"Make the contractors come to you."

Her mother hugged her. "Let her be, Barry." She looked her daughter over. "You look terrible! Have you been sleeping?"

"It's good to see you, too."

"Don't touch that!" Her mother slapped her father's hand away from the remnants of a birthday cake. "Your daughter hasn't had a piece yet."

Cousins, nephews, and nieces called out from the living room on seeing her and hugged her hello. "Hello, sweetheart!"

"Better late than never!"

"Shame you missed dinner."

Her cousin Ron showed off his infant boy—who was adorable. Ron was in his early thirties and worked as a technician at the SMAB—the Solid Motor Assembly Building—out on the cape. Before the shuttle program was canceled, her father had had a lot of pull there. Lisowski, too, was third-generation NASA.

Her father leaned close as she entered the kitchen again. "Go out and say hello to your grandfather. He'll be happy to see you. Remember: it's his ninety-fourth."

"I know how old he is, Dad."

Lisowski opened the familiar sliding screen door, and as she moved into the backyard, she could see toddlers moving about with their young parents. She spotted her grandfather watching from his wheelchair near the garden.

Gerard Zygmunt Lisowski, PhD—Gerry to everyone who ever knew him. His parents had immigrated to the United States during World War II, bringing her grandfather along with them as an infant. A mathematics prodigy, Gerry had altered the trajectory of the entire family—graduating from Princeton and joining the Apollo program as a young aerospace engineer.

After years of having him look over her shoulder while she did her math homework, Lisowski knew just how sharp his intellect still was.

He regarded her through rheumy eyes as she approached—and finally deciphered her face in the semidarkness. His craggy face brightened, and he croaked, "Erika, sweetheart."

She walked over and hugged him gently. "Happy birthday, Dziadek."

"Now I am happy. Where have you been off to?"

"California. I had meetings with commercial space firms there."

"Ah. Anything interesting?"

"The usual boring stuff. Did you have a nice birthday dinner?"

He waved her off. "I don't enjoy food like I used to." He looked up at the night sky. "Okay, let's see how well you remember. What star is that?" He pointed.

"You know that's not a star. It's Jupiter. And that's Mars over there."

He snorted. "Very good. Can you still find Sirius?"

She got her bearings in the night sky and pointed. "Canis Major . . . and there's Sirius right there. The brightest star. That's an easy one." Lisowski looked down at him and smiled in contentment. It had been so long since she felt like an eight-year-old girl. Back then her world was full of dreams without complications.

Her grandfather searched the night sky, but soon his smile faded. "My time's running out, Erika."

"Please don't say that. You know it upsets me."

"It upsets me, too." He squeezed her hand—then paused as he noticed her other hand was behind her back. "What do you have there?"

"Nothing."

He sat up in his wheelchair. "Now, come on. If it's a gift, you'd better give it to me now, or I might not live to see it."

"Stop joking like that."

He waved an arthritic hand. "You know how much I look forward to your gifts. You're the only one who knows what to get me."

"Well, in that case . . ." She held out a small box wrapped in blue foil. "It is a gift."

He looked at her. "Is it, now?" He extended his hand.

"Careful. It's heavy for its size. Do you want me to open it for you?"

"Not on your life." He hefted it in both hands. "Ooh. It is heavy." He examined the box's weight distribution by turning it one way, then another. "Not titanium. No . . . Now, let me guess."

"You won't guess. You'd better just open it."

"Hmm. I say it's . . . a challenge coin from the Blue Gemini project."

"Now, where on Earth would I get that?"

"eBay. Some might even be authentic."

"Interesting guess, but wrong."

"How about a model of the Dyna-Soar?"

"Wrong again. You're thinking in the wrong era."

"Really?" He looked even more curious. "Not a shuttle tile, I hope. But, no—this is too heavy."

"Dziadek, please open your present."

"If you insist . . ." His spotted hands scraped away the foil. Underneath was a rosewood box. He looked up at her one more time and then opened the lid to reveal an expertly milled piece of metal the size of an avocado. He lifted it from its blue velvet pedestal. It had intricately curving metal tines. He turned it end over end, studying its surface. "How was this cast?"

"It wasn't. It was formed by laser chemical vapor deposition."

He appeared to have lost his world-weariness as he studied its surface. "It's beautiful. So perfect."

"It's made of Inconel."

He looked up. "And what is it?"

"It's a sensor housing—made for the prow of the first commercial deep space vessel. A gift to you, Dziadek, from the ship's builder. He wanted you to have it."

His hands trembled as he held it. "Oh, Erika . . . it's magnificent." After a few moments he gazed into the night sky. His eyes teared up. "Goddamnit . . . I'm sorry."

"Don't be sorry." She put her arm over his shoulder and looked up at the sky with him.

"We were right there, Erika." He looked to her. "We could have done it. I'm so sorry that we didn't. I'm so sorry, Erika."

"No, no." She hugged him. "No, Dziadek, please."

"We could have done it."

"I *know* you could have." She looked him in the eyes. "I know." She leaned her head against his and then sat with him, watching the heavens.

CHAPTER 19

Decompression Cycle

OCTOBER 18, 2033

After a week of windsurfing and relaxation on Hamilton Island in Queensland, Australia, James Tighe was beginning to put his half year beneath the Antarctic ice sheet behind him. Part of the Whitsunday Islands near the Great Barrier Reef, here it was hard to imagine that cold even existed.

Tighe strolled the warm sand of Whitehaven Beach with Eike Dahl and David Morra. A little ways behind them Isabel Abarca and Jin Han laughed as Nicole Clarke chased Amy Tsukada with some sort of sea creature held in her hand. As usual, Tsukada had her earbuds in.

"Stop!" Tsukada raced through the shallows.

"I just want to show it to you."

"Get away!"

Clarke had anchored their rental sailboat—a forty-four-foot Sunsail—just off the beach with practiced ease. She'd captained much larger vessels. Adedayo Adisa waved to them from the boat. Yakovlev and Chindarkar were sunning themselves on the deck.

Tighe realized it might seem odd to outsiders that, after spending nine months in training together, the group would spend their R & R together, too. But it felt natural.

He wasn't normally fond of the beach scene, but Whitehaven Beach was different—part of a marine park, it was pristine, perfect, and unpopulated. There wasn't a house or building anywhere on the island—just 5 kilometers of tranquil sand.

For the first time in his life Tighe was actually on vacation. He wasn't here to explore a new cave or to wrangle his way onto an expedition—or to crash on a friend's couch. He came here to enjoy life. And friendship. It felt good.

Morra shouted, "Hey, Nic, give it here . . ." He sprinted on his carbon fiber prosthetic legs, grabbing a starfish from Clarke and swiftly catching up to Tsukada—who dove into the water to escape.

"Coward!"

Dahl watched, laughing. At some point Tighe's eyes met hers.

She brushed against his arm. "You seem happy." Her barely detectable accent did mysterious things to him.

"This is all new to me. Relaxing, I mean."

She wore a red one-piece bathing suit that was practical yet did not leave much to the imagination. The fragrance of sunblock on her skin quickened his pulse. Over the long months in Antarctica her blond hair had grown, and she now kept it in a French braid. She stroked it. "Feel like exploring the island?"

"Hell, I'm up for anything."

That evening the group stared at a star-filled sky as they sipped wine on benches at the sailboat's stern. Anchored just off the coast, they had extinguished the lights and listened as gentle waves lapped against the hull. The sound seemed to soothe even Tsukada, who for once didn't have her earbuds in.

Abarca spoke to Jin's silhouette. "You decide on that job with FSG yet?"

"I am considering it."

"Where are they based?"

"French Guiana."

Morra grunted. "Bloody hell. It's about time. Can they get you into space?"

"They say they can. There is a spot in an orbital certification class in late November."

Yakovlev looked up. "The one run by Evenstar? At Hotel LEO?"

Jin nodded.

Yakovlev laughed. "Could be same class J.T. and I are taking."

Tighe cleared his throat. "Harbinger hasn't sent us to orbit yet. They could be all talk, Yak."

"Maybe. Maybe not. It is a few million dollars. For tech company this is nothing."

Chindarkar pointed up. "Look, a meteor!"

The others oohed as they watched it streak across the heavens.

Abarca asked, "Priya, will you be going back to the ISRO?"

"I don't know yet. I'm talking to a couple startups. I figure if J.T. can get into orbit, a person with my skills should have no problem."

Dahl laughed.

"You're hilarious." Tighe tossed a napkin at Chindarkar.

Adisa suddenly said, "Do any of you recall a woman named Rachel Gardner?"

Everyone turned to him.

Clarke asked, "Who's Rachel Gardner?"

"She was on Ascension with us—a former war correspondent."

Yak made a cutting motion across his throat. "Yegorov dismissed her as corporate spy."

Adisa turned to him. "For being a journalist, but yes, she was dismissed from candidate selection. She is writing an article on Catalyst Corporation—but really about Nathan Joyce, I think. She contacted me with some questions."

Abarca put down her glass of wine. "Recently?"

"Today."

"I hope you didn't tell her anything, Ade." Dahl leaned against Tighe. "Remember the confidentiality agreement."

"I have not spoken to her." He paused. "But she did say something interesting in her text. She said Catalyst is in financial trouble."

Morra laughed. "Ha! No shit."

"She said that Catalyst did not actually purchase seats into orbit from Burkett or Macy—Catalyst only put down a deposit."

Tighe whistled. "Wow. So it's like I thought—a publicity stunt."

Chindarkar asked, "Where does that leave the chosen ones? Joyce still has them doing publicity all over."

Clarke nodded. "And under contract. I'll bet we stand a better chance of getting into orbit than they do. It almost makes me feel sorry for them."

There was a moment of silence.

Morra said, "Almost."

CHAPTER 20

Escaping Earth

NOVEMBER 26, 2033

James Tighe emerged from a microbus into Florida sunshine, wearing his bright-blue flight suit and carrying a battery-powered breathing apparatus. His helmet was zipped shut and his suit pressurized to maintain quarantine.

Behind him Sevastian Yakovlev disembarked, followed by Priya Chindarkar, both of them in identical pressurized blue flight suits. Each of their names was emblazoned on a fabric patch over their hearts, beneath the logo patch of their respective employers—Harbinger Aerospace for both Tighe and Yakovlev, and a Swiss company named PsiStar for Chindarkar. A patch of their national flags was also stitched onto their left shoulders.

The three of them stopped and stared up at the Starion Block 9 Zephyr rocket towering over the launchpad—George Burkett's rocket. Their employers had made them Burkett's paying passengers this morning.

Yakovlev was happier than Tighe had ever seen him—giddy, in fact. The Russian took a deep breath of filtered air and shouted, "It is beautiful day to fly!"

Elizabeth Josephson, the former ESA flight surgeon, Katsuka Akira, the round-the-world solo sailor, and Michael Harris, the geologist, exited the microbus, likewise in pressurized flight suits. Harris was also flying for PsiStar, Josephson and Akira for a Japanese pharmaceutical company named Mobio.

Uniformed NASA security officers carrying computer tablets greeted them. One pointed downward. "Spaceflight participants, to this line, please."

One of the guards scanned the ID badge hanging on Tighe's flight suit, while the other officers approached his companions. "Passport and launch certification please, Mr. Tighe."

Tighe withdrew his passport and certification from a Mylar envelope on a lanyard around his neck. It contained all his documentation.

The officer took photos of Tighe's documents with his tablet. "Class 3 Medical Certificate, please."

Tighe searched through his packet and handed it over.

Two officers examined Tighe's paperwork.

"Confirm for me your employer and the purpose of your visit to space."

"Harbinger Aerospace. Orbital flight training."

"And your destination?"

"The Hotel LEO."

"The duration of your stay in orbit?"

"Two weeks."

"Your PPK, please."

Tighe passed along his Personal Preference Kit, a sealed polymer bag containing his personal effects.

The officer weighed the bag on a digital scale and it came up just shy of 1 kilogram. He handed it back to Tighe.

Another officer placed his tablet in front of Tighe. "Your signature on this affidavit indicates your agreement to comply with international rules concerning alteration of the natural orbits of celestial bodies and/or orbital objects capable of impacting Earth and/or lawful spacecraft. Should you create space debris, you are hereby legally bound to report such incident, detailing the object's mass, estimated trajectory, and all pertinent details. If you agree, sign here."

Tighe signed the tablet with his gloved finger.

Just then Yak and Harris called out, pointing skyward.

Tighe turned to see a rocket lifting off miles away, its brilliant flame riding a tower of white smoke into the dawn sky. It performed a gravity turn as it headed east across the Atlantic.

It was Jack Macy's rocket—built by his aerospace company, Zenith—and on board were Isabel Abarca, David Morra, Eike Dahl, Nicole Clarke, an American chemist named Caitlin Long, and Amy Tsukada. They'd all signed up with different NewSpace companies in various industries—communications, fiber optics, and pharmaceuticals—and were going into orbit as paying passengers, too.

Harris said, "There they go."

Tighe willed the rocket to keep climbing.

Yak applauded. "Ha! Go, my friends!"

Suddenly a series of deafening *booms* reached them, like the drum solo of the gods. It was as if the sky was being torn asunder.

Yak reveled. "Now is our turn."

As they waited for liftoff in Burkett's sleek Starion capsule, Tighe watched the capsule commander, their seventh launch passenger, run through launch checklists. Major Eileen Willis—a former NASA astronaut—was headed into orbit to help run Evenstar's orbital training class at the Hotel LEO. The journey was automated, but in the event of a malfunction with the autodocking system, they'd have Major Willis on board to bring them in manually.

Harris turned to Yak. "Why was it so important to watch that film last night?"

"*White Sun of the Desert*? Wery important film."

"It had nothing to do with space."

"It is tradition."

Major Willis turned to them. "Make ready! T minus one minute and counting."

Tighe took a deep breath. This was really going to be an experience—and if anything went wrong during the launch, a short experience.

As the countdown closed toward zero, a deep rumbling began and the capsule vibrated. Then it felt like a horse kicked Tighe in the back as the cabin shook. Glancing out the porthole window, Tighe could see they were already clear of the launchpad.

Yak whooped with joy.

The others responded in kind.

"*Throttling to 70 percent.*"

In a half minute or so the vibrations slowed, and the voice of mission control came through Tighe's earphones. "*We are at max Q.*"

Major Willis responded on the radio. "Max Q confirmed."

After a few more moments, mission control said, "*Throttling to one hundred percent.*"

The g-forces increased, and the slipstream outside wailed like a lost soul.

In a couple of minutes the vibrations eased entirely, but the g-forces kept increasing. Then they relented momentarily.

"*MECO.*"

The capsule jolted.

Mission control's voice: "*We have first-stage separation. Second-stage engine start confirmed.*"

The capsule commander tapped at touchscreens. "Roger that, mission control."

The g-forces increased again, but Tighe recalled the human centrifuge back on Ascension Island. This was nothing compared to that. Outside it was now both day and night at the same time, with the curving blue rim of the Earth spreading out below against a wall of blackness.

Finally the engine noise stopped and the g-forces faded away. They now coasted in complete silence. In freefall.

"*We have SECO.*"

The commander turned to her passengers. "Ladies and gentlemen, welcome to space."

Truly in microgravity for the first time, Tighe felt good. Looking out the porthole, just beyond Chindarkar's seat, he could see the Pacific Ocean gliding past 400 kilometers below.

She turned to him and grinned. "I knew it would be beautiful. I just can't believe how—"

The sound of retching came to them, and they turned to see Harris with his helmet unzipped, heaving into a microgravity vomit bag. The geologist looked miserable, with small globules of vomit floating near his face.

Tighe stopped turning his head so much—at least this early on. Sudden movements could bring on disorientation and what the instructors called "space adaptation syndrome."

Yak spoke in soothing tones to Harris. "Space sickness wery common, Michael. I was sick myself, first time."

Harris gasped for air. "Just stop talking about it, please. . . ."

Six hours later the Starion capsule closed in on the Hotel LEO's orbit. Financed by billionaire Ray Halser, and lifted into orbit by Jack Macy's rockets, nowadays the world's first orbiting hotel hosted more employees of space start-ups than rich tourists.

The "hotel" consisted of eight large inflatable habitats rounded on both ends. Each had a single window on the side facing toward Earth. The habs were joined in an irregular pattern by aluminum connecting modules, with solar panels and antenna dishes jutting out in places. There were several docking ports, one of which was already occupied by a Zenith capsule.

The automatic docking system brought them in as the capsule commander stood by, her hand hovering above a joystick, ready to take control in the event of a malfunction. However, moments later there was a slight bump into the docking port, and then the *thunk* of locking bolts. The passengers clapped—except for Harris, who was still zombified by misery.

A soothing male voice came in over the radio. "*Starion-4-6, the staff of the Hotel LEO welcomes you.*"

CHAPTER 21

Hotel LEO

M ost people on Earth had heard of Raymond Halser's orbiting hotel. It was the sort of place that eventually wound up profiled by just about every current events or celebrity news show—the most exotic of destinations for the adventurous rich. The Hotel LEO (short for "low Earth orbit") had been assembled across dozens of rocket launches throughout the late 2020s, and an imitation neon sign glowed outside the docking port declaring it "Open."

However, the Hotel LEO was evolving into a business hotel for NewSpace companies. It had roughly twice the pressurized volume of the old International Space Station, and the individual compartments were much roomier—perfect for EVA training sessions.

As Tighe and his capsule-mates floated in through the airlock, they were greeted by the hotel manager, Kaspar Eld, a gregarious Swede in his thirties, who was dressed in a pinstripe flight suit and painted-on necktie. The outfit was clearly meant to evoke the hospitality industry but was also a mark of Eld's sense of humor. He was immediately likable—which was no doubt why he'd been selected for this job.

Eld's staff—a chief engineer, a flight surgeon, a nurse, two hospitality stewards, and two engineering/day porters—were cordial but professional, as would be the staff of any five-star hotel on Earth, and judging by the way they took charge of Harris, they also seemed to be experts on space sickness. No doubt ensuring rogue globules of floating vomit didn't invade brunch probably kept the staff busy. Eld escorted the staff into the Commons Hab, a lobby-like open area about 7 meters high and 14 meters long. It had two sizable windows that opened on a breathtaking view of the Earth rolling past below. It reminded Tighe of photos he'd seen of old-time zeppelin travel in the 1920s.

Eld gestured. "We orbit Earth sixteen times a day—forty-five minutes on the dark side, forty-five minutes on the dayside." He gestured to telescopes mounted on pedestals around the thick laminate windows. "When you are not in training, I recommend having a look. For now, please follow me. . . ."

Tighe and his companions moved through connecting hatchways and were led to their minuscule semiprivate cabins in other habs. Eld knocked on a plastic doorframe, and Tighe was surprised to see Adedayo Adisa's face appear as an accordion door slid aside.

Adisa smiled. "J.T.!"

They hugged and slapped each other on the back.

"Looks like we're roommates." Tighe read the company patch on Adisa's flight suit. "Neocom. Let me guess: communications satellites."

Adisa laughed. "I have come full circle. I am to work on enhancing satellite security."

"They hired the right guy."

"Have you looked through the telescopes yet?"

A few minutes later Tighe and the others gathered around the hotel's windows to take in the awe-inspiring sight of Earth. Morra, Abarca, Jin, Clarke, and many more of his colleagues from Concordia training gathered around the window's edge. Still excited by the novelty of microgravity, some of them laughed and tumbled in midair as they awaited their turn on a telescope.

Tighe noticed Tsukada smiling as she floated past with Yakovlev. Far from looking sick in microgravity, she seemed at home in space—although with all the fans distributing air, it was hardly silent inside the hotel. Yak put his arm on Tsukada's shoulder and pointed out sights below.

Tighe finally got his turn at one of the telescopes and found that he could spot individual ships plying the Pacific. Then he focused on cities—New York, London, Paris. It was extraordinary to see them live and in their entirety. It felt oddly godlike.

Eld gathered the Evenstar students for a group photo around the window, and everyone smiled—except for Harris and Long, who were both still sick in their cabins.

The hotel was near its thirty-six-person capacity, including staff. Eighteen guests from half a dozen NewSpace companies had arrived on three capsules for Evenstar's orbital certification training class. Most of the other guests were business travelers—techs up to repair satellites or to service automated fiber optic and pharmaceutical manufacturing platforms.

However, as Tighe and Jin floated toward the far end of the lobby, they were startled by the sound of Chinese rap music. Two cameramen were filming a teenage Chinese rapper wearing a gold space suit with a Prada logo. He had a diamond-studded gold yuan symbol on a chain and scarlet sneakers with golden accents. He floated above an Earth-facing window, lip-synching to lyrics played over speakers as he made hand signals with his fingers, emphasizing the chorus.

"*Mashang*, motherfucker, *méi bàn fâ!*"

Adisa floated alongside Tighe and Jin, grooving to the music. He said, "You know who that is?"

Jin glared at him.

"Smoov-OB. He is quite popular in Lagos. Eld told me it is the first music video ever filmed in space—and we are here to witness it."

Jin just shook his head in disgust and floated away.

After four days of classroom training sessions Tighe was informed by the instructors that he and Jin would be going out on their first EVA. They'd be tethered to the hotel and each would have an instructor alongside, but the trainees were also warned that space sickness was a possibility; with the surface of the Earth in view, they would get the strong sensation they were falling toward it—because they were. Willingly stepping out over a 200-mile drop alarmed most people.

The instructor held up a diagram of their space suit. "Remember, if you vomit while on an EVA, do not panic. Your suit has five air returns, so they are unlikely to become blocked. However, if by some chance they do, shut down your fan and switch to purge, and vent out to the Display and Controls Module purge valve, continuing fresh oxygen flow from the tanks."

Finished, the instructor looked at the gathered faces arrayed in every direction. Everyone was suffering headaches from the CO_2 accumulating in the microgravity classroom. "All right, then. Let's get our first two trainees pre-breathing oxygen in prep for EVA."

———

Tighe listened to his own breathing as he gazed at his surroundings. Jin floated next to him, also in an orange clam suit. Both of their helmets seemed transparent—both to themselves and to each other—due to the light field software. The situational awareness it provided was astounding.

Jin cast a slight grin toward Tighe as the instructor began to turn the airlock hatch. The astronaut instructors stood ahead of and behind them in more traditional, white EMU space suits.

Then the hatchway was open, and the entire world appeared below them.

"Okay, J.T., you're up. Move through the hatchway."

Tighe gave a thumbs-up to both instructors.

Jin's calm voice came in over his radio. *"Right behind you."*

Tighe stepped to the edge of the hatchway and looked "down."

The state of Florida slowly passed 400 kilometers below his toes. He slid the visor of his helmet up to reveal the clear composite faceplate beneath, then looked down again.

Nope. Not a software simulation.

He closed the visor, and his view widened dramatically. The helmet's software was far preferable to the naked visor. Tighe felt his stomach leap as he stepped out into nothingness.

"Watch your pulse. Steady your breathing."

Tighe regained his calm, quickly acclimating to the fact that he was floating alongside the Hotel LEO. Below him cloud-swirled continents glided by.

Tighe became so engrossed that he didn't notice he was floating away from the hotel. Suddenly the tether tugged him back. He grabbed the tether in his gloved hand and began to pivot himself around. As he waved his arm, he could feel the stiffness of the suit against its internal pressure.

A laugh came over his radio. Tighe turned to see Jin's smile as he moved out into the space outside the airlock. The virtual bubble the clam suit software created around their heads made it possible for them to see each other's expressions clearly.

"Well, you're spacewalking, Han."

Jin laughed again as he came up alongside Tighe to look upon the Earth. *"It is more beautiful than I ever thought possible."*

CHAPTER 22

Full Disclosure

After a week at the Hotel LEO, each of the Evenstar students had performed at least one space walk, with a few, like Jin, Morra, Yak, and Tighe, going out for a second. Geologist Michael Harris was already gone, having been sent down to Earth on a departing supply capsule on day four, every bit as sick as the day he arrived. Caitlin Long vomited during her space walk and then thrashed like a drowning swimmer, clawing at her helmet. The instructors had a struggle to get her back to the airlock. Since then, she hadn't left her cabin.

At six a.m. on the eighth day, as Tighe was brushing his teeth and trying not to make a mess in microgravity, an announcement came over the hotel's PA system. It was the voice of Evenstar's lead instructor.

"The following trainees have earned their microgravity operations certification and are to report to the hotel lobby at eight a.m. UTC for return to Earth."

Tighe and Adisa exchanged surprised looks.

"The graduating trainees are as follows: Adedayo Adisa—"

"Congratulations."

Adisa put a finger to his lips.

"Isabel Abarca, Katsuka Akira, Priya Chindarkar—"

A *whoop* of joy came from a nearby cabin.

"Eike Dahl, Jin Han, Elizabeth Josephson, Nicole Clarke, David Morra, James Tighe, Amy Tsukada—"

A muffled *No!* was audible nearby.

"—and Sevastian Yakovlev. Please pack your PPK and be in the hotel lobby by eight a.m. UTC. That is all."

Tighe stowed his toothbrush and sighed. "Leaving a week early. That's a bummer. I was hoping to get another space walk in."

"Our employers are no doubt paying a great deal every day we are here."

Tighe looked around the cabin, committing the sights and smells of the famous hotel to memory.

Two hours later both he and Adisa floated in the Commons Hab in their blue flight suits alongside ten other students.

The lead instructor said, "Congratulations on achieving your orbital operations certification."

There was a smattering of applause.

The two instructors held an informal ceremony, which involved applying a patch onto Velcro tabs on the shoulders of each student's flight suit. The patch depicted a lion's-head profile with the letters "LEO" against the curvature of the Earth.

One of the instructors took video on his phone as hugs and handshakes were exchanged. Graduates waved at the camera.

Amy Tsukada did not wave. Neither did she smile. Instead, she floated above the viewing windows, staring down at Earth—her tormentor.

Abarca floated alongside Tighe and watched. "It's unfair they're sending her back a week early. Her most of all."

"The irony is that if she were less of a natural up here, she'd get to stay longer."

Eike Dahl came up and hugged Abarca, then hugged Tighe, kissing his cheek. "I can't believe we're going back already. I love it up here."

"Hopefully we'll be in space again soon."

The instructor shouted, "Five minutes! Be ready to depart in five minutes, graduates!"

There was a scrum to purchase Hotel LEO–branded lapel pins from the hotel gift shop; then the trainees were divided into two groups of six. Tighe's group—which included Elizabeth Josephson, David Morra, Amy Tsukada, Sevastian Yakovlev, and Priya Chindarkar—zipped up their helmets and then made their way through the airlock and into a waiting Starion capsule. With its propulsion module still attached, it would be able to depart from the station and position itself for Earth reentry.

The second group would depart an hour and a half later—the time it would take for their landing zone in the remote New Mexico desert to come around again.

Tsukada had a look of dread on her face as she passed by Tighe and entered the return capsule. The passengers strapped in to their seats and hooked their suits into the spacecraft's life support and comm links.

Major Eileen Willis was their pilot again for the return journey. She ran through her preflight check.

The hotel manager's voice came in over the radio as the capsule undocked. *"Thank you for choosing the Hotel LEO, and we hope to see you again soon. Be sure to leave a review on our website . . ."*

Tighe gazed out the porthole at the rim of the Earth and noticed just how thin the atmosphere was—barely a film on the Earth's surface. Everyone who had ever lived had been born in that narrow gap between Earth and space. It seemed alarmingly fragile.

There was a *thunk* as the docking bolts retracted. Thrusters gently pushed the capsule away from the hotel.

The reentry approach would require three hours—waiting for the precise target window. The capsule commander told her passengers to prepare for a deceleration burn and moments later there was a throaty rumble as Tighe was pressed back into his seat for a minute or two.

After the engine cutoff they coasted for more than three hours. Tighe pondered the blue panorama of Earth spread out below, clouds swirling over the Pacific. He was looking forward to seeing this view again and wondered when that would be.

Chindarkar craned her neck to look out the porthole over Tighe's shoulder. "Shouldn't we be getting closer by now?"

Tighe turned to her. "Hmm?"

Morra also leaned forward to look. Puzzled, he turned to Willis. "Hey, Commander, you get lost?"

Willis tapped at a computer tablet console. "Negative, Mr. Morra. We just need to make a stop along the way."

The passengers exchanged bemused looks.

Chindarkar shifted her view and pointed out the window. "Look! Ahead in orbit—it's a spacecraft."

Capsule commander Willis spoke into her comm link. "Cycler 1, this is

Starion-6. I am six klicks out from your forward airlock. Request permission to dock."

A male voice with a German accent came over the comm link. *"Copy that, Starion-6. You are cleared to dock."*

"Switching to auto. Confirm signal lock."

"Signal lock confirmed."

The spacecraft's thrusters popped now and again as the capsule glided toward a large inflatable hab—a very large hab. As the thrusters turned the capsule around, the rest of the passengers got a look through the portholes.

Judging from the logo on its side, this was another of Halser's inflatable craft. However, a second, larger logo read "Lunargistics, LLC." The name "Rosette" was also printed in black letters on the hull, along with what appeared to be license numbers. At the front of the craft was a much larger airlock than the one at the Hotel LEO. The vessel had a propulsion module in the aft section as well as four large solar arrays. Two small windows glowed with a welcoming light in the hab's flank.

Morra narrowed his eyes. "We're not doing a reentry today, are we, Commander?"

"You are quite observant, Mr. Morra."

Yak laughed and clapped his gloved hands. "Is good news, Amy! Yes?"

A cautious half smile appeared on Tsukada's face. "We're not doing a reentry?"

"Leave your seat belts fastened, please."

Several minutes later the capsule docked with a sharp *clunk* of metal.

"Testing dock seal." Willis waited several moments, watching readouts.

Another voice over the radio said, *"Seal is good. Opening hatchway."*

The commander unbuckled, as did the others.

They moved hand over hand through the hatchway and into a large airlock lined with utility space suits, aluminum tool harnesses, emergency breathing apparatuses, and small robotic craft studded with thrusters and cameras. The place smelled of ozone.

A bearded Caucasian man in a gray flight suit with the name "Schultz" stitched beneath a Lunargistics company logo motioned for them to all come inside. He wore a Berlin Sluggers baseball hat and spoke with a slight German accent. "Come inside. We must clear the airlock. The next spacecraft is en route."

As they entered the main compartment of the ship, Tighe and his companions stared around in amazement. The space was larger than the Hotel LEO's Commons—about 20 meters long and 13 meters in diameter, with the entire volume visible around them. Instead of walls, the interior was sectioned off with black carbon fiber grillwork, punctuated with small openings meant for people to float through. The compartments were lined with lockers, storage units, and metalworking and electrical equipment, all visible at once, as though a dollhouse. Half the space was dedicated to living quarters—with room easily for a dozen or more people.

Two more crewmen—a man and a woman—glanced up from soldering a circuit board on a workbench. They "stood" upside down, feet on the ceiling in microgravity.

Schultz gestured. "That is Martin, chief engineer, and Petra, first mate."

They both nodded, then got back to work.

Schultz floated forward. "I am Gervas, captain of the *Rosette*."

Clarke asked, "What is this ship?"

"It is a lunar cycler—usually unmanned due to cosmic radiation—in a two-to-three resonance with the Moon."

"For what purpose?"

"That is not for me to say." He grabbed the compartment wall grid to move about and led them into what looked like an omnidirectional microgravity conference room at the far end of the ship. "Wait here. The others will rendezvous soon."

Tighe asked, "What others?"

"Just wait. All will be explained."

With that the six of them gathered in a circle. For nearly an hour they mused on why they were here, until they heard Schultz's voice talking on the radio elsewhere on the ship.

"Zenith-3, you are cleared to dock."

A few minutes later the airlock opened again, and Adedayo Adisa, Isabel Abarca, Katsuka Akira, Eike Dahl, Jin Han, and Nicole Clarke floated in. The same gobsmacked look was pasted on their faces.

Yak called to them. "Down here!" He grabbed the doorframe and laughed heartily. "Is this place not wonderful? What I would have given for this much room when I was on ISS!"

The new arrivals floated "down" to them, followed by Captain Schultz.

"Everyone inside the meeting room, please. The conference call will begin soon."

Dahl edged past Tighe's shoulder. "Conference call with who?"

Schultz switched on a holographic projector—not unlike the one Tighe had seen back on Baliceaux.

Abarca folded her arms and observed, her expression unreadable.

Jin floated up to Tighe and Morra. "What is going on?"

"We know as much as you, Jin." Tighe gestured toward the projector.

After focusing several lenses, the captain got onto a comm line and started reading out codes to someone. He then exited the meeting compartment and pulled curtains shut behind him. The twelve passengers were now by themselves, floating at all angles around a central projector.

Moments later the lasers glowed and a larger-than-life bust of Nathan Joyce appeared as a smiling apparition. Signal interference occasionally rippled him as he looked around the room. Joyce could apparently also see them. "I've waited years for this moment. And here we all are."

Jin glowered. "What is going on, Mr. Joyce?"

"Please, Han, call me Nathan. My apologies, but a certain degree of misdirection was necessary during this training process."

Clarke looked incredulous. "What training process? We work for other companies now, Nathan."

"The illusion that you all work for different companies was one of the misdirections, Nicole . . ."

Tighe and the others glanced around at the various employer patches on their flight suits—Harbinger, PsiStar, Neocom.

". . . when you are all, in fact, still working for me."

Morra leaned in. "I signed a contract with BKG."

"Which is owned by a shell company that's controlled by a sovereign fund, which has invested in my project. All that's required to reactivate your Catalyst Corporation contract is your signature."

Tsukada frowned. "You control the companies we work for?"

"Through proxies, yes."

Clarke floated forward. "But why? You already selected your asteroid-mining crew. They're all over the media."

"That's correct. I needed people who *truly believed* they were my asteroid-mining crew. People who could distract the media while my *real* asteroid miners quietly left the Earth."

Tighe narrowed his eyes. "Your *real* asteroid miners? What are you talking about?"

"Again, I apologize, but deception was necessary to maintain a secret that very few people on or off Earth are aware of: namely, that the much-publicized space-craft for my proposed asteroid-mining expedition is not just an idea—it is already built, operational, and even now awaiting its first crew in a lunar distant retrograde orbit." He spread his spectral hands. "Awaiting you." A pause.

This news stunned everyone.

Morra stared hard at Joyce's hologram. "I'll believe that when I see it."

"You'll be seeing it soon enough, David. At this very moment you're all cycling for a rendezvous with the *Konstantin*."

"The *Konstantin*?"

"The name of my mining ship. I named her after Konstantin Tsiolkovsky, the visionary genius behind the rocket equation, and the first human being to envision asteroid mining as well as artificial gravity way back in 1900."

"You're telling us you built a spaceship the size of the mock-up we trained on in Antarctica—and it's *already* in orbit around the Moon? And nobody noticed?"

"It's called 'space' for a reason."

"That wouldn't hide its infrared signature."

Joyce looked impatient. "Which is why a thermal shield was placed in a strategic orbit—to conceal the *Konstantin*'s heat signature from certain sensor arrays."

"That ship was at least—"

"Five hundred and sixty-three metric tons, fully fueled. Three hundred and forty-six tons dry. Lifted in pieces over three years by two dozen separate companies to a lunar DRO at a cost of nearly nine billion dollars; however, the fully amortized cost including construction and R and D was more like twenty-four billion."

Clarke whistled.

Morra stared. "Like I said, I'll believe it when I see it."

"In slightly more than forty-eight hours you'll all be near the Moon, and you can have a look yourself."

Amid gasps from the others, Abarca remained silent and listened intently.

"The Moon?" Jin stared in disbelief at Joyce's hologram. "We are heading to the Moon right now?"

"Yes—or at least to a lunar orbit 40,000 kilometers from the surface."

"You're kidnapping us?"

"Absolutely not. Commander Willis and Commander Mendoza are standing by to bring back down to Earth anyone who wishes to leave.

You can either take a weeklong trip to the Moon or you can return to Earth right now."

No one budged. No one spoke.

"I see there are no takers."

Tighe said, "Then the mining expedition to Ryugu . . . is really happening?"

Joyce's hologram pivoted to look at Tighe. "Yes. It is, J.T."

The team struggled to process this news.

Yak looked up. "But crew of *Konstantin* would need only eight—four in each hab." He glanced around the compartment. "Why are there twelve of us?"

"Good question, Sevastian. The company psychologists have already selected the optimal crew of eight individuals from among you twelve. Four women and four men, chosen for key personality traits, group cohesion, critical skill sets, and poise under pressure. When we reach the *Konstantin* two days from now, those who are willing will participate in one week of dress rehearsal training with the real ship's systems. You'll work with your mission controllers on Earth, test equipment, inventory supplies, troubleshoot last-minute problems, and then . . ."

Everyone hung on his words.

". . . the crew of eight will be announced. The other four are alternates—in case we have any who decline the honor."

Tighe asked, "And then what? The *Konstantin* leaves for deep space?"

Joyce nodded. "On December thirteenth."

More gasps.

Dahl said, "That's nine days from now!"

"Yes. There is an ideal orbital window to Ryugu on December thirteenth—one that won't happen again for another century. On that day, from a lunar DRO the *Konstantin* can reach Ryugu in just forty-eight days with a delta-v of only 1.7 kilometers per second, and a postinjection burn of 1.9 kilometers per second to circularize your orbit as you arrive on January 30, 2034."

Adisa said, "Less acceleration than it takes to reach our own Moon."

"Very good, Adedayo." Joyce studied the faces around him. "And that circumstance will not occur again in our lifetimes. It's a singular opportunity for the right people."

The crew floated in silence for several moments.

Clarke spoke first. "What if the whole thing doesn't work? What if there's a problem when we get there?"

"After you arrive, you'll have a ten-day window to prove whether we can extract water and other resources from Ryugu. If not, you turn back before Earth gets too far away in its orbit. If you *can* extract resources from the regolith, then you'll have plenty to sustain yourself until the Earth comes back within range four years later—and you'll also have plenty of fuel. All that's required to change humanity's future are a few people with the courage to carry out this plan."

The crew considered this.

Dahl glided up next to Tighe. "The news said your plan is reckless, bordering on insane. To stay in deep space for *four years*. It's never been done."

"Then why did you sign up, Eike?"

Josephson answered in her British accent. "Frankly, we didn't think you were serious, Nathan."

Jin scowled. "The record stay in space is just 438 days—and that was in low Earth orbit, within the protection of Earth's magnetic field."

Yak nodded. "Cosmonaut Valeri Polyakov. My father knew him."

Jin stayed focused on Joyce. "You really think we'll survive solar flares and galactic cosmic rays for *four years* out in deep space? We will be receiving a year's worth of radiation every nineteen hours."

Joyce remained serene. "My engineers have specifically designed the *Konstantin* to sustain you, sheltering in the shadow of Ryugu against solar flares, and using the materials you harvest and process to create a shield against cosmic rays. If you mine Ryugu successfully, you will not only have performed the most incredible feat in all of human history, but you will also never want for money again. For those willing to go, Catalyst Corporation is offering quadruple the completion bonus: six million US dollars each—plus production bonuses. Our estimates show it's possible to produce 3,000 tons of water ice, 3,000 tons of iron and nickel, 600 tons of cobalt, 1,200 tons of ammonia, 1,200 tons of nitrogen—this could amount to hundreds of millions in crew bonuses."

That news took the edge off.

Clarke grabbed at nearby grillwork to steady herself, even though she was already floating. "We're heading toward *the Moon* right now?"

"Two and a half days, then you'll transfer to the *Konstantin*."

Adisa asked, "What do we do until then?"

Joyce shrugged. "I suggest you decide whether you want to go on the greatest voyage in history."

Adisa nodded. "I see."

Joyce pivoted to take in the assembled crew. "We'll speak again after you're aboard the *Konstantin*. Get to know your ship. Until then, safe travels."

With that, Joyce's hologram winked out.

The miners exhaled, as if having suddenly remembered to breathe.

Morra stared at the spot where Joyce had been. "Hard. Fucking. Core."

Tighe kissed Dahl gently as he floated next to her in a cocoon bag. He tried to rest his head on her shoulder—although she kept floating away whenever they moved. He could feel how frustrated she was.

"Microgravity sex is awful."

He looked around in the semidarkness. "I think we both need to grab on to the grillwork."

Tighe noticed Dahl's mind was elsewhere. "What's wrong, Eike?"

She looked at him and spoke softly. "You're seriously considering this, aren't you?"

He floated next to her, feeling her warm skin against his cheek. "Someone has to be first."

"Yes, but *next week*? This isn't the only deep space expedition in the works. Burkett and Macy are preparing to mine the Moon."

"But they *aren't* doing it—not yet. Joyce says it'll be stuck in litigation for years. Those years could make the difference."

"Can we even trust Joyce? Everyone says—"

"That he's irresponsible. I know."

"This isn't just money he's risking—it's our lives."

"Eike, you jump off of cliffs in a flying squirrel suit and glide between trees, where one wrong move means instant death. For what?"

"That's different. The variables are known. I can ride the edge of those variables to express my joy at being alive."

"But someone had to do it first, right? It was insane until someone proved it wasn't. That's what this expedition is."

"This isn't a wing-suit dive, J.T., or a cave dive. This isn't a few minutes or hours. This is *years*. The novelty will wear off, believe me. And there are so many moving parts. Even the *mock-up* of the ship had problems. The real ship will be even more complex, and it's not flight proven. So many dangers. Radiation. Micrometeors. The unknown." She gripped his shoulders. "It's almost certainly going to fail. You do realize that? And even the smallest failure out there will kill us."

He contemplated her face for several moments. "I know."

After a few sleepless hours Dahl finally took a pill to fall asleep. Tighe was still wide awake and floated "down" to the rec/meeting compartment. There he found Morra and Jin levitating in silent contemplation. Tighe nodded to them.

Morra was gazing at a family photo floating in front of his face, stowed among the kilo of personal effects he had taken to orbit.

This was the first time Tighe had seen Morra's family. The daughters looked to be about six or seven—twins—and adorable. Morra's ex-wife was a red-haired Caucasian woman, in a polka-dot dress, as she smiled, hugging her girls on a sidewalk.

"Beautiful children."

Morra nodded. "Thanks. They're older now." A shadow crossed his face. "I want to leave them something." He paused. "My wife, too." Another pause. "Ex-wife."

"It might be a lot more than just something." Tighe noticed Morra was holding a plastic squeeze bulb filled with caramel-colored liquid. "Is that what I think it is?"

Morra nodded. "It cost a few thousand dollars to put this much kinetic energy into a bottle of scotch. So they sent the good stuff." He turned and called out, "Captain! Can J.T. get a grog ration?"

A voice returned, "Yes. I vill bring it in a moment."

"Thanks." Morra looked over at Jin. "Hey, Han. You sure you don't want a jolt?"

Jin spoke without turning. "I told you, I do not drink."

"Not even to celebrate going to the Moon?"

"Especially not then."

"Han. Han Solo!" Morra laughed.

Jin turned and frowned at him.

Morra grunted. "Not a *Star Wars* fan. All right. I'd pack a sense of humor if you're going on this trip."

Tighe addressed Jin. "What do you think about all this, Han?"

The taikonaut rubbed his face.

"If you do go, you'll come back with more experience than the entire Chinese space program."

Jin hesitated and then said, "I am ashamed. That is what I think."

"Ashamed?" Morra frowned. "What do you mean, ashamed? About what?"

"I had every advantage. I even had *guanxi*. And still I failed as a taikonaut."

"I don't know what guanxi is, but bureaucracies are unfathomable. Besides, look how far you've come on your own."

Jin seemed vexed. "It is your Western mind that says this. It is not only about me. I am my parents' son. Their only child. They put all their hopes into me. I should remain on Earth."

Tighe and Morra exchanged looks. Tighe asked, "So, if you're asked, will you go?"

"It would be selfish for me to go." Jin struggled mightily with something. "But I want to go. More than anything. To show them they were all wrong. This is antisocial behavior. To put my own desires ahead of others. Ahead of my nation. Ahead of my parents. To simply leave."

Tighe and Morra said nothing. When it came down to it, each of them would decide for themselves whether they would go. Instead, the three men floated in silence, lost in their own thoughts.

CHAPTER 23

Konstantin

James Tighe caught his breath at first sight of the *Konstantin*. The ship's massive solar array gleamed in the sunlight, as did the Mylar sun shield near the stern that shadowed a cluster of spherical fuel tanks.

Their transfer capsule approached the *Konstantin* from the bow and glided along her length at a distance of 200 meters. It was hard to get a sense of scale until Tighe caught sight of two workers in orange clam suits, silhouetted by welding flash.

The ship looked different from the holographic models that Tighe had become so familiar with in Concordia because the radial arms were presently folded up against her central axis. At just over 250 meters from rocket nozzle to antenna tip, she resembled a massive folded construction crane, made from carbon fiber box-truss girders. There were the inflatable hab units, manufactured by Halser's company—for real this time, not mock-ups or computer models.

The Central Hab was in the same position, but with the three radial arms folded upward, toward the solar mast, their hab modules were bundled together like a cluster of marshmallows stabbed onto erector set girders. The name "Konstantin" was painted across the outer surface of the Central Hab in gray letters. License numbers were printed in smaller letters below that, as well as a national flag consisting of three horizontal bars: red, white, and blue.

"Luxembourg." Abarca gazed out the porthole alongside Tighe.

"So Luxembourg is leading the world in space exploration now?"

"Apparently."

The transfer capsule's thrusters popped intermittently as the commander piloted them toward the docking port above a module labeled "Hab 1."

After a few minutes they heard the *clunk-clunk* of the docking collar clamping down, followed by checks for the integrity of the seal before capsule commander Willis unbuckled and moved to open the hatch door. She turned to her passengers.

"Welcome aboard the *Konstantin*."

Still in their blue flight suits and helmets, Tighe, Abarca, Morra, Jin, Yak, and Adisa gathered near the hatchway.

Yak was first through, and he called out as he entered, "Now, *this* is a spaceship!"

Tighe followed and entered an all-white circular airlock that he remembered well. It was identical to the mock-up in Antarctica—a squat aluminum cylinder 6 meters tall and 5 meters in diameter, lined with storage compartments, emergency gear, and batteries in charging units. Tighe floated across the compartment to gaze out of the fused silica and borosilicate porthole. The Sun's glare was so bright no stars were visible in the void beyond, only the nearby Moon and irradiated blackness.

"Look."

Yak and Abarca joined Tighe to gaze at the Moon. At this distance, about 40,000 kilometers, it was the size of a golf ball held at arm's length.

The distances out here were unfathomable. The team was "close" to the Moon, but you could still fit eight widths of the continental United States in the gap. No wonder nobody had spotted the ship. Tighe didn't resolve the *Konstantin* with his naked eye until they were within 50 kilometers. Even then the ship was a speck.

Glancing over his shoulder, Tighe saw the other team members had entered, too. Jin was helping the capsule commander secure the airlock hatch, while Morra stared at the reality of the ship.

"It is real!" Yak laughed and did a somersault in midair, then broke out in an exaggerated microgravity Russian dance. His shout echoed. "Joyce, you magnificent bastard!"

Tighe pointed quizzically at a hatchway marked "Transfer Tunnel 1."

The commander instead gestured "down" at a hatch marked "Hab 1." "Keep your helmets sealed until we're in the crew hab."

Adisa helped Tighe with the interior hatch—which, unlike in Antarctica, was easy to lift in microgravity.

The capsule commander glided up to them. "With twelve crew instead of eight, we'll be doing a warm-bed rotation. Sleep schedules will be posted on the duty roster. The other capsule's headed to Hab 2."

Tighe looked through the open hatch and realized he didn't have to worry about falling down the ladder. Instead he glided straight in.

As he reached the Hab 1 vestibule, he looked back "up" at the commander. "When do we spin her up and get some gravity in here?"

The others murmured in agreement.

Willis waved them off. "Not for a couple days yet. There's lots to cover on the punch list first."

Tighe continued "down" into the familiar aluminum-walled inner core of the hab unit. Here, the circular walls were lined with numbered supply cabinets. A couple of beds occupied the floor to either side, with a smaller interior hatch in the decking between. This led to the first-floor sleeping quarters.

Ahead of him was the lozenge-shaped pressure door with a laminate porthole. He braced himself against the bed frames to either side and gripped the circular metal wheel in the door's center. He glanced back at Adisa, who had just floated into the chamber. "Turning this wheel isn't as easy in free fall."

After a bit of struggling, they both got the pressure door open, and Tighe moved out into the upper floor of the hab—straight into the surreal sight of a modern-looking apartment—complete with curving sofa and egg-shaped reading chairs.

He looked around as the others floated in behind him. "I'll be damned . . ."

To the left, on the far side of a folding wall, he could see the edge of the hab's medical bay, with exercise equipment in the next section. To the right, past the reading chairs, was a galley table with chairs stacked against the curving hab wall, and an actual kitchen counter, cabinets, sink, and a microwave, with a pantry just beyond.

Adisa, Abarca, Morra, and the others spread out, floating like ghosts through the living space.

Morra gazed down on the galley table. "I'll like it better when we can have a proper seat."

Suddenly the crystal Tighe wore came to life—scrolling computer script information before presenting a display of software-defined light.

Adisa nodded. "There we go."

"Your crystal just linked to the ship?"

"Yes. We should be able to interact with the *Konstantin* now."

Tighe gestured to navigate familiar virtual UIs until he reached atmospheric readings for Hab 1's atmosphere. He examined the values. "One thousand thirteen millibars pressure. Seventy-eight percent nitrogen, 21 percent oxygen, 1 percent argon, and 0.04 percent carbon dioxide. O_2 partial pressure of 21 kilopascals. N_2 partial pressure, 49 kilopascals." Tighe looked to his companions. "Air looks good." He popped the pressurization seal on his flight suit and unzipped his helmet—then took a deep breath of the hab's air.

The others looked at him.

"Furniture's off-gassing a little, but it's nice. Smells like a furniture store."

The others depressurized and unzipped their helmets, pulling them back like sweatshirt hoods to rest between their shoulder blades.

They all floated in the living room and kitchen, hovering above furniture designed for normal Earth gravity.

"Let's check out the downstairs." Tighe pulled himself along to the gangway hatch that he knew lay just beyond the kitchen.

Morra and then Adisa followed.

Tighe sailed down through the hatchway, ignoring the ladder rungs, and came out on the lower floor, next to three rows of aquaponic units—healthy green lettuces, herbs, and other plants growing in receptacles set in thick PVC pipes. Reflective Mylar and indigo-colored LED lamps were suspended above and around them.

Straight ahead, against the core wall, were the hab's computer racks. Adisa examined these, making gestures that indicated he was using his crystal to inquire as to the system status.

Tighe glided rightward, past the industrial-grade clothing washer and dryer and an on-demand water heater, and stopped alongside an accordion door for two cubicle-like workstations. He opened the first to see a familiar ergonomic office chair bolted to a slot in the deck. The desk was empty, except for the lidar sensors built into each corner.

Morra floated alongside. "Looks just like our desks back on Earth."

Tighe floated onward past twin oxygen generators consisting of tubes, tanks, and clear plastic cylinders. Past water-treatment equipment and a 1,000-gallon plastic water tank.

He continued around the circular core to the bathroom door. He touched the lever handle and looked inside at the aluminum toilet, sink, and shower. This room had always seemed suspect in the training mock-up—as if a normal bathroom had no business being on a spaceship.

Morra looked over his shoulder. "I don't know about you, mate, but after two weeks of shitting into a vacuum nozzle, that's a welcome sight."

They both rounded out the tour by inspecting the secure storage compartment—which held the time-release lockers. Part of Dr. Bruno's "psych regimen," these would be opened at intervals by the ship's system or by the mission control managers. The lockers contained goodies, surprises, and other items of interest to keep up crew morale. It was a minor issue in Antarctica training, since they were only doing two-week stints with each team. However, Tighe suspected these lockers would be a lot more important on a mission that spanned years.

They floated past the other two workstation cubicles. Morra cranked open the wheel of a heavy pressure door and gazed into the ground-floor crew quarters. He called out to the others, "Everything looks shipshape!"

Tighe pointed at a yellow hatch-shaped line in the floor of the lower level. "Bilge storage."

"Ah. After you . . ."

Tighe pulled on the hatch ring and it opened easily in microgravity. He switched on his suit's chest-mounted LED light and gazed down into the dark crawl space.

"Do we put on our helmets?"

Tighe glanced at the air indicator at the edge of his crystal display. "Oxy levels look good." Tighe floated down into the meter-high circular space, 2.5 meters wide, that arced around the aluminum core. The bilge was lined with plastic storage units. Tighe activated the manifest in his heads-up display, and now each storage unit he looked at displayed a pop-up window revealing its contents.

The bilge was chilly—he could see his breath as a mist—but that was by design. It wasn't a freezer, since their food was dehydrated, but there was no need to heat the space to room temperature either. Tighe read the contents of one food container that popped up in his crystal.

"Hey, Dave."

"What?"

"Did we have dehydrated beef lasagna at Concordia?"

"No, we did not."

Tighe opened the case and took out a plastic pouch with attractive hikers smiling on the package. "I know this brand—not bad. Expeditions didn't usually spring for this one. Pepper steak. Blackened chicken. Thirty-year shelf life."

Morra glided next to him and looked at the labels on the vacuum-sealed packages. "I suppose when it costs six thousand dollars a kilo to bring anything up here, choosing the good brand doesn't bump up the price much."

Tighe stored the packet again. "Still, they could have been assholes about it."

After an hour refamiliarizing themselves with a hab they'd spent months on in Antarctica, the crew started customizing their living space through the ship's virtual UI. Adisa navigated the ship menus and instantiated a 3-meter-wide virtual picture window onto the wall of the hab. He brought the live image in from one of the ship's external high-def cameras, then shared the layer to everyone else's crystal so they would all see it in the same place.

"Whoa! Great idea, Ade."

"That's really something . . ."

They now had what looked like a massive picture window in the wall of their hab, revealing a breathtaking sight: the nightside of Earth—sprawling coastal cities glittering. The partly illuminated pockmarked surface of the Moon appeared somewhat larger in the foreground. The stars, by contrast, were obscured by the Sun's glare.

Along with the others, Tighe gazed at the sight for a minute or so, but eventually he got busy inventorying supplies and tools. At some point they broke for a subpar microgravity meal while they all floated above the useless kitchen table.

Microgravity tended to dull the taste buds, and the requirements of eating in free fall also limited the menu. By comparison, the dehydrated rations in the ship's hold looked delicious.

Abarca squeezed "beefsteak" out of a brown plastic sleeve into a folded tortilla.

Tighe chewed rehydrated spinach. "I can't taste any of this. Can you pass the hot sauce?"

Morra batted it over to him.

Tighe caught it. "Could you imagine a four-year-long trip in micro-gravity?"

Everyone groaned.

An hour or so later, a virtual screen opened in their crystal displays, and a familiar face appeared: Gabriel Lacroix, mission control manager. He wore a Catalyst Corporation polo shirt. At first, he was unrecognizable due to the broad smile on his face. His French accent sounded in their ears. "Greetings, crew of ze *Konstantin*."

The team laughed and clapped. "Gabriel!"

Morra called out, "So, were you in on this from the start?"

Lacroix turned serious. "I would like very much to discuss that, David. How-ever, we have a long checklist to get through."

Morra turned to Tighe. "That didn't last long."

> "Our December thirteenth orbital window to Ryugu is immovable,
> and we dare not skip any preflight procedures. Let us get to it."

The days leading to t minus zero were filled with a seemingly endless list of tasks. The crew paired up with Catalyst Corporation's four-person construc-tion team to inspect every corner of the ship.

Tighe and Jin met with the *Konstantin*'s construction manager, Julian Kerner, an aerospace engineer from Cologne, Germany. A no-nonsense type, Kerner hit it off with Jin immediately as they commenced discussing the *Kon-stantin*'s orbital assembly from seemingly separate vessels.

Crew inspections developed a growing punch list of technical concerns, and it soon became obvious that the *Konstantin* had some issues. In various places interior access panels did not close properly, pieces of equipment were missing, and elements of the ship's operating system were buggy. Sensors and actuators malfunctioned.

The ship's largest pressurized compartment—the inflated Central Hab—served as a junction for the three radial tunnels, as well as the z-axis tunnels running the length of the *Konstantin*. When the ship was spun up, the Central Hab would rotate slowly around an axle-like core.

Tighe and Morra floated among built-in shelving along the interior walls of the Central Hab, carrying water vapor dispensers and closely watching tiny wisps of vapor to see if they were sucked out through pinhole leaks in the exterior walls. They found and marked forty-six minor air leaks in all, but the construction team insisted this was within the design specification and that the oxygen generation system would be able to keep up.

During their next shift, Tighe and Morra ventured back to the Central Hab and then up the vertical transfer tunnel to the upper airlock. This was where the four mule utility craft, four clam suits, and four Valkyrie humanoid telepresence robots were docked.

Tighe and Morra spent twelve hours cycling through the diagnostics for each of the systems, then remotely operated the mule and Valkyrie units—utilizing their autodocking capabilities—as they'd trained to do on simulators in Antarctica. It was remarkable how faithful that simulation turned out to be.

The highlight of the testing, though, was when Tighe and Morra began their two-hour oxygen prebreathe in preparation for their own EVA. Slipping out of their lightweight blue flight suits in the suit airlock, they each climbed through the back hatch of their docked clam suits.

Going through the suit's power-up checklist, Tighe closed the carbon fiber hatch behind him and pressurized the suit with pure oxygen. He then activated the helmet—making it virtually transparent.

Tighe now gazed out into space, his suit docked like a gargoyle on the side of the *Konstantin*. After checking that the suit's two tethers were hooked into eyelets, he radioed to mission control. "Undocking, EMU-2."

"Undocking EMU-2. Copy."

Morra's voice came in on the radio. *"Undocking, EMU-4."*

"Undocking EMU-4."

After a clunking sound, Tighe floated slowly away from the ship, his umbilical lines uncoiling behind him. He gazed up at the solar array towering "above" him, then turned to see Morra floating in from the far side of the airlock tower. They clasped gloved hands and laughed as they met.

"Looking good."

Morra pointed at the distant Earth. *"Can you believe this is real?"*

Tighe followed Morra's gaze. "Not entirely. No."

Two days later the crew of the *Konstantin* was strapped into seats bolted to the Central Hab's core.

Abarca shouted, "All right, who's up for some fake gravity?"

The other crew members clapped and whistled.

For the moment the crew included four extra members, and they had to use folding jump seats bolted to the storage racks. However, strapping in was just a formality. Tighe knew from training exercises that in the event of a major structural failure of the ship while spun up, seat belts were just a way to find the bodies.

The capcom's voice came over the line. *"Radial arms confirmed unlocked. Deployment thrusters firing in three, two, one . . ."*

Tighe watched external camera screens as plumes of gas issued from dozens of thrusters set along the length of each radial arm. Each burst was computer controlled to slowly bring the long box trusses outward and downward, extending them perpendicular to the ship's z-axis. Opposing thrusters occasionally fired to slow their descent, ensuring the process did not exceed shearing-force tolerances.

Tighe smiled to see the *Konstantin* he knew so well from training take shape before his eyes. Soon, the three habs were each more than a hundred meters away from the spine of the ship.

The capcom said, *"Radial arms deployed and locked."*

"Konstantin, *prepare for spin-up in three, two, one . . ."*

As mission control counted down, fourteen CO_2 thrusters on each radial arm fired. The entire ship vibrated as the box trusses began to spin slowly along the z-axis. The outer wall of the Central Hab began to rotate around the crew, the entrance hatches to all three transfer tunnels along with it, vacuum seals cushioned by electromagnetic levitation.

The sound of metal or some other structural member shrieking and groaning occasionally came to them as the ship's rotation increased in speed.

Adisa looked around. "That sounds alarming."

The *Konstantin* flexed and rumbled as though in a storm.

A sudden loud *clunk*, followed by another metallic groan, caused the miners to exchange concerned looks.

Morra said, "Mission control, is this erector set going to hold together?"

The capcom's soothing voice returned. "*Spin-up proceeding within design parameters. Stress factors nominal.*"

The thrusters continued to fire for several minutes until finally the outer wall was rotating around them once every twenty-one seconds. The mysterious noises had ceased, replaced by the mild *whoosh* of the Central Hab's rotation.

"*Mission control to* Konstantin: *spin-up procedure complete. You now have a-grav.*"

The crew cheered and clapped.

A few minutes later Abarca, Morra, and Tighe hung from a steel cable on a cluster of carabiners clipped into their suit harnesses as a planetary winch lowered them into Tunnel 1. They'd all been assigned to Hab 1 along with Akira, Clarke, and Dahl and were the first group of three to make the transit.

There wasn't much sensation of gravity at first, so they used ladder rungs to pull themselves along the tunnel. However, as they kept going, the sensation of "down" became more pronounced, and they naturally floated back toward the center of the tunnel. Eventually they were all suspended from the end of the steel cable as if being lowered into a well.

Tighe looked around at the 100-meter-deep transfer tunnel. "This feels different from the mock-up."

Morra monitored their progress. "Because that was in real gravity. You ever swing a rope around your head?"

Tighe nodded.

"This cable's like that. We hook up, and as long as we're on the end of it, we're swinging in a circle from the ship's center."

Abarca said, "And if we let go—"

"We fly in a straight line. We don't fall straight down—at least until the tunnel wall catches up to you. Then you'll slide down the wall with increasing speed."

"I don't plan on finding out."

Abarca flexed her arms up and down. "You feel that? Like gravity."

Tighe did the same. "Yeah, I feel it now."

One hundred six meters down, the planetary winch clicked to a stop. They now stood in what felt like one Earth gravity atop an aluminum airlock with a hatch in the center of the floor. The group held on to one another unsteadily.

"Coriolis effect?" Morra sat.

Abarca knelt close to him. "Could be orthostatic intolerance."

"Is that serious?" He took a deep breath.

She took out a light pen and examined his pupils through his visor. "Should go away soon. It's caused by changes in the autonomic regulation of blood pressure and loss of plasma volume from microgravity."

"So it's normal."

"Affects everyone differently." She got on the comm link. "Crew, be aware, if you feel dizzy when you get into gravity, sit down immediately until it goes away. Otherwise you might faint. Doctor's orders."

Chindarkar's voice came back. *"We copy you, Isabel."*

Abarca turned to Tighe. "How about you?"

Tighe gave the thumbs-up. "Feels like gravity to me."

As Morra stabilized, they strained to get the hab airlock hatch open in 1 g. Then they lowered themselves into the airlock using the winch. After unclipping, they raised the winch line and closed the upper hatch before pressurizing the airlock. Only then did they open the hatch into Hab 1.

Tighe checked the air. "Still looks good. We can unzip."

He and the others depressurized their flight suits and unzipped the hoods.

After they shakily descended the ladder into the upper crew quarters, Abarca immediately dropped onto one of the beds.

"Thank god. A real bed."

Morra collapsed onto the bed across from her and let out a groan of relief.

Tighe walked slowly across the floor. From his frame of reference the acceleration of a-grav felt natural. "I'll be damned."

Abarca rolled onto her side. She smiled. "We can do this."

Tighe looked around. There were no vibrations. No hint of motion. "I gotta tell you, until this very moment, I wasn't sure." He turned to face Abarca. "But I think this could work."

Abarca got up, still wobbly. "Well, if you'll excuse me, I'm about to take the first hot shower in space." She turned the wheel to the pressure door.

Tighe helped her push it open, and they moved out into the living quarters.

Abarca started singing "*Gracias a la vida*" in Spanish while she headed downstairs.

Tighe was surprised (and relieved) that she had a beautiful voice. He then walked over to the kitchen sink and stopped in front of the water dispenser. As he listened to Abarca sing, he grabbed a plastic cup and pressed it against the dispenser, filling the cup. He sloshed the water around, studying it.

Air bubbles rose to the surface. It looked like any glass of water on Earth. Tighe laughed and tipped it back, drinking deep. He put the empty cup on the counter. "I am so evolved for this."

He heard the shower start on the floor below and listened to the singing.

As the days passed, they crossed off more and more of the items on Lacroix's checklist.

Sitting around the galley table one night in Hab 1, Tighe recalled them all breaking bread around a table off Australia's Sunshine Coast. Now the six crew members in Hab 1 were having rehydrated chicken and noodles, but Abarca shared out six glasses from a bottle of Chianti. The wine was a luxury afforded to them on this last night in normal gravity before the *Konstantin*'s departure.

Tomorrow they'd spin down the ship, refold the arms, and prepare for a burn to Ryugu. And they still didn't know who was going to crew her and who was not. There would likely be losses at this table.

Abarca held up her plastic cup. "Here's to the crew of the *Konstantin*— whoever they may be."

Everyone clinked plastic cups. "To the crew of the *Konstantin*."

The next day, after spinning down the ship and going through lockdown procedures, all twelve miners were called to the Central Hab. As they floated in microgravity, the construction team joined them. What everyone had worked so long for was about to happen, and there was a festive atmosphere.

However, a thinly veiled tension was present among the crew. Not everyone was going. Whether that was good or bad was impossible to know.

At six p.m. UTC, mission control manager Gabriel Lacroix's head and shoulders materialized in holographic form, floating near the center of the hab. "Attention, crew of the *Konstantin*. Attention, please."

Everyone fell silent and floated to the periphery so all could see.

"Thank you." Lacroix paused. "Before we begin, I want to say how well you have all worked together in the past week. This ship could not have been made ready in time were it not for your teamwork. And tomorrow the *Konstantin* will begin an historic voyage."

The assembled crew and workers clapped and whistled. Several of the construction workers recorded the moment on their phones.

Tighe tried to contain his nervousness. Looking out across the faces, he realized these people were as close to family as any expedition he'd ever joined.

Morra grabbed him by the shoulder. "All right, you wanker. Shall I put in a good word for you?"

Tighe laughed. "If you think it'll help."

Lacroix's hologram gazed off camera for a moment and then said, "Before I announce crew assignments, a brief word from Mr. Joyce."

As Nathan Joyce's hologram glowed into place, the workers and crew applauded. Some whistled. Tighe couldn't help but notice that Abarca again floated at the edge of the group with her arms crossed, expression unreadable.

"Good evening." Joyce gazed out at the assembled crew and the ship's builders. "Consider this: for decades humanity has possessed the capability to expand into our solar system—but we have not." He let his words sink in, looking from face to face. "It's not because explorers like you weren't willing to shoulder the risk. Instead it was a blindness among our leaders that prevented them from seeing the true risk. And yet on Earth, we spend a trillion dollars on war without blinking an eye. With each passing year, the chance of a global catastrophe mounts—the climate, an epidemic, a financial crash, or a war that shrouds Earth in space debris and prevents us from reaching space. Possibly ever again. Humanity's future depends on going—now, not later. I have invested literally everything

I possess to provide you—courageous people—with this ship that can carry you to the most promising asteroid in the inner solar system—one that contains enough resources to jump-start an entire cislunar economy. Enough to establish a toehold in space."

The enormity of the moment was now fully apparent to those gathered around.

"All of you have taken lethal risks before for so much less. I ask you to take this risk for the best reason of all—to secure the lives of countless generations to come. To finally embark humanity into the cosmos." With one more gaze at those assembled, Joyce nodded and then disappeared.

Lacroix returned. He focused on his crystal as he spoke. "After careful consideration of all relevant factors, the first crew of the *Konstantin* consists of the following individuals."

Tighe tensed. So did those around him.

Lacroix took a breath. "Nicole Clarke."

Clarke blanched but nodded.

"Isabel Abarca."

Tighe noticed she had no reaction.

"James Tighe."

And then Tighe felt a flash of shock—but also of joy.

"Katsuka Akira."

Sighs of relief and gasps of shock.

"Jin Han. Adedayo Adisa."

Jin remained grim-faced, but Adisa's bright smile flashed immediately. "Amy Tsukada."

She screamed in joy, and the others laughed.

"Eike Dahl."

Dahl stared into space.

That was eight. *The* eight.

Tighe snapped a look at Morra—who appeared devastated by not having his name called. Tighe looked around the room and saw everything from anguish to joy. He caught Dahl's eye and smiled slightly, but she turned away. Yakovlev wrapped his head in his hands at being left behind, as did Josephson. The room began to buzz with murmured discussions. Tighe and Morra locked eyes.

Morra made a brave face and gave a thumbs-up. "Congrats, brother."

Lacroix shouted. "Quiet, please. Thank you."

The hab quieted down.

"Among the eight crew members chosen, are there any who, after considered reflection, do not wish to accept?"

Dahl's voice immediately answered, "Me."

Katsuka raised his hand as well.

Dahl turned to Tighe again but spoke to Lacroix. "I can't do this. And there are others who want to go."

Tighe realized he wasn't surprised. It was a moment he'd known was coming.

"Are you certain, Ms. Dahl?"

"I am."

"Mr. Akira, are you certain you wish to decline your position?"

Katsuka nodded. "I am certain, Gabriel. Thank you."

Then Lacroix announced, "Very well, the replacement crew member for Eike Dahl is . . . Priya Chindarkar."

Chindarkar put her hands to her mouth momentarily, but when she lowered them, there was a smile of relief. She floated over to Tsukada and they hugged.

"Will you accept this honor, Priya Chindarkar?"

She looked up. "Of course! Yes."

Lacroix continued. "Very good. The replacement crew member for Katsuka Akira is . . . David Morra."

"Yes!" Morra shouted and raised his arms and brought them down as fists. "Goddamnit, yes!"

Tighe and Morra embraced, slapping each other on the back. "Holy shit."

Lacroix looked around. "Tonight is the last night for any changes of heart. Barring such changes, we now have the first crew of the mining ship *Konstantin*. Congratulations to you all."

Those in attendance clapped and hugged one another. They even hugged Jin, who didn't seem particularly comfortable with the familiarity, but he went along with it, acknowledging the historic nature of the moment.

Kerner took photos of the gathered crew, floating arm in arm, smiling.

On the periphery, Yak now looked devastated.

Lacroix let the group celebrate a bit, and then he said, "For those not called or who declined, please know that you are still under contract with Catalyst Corporation, and aside from being at the top of the list for future expeditions, your services will be required to aid your former crewmates in a capcom role. This evening is not good-bye. It is simply, until you meet again."

This brightened Yak's expression considerably. Tsukada floated over to console him further.

Near Tighe, Josephson floated up to Abarca and extended her hand. "Congratulations, Isabel. I suppose the *Konstantin* doesn't need two surgeons. I hope we meet again."

Abarca kissed Josephson on both cheeks and hugged her in true Argentinian fashion.

Lacroix then said, "One more piece of business."

Yak called out, "Quiet, everyone! Quiet!"

"Although mission control will remotely handle piloting and astrogation for the *Konstantin*, it is nonetheless important that the first commercial asteroid-mining ship have a captain." Lacroix looked to Clarke in the crowd. "Nicole Clarke, as a licensed ship captain back on Earth, Catalyst Corporation has determined that you possess the expertise most suited to this role. Will you accept the position of captain of the *Konstantin*?"

Clarke stared dumbfounded, but then looked out at the seven others searchingly. Tighe gave her a thumbs-up, as did Morra, then Abarca, and the rest followed suit—although Jin looked a bit put out, considering he was actually a trained astronaut. However, he finally did as well.

Still stunned, Clarke said, "I . . . accept?" She resolved. "Yes, I accept."

CHAPTER 24

Confidant

I t was the self-assured calm Nathan Joyce projected with investors that impressed Lukas Rochat most. As Rochat had become more knowledgeable about Joyce's business over the last six months, he had realized one of the keys to Joyce's success was managing what his investment partners knew, and when they knew it—all without seeming to care. Yet, it was this information imbalance that Joyce guarded even more closely than his percentage of a given enterprise. The confident demeanor, the patter before and after meetings, even a dropped pen while signing contracts were all intended to misdirect attention from what mattered. Joyce's proven track record encouraged trust, from which he wove his future success, stretching its fabric thinner each day.

As a result, the ouroboros tattoo on Joyce's bicep had taken on new meaning for Rochat. The billionaire's empire was as much temporal as it was financial. As one venture faded, another rose. Administering Joyce's business interests was like juggling chainsaws: one miscalculation would bring disaster. That Joyce managed it at all was astounding—without even factoring in Joyce's biggest play: the asteroid-mining ship, *Konstantin*.

Rochat wasn't privy to Joyce's entire plan, but he had begun to piece together the basics from government filings and contract negotiations he'd carried out on behalf of Catalyst Corporation. Joyce planned to vault ahead of the other Space Titans by taking bigger risks—principally by sending human beings to figure out things in situ. It was bold even by Joyce's standards, and now that Rochat knew the scope of it, he also knew that its success meant life or death not just for the asteroid miners but for Joyce as well. The money invested in the *Konstantin* was supposed to be invested elsewhere and would sooner or later be missed.

In the meantime, Rochat's space-law practice was now a success. He'd staffed up and opened offices not only in Luxembourg City (just off Space Row) but also in Washington, DC, and Los Angeles. Other NewSpace start-ups had noticed Rochat's rise and started hiring Sirius Legal Services as well. A dozen admins, paralegals, and junior associates now managed thousands of pages of filings and revisions for Catalyst. With Joyce's asteroid-mining scheme widely derided as unserious, those filings were met with bemused skepticism by Luxembourg officials, who barely had a chance to evaluate them before Rochat's firm submitted still more—totaling hundreds of thousands of euros in fees.

As the departure date neared for Joyce's secret spaceship, he had insisted Rochat stay physically close by him. Whether it was caution, suspicion, or, as Rochat preferred to believe, a growing bond between them, was unclear.

From Hong Kong to London to New York, Rochat accompanied Joyce as his "associate" and watched Joyce good-naturedly brush aside questions about his space ambitions from the many business and political leaders with whom he met—clarifying for investors that his real business was here on Earth.

However, in private Joyce appeared to relish Rochat as a confidant—the only one who knew their true purpose.

One evening, at a cocktail party on the eighty-eighth floor of a glass tower overlooking New York's Hudson Yards, Joyce leaned on a terrace railing and gazed at the Moon in the evening sky. Rochat stood next to him.

Joyce seemed contemplative. Behind them a glass wall revealed party guests chatting in a penthouse flat while a beautiful Asian woman played Gershwin's "Rhapsody in Blue" on a grand piano. The movers and shakers were all inside, but Joyce seemed to have limited interest in Earthly matters.

"Lukas, you probably think I'm insane."

Rochat cocked his head. "Do you really think me so judgmental?"

Joyce smiled and grabbed Rochat by the scruff of his neck affectionately—momentarily crumpling the collar of his Brunello Cucinelli cashmere suit.

Rochat wondered if others suspected they were lovers. They were not, of course, but perhaps if outsiders knew the secret they both carried, the intimacy of their discussions would make more sense. And although Rochat was not physically attracted to men, he did not find it entirely unappealing for others to think that Joyce held special affection for him.

Joyce looked up at the Moon again. "This leap . . . this great leap that humanity must make. It's necessary. More than anything we've ever done before." He was obviously struggling. "I'm not a monster. You know that, right?"

Rochat nodded. "Of course, Nathan."

"Remember this, Lukas: I'm sending *people* for a reason; agile aerospace—faster failure. The ability to adapt in situ will increase the overall chance of success. Humans can pick up a malfunctioning robot, fix it, change it, improve it, and try again without having to launch a whole new mission. I know it's dangerous, but I'm sending them for a reason."

Rochat just listened.

"Yes, I'll leapfrog Burkett and Macy and the others, but that's not the purpose. Doing so will force *them* to take bigger risks, too, and that will pick up the pace of this entire process." He looked away.

Rochat knew that Joyce wasn't wrong—but he also knew it wasn't the entire story. The big picture was the Hail Mary pass this expedition represented for Joyce's enterprises. Rochat suspected it was why the economist Korrapati's message resonated so powerfully with Joyce—Korrapati was a financial high priest offering absolution.

Among the few financial statements Rochat had seen from shell companies and Catalyst subsidiaries, Joyce's enterprises were an iceberg of debt. And his working cash flow seemed to stem from difficult-to-untangle international deals—particularly reverse mergers with Chinese companies.

Rochat's tenure in mergers and acquisitions back in Vevey meant he was well acquainted with the practice of merging with offshore firms that had ceased business operations but were still publicly listed on US exchanges—thus avoiding the lengthy vetting process for an American IPO, and using a fictional balance sheet to attract investors. The big accounting firms would confirm that the fictional numbers added up, but eventually the companies would collapse. Hundreds of billions had been funneled to unseen hands this way over the years.

As Rochat listened to Joyce, he knew the truth: Joyce had secretly funneled so much into his space ambitions that his other ventures were getting impatient for expected returns. No doubt he hoped that the *Konstantin* would settle all accounts. In truth, Rochat could think of nothing else that could.

Joyce was a convincing liar because the first person he lied to was himself. Undisciplined, egotistical—and yet, willing to risk everything for a greater purpose. It was finally clear to Rochat why so many people both hated and loved Joyce. Rochat was one of them.

Joyce spoke to the Moon. "I need to keep my ship afloat for at least another year, Lukas. One more year."

Rochat knew Joyce wasn't referring to the *Konstantin*.

"If you don't know certain things, then you can't be held responsible for them." He turned to Rochat. "So do yourself a favor and stop looking."

This was as sincere a communication as Rochat had ever had with Joyce.

"Do you know why I trust you, Lukas?"

Rochat did not.

"Because, like me, you know what it's like to be seen as no one of consequence. And like me, I don't think you ever want to go back."

They regarded each other.

"Protect me, Lukas. On the other side of this, there is a future. I promise you."

CHAPTER 25

Departure

James Tighe slept fitfully in microgravity, his cocoon bag velcroed to a bed in the second-floor crew quarters of Hab 1. As he floated in the semidarkness, he thought of all the things that could go wrong on the journey he was about to embark upon. Yet no matter how many ways he thought the expedition through to disaster, he never imagined himself not going.

He glanced across at Jin Han, who was cocooned on his own cot a meter away. The dim light of charger LEDs revealed that Jin's eyes were also open.

"Can't sleep either?"

Jin slowly shook his head.

"You're not thinking of backing out, I hope."

Jin stared at the ceiling. "I am going."

"Once you do, there's no looking back. Agreed?"

Jin paused a moment, then nodded. "Agreed."

The next morning the capcom on duty summoned the eight-person crew of the *Konstantin* to gather in the Central Hab. Tighe, Abarca, Jin, Morra, Adisa, Tsukada, Clarke, and Chindarkar transferred from their habs in the now-folded ship. They noticed that all but one of the construction crew capsules had departed from *Konstantin*'s docking ports.

In the Central Hab they found the construction manager, Julian Kerner, floating alone, tapping at a virtual UI. He looked up and nodded. "We have some legal matters to finalize."

The crew exchanged doubtful looks.

Kerner made one last tap and a hologram of a young blond man in a fashionable suit and tie floated before them. "You're on, Mr. Rochat."

After a several-second transmission delay, the young man nodded. "Greetings from Earth." He chuckled at his own joke. "I am Lukas Rochat, Catalyst Corporation's legal counsel for space affairs."

Morra sighed. "I told you the space lawyers would come."

Rochat was still talking, oblivious due to the delay. ". . . you depart. Captain Clarke, as a commercial vessel under the legal jurisdiction of the Grand Duchy of Luxembourg, the crew of the *Konstantin* will need to maintain hard copy of its Maritime Supervisory Authority Endorsement on board at all times."

"Is he kidding?"

Kerner passed Clarke a zipped polymer documents bag.

She laughed. "Sure, in case we're boarded by customs officials. Thanks."

". . . in accordance with EU regulations. Company management will need those documents out at the work site. In coming years it may avert litigation. Next, the foreman should supply you with your captain and crew shipping licenses."

Kerner passed her a packet of documents with ID cards for each of the crew.

She turned to them. "Guys. Your shipping licenses. I know you were concerned we'd leave without them."

Tighe glided close to check his out. "Goddamnit. I can never get away from this DMV photo. I look half asleep in this picture."

"You look high." Morra laughed.

Rochat examined the faces of the crew. "At this time, I need to hear a positive proclamation that each of you are embarking on this journey of your own volition and that you reached this decision free of all coercion. Please state for the record, beginning with you, Captain Clarke."

Clarke did so, as did the rest of the crew.

Satisfied, Rochat nodded. "That is all. I wish you a safe and successful expedition." With that, Rochat's image faded.

Kerner turned to them. "Well, the *Konstantin* is all yours." He pounded the central core's aluminum-zinc wall. "She's a sound ship, and she'll look after you. Please, if you do not mind . . ." He reached into his flight suit and pulled out a photo of the *Konstantin*'s first crew floating in this compartment the day before. He then produced a marker pen. ". . . can I ask you to sign this for posterity?"

The crew exchanged looks. Clarke grabbed the marker and held the photo against the wall as she signed beneath her image. They passed the photo from one crewman to another, each signing it with their own unique flourish.

When they were done, Kerner took care to place the photo in a sealed sleeve, then had them pose for another group photo, which he took with his crystal's integrated camera. "The departure countdown has begun. . . ." He checked his crystal. "I am synchronizing your displays. We are at t minus three hours, six minutes and counting."

The digital countdown appeared in the upper right corner of all their displays.

"When we reach t minus zero, the *Konstantin*'s main engines will fire, and she will accelerate on a trajectory to Ryugu. Mission control will be in contact within the hour to make sure you're strapped in and prepared for the injection burn." He looked at them. "Any questions?"

They shook their heads.

Kerner held up a phone handset. "I have here a comm link to mission control. They can connect you into Earth's phone system. If any of you wish to call someone before you depart, now is the time. There is a one-and-a-half-second delay due to the distance from Earth, and I should warn you that Dr. Bruno will be monitoring your call to ensure that no confidential information is divulged. You will be cut off if you reveal anything about this mission or your location." He held up the phone again. "Anyone?"

Adisa raised his hand, as did Tsukada, Clarke, and Tighe.

Since Tighe was closest, Kerner passed the phone to him. "Five minutes."

"Right." Tighe moved hand over hand to the far section of the Central Hab and held on to the storage shelving. He then turned on the phone.

A mission controller's voice came on the line. "*Who am I speaking with?*"

"James Tighe."

"*What number would you like to call, Mr. Tighe?*"

Tighe was surprised he remembered the number so readily—or maybe he wasn't surprised. He repeated the country code and phone number to the mission controller.

"*Stand by, I'll connect you directly. Please remember: your call will be monitored.*"

"I know."

After a few moments he heard the line ringing.

His mother's voice answered on the third ring, speckled by static: "*Hello?*"

Tighe took a breath. "Mom. It's Jim."

A pause.

"James?"

Another pause.

"Yes, it's Jim, your son."

Several moments of silence passed. Too many.

"Are you there?"

"Well, James, you call out of the blue. I haven't heard from you in years."

A pause.

"It's been a while. I know."

A pause.

"What's that? There's some sort of delay."

A pause.

"I know. I'm far away."

A pause.

"I can guess why you're calling."

Tighe looked around at the spaceship and his fellow miners—some of them floating upside down. "No, I don't think you can, Mom."

"Are you in trouble?"

"I'm not in trouble. I just—"

"Is it money?"

"I'm going away, and I wanted to call you before I left."

A pause.

"You can't think that just by calling you'll be in our lives. You have to be present to be part of people's lives."

"I know. But this is—"

"—doesn't do you any good, and it doesn't do us any good either."

"Mom, listen for a second!" Tighe noticed the other crew members look at him, but then they purposely turned their attention elsewhere.

Tighe looked away from them and spoke more softly into the phone. "I called because we might never speak again."

Pause.

"That's the way it's always been."

"Believe me, this is different. Things haven't been perfect between us, but I wanted to talk before I go."

"Have you been arrested, James?"

Tighe pinched the bridge of his nose.

"*I can't waste more help on you. I have grandchildren to—*"

"I just wanted to say that—"

The delay caused them to step on each other's words.

"*—you finally grow up and become a functional adult? Your brothers and sisters all have families. What have you accomplished with your life? There's no purpose in it at all as far as I can see.*"

A familiar numbness came over Tighe as he listened to her voice. It was as though he were fifteen years old again. He began to hear only the tones of her voice, not the words.

"Mom." A pause as she still talked. "Mom." Another pause. He nodded to himself and spoke without emotion. "I have to go."

The delay again.

"*Of course you do. You always had to go. I have to go, too.*"

With that the line disconnected.

Tighe gripped the phone and rested his head against the cold carbon fiber of the shelving. He floated there for several moments.

Abarca eventually moved over to him. "Hey, are you done?"

He looked up and nodded. "Yeah. Sorry for the wait." He handed her the phone.

She gripped his arm to stop him from floating away, pulling their faces close. "For what it's worth, you matter a lot to me, J.T.—to all of us."

Tighe nodded.

She embraced him. "People back home don't understand us. They can't help it."

As the countdown reached t minus two hours, mission control instructed the crew of the *Konstantin* to don their blue flight suits and strap in to the eight seats bolted to the Central Hab's core wall.

Tighe looked around at his crewmates. They appeared to be contemplating the magnitude of what they were about to do. Abarca had summited the highest mountains in the world. Morra had experienced combat. Tighe had dived to the limit in unexplored caves. Most of them were intimately acquainted with danger.

However, intercepting an asteroid as it passed a few million kilometers from Earth, rendezvousing with it, and drifting away from Earth for *years*—traveling to the far side of the Sun—well, no human had ever gone even a thousandth that distance from Earth. This was an expedition unlike anything anyone had ever attempted.

The capcom's voice finally came over the laser comm link. *"Stand by for message,* Konstantin."

Suddenly a hologram of Nathan Joyce appeared before them. He sat behind his desk at Baliceaux and nodded. "I won't speechify much before you go. We'll be talking later anyway. Just remember this: we all know things will not go according to plan—but that's why we're sending you. To rewrite the plan as needed. Surprises are to be expected. The entire mission control team and myself will be ready whenever you need us. If you do your jobs correctly, a few years from now you'll be able to afford a ship like this yourself—and there's more than enough asteroids up there for all of us." He studied their faces. "You may have wondered why I kept this ship a secret. It's because I didn't think Earth would let us go. I didn't think they'd understand. You go now with our confidence in your ability to do what no one else has ever dared. Safe journey, and I will see you all again soon."

With that, Joyce faded away.

"T minus five minutes and counting."

As Tighe waited, strapped to his seat in free fall, he listened to the countdown over the mission control comm line. Tighe looked over at Jin, Tsukada, Clarke, Morra, Adisa, and Chindarkar, some with their eyes closed, others looking tense. Abarca, by contrast, looked calm, determined. He imagined her charging to the summit of K2 in the dead of winter. Her father's ax in hand.

These were the most important people in his life now.

Tighe was ready. He'd been ready to leave for a long time. If death awaited him on this voyage, so be it. In the meantime, he would help his crewmates however he could.

Abarca held out her arms, and the crew did likewise, joining gloved hands. "Here we go . . ."

The final countdown began.

"T-minus 10, 9, 8, 7 . . ."

As the countdown reached zero, the ship vibrated almost imperceptibly, easing them back against their seats with about a half g of force. The sensation was minor compared to the violence of launching off the Earth.

The crew clapped—followed by nervous laughter.

"I guess that's it, then."

Mission control's voice came in over the comm link. *"Fair winds and following seas, Konstantin."*

Clarke answered: "Roger that, mission control. See you in four years."

"All engines throttling to 70 percent . . ."

Erika Lisowski pored through a worksheet of project costs in her cramped office on the ninth floor at NASA headquarters in Washington, DC. Her door stood open and colleagues walked past or clattered away on keyboards in cubicles nearby.

Just then Lisowski's mobile phone chimed, indicating an incoming text.

She pulled it out of her jacket pocket and looked at the display.

A single line of text from a restricted number read:

Heading out—do you need anything?

Lisowski gasped and stood up, pushing her office chair back. She breathed fitfully and put the phone down on the desk, bringing her trembling hands to a peak against the bridge of her nose. After a moment she moved to close her office door, then turned to face the wall. She struggled to restrain herself from shouting in joy.

After a few more moments, Lisowski picked up the phone and texted back:

Bring back water.

Then she slipped the device into her jacket and picked up her desk phone. She tapped in an unlisted extension. When the line picked up, the only words Lisowski said were: "Let's grab a coffee."

CHAPTER 26

First Passage

Throughout history, most of a sailor's time was spent performing maintenance or in training drills. It seemed the life of an asteroid miner wasn't going to be much different. Very little of the seven-week transfer orbit to Ryugu was spent in relaxation. Despite all the automated systems, Tighe and the rest of the crew were kept busy performing upkeep on CO_2 scrubbers, oxygen generators, water-processing systems, and moisture-removal systems. The crew also maintained three banks of aquaponics units, growing leafy plants in each of the two residence habs and harvesting fresh greens for their evening meals. They rotated domestic chores, cleaning living spaces and lavatories and restocking pantries and consumables.

Whenever possible they remained in the crew quarters behind the core's radiation protection and wore AstroRad vests while moving about the hab.

With the ship spun-up the habs were run on a twenty-four-hour cycle in Earth's UTC time zone, and as artificial twilight approached each evening, hab lighting would imperceptibly change to a softer hue. The company psychologists also instantiated virtual windows in the hab walls, displaying hours of ultra-high-def video overlooking vistas on Earth, with the effect that the ship's crew seemed to be living in a circular tower overlooking first a Swiss valley, followed a few days later by Lake Como in Italy, and the following week by a view of the Caribbean. The frequency of the hab's lighting matched natural sunlight, and in a-grav while tending to the plants in the aquaponics bay Tighe could almost convince himself he wasn't on a spaceship at all.

A few times Tighe opened a private virtual window to look out upon space from one of *Konstantin*'s external cameras. Exposed to direct sunlight as the *Konstantin* was, space looked more like a faded black, endless void, with only a few of the planets and no stars visible. Earth and the Moon were now no more than white disks behind them, difficult to distinguish from Jupiter, Venus, or Mars.

The crew was also kept busy tracking down dozens of error and trouble codes that sprang up throughout the *Konstantin*'s operating system—most of which turned out to be false alarms. This resulted in several corner-to-corner inspections of the ship as well as sending out video drones to glide along the length of *Konstantin*'s z-axis box trusses.

Mission control also ran the crew through emergency drills, extinguishing virtual fires and simulating medical emergencies—rushing simulated injury victims to one of the two medical bays.

Immediately after departure the company psychologists implemented a habitat crewing schedule as part of their "emotional hygiene" regimen; every two weeks the crew assignments for Hab 1 and Hab 2 would change, following a "Social Golfer" algorithm to mix people with maximum variety.

The biweekly crew shuffle was treated as a "fun" event by mission control, and it was a sound idea; being in close quarters with the same people constantly could get old, and moving between habs required at least fifteen minutes. That meant Tighe would go a week or more without seeing the other hab crew in person.

The first rotation found Tighe, Han, Abarca, and Clarke in Hab 1, with Adisa, Morra, Chindarkar, and Tsukada in Hab 2. The sleeping arrangements within a hab were up to the occupants. As of yet, no shipboard romances had begun.

Not long after the *Konstantin* departed cislunar space, the company shrinks also suggested the crew determine their preferred holiday schedule. Holidays were important, they noted, to maintain "rootedness" to the passage of time and to have events to look forward to.

Toward that end Captain Clarke held a crew meeting, with each hab using augmented reality to virtually extend their galley table to include crewmates from the other hab. Christmas was only a few days away, but Clarke suggested that, since none of the crew was particularly religious, they should implement their own holiday schedule based on Earth's celestial events: the equinoxes, solstices, and New Year. They could celebrate birthdays as well. That way the holidays were based on something they all shared (and in truth many religious festivals on Earth were variations on these celestial events anyway).

Thus, the first shipboard holiday occurred a little over a week after they left lunar DRO, on December 21: the winter solstice. The crew strung LED emergency lights and held a rehydrated feast of sorts—with steak, noodles, turkey, and vegetables, all of it rather similar in consistency.

They had another feast on New Year's Eve—although for this, mission control maintained a videoconference link and also remotely unlocked one of the gift lockers to reveal a bottle of brandy. The entire crew toasted in the year 2034 along with mission control.

Helping to liven things up was news from Earth, TV shows, movies, and especially capcom shifts by their colleagues Eike Dahl, Sevastian Yakovlev, Elizabeth Josephson, and Katsuka Akira. The four of them were still employed by Catalyst Corporation, and a couple of days after the *Konstantin*'s departure they'd caught the lunar cycler *Rosette* back toward Earth, where they now checked in regularly with the crew. Early on, the transmission delay wasn't more than a few seconds, so conversations were still normal.

Sometimes, during his one hour per day of personal time, Tighe would go to his quarters and make use of a separate channel from the *Konstantin*'s 1.3-gigabit laser comm connection to chat with Dahl after she'd clocked off for the day as a capcom.

No doubt the company was monitoring their calls, but their mutual attraction was too strong to ignore—and sadly pointless. They both knew nothing between them would ever be the same, yet they resisted acknowledging this as long as possible.

In the darkness of his quarters Tighe asked her image, "Are you flying again?"

Dahl shook her head. "*I'm planning a trip to Stryn, but first I have to recondition, make certain all this microgravity work hasn't messed with my flying instincts.*"

"I have no right to say this, Eike, but . . . be careful."

She laughed. "*Says the guy on a spaceship heading 200 million miles from Earth.*"

He chuckled. "We're both terrible at the 'careful' thing."

She grew serious. *"But I appreciate the sentiment."*

Invariably their video calls would end reluctantly, and Tighe would feel an irresistible emotional pull toward Earth for an hour or more afterward. However, he knew that bittersweet taste was as good as it got for him. Experience had shown he was not suited to long-term romantic relationships. Tighe had a feeling Dahl was wired the same way. They'd just never had the chance to enjoy the bloom of their romance, and that stung more than he expected it would. She was an extraordinary person and often on his mind.

Yet, the *Konstantin*'s journey continued, week in and week out—as did the maintenance and training that kept the crew occupied.

A month after departure Tighe was sitting at his workstation, running through a VR training exercise, when alarms suddenly whooped throughout the hab. The VR environment dissolved in Tighe's glasses, and he suddenly looked up at real-world emergency strobe lights.

A calm female computer voice said, *"Warning: Central Hab fire. Repeat: Central Hab fire."*

Tighe spoke into his comm link. "Anybody know if that's real?"

Morra's voice: *"Ade, you near the core?"*

Alarm codes scrolled by in Tighe's crystal. He tapped the first one, bringing up a surveillance camera image of the Central Hab.

On the screen globules of orange plasma roiled among the food storage racks in microgravity.

"Shit! We've got real fire!"

The alarms muted.

Adisa's urgent voice came in over the comm link. *"Fire in the hub!"*

The CCTV camera image showed Adisa floating past in his blue flight suit, headed toward a fire extinguisher mounted on the aluminum core wall—next to oxygen packs.

Tighe was already running, headed toward the transfer tunnel. His virtual workspace moved with him. "Ade, forget the extinguisher! Grab the O_2 packs and seal yourself in the core!"

On the surveillance camera Adisa was already floating toward the flames with the fire extinguisher. *"If we lose the Central Hab, we all die!"*

Clarke cut in. *"Ade, seal yourself in, and we'll purge the atmosphere!"*

The fire suddenly bulged over Adisa, and he shouted as he held his arms up.

The arms of his blue flight suit were now on fire—the flames almost unrecognizable in microgravity. Adisa tried to aim the extinguisher at himself.

Abarca suddenly appeared on the surveillance image and grabbed him by the harness as she pulled him backward toward the central core's pressure door. *"I've got him!"*

Adisa shouted, *"Forget me! We must contain the fire!"* He slapped at plasma-like flames pulsating across his belly.

"Don't worry about that." She pushed him inside and pulled the pressure door closed after them. On the CCTV image the door's wheel spun. *"Purge the Central Hab!"*

Clarke was already on it. In seconds blowers started evacuating the compartment's air, and on-screen the fire dimmed.

The ship's voice said, *"Central Hab emergency purge in progress."*

By the time Tighe reached his own hab's airlock, the flames in the Central Hab were out.

Alarms started clearing from the queue.

Jin's voice said, *"According to the system log, there was an electrical short in Trunk Line 2. We should cut power to it."*

Clarke asked, *"What systems will that affect, Han?"*

After a few moments: *"Line 2 supplies power to the refinery, which is dormant."*

"Okay, cut the power. We need to check the whole system with mission control."

Morra's voice asked, *"How's Ade, Isabel?"*

"I'm assessing. He's got at least second-degree burns on his forearms. His suit's also been compromised. J.T. . . ."

"Yeah, Isabel?"

"You're closest. Help me get Ade to Med Bay 2."

Tighe radioed back, "On my way."

An hour later Adisa lay on a medical table with his arms bandaged.

Abarca checked his pupils, looking for signs of shock, as Tighe stood nearby.

"Stupid, stupid, stupid!" Adisa struck his forehead repeatedly with his bandaged arms. "I did not follow protocol. I could have doomed us all."

"Hey! Be careful with your arms."

"We have not even reached Ryugu, and I am already disappointed with myself."

Abarca grabbed Adisa's chin. "Look at me. We need you for your brain, not your firefighting skills. No unnecessary heroics next time. Understood?"

"Understood, Isabel."

Within twenty-four hours Catalyst mission control engineers helped Jin and Morra locate the source of the fire—faulty wiring. That necessitated an inspection of all electrical lines in the ship, expanding their already long list of duties.

During one of their weekly all-hands meetings with mission control, Clarke raised an issue that was on the minds of the entire crew. She looked at the virtual image of Gabriel Lacroix and asked, "When is Catalyst going to issue a press release announcing the *Konstantin*'s existence, Gabriel? And her mission, and the identity of her crew? This journey is historic."

The crew in both habs voiced their agreement.

After a short transmission delay, Lacroix looked up from his meeting agenda. He motioned for the other mission controllers to leave the room and then held up a hand to ward off more questions until he was alone.

Finally, he looked at Clarke through the video link and spoke with his slight French accent. "We all want to announce to the world what we are doing here. And of course, it is historic." Lacroix frowned. "However, we cannot do this. Not yet. As you know, certain international laws were broken by launching the *Konstantin* without the approval of a sovereign state. If this was made public at this point, Mr. Joyce may be forced to resign as CEO and might also be removed from the boards of his other companies. Given his commitment to this project, that would be a catastrophic development."

After the transmission delay Tighe said, "Then at what point *does* Catalyst tell the world about us, Gabriel?"

Another delay, then, "We tell the world, J.T., once we have proven that you can harvest Ryugu's resources and send them back toward lunar DRO. At that point, it will become obvious that Mr. Joyce was not reckless—but instead a visionary. A visionary who will, at that moment, be sitting on top of a strategic resource worth a great deal of money to his investors."

Morra said, "I get it—better to ask forgiveness than permission."

"Precisely, David." Lacroix looked at the crew's faces. "However, once you prove asteroid mining is practical, it will indeed be in Catalyst's interest to announce this expedition to the world. You will all become quite famous."

In the third week of January, while he was scrubbing the hab's aluminum toilet, Tighe heard a strange whistle over the comm link. Then a message from Clarke popped up on his crystal.

Land ho!

Tighe put down his brush and opened the message.

Check it out: first sight of Ryugu...

He heard cheers elsewhere in the hab.

Tighe tapped at the link, which opened a video window showing a grainy white dot against a black background. The image was a live feed from a forward camera, but it looked more like a dead screen pixel.

As the days passed, the dot did not grow in size, but it did increase in brightness, the asteroid reflecting light from the Sun behind them.

At night Tighe would lie in bed staring at the image of Ryugu. He wondered what awaited him there. What awaited them all.

On January 29 the *Konstantin* was 100,000 kilometers away from Ryugu. Mission control gave the order to begin spin-down procedures in preparation for a postinjection burn that would circularize the *Konstantin*'s orbit to match Ryugu's.

The entire crew strapped in to the bulkhead seats outside the central core. They all wore oxygen masks, prebreathing in the event an emergency EVA was necessary.

Mission control fired the radial-arm thrusters for several minutes to halt their rotation. Tighe watched the rotating wall of the hab around them slow and finally stop. Mission control then unlocked the radial arms and fired vertical thrusters to gradually fold them upward until they were flush against the *Konstantin*'s z-axis. Locks then engaged to secure the arms in preparation for the burn.

The *Konstantin* had covered a long enough distance from Earth over the past seven weeks that there was now a forty-seven-and-a-half-second transmission delay with mission control. This meant an effective ninety-five-second response delay to any questions or emergencies. That would only increase in coming months.

A countdown for the postinjection burn appeared in all their crystal displays.

"Konstantin, *we are at t minus ten minutes local time for a 1.9-kilometer-per-second postinjection burn.*

"*Fuel systems are go.*

"*Engines are go.*

"*Comm systems are go.*

"*Telemetry looks good.*"

A verbal countdown began ten seconds before engine ignition—which mission control called correctly despite the transmission delay, and at t minus zero a gentle vibration reached the crew as they were gently pressed into their seats. After a ninety-five-second delay the radio confirmed what they already knew. . . .

"*We have main engine start.*

"*Throttle at 30 percent.*

"*Trajectory nominal.*"

Attitude thrusters fired occasional corrections as they closed in on Ryugu.

They all watched with rapt attention as a gray, top-shaped rock increased in size on their virtual screens, at first imperceptibly, and then noticeably.

There it is.

Past tense radio chatter from mission control filled their ears. They listened as the *Konstantin*'s remotely controlled flight systems brought them in.

Tighe flipped through standard optics and into infrared, ultraviolet, and radar imagery of Ryugu. As he did so, he could see small flecks gliding slowly around the irregularly shaped kilometer-wide rock—cube sats from the Hayabusa2 mission back in 2018, circling 10 kilometers above Ryugu's day-night terminator.

Still the *Konstantin* drew closer.

A hundred kilometers out the asteroid was the size of Tighe's thumbnail at arm's length. The ship rumbled against its rocket exhaust.

"Reducing throttle to 20 percent."

Fifty kilometers out, surface features were now visible to the naked eye. The asteroid had a pronounced equatorial ridge and pointed poles—as though two mountains had been pushed together, base to base. The asteroid rotated level with its orbit and too slowly to be noticeable.

The *Konstantin* began to pass toward the asteroid's left side.

Twenty kilometers out and Ryugu's surface looked speckled by crumbs— boulders tens of meters in size. One particularly large crumb—what the trainees had called "the Castle"—was located on the asteroid's north pole. But it was impossible to get a sense of Ryugu's real proportions. It looked for all the world like a fist-sized clump of ash floating 2 feet in front of Tighe's face.

Ten kilometers out and Ryugu was basketball-sized in Tighe's crystal display. However, the true immensity of the rock was starting to become clear as ever more detail resolved on its sunlit side.

Five kilometers away, and the enormity of this mountain was now obvious: almost a kilometer in diameter and estimated at 450 million tons. Its geology was entirely alien to a caver's eyes. No limestone formation. No volcanic origin. No erosion. Yet, according to Clarke, this primordial stone was older than the Earth.

And then the *Konstantin* came under the shadow of Ryugu.

Suddenly the disk of the Milky Way and a trillion individual stars blazed to life at the edges of the screen, while a consuming blackness occupied the center.

The crew let out gasps of awe. The stars were beautiful.

The ship rumbled for several more seconds and then went quiet.

Forty-seven and a half seconds later:

"MECO.

"Bang-bang control activated.

"Bang-bang looks good."

Soon Gabriel Lacroix's voice came in over the laser link. "Konstantin, *you are now on station in the shadow of Ryugu, 3 kilometers above the asteroid's equatorial ridge. Congratulations. You have now traveled farther from Earth than any human beings in history."*

The crew cheered as they unbuckled and floated clear of their seats. They hugged and slapped one another on the back.

"*Note your display*, Konstantin. *You are at t minus two hundred sixteen hours, twelve minutes and counting for a mission go, no-go.*"

Tighe noticed a new countdown in the corner of his crystal display.

"*You have until that time to confirm the viability of water extraction from asteroid regolith. Failure to do so will require a mission abort before the Earth-return orbital window closes. We are activating the countdown timer now.* . . ."

Clarke responded, "Roger that, mission control. Be advised, we have warning codes for Radial Arms 1 and 3. Request permission for a manual arm deployment. I want human eyes to inspect *Konstantin*'s structural integrity before we spin up. Over."

They floated for a minute and a half waiting for a response. In the meantime, they pointed out Ryugu surface details in infrared and ultraviolet frequencies. Finally the capcom's voice came through.

"*Affirmative*, Konstantin. *You are cleared for manual arm deployment.*"

Clarke turned to the crew. "Dave, Han, J.T., get out there and make sure the *Konstantin* is safe for spin-up." She checked the countdown clock. "We've got slightly less than ten days to prove this entire trip wasn't for nothing. So let's get busy."

CHAPTER 27

Dowsing

Tighe eased himself into his clam suit through the hatchway and then instantiated a virtual EVA checklist. He closed the hatch behind him, and the suit pressurized with a hiss. About halfway down his checklist he activated the system to render his helmet invisible. Suddenly his checklist ground to a halt.

In the shadow of Ryugu the sheer number of stars that spread out and away from Tighe left him spellbound. He stared slack-jawed for several minutes.

Over him arched the brilliance of the Milky Way. Its intricacy and clarity were more stunning than anything he'd ever imagined.

Morra's voice finally came over the radio. *"Are you guys seeing this?"*

Jin's awed voice responded. *"Yes."*

Morra's voice came next. *"Happy birthday, J.T."*

Tighe laughed. He'd forgotten it was his thirty-eighth birthday. "Thanks." Tighe activated a virtual info layer and labels appeared on celestial bodies as he focused on them. Several glove widths to the left was a swirl of blue, white, and red gas that bore the label "Large Magellanic Cloud." Above that, the bright red Carina Nebula was set like a ruby on the glittering chain of the Milky Way, which spanned the cosmos before him. Tighe's home galaxy bulged into a pointillized cloud of light, more finely detailed than anything he'd ever conceived. Its glowing center was 28,000 light-years away, and it nonetheless dominated his view.

Over the dark shoulder of Ryugu to his extreme right, Tighe could see the bright disks of the Earth and Moon, nearly equal in brightness as they caught the Sun's light.

They were so small. Insignificant.

Awed murmuring in Mandarin came in over Tighe's radio as he continued to stare, transfixed.

No matter what happens, now it was already worth it.

Tighe opened up his helmet visor so that he could behold the universe not through a light field display but with his own eyes. As he did so, he gasped with renewed awe.

No cathedral could ever compare. No subterranean flowstone sculpture. Nothing in his adventurous life could have prepared him. A wave of gratitude swept over him.

Clarke's voice came in over the radio. "*Dave, Han, J.T. What's happening? Why aren't you moving?*"

Morra laughed, followed by Tighe and Jin.

Tighe closed his visor and reactivated the helmet's external camera system. He glanced at the go, no-go countdown timer. They'd been gawking at the cosmos for a full ten minutes.

"Sorry. Just paralyzed by the indescribable beauty of the cosmos. We'll get to work."

Tighe tore his eyes away from the stars and undocked his suit. As he floated free, he reeled in his tether and made his way to a waiting mule utility craft. A virtual label indicated the mule was piloted by Chindarkar. Tighe waved a gloved hand to Morra and Jin as they approached around the upper airlock. They grabbed the mule's handles and stepped onto the running board across from him. The three of them exchanged smiles at what they were witnessing.

The mule's thrusters popped and brought them up toward the summit of the ship—where the solar array was even now unfolding and focusing on the Sun's light over the horizon of Ryugu. As it caught the Sun, the panels blazed like gemstones.

Morra said, "*If everyone could experience this . . .*"

Jin finished, "*It would change them.*"

The mule brought them forward along the length of the ship, past the folded radial arms, to the three locked-down hab units. As they disembarked and got to work, the black silhouette of Ryugu blocked out a third of the universe behind them—its immensity palpable.

The error codes for Arms 1 and 3 turned out to be false alarms. The locking bolts securing the habs retracted without incident. Within an hour the three of them returned to the upper airlock. It was with regret that Tighe opened the rear hatch of his EMU and pulled himself back aboard the *Konstantin.*

Once inside, Tighe exchanged knowing looks with Jin and Morra, and they clapped one another's shoulders. Words were unnecessary between them even hours later.

After the *Konstantin*'s spin-up, the crew quickly "descended" into their habs—with Clarke and Tsukada heading to the workshop, or Fab Hab, where they began activating and running diagnostics on laboratory, refinery, and additive manufacturing systems.

Mission controllers launched three cube sats from racks on the *Konstantin*'s spine, placing them in different orbits around Ryugu to act as communication relays.

By the first evening, the crews in both habs sat around their galley tables for dinner, using the AR conference system to virtually extend their four-person tables into one eight-person gathering. Lacroix and the other mission control managers also joined them via a virtual video.

Lacroix led a toast as the crew held up plastic cups of rehydrated apple juice. Awkwardly, they received his words nearly a minute later. "To humanity's next great leap."

"Hear! Hear!"

After dinner Captain Clarke activated the *Konstantin*'s exterior lights, kicking on a million-lumen searchlight located on the lower spine of the ship. The brilliant beam stabbed out at the asteroid's surface, landing as a small but brilliant ellipse. Shadows played across the irregular regolith as the beam searched.

Sitting in the galley of Hab 1, Tighe, Abarca, and Jin watched a virtual screen showing a close-up of the beam's span. Clarke guided the searchlight through the coordinates of surface boulders ranging in size from 8 to 4 meters in diameter, chosen from 2018 Hayabusa2 mission imagery and current radar scans. She worked through a list of candidate rocks supplied by mission control—boulders that looked easy to separate from the surface and enclose in one of their 15-meter asteroid bags.

Due to Ryugu's slow rotation, it took more than seven hours to lay eyes on them all. Afterward, Clarke and mission control geologists narrowed the list to only six candidates for follow-up muon tomography scanning—which would confirm that the boulders did not extend deep into the regolith.

The crew went to bed just after one a.m. UTC.

As Tighe lay in his cot, he was so excited that he could barely close his eyes. He was in deep space, alongside Ryugu, and still alive. Tomorrow they would try to do something no one had ever attempted: harvest water in deep space. He smiled as he recalled the breathtaking view outside the ship, then grabbed his crystal to check the countdown:

211 hours, 4 minutes until the return window to Earth closed.

If they could not derive the necessities of life from this mountain of dust within the next nine days, they would need to head home.

The failure of the expedition would spell financial ruin for Joyce, of course, but that didn't seem all that important. Tighe suspected people like Joyce would always find a way to be rich. What did concern Tighe was what their failure would mean to the future of exploration. How long until someone tried again? Decades? A century? Would it even be possible ever again?

They must succeed. There was no other choice.

Tighe finally fell into a restless sleep, his dreams filled with visions of falling down a cliff face back on Earth—as Abarca, Morra, Jin, and the others gazed down on him from a high ledge.

Tighe was awakened at six a.m. by mission control playing music throughout both habs—the guitar riff, horns, and strings of "Papa Was a Rollin' Stone." Tighe and Morra got up and stretched as the overhead lights came up.

Morra glanced at the ceiling. "I get the stone analogy, but does mission control realize it's meant as a metaphor for bad parenting?"

"Pretty sure that's not what they were going for."

Not much later Abarca, Tighe, Morra, and Clarke sat around the galley table sipping freeze-dried coffee and eating rehydrated oatmeal. Mission control managers appeared on a video feed—with one of them standing in front of a green screen of Ryugu, pointing out key surface features like an off-world weatherman.

The other four crew members from Hab 2 beamed in via the AR link, and thus appeared to be having breakfast on an extended virtual table in the wall alongside them. It was a surreal caricature of a normal household starting their day.

A virtual Adisa looked up from a UI only he could see. *"We are 215,000 kilometers farther from Earth than yesterday. Relative velocity is, for the moment, 8,941 kilometers per hour and will reduce slightly each day for some time."*

Abarca glanced up from reading. "Which means what to us, Ade?"

"Which means the communications delay with Earth will increase by roughly a second and a half every day for the next several months. Today it is forty-eight seconds—with a mission control response time of ninety-six seconds. I can place the current comm delay in the lower left corner of the group main screen, for ready reference, if that is helpful."

Clarke nodded. "That is useful, Ade. Thanks." She looked over her bowl of oatmeal to a virtual Chindarkar, who was also tapping at invisible objects while sipping tea. "Priya, this morning I'd like you to take the muon tomography scanner and get detailed subsurface maps of our boulder candidates. We'll regroup with mission control once you have that data."

"You got it."

Adisa spoke to Chindarkar. *"Priya, please use Mule 3 or 1. The other two have error codes I am still tracking down."*

Chindarkar looked to Clarke. *"Which boulder do you want me to start with?"*

"Whichever's closest when you launch." Clarke spoke through a comm link. "Mission control, we're preparing a mule for surface scanning. If you have suggestions, now's the time."

Everyone knew an answer wouldn't be coming for another minute and a half.

Clarke turned to Tighe, Morra, and a virtual Jin. "Mission control wants us to hook up the magnetic rake and try to harvest enough regolith for an initial assay. They've marked a promising iron-rich dust pool on the coordinate grid. Han, you're on the pilot roster today. Dave and J.T., you manage the rake."

Tighe perked up. "EVA?"

"Negative. Telepresence only. No unnecessary radiation exposure. Let our machines do the work. Use a mule ."

"Any Valkyries?"

"*One* Valkyrie. And keep it clamped to the running board unless absolutely necessary. Return to the ship when you've got at least fifty kilos of regolith—the most representative sample you can find."

"Aye, aye, Captain."

Morra spoke to Jin's AR image. "Han, conference us after breakfast."

"*I'll be there.*"

After eating, Tighe and Morra headed down to their workstations. There, Tighe jacked in to the 3D telepresence system with his crystal and could see that Chindarkar had already checked out Mule 3, leaving Mule 1 as the only green-status unit. He glanced up to see Morra slip in to the chair of the workstation opposite, a cup of tea in his hand.

Tighe spoke while manipulating the holographic UI floating between them. "And to think my entire life has been one long effort to avoid working in a cubicle. . . ."

"I reckon most people would be jealous, mate."

Tighe spoke through the comm link. "Priya, we'll wait until you're clear of the dock before we power up."

"*Grabbing the scanner now. I'll just be a minute.*"

"Take your time. Jin, you with us?"

Jin's voice came in over the comm link. "*I am here.*"

Tighe looked to Morra. "You want the Valkyrie?"

Morra raised his mug. "You take it. Royal Engineers will act in an advisory capacity this morning."

"Han, Dave's got the jitters, so it looks like I'll be your Valkyrie."

Morra chuckled. "Wanker."

"Come by and pick me up. I'm Unit"—Tighe examined a row of Valkyrie icons—"V-2."

"*Unit V-2. Copy.*"

Tighe tapped Unit V-2 in his display. After a brief delay his crystal became a virtual reality headset, filled by a first-person view of the Valkyrie's stereographic cameras. It was fully immersive, and just like yesterday the starscape was spectacular.

"I don't ever want to get used to this." Tighe turned his robotic gaze upward to see Mule 3 silently navigating just overhead, its cold-gas thrusters popping occasionally. Tighe watched as the mule's robotic arms grabbed the muon tomography scanner from the tool rack atop the ship's docking port. The scanner was a box the size of a refrigerator. It detected "coulomb scattering" of subatomic particles to derive imagery inside solid objects. The same technology had been used to locate hidden burial chambers in the Egyptian pyramids.

After a few more moments, Chindarkar piloted Mule 3 away. *"All yours."*

"Happy scanning."

Jin then piloted Mule 1 in front of Tighe's robot avatar. Tighe extended his real-world arm, and scanners on his desk transferred the gesture to his Valkyrie, grabbing the metal handle that ran along the length of the mule. Tighe undocked his robot from its charger and lifted the Valkyrie's feet onto the running board, clipping its tether into an eyebolt on the mule's hull. "I'm clipped in, Han."

"Maneuvering . . ." The view shifted as the mule's thrusters popped. Jin navigated to dock with the folded magnetic rake, locked down, and then pulled the tool free from its storage clamps.

Jin's voice came over the radio. *"Mule 1 ready to deploy rake."*

Clarke's voice replied. *"Roger that. Jin, I've marked the coordinates of Dust Pond 3 on your display."*

"I am maneuvering . . ."

The mule's thrusters popped once more, and Tighe's view turned toward the black shadow of the asteroid. The surface was 3 kilometers away on his readout. The mule thrust straight toward it, getting clear of the *Konstantin*'s rotating radial arms, the ends of which held blinking navigation lights. The three habs silently swept past at 124 kilometers per hour.

Tighe watched the dark wall of the asteroid approach. "This is pretty intense, Dave. You sure you don't want to spectate?"

Across the desk an unseen Morra said, "Already am."

Jin kicked on the mule's bottom lamps and rotated Mule 1 so the rake faced Ryugu. It now seemed like they were descending to the asteroid's surface, rather than gliding toward an immense wall.

As they got closer the mule's lights began to illuminate a level, irregularly shaped area of regolith no bigger than a wading pool. It was bordered by low ridges of ashen rock.

Jin's voice: "*Mule 1 on station.*"

After a brief pause, Clarke said, "*Deploy the rake and proceed, Mule 1.*"

Tighe lowered his real-world chin to have the Valkyrie look down at its feet. Below the mule the wire grid of the magnetic rake unfolded out to a 5-meter square.

"*Rake deployed. Electromagnets . . . powered on.*" The thrusters popped to gently lower the mule toward the asteroid. "*Descending to Dust Pond 3.*"

"Keep the mule above the regolith, Han. Mission control says Ryugu's dark side has a significant electrical charge."

"*I copy.*"

Tighe watched the approaching surface of the asteroid through the grid of magnetized wire. Illuminated by the mule's work lights, the dust looked impossibly fine. "If that's got iron in it, it should be easy to collect with a magnet."

As the magnetic rake descended, particles suddenly coalesced along the lines of the magnetic field, making the dust almost seem alive. It swarmed around the wire grid and extended ferrous tendrils toward the mule's running board.

"Look at that."

Jin's voice: "*I'm getting pulled in.*"

Morra's voice: "Heads up."

A blue bolt of electricity arced along the rake, and suddenly Tighe's Valkyrie link went dead. His crystal went transparent again, and he and Morra stared at each other in the workstation.

Tighe keyed his mic. "Nicole, V-2 is down. Just lost my connection." He opened Mule 1's video feed, which skipped with signal interference but was still online.

Jin said, "*The rake dragged the mule down into the regolith.*"

Clarke answered. "*Pop thrusters. Get the mule out of there.*"

As the mule's downward thrusters fired, the entire screen filled with blinding dust. Then the link to the mule was gone.

Jin's voice: "*Lost mule signal.*"

"You have got to be shitting me. . . ."

But then it came back.

"*Wait. I'm back up.*"

Morra shook his head and groaned. "Oh, man. What are we doing . . . ?" He tapped at a virtual UI and brought up a distant CCTV image of the mule as seen from the *Konstantin.* "Jin, I think you should return to the ship." He rewound the video and tapped "Play." "Nicole, watch my video layer. . . ."

Tighe and Morra watched the recording as the distant mule's work lights momentarily became obscured by a cloud of dust as its thrusters blasted downward. By the time the craft rose above the cloud, the rake was empty.

Morra spoke over the comm link. "Nicole, the rake is useless. When we turn on the electromagnet it pulls us in, and when we pop thrusters it creates a metallic cloud that acts like a Faraday cage—and also blasts the rake clean. It needs a redesign."

Clarke replied, *"How long do you need?"*

"I'll sort that out with Ade." Morra closed the video window. "In the meantime, we could use the Archimedes' screw to pull up a regolith sample. That should hold enough for an assay."

"But would the screw cut into rock?"

Adisa answered instead. *"Hayabusa2 data shows rock density to be low— 1.5 grams per cubic centimeter. You could crumble it in your hands."*

Morra nodded. "Right. So we drill a core sample from a boulder. Bring it back to the refinery and cook it. The sooner we get a sample, the sooner we know whether this entire expedition is possible. The clock's ticking."

They all glanced at the countdown, hovering at the edge of their vision.

After a few moments Clarke said, *"All right. Let's do it."*

Two hours later Tighe and Morra again sat at their workstations watching a shared holographic display of Mule 1 hovering above a boulder on Ryugu's surface. Except this time the mule had a different tool attached to its lower docking port. The Archimedes' screw consisted of a polymer tube, 20 centimeters in diameter, inside of which was an aluminum auger, the sharp point of which jutted out like a corkscrew.

The mule's work lights illuminated a massive boulder rising tens of meters above the surrounding terrain—high enough that the surface was mostly lost in shadow.

Jin's voice came in over the comm link. *"Twenty meters."*

The ashen, irregular surface of the boulder came into view.

Clarke said, "*Aim for the highest elevation, Han.*"

"*Maneuvering . . .*"

The mule popped thrusters as Jin piloted the vehicle in, guiding the auger tip. Thrusters fired course corrections occasionally. Finally, the auger touched down with the full mass of the mule behind it, penetrating the surface.

"*Activating auger . . .*"

The blade bit into the ashen rock and started sinking from sight. Ryugu's rock appeared to be as porous as anticipated.

Jin's voice came in. "*We are getting regolith in the sleeve.*"

Tighe and the others applauded. He and Morra high-fived across the workstation.

The auger began to sink deeper into the rock.

Tighe watched the hologram. "Why don't we just keep doing this?"

Morra studied the image. "Burning 20 kilos of thruster gas to get 50 kilos of regolith isn't exactly efficient."

They watched for another minute or so until Clarke announced, "*Jin, that should be plenty. Bring the core sample back to the bottom airlock and offload it into Pressure Vessel 1. Amy?*"

Tsukada's voice came over the comm link. "*Here, Nicole.*"

"*Work with Jin to make sure the sample gets into your refinery. Tell me when you're ready to begin the assay. I want every step on video for mission control.*"

By early afternoon Tighe, Abarca, and Morra sat around the galley table as Clarke arranged virtual video windows to reveal every corner of the *Konstantin*'s refinery.

The refinery was located in the aft section of the ship, just forward of the engine room. Surveillance cameras showed branching groups of color-coded piping and conduits running in and out of a central chamber. Neither the refinery nor the engine room of the *Konstantin* was pressurized, to limit the risk of fire.

Like all of the crew, Tighe had been trained to process asteroid regolith—but up until now it was theoretical, only having been done with asteroid simulant back on Earth.

Clarke spoke over the comm link. "Amy, Gabriel tells me that Nathan

Joyce is watching. So I want you to bring us through each step of the refining process. Understood?"

Tsukada replied, "*Understood, Nicole. Stand by.*"

A virtual window expanded, providing a view into what looked like an industrial clothes dryer with metal fins set into the walls. The chamber was filled with a cloud of floating ash.

Tsukada said, "*Assay 1, Ryugu, January 31, 2034, 1321 hours UTC. Initial sample mass: 87.32 kilos. Note that the regolith sample has been pulverized to increase surface area for chemical reactions.*" She was silent for several moments. "*Spectrometer readings confirm composition consistent with carbonaceous chondrite—which is what Catalyst mission planners were expecting.*"

Tighe, Morra, and Abarca applauded.

Clarke's voice broke in. "I'm sure they'll be happy to hear that, Amy."

A reddish glow appeared in the interior of the pressure vessel.

"*Heating sample to 500 degrees Celsius. This will cause the hydrates to release their volatiles—that is, chemical compounds with low boiling points.*"

Tighe and the others watched a mist forming amid the dust.

"*What you see being released here is mostly water vapor.*"

Again the crew applauded and hooted.

"*However, this vapor also contains impurities—ammonia, carbon monoxide, nitrogen, methane, hydrogen cyanide, hydrogen sulfide. We'll need to filter these out using in situ chemical oxidation—fortunately I should be able to synthesize the hydrogen peroxide and potassium permanganate necessary for that from Ryugu's regolith.*"

After several minutes the pressure vessel cooled, then spun like a washing machine, flattening the material into a blur against the circular wall.

"*The volatiles will be condensed into a liquid and piped to storage for later purification.*"

The pressure vessel stopped spinning, and soon the powder began to float again.

"*At this point we begin a process called 'beneficiation'—which simply means concentrating the mineral content in the ore. This will also extract the more stubborn volatiles. I begin by pressurizing the vessel with pure hydrogen . . .*"

The particles in the vessel swirled around violently.

"... *and cranking up the heat to 800 degrees Celsius."*

The powder in the vessel began to swirl once more.

"The final volatiles extracted here include hydrogen, carbon dioxide, sulfur, nitrogen, hydrocarbons, chlorine, sulfuric acid, hydrochloric acid—but also amino acids; organic compounds that will prove useful. I'm removing all of these for later filtration as well."

By now the pressure vessel on-screen was an orange, swirling cloud of gas and particles. Tsukada left it that way for several minutes, and then the heat dropped as the vessel again spun rapidly—extracting the gas mixture through centrifugal force. When the walls stopped spinning, much less material remained and some of the particles now had a metallic sheen.

"The regolith mass is now 42.13 kilos—about half what we started with. We performed the heating in an atmosphere of hydrogen to allow the organic molecules to react with magnetite in the ore. This released two very useful gases—carbon monoxide and carbon dioxide—but notice that it also produced what's called 'free metal,' the concentrated iron you see glittering in the powder."

Tighe studied the screen. The material in the vessel was far different from the gray asteroid dust with which they began.

"What we have now is an involatile residue—about one-third iron-nickel-cobalt alloy, which we need to purify still further through an acid leach. . . ."

On-screen, globules of liquid were injected into the vessel; they immediately reacted with the powder, bubbling violently. The heat rose again to several hundred degrees Celsius as the vessel began to spin, flattening the powder against the walls while the reaction accelerated.

"We can use acids obtained from earlier steps in the refining process to make this process sustainable long term. The reactions you're seeing are extracting phosphorous, sodium, potassium, calcium, and magnesium, all of which we can use."

The reaction continued on-screen until the vessel began to fill with smoke.

"White fumes indicate the process is nearing completion, and we again filter and store these compounds for later purification."

After a while the vessel stopped rotating.

"All that remains now of the original regolith is powdered ferrous metals and silicates. We could melt this down, but an iron-smelting furnace is a bad

idea on a spaceship. Plus, smelting requires a large amount of energy. Fortunately, there's another way...."

The temperature in the vessel now plunged to 100 degrees Celsius.

"Gaseous carbonyl extraction involves transforming metal into a gas."

On-screen, the powder began to swirl again, and pressure in the vessel increased to 2 atmospheres.

"Our ore sample contains three key metals—iron, nickel, and cobalt—all bound to each other. However, when we introduce carbon monoxide into our chamber under precise pressure and temperature, the metals within the ore begin to transform. Nickel reacts first, combining with four carbon monoxide molecules to form nickel tetracarbonyl, a highly toxic gas."

The pressure in the vessel slowly increased.

"As the temperature and pressure increase, the iron in the ore reacts next, combining with five carbon monoxide molecules to become iron pentacarbonyl, another impressively toxic gas."

The temperature in the vessel increased still further to 200 degrees and the pressure to 10 atmospheres.

"And now the cobalt combines with eight carbon monoxide molecules to become gaseous dicobalt octacarbonyl, yet another toxic gas."

The vessel then spun fast, extracting the carbonyl gases from the chamber, and after a minute or so the spin cycle slowed and stopped. Now all that was left floating in the chamber was sandy powder, less than a quarter of the original regolith sample.

"Leaving us with a harmless silicate residue. We can pack this into containers as radiation shielding. However, in coming years, we may be able to economically extract small quantities of platinum-group metals or synthesize silicon, glass, or other useful compounds from it."

The chamber flushed with air, blowing the sandy powder down a pipe. The entire chamber was now empty.

"At room temperature and pressure, nickel and iron carbonyls condense into liquids, allowing us to pipe them around the refinery or store them without the need to keep metal in a molten state. Cobalt carbonyl becomes a powder at room temperature but returns to gaseous form at 52 degrees Celsius, meaning it, too, can be easily piped around the refinery. Transforming them back into solid metal is also not difficult."

The video window now showed a surveillance-camera view of Tsukada standing in her lab.

"In short: Ryugu's regolith is everything we hoped it would be. Now you just need to prove you can get me thousands of tons of it—without killing yourselves or destroying the ship."

CHAPTER 28

Inertia

S itting around the galley table in Hab 1, Tighe, Morra, and Clarke stared at a holographic scan of a section of Ryugu's surface. A large boulder was highlighted in red as the image rotated to reveal its dimensions.

Chindarkar's voice came in over the comm link. *"Muon tomography scanning shows Boulder 4 as the most promising pull candidate."*

Boulder 4, 6 meters in diameter, was egg-shaped, and only a quarter of it was sunken into the asteroid's surface. The rock looked solid, and its chemical composition was straight out of the *Konstantin* mission plan.

Clarke stared at the image. "Estimated mass . . . 214 tons. Just about perfect."

Tighe leaned in next to her. "In Ryugu's gravity that's about 30 kilos."

Morra grimaced. "Too bad about inertia."

There was a pause as Clarke opened the laser comm channel. "Mission control, we've selected Boulder 4 and are ready to move it to a terminator orbit. Please advise."

What followed was a half-hour transmission-delayed discussion with mission control managers, engineers, and geologists. Eventually Clarke got a green light to pull Boulder 4 from Ryugu's surface.

Chindarkar activated one of the ship's two ARS robots after uploading the mission profile into its job queue. The 2-ton robot was shaped like a hexagonal cylinder with twin solar panels resembling mouse ears. It undocked from its perch near the upper airlock and activated thrusters that sent it toward Ryugu's surface.

As the ARS descended, it unfolded long robotic legs at its front. The legs consisted of interlocking aluminum-frame triangles whose angles to one another were adjusted by linear actuators, enabling them to "curl" like the fingers of a claw in an arcade game—but also to push off a surface. At the moment these legs were bowed out for landing, their base plates extended for impact. On-screen it was hard to tell that this spindly robot was 15 meters tall.

A nearby mule remotely piloted by Chindarkar illuminated the target boulder with work lights as the ARS touched down like a three-legged spider standing around and over Boulder 4. A small amount of dust kicked up as the legs of the ARS flexed to absorb the 1-meter-per-second impact without rebounding back into space.

"ARS 1 has landed over Boulder 4."

They watched monitors as ARS 1's scanners made a 3D model of the boulder beneath it, and then a pair of smaller, tool-equipped arms descended from its belly. These began to drill into the rock in several places at opposing angles.

The robot's onboard cameras offered a close-up of the process. After several minutes drilling a dozen holes, bolt-studded clamps descended into them and held Boulder 4 fast.

"Boulder 4 secured. ARS 1 preparing to push off the surface."

ARS 1's legs started bowing outward as the linear actuators tightened, lowering the craft in preparation for its vault away from Ryugu. This design used leverage instead of rocket fuel to move the boulder—which was important when that boulder was two-thirds the mass of the entire Konstantin.

"ARS 1 standing by."

They had to wait another two and a half hours until Ryugu's rotation brought the site into sunlight. Once dawn crested on Boulder 4, Clarke gave the order.

Adisa activated the robot. "ARS 1 pushing from surface."

Suddenly the spacecraft's tall legs flexed upward—but instead of pushing off Ryugu's surface, one of the legs thrust through the regolith, sinking meters deep. This caused the ARS to topple as the other two legs pushed—causing the boulder to roll and partly trapping the robot. Regolith kicked up in a huge dust cloud.

Tighe and Morra winced.

Clarke rubbed her face. "Goddamnit!" A long pause. "Dave. J.T." She looked up. "I need you guys to go down there and unfuck that equipment."

Morra gave a thumbs-up to Tighe as he answered. "We'll need a couple hours for the prebreathe. The dust should have settled by then. You want to send the other ARS out to try a different boulder in the meantime?"

"Negative. We'll hold that in reserve."

Morra nodded. "Ade, what's the weather report?"

Adisa answered, *"No solar flares predicted."*

Clarke frowned. "Belay that. Let's play it safe and wait. By 1400 hours, Boulder 4 will be back at the terminator line, and you'll have another three and a half hours of darkness to work the problem before it rolls into sunlight again."

"All right. We'll come up with a plan in the meantime."

Clarke added, "Han, I want you prebreathed and in the upper airlock when they go out—ready to provide rescue if necessary."

Jin replied, *"I'll be ready."*

An hour later Tighe, Morra, and Jin floated in the upper airlock, examining live imagery of the Boulder 4 site. The ARS was toppled onto the surface with both its free legs and its rocket motor pointed the wrong way.

Tighe looked to Morra. "Well, Royal Engineer, what's the plan?"

Morra studied the scene.

Jin pointed. "It is only the one leg that is caught. We could dig it out. The regolith is not dense."

"I want to stay clear of that regolith if at all possible. It can have up to a two-hundred-volt charge on the nightside."

Tighe suggested, "How about winching ARS 1 to the side—from another rock?"

Morra pondered this. "It could do more damage." He thought for a moment. "What if we detach the trapped leg? Then the ARS is just a couple tons to pull away from the boulder in microgravity. We could use a mule for that."

Jin added, "Then we bring in the second ARS to pull Boulder 4."

"We should bolt panels to the feet—like snowshoes. To keep it from sinking during the pull."

With a half hour remaining until Boulder 4 rotated around to them again, Tighe and Morra slipped through the hatches of their clam suits, pressurized, and then undocked from the *Konstantin.*

Once outside the ship, they grabbed the handles of a mule utility craft remotely piloted by Chindarkar.

Tighe and Morra placed tools and spare gas canisters onto the equipment rack atop the mule, strapping them down with polymer cord. Then they clipped their tethers to eyebolts on the mule before climbing onto the running board.

Tighe rapped on the hull of the mule to indicate they were ready—and it made no noise whatsoever. Neither was Chindarkar actually inside. He rolled his eyes at the mistake and spoke over the radio. "We're ready, Priya."

"Next stop, Boulder 4. Mind the gap. . . ."

Thrusters sent the mule heading toward the dark surface of Ryugu.

Tighe noticed the return countdown timer in his crystal display. He looked across the top of the mule at Morra. "Thirty-six hours gone so far."

Morra drummed his gloved fingers impatiently on the hull of the mule. *"Plenty of time left before the return window closes."*

Clarke's voice came in over the comm link. *"Dave, J.T., I don't need to say this, but be careful down there."*

Tighe answered, "Aye, aye, Captain."

Suddenly a pressure alarm appeared in Tighe's crystal display. It was for the *Konstantin*'s upper airlock.

Tighe glanced back at the *Konstantin*.

Adisa's voice came through. *"Han, can you confirm a fault in the upper airlock?"*

Jin answered, *"Stand by."*

Several more pressure alarms activated in the upper transit tunnel. It was starting to resemble an expanding ship depressurization.

Tighe looked to Morra. "That's crossing two airlocks. Hull failure?"

Morra shook his head in disbelief.

Adisa's voice: *"Air quality still looks fine. This doesn't make sense."*

"Great." Tighe muted the alarms. "Tell us when you sort it out. We're going to need that airlock to get back into the ship."

"Wilco."

Chindarkar brought the mule down to 15 meters above Ryugu's surface, floating over the toppled ARS. In microgravity the asteroid seemed to be straight ahead of them—like a cliff face.

Tighe knew that mission control back on Earth would be watching their transmission-delayed video feed—that Joyce himself was probably watching. He tried not to sense their eyes on him and instead concentrated on the job.

Morra said, *"Priya, turn on the work lights, please."*

The mule's forward lights kicked on, illuminating the entire scene.

Tighe grabbed tools from the cargo rack and clicked them into his chest harness.

Morra activated the mule's forward winch, paying out cable.

Tighe checked the distance to the surface with his helmet's laser range finder. "Sixteen meters."

"Thanks." Morra clicked the winch line's carabiner onto his utility belt. *"Whenever you're ready, mate."*

Tighe clipped in to Morra's harness, linking the two of them. "Let's do it."

"Remember: the regolith has an electrical charge. Stay clear of it, or you might short out your suit."

"Can that really happen?"

"Who knows? But let's not find out."

Morra gripped Tighe's gloved hand as Morra fired his clam suit's SAFER unit. Cold-gas thrusters brought both of them the short distance across the gap to the toppled ARS and the wall-like surface of Ryugu.

As Tighe bumped into the aluminum hull of the ARS, he reached for one of several maintenance handles built into its side—but missed. The EVA space suit was nowhere near as flexible as his flight suit, and he bounced off, slowly floating back into space.

"A little help . . ."

Morra grabbed a handle and reeled Tighe in by his tether. *"I guess I'm the first human on Ryugu."*

Tighe laughed. "Shit, I guess you are." He spoke into the comm link. "Ade, you writing that down?"

Clarke's voice replied instead. *"Please concentrate—the both of you."*

Morra unclipped the winch line from himself and clipped its carabiner onto an eyebolt on the toppled ARS. He gestured to the mule's camera. *"Priya, carefully take up the slack on this cable."*

They both moved aside and clipped their tethers to the ARS. Tighe then moved hand over hand along the hull of the ARS until he reached the base of the leg trapped under Boulder 4. This close, the boulder was the size of a small house and the robot not much smaller.

"Wait a sec." Tighe held up his gloved hand. It was somehow coated with fine black iron filings. They stuck to him like magnets. "Christ, I barely brushed the surface of the boulder and got my whole glove coated."

"Any electrical shock?"

"No. I guess the suit's a poor conductor." Tighe examined his glove closely under the helmet-mounted work lights. The regolith consisted of prickly splinters. It was almost impossible to believe these mineral hydrates contained water. They looked the opposite of life-giving—more like a magnified virus. His helmet-mounted camera, he knew, would be relaying the image back to the ship. "This is some evil-looking shit. I don't want to get buried to my waist in this. The suit would probably get compromised pretty quickly."

Morra said, *"Ade, just for the record books: J.T.'s now the first human being to touch an asteroid."*

Tighe stopped and was surprised this hadn't occurred to him. He turned and smiled at Morra. "Hey, Ade, we should write these on the hab wall."

Clarke's voice came through. *"There are going to be a lot of firsts on this expedition. Let's try to focus on the job, please."*

"Right . . ." Tighe pulled a can of compressed CO_2 from his harness. The crew had taken to calling these "cans of delta-v." He aimed it away from him and Morra and sprayed CO_2 to clear the regolith off his glove. The black cloud whirled away into the distance. He grabbed the ARS again and stowed the can.

Tighe brought up an AR display of the ARS's tech schematic in his crystal. The virtual animation glowed comfortingly in the darkness next to him, demonstrating the steps of his task superimposed over the real machine. He followed the procedures to power down the ARS's system, then detached the electrical and data lines from the huge machine's trapped limb. Several times he had to spray CO_2 to clear away encroaching, electrically charged regolith. "Ryugu keeps trying to eat me."

Removing the power and data links took more than an hour. Once he got the power lines removed, he started loosening the superstructure bolts with a meter-long socket wrench, which was exhausting and took another half hour.

Clarke's voice came in over the comm link. *"We chased down those airlock alarms. Ghost alerts. I reset the panel, and they went away."*

Tighe struggled with a bolt. "So the upper airlock's operational?"

"*Affirmative.*"

Chindarkar's voice came in over the comm link. "*One hour until the terminator comes around again.*"

"That sounds ominous." He looked up at Morra. "You ever see those movies?"

"*What,* The Terminator?"

"Yeah." Tighe reached down to turn a loosened bolt.

"*I'm not really into sci-fi.*"

Tighe laughed. "You hear that, Priya? He's not into sci-fi."

Tighe placed the last bolt in a cinch bag on his belt. He then turned around and held on to one of the ARS's maintenance handles as he began to kick the frame at the base of the huge robot's trapped leg.

Morra came over and joined him, and they both started stomping on it while holding tight to the ARS's body.

Chindarkar's laughter came in over the comm link. "*You look like a couple of astronauts beating the shit out of a robot.*"

Tighe went with it. "You pay . . . on the first of the month . . . like everybody else!" He kept kicking.

The leg finally slipped loose from its mounts.

"There we go."

After they'd climbed back aboard the mule, Chindarkar popped thrusters to pull the now two-legged ARS robot away from the surface, scattering a modest amount of regolith behind it.

Tighe and Morra turned to see the second ARS unit coming in.

Clarke's voice came over the comm link. "*Dave, J.T., good job. Return to the ship.*"

"Copy that."

As Chindarkar piloted the mule back to the *Konstantin*, Tighe and Morra took in the impressive view of their ship, silhouetted against the question-mark-shaped red nebula of Barnard's Loop and the diagonal sprawl of stars that was the Milky Way.

Tighe couldn't help but laugh.

"*What's so funny?*"

"When Nathan pitched this job to me, he said it came with one hell of a view." Tighe stared forward. "He undersold it."

After catching some shut-eye, Tighe and Morra were back at their cubicle workstations at four a.m. Earth UTC to join the others watching the second ARS attempt to pull Boulder 4 from Ryugu's surface. Mission control managers stood by on transmission delay.

As the first rays of sunlight touched the ARS's mouse-ear solar panels, the robotic legs tensioned—and then the huge machine sprang away from the surface.

The crew broke out in applause as the ARS, clutching Boulder 4, rose into the sunlight, 100, then 200 meters above Ryugu's surface.

"I'll be damned, that Rube Goldberg contraption actually worked."

The ARS still rose, its main legs slowly curling around the boulder. At 400 meters' altitude the ARS began slowly tumbling. The sheer mass of its cargo overpowered the intermittent puffs from attitude control thrusters.

"Aww, fuck's sake . . ." Morra lowered his head onto his desk.

Adisa's tense voice came in over comms. *"We've got a 200-ton boulder tumbling out of control. It could collide with us."*

Clarke spoke over the comm line. *"Ade, we need to arrest Boulder 4's tumble immediately."*

"The software seems to be miscalculating."

On-screen the ARS's thrusters were still stabbing in various directions trying to stabilize the craft.

Chindarkar's voice cut in. *"Nicole, if the ARS runs out of thruster gas before that boulder stops tumbling, we'll lose the robot, too."*

In the virtual display before them, cameras on the *Konstantin* zoomed in to track the ARS in orbit. Its thrusters fired plumes of gas frantically.

Clarke sighed. *"Why the hell is it making it worse?"*

Adisa's voice: *"I suspect it is trying to calculate the boulder's precise center of gravity."*

Chindarkar's voice: *"Thruster gas at 23 percent."*

On-screen the ARS and its boulder shifted erratically. However, after a couple of minutes it began to slow its tumble, and finally, with a few last thruster blasts, it stabilized.

Morra slumped.

The ARS was finally able to place Boulder 4 in a terminator orbit 5 kilometers from Ryugu. It then released its legs and managed to get within a few meters of the ship's robot dock before its cold-gas thrusters were exhausted. It took hours of EVA work for Tighe, Morra, and Jin to nudge the two ARS robots back into their docking ports—one robot still missing a leg.

With Boulder 4 now in position in orbit around Ryugu, mission control cleared the crew to deploy one of the four Honey Bee optical mining robots to bag the rock.

The Honey Bee was not a small robot, with twin sunlight-focusing thin film parabolic reflectors—each 15 meters across—a central propulsion module, and resource containment bags spanning 5 meters in the center.

With a 3D model of the boulder programmed into the Honey Bee, it automatically cinched its containment bag open, fired thrusters to bag the rock, and cinched the bag closed again.

After high-fives among the miners, a series of glitches plagued the start of the optical mining process. There were freeze-ups with the centrifugal sorter, hiccups with the software that mission control had to patch and upload.

Finally, they partially pressurized the boulder containment bag with CO_2 so that blowers would be able to direct the volatiles and other materials into the centrifugal sorting unit.

By the time they'd gotten everything set up, Jin, Tighe, and Morra had spent nearly seventy-two hours on space walks, leaving just three days before their return window to Earth closed.

The countdown in their visor display weighed heavily on them all, and Lacroix gave Abarca approval to issue the crew what Tighe could only assume were amphetamines to keep them working around the clock as the deadline approached.

Eighteen hours later, when the revised software finally rotated the Honey Bee's optical mining lenses toward the Sun's light, a white flash guttered from within the containment bag, and searing heat spalled the boulder's surface in millimeter-deep blasts. It was the first time the machines had ever been used in deep space.

Tighe, Morra, and Jin clung to their mules half a kilometer away as they waited in fatigue for the readings to come back from the mining rig.

It was several minutes until they heard Clarke's voice.

"*The Honey Bee is harvesting large volumes of water vapor, ammonia, and nitrogen!*" Cheers were audible in the background back on the ship. "*This is gonna work.*"

Tighe, Morra, and Jin exchanged weary smiles.

Tighe said, "We did it."

Morra nodded. "*So it appears.*"

Clarke's voice again. "*Dave, Jin, J.T., return to the ship. You'll need to get some rest for what comes next.*"

"What comes next?"

"*We have an important decision to make.*"

CHAPTER 29

Go, No-Go

For the first time humans had harvested—in fact, *were still* harvesting—life-giving resources from a celestial object. Tighe knew this moment was historic. Now that they'd proven asteroid mining viable, the plan was for Catalyst Corporation to publicly announce their expedition to the entire world. Tighe wondered how that would change his life and the lives of his crewmates.

In the meantime, the entire exhausted crew of the *Konstantin*, along with mission control managers on Earth, hugged one another in joy. Gabriel Lacroix remotely unlocked one of the reward lockers in both habs to reveal a bottle of actual French champagne. Clarke opened Hab 1's bottle, and they cheered as the cork ricocheted off the carbon fiber ceiling tiles. Tighe had become so space-focused that he reflexively estimated the delta-v of the champagne cork.

Cups were poured, and Clarke raised her glass for a toast. "To the first of many firsts."

"Hear! Hear!"

Suddenly a familiar—and very relieved-looking—face appeared on the video-conference screen. Nathan Joyce looked tired and unshaven—but all smiles. After a transmission delay he said, "I won't deny that up until now I was trying hard not to think about what would happen if I was wrong."

The crew and mission control team laughed—although the delay made interaction with their boss slightly awkward.

Joyce waited before he said, "What you have achieved is monumental. It will change everything." Joyce then raised his own glass of champagne. "To the crew of the *Konstantin*. The greatest explorers who ever lived."

Mission controllers raised their glasses.

The crew bumped plastic cups again.

After they finished the champagne and cleared their respective galley tables—Clarke, Tighe, Morra, and Abarca in Hab 1; Jin, Chindarkar, Tsukada, and Adisa in Hab 2—both groups placed a clear plastic pitcher of cold water on the table in front of them.

Asteroid water—harvested the previous day and purified through Tsukada's refinery. She had tested the water in her lab overnight and found it potable. Trying it—yet another first for humanity—Tsukada decided it even had a pleasant taste.

Clarke lifted the pitcher and poured a cup of water for each of her crewmates. In Hab 2, Adisa did the same.

Lacroix, mission managers, and Joyce observed the proceedings via videoconferencing windows.

Clarke looked to the crew. "The purpose of this meeting is to arrive at a go, no-go decision for this expedition." She gestured to the countdown timer that every crew member had in his or her own crystal display. "In twenty-five hours and twelve minutes we will lack the delta-v necessary to return to Earth until February 10, 2038—over four years from now."

Several crew members took a deep breath upon hearing it said out loud.

Clarke looked up at Lacroix and Joyce. "Witnessing this discussion, we have mission control manager Gabriel Lacroix, Catalyst CEO Nathan Joyce, and Catalyst Corporation legal counsel. They are also recording this meeting for posterity."

Morra looked to the virtual screens. "The decision is ours, not theirs."

Clarke nodded. "You're right, David . . ." She muted the Earth feed so mission control could hear the crew but would be unable to speak. "Per our employment contract, the decision to stay or to leave is ours to make. Not theirs." She studied the faces of her team. "Do we remain at Ryugu for the next four years and prove the long-term viability of commercial asteroid mining, or do we return to Earth before the transfer window closes? That's the question— and any decision to stay must be unanimous."

Tighe looked up at Joyce and Lacroix, who were not yet aware they would be muted a hundred seconds from now. He turned back to Clarke. "I wasn't aware it had to be unanimous."

"Did you really not read your contract, J.T.? In compliance with the Universal Declaration of Human Rights, no one can be held here against their will."

Chindarkar spoke from Hab 2. *"So one vote against and we leave?"*

Clarke nodded. "That's the only way this is going to work. We all have to agree that we're staying—because every one of us will be needed to make sure we succeed."

Morra examined his half-full cup of water. "Mr. Joyce up on the wall there spent twenty-four billion dollars getting us here, but I don't give a damn about that." He held up the water. "Look at this. It means Earth isn't the only place humans can be. Right here is a future for my children's children. We've been here nine days. Think what we can do in four years." Morra looked over at Tsukada. "Does Ryugu give us everything else we need to survive?"

Tsukada considered the question. *"Water, nitrogen, ammonia—we can provide fertility to plants. Restore atmospheric pressure for the N_2 lost in the habs. We can restore losses from CO_2 scrubbing and electrolysis. We can make methalox rocket fuel, manufacture metal parts, create polymer plastics, radiation shielding. And we have construction materials—millions of tons."* She nodded. *"Yes, everything we need."*

Morra nodded to himself. "Plus our production bonuses—based on the sale price of whatever we produce over the next four years. A few thousand tons of resources at the top of Earth's gravity well would be worth a fortune. Are we really going to just turn around and fly away from that? Joyce is right; we could jump-start an entire new economy in space, and we'd all be worth a hundred million when we return."

Clarke looked around the table. "I want to make certain everyone is heard before we vote on this."

Tighe sat up. "Is the vote final?"

"No. We keep voting until—"

Chindarkar interjected, *"Until what? Until you get the outcome you want?"*

"It's like a jury, Priya. We keep trying to come to a unanimous decision."

"A decision for, you mean."

Abarca leaned forward. "Priya—do you not want us to stay?"

There were several seconds of silence as Chindarkar stared at the table.

Morra looked stunned. "You're takin' the piss . . ."

Clarke frowned at him. "Keep it professional, Dave."

Chindarkar said, *"I haven't made a decision either way."*

Tsukada stared. *"Priya, seriously?"*

Everyone started talking at once, and Clarke waved everyone to silence again.

Jin interjected, *"I am not certain about staying either."*

The other six groaned and threw up their hands. Tighe actually pushed away from the table for a moment to pace nearby. He narrowed his eyes at Jin. "This better not be about your 'duty' to—"

"What would you know about duty?"

The others howled.

Clarke waved everyone to silence again. "Han, help me understand. What do you mean, you haven't decided?"

Jin sighed. *"Getting rich is not why I came here. I came to prove that this was possible. And we have done that."*

"Oh, you got what you wanted, so everyone else can fuck right off, is that it?"

Clarke called out, "David."

Morra leaned in but spoke more calmly. "Not everyone thinks money's evil, mate. Joyce is right; it's financial opportunity for investors that will open up space—not another Apollo landing. And there's nothing wrong with me wanting to leave behind something for my girls. You think I came all this way just so I could cruise down King's Road in a Lambo?"

"How do you know we will be able to keep what we earn?" Jin turned to Clarke. *"You speak of human rights law, but I have been thinking about all the laws Nathan broke in sending us here. Do you really think we can just do as we wish without consequences?"*

Tighe sat back down. "You knew this before we left. Returning now accomplishes what, exactly? What does it fix, Han?"

Tsukada glared. *"As if governments follow laws."*

Chindarkar said flatly, *"We're all going to die if we stay here."*

Everyone turned to face her. There was sudden silence.

Chindarkar continued. *"I just thought most of you felt like I did. That we'd give this a try, achieve some firsts, and then . . . go back to Earth."*

Morra looked closely at her. "Bollocks."

Tsukada said, *"Screw Earth."*

Abarca asked, "What's going on, Priya?"

Chindarkar stared at the tabletop. "*I found a golf-ball-sized hole on an EHD cooler enclosure last week—outside the upper airlock. Spotted it with a mule. Whatever hit the enclosure struck with enough velocity that the metal wasn't even deformed—it was just a hole, clean through the panel. In one side, out the other. No alarms went off either. If it had hit a structural support or a fuel tank or a piece of critical equipment, we'd all be dead.*"

She looked up at the images of Joyce, Lacroix, and now mission management psychologists on the virtual screens trying to get the crew's attention with their mics muted—holding up written signs demanding attention.

"*Look at them. They have almost no idea what they're doing.*" She turned back to the crew. "*We're getting critical alarms constantly. I can feel the hab shake—literally shake—when people hop onto the deck above me. The Konstantin is about as solid as a tent.*" Chindarkar took a deep breath to steady herself. "*We're going to die if we don't take this one last chance to get back to Earth. We've already made history. Isn't that enough?*"

Morra said, "No. It isn't."

"*We'll be famous when we get back to Earth. You can make—*"

Tsukada shouted, "*How does that solve my problem?*"

Clarke once more held up her hands for silence. "Why didn't you report that meteor strike, Priya?"

"*What difference would it make? It didn't hit anything critical. I didn't want to freak everyone out, but the more I've thought about it, the more it's freaking me out.*"

"That's why you report it."

"*Why, so the shrinks can tell me to meditate—or pop an anxiety pill? That enclosure was supposed to be shielding, Nicole. It might as well have been tissue paper. I did the math. Something hit us going at least 40,000 kilometers an hour.*"

Adisa shrugged. "*I would say we were lucky.*"

"*We've been out here for two months, Ade! What do you think is going to happen over the next fifty months? What if we encounter a micrometeor storm? And what about cosmic radiation?*"

"*We are harvesting water.*" Adisa gestured to the walls. "*We can fill the bladder tanks to shield us.*"

Jin stared hard across the table at Chindarkar. "Fear *is not a valid reason to return to Earth.*"

"*Oh, and your reason is—because we broke the law? Han, if I always obeyed authority, I would have been disposed of in some arranged marriage.*"

"You took up a spot on this expedition." Abarca looked to Chindarkar. "Priya, remember that day out on the cliff back at Ascension Island?"

"*Of course.*"

"You didn't panic on that rock face—although you were facing death then, too."

Chindarkar stared into the memory. "*That was different.*"

"How was it different?"

Chindarkar looked up. "*I was in control on that cliff. Here we can be snuffed out any second. It's only a matter of time. There could be a supernova, or a—*"

"It's the same back on Earth, Priya. And I have news for you: it's the same everywhere. You could get cancer, you could die in a tsunami or an earthquake. You could get struck by a car. We just accept this is a risk, and we get on with it. You've had too much time to obsess over this meteor strike, and Nicole's right; you should have shared the information so we could help give you some perspective. We're all in this situation together, and as far as I can see, you're the only one who's panicking."

Chindarkar stared at the table again.

"I've seen this happen to the bravest climbers I know. When you start to obsess, start to believe you can control for everything—that's when the fear strikes."

Chindarkar said nothing.

"Let me spoil the ending for you, Priya: you're going to die."

Everyone around the table looked up in surprise at this tack.

"I'm going to die, too. So is J.T. So is Nicole . . . So is everyone at this table and everyone on Earth. But strangely, we're not panicked about *that*. It's a given. You want control? Living your life to the fullest is the *only* thing you can control, and I don't think you'll find a better chance to do that than here."

The crew sat in silent contemplation for several minutes.

Eventually Tighe poured himself another cup of water. He swirled it around and studied the bubbles forming, then rising in the artificial gravity. He looked around the table. "You guys can decide to do whatever you want, but

I'm staying. I don't care if I have to set up camp on the side of that rock. I will mine it with a fucking pick and shovel, if I have to—because this is what we humans need to do."

The others remained silent.

"I've taken risks before, but never for a very good reason. I lost . . ." The words caught in his throat for a moment. ". . . my dearest friend—a man who was a father to me—just for a chance to see what was around the bend in a cave. Well, for once in my life, I not only know why I'm here, at this place, I finally know why I *exist.* I've always wondered why I was so odd. What possible evolutionary purpose could a person like me serve? No kids. Focused on my own experiences." He pressed his hand on the table in emphasis. "*This* is my purpose. This has always been the purpose of people like us. We blaze trails. We chart oceans. We push back frontiers. Without us, humanity slowly dies."

The entire crew stared at him.

Eventually Clarke looked around the table. "If we are going to do this, we must be able to rely on one another absolutely." She took a steadying breath. "So . . . please, do not vote yes unless you truly mean yes." She checked the countdown clock. "We've got hours more. There's no reason to vote yes now if you are not ready." She looked to Chindarkar. "Or ever, if you are not."

The crew of the *Konstantin* stared at one another.

Clarke raised her hand. "Who here wants us to stay, to see this out for the next four years? To fully commit to this expedition—though it might bring our death?"

Chindarkar looked Tighe in the eyes and, to his surprise, raised her hand.

Clarke was taken aback. "You're certain, Priya?"

She nodded. "Just lost my perspective there for a moment. It's sometimes easy to forget that the purpose of life isn't just to stay alive."

Tighe also voted to stay, as did Morra, Abarca, Adisa, and Tsukada. Everyone turned their eyes toward Jin.

Jin took a deep breath. "*I have complete faith in all of you. I just—*"

Morra leaned in once more. "Would you just raise your hand already?"

Clarke glared at Morra. "Don't pressure him, Dave. Everyone must decide on their own."

Morra threw up his hands. "He *knows* he wants to. He just won't admit who he really is. If I thought for one second I was wrong, I'd shut my mouth, but, Han, I've lived with you long enough to know you were made for this. I haven't seen a smile on your face more than two seconds in the past year, and we get outside in a space suit and you're like a six-year-old in a candy store. I hate to be the one to break it to you, but you're not an obedient son. Or a follower of rules. You're an adventurer. It's in your blood. If you go back now, you will be miserable for the rest of your life. And you will make everyone around you miserable, too. Believe me. I know."

Jin gave Morra a sideways look. After nearly a minute Jin said, "*I am selfish.*"

"Yes. You are. So am I. So is everyone."

Jin shook his head. Then he raised his hand.

Clarke asked, "Are you certain, Han?"

"*I am certain. I wish I was not, but I am.*"

Clarke nodded. "Then it's official: we're staying for the duration."

With that, the crew stood. They looked from one face to another—and finally breathed a sigh of relief, hugging and slapping one another on the back. Jin alone remained stone-faced.

Clarke looked up at the agitated faces of Catalyst mission controllers and a now snow-filled Nathan Joyce video feed. She turned off the mute button. "They'll find out in a hundred seconds or so." She looked up at Lacroix's image. "Mission control, the crew of the *Konstantin* has made a go, no-go decision. We are here for the duration. The Ryugu mining expedition is a go."

Nathan Joyce's San Luis Valley, Colorado, ranch was more than 50,000 acres. Nestled in the Rocky Mountain Foothills and surrounded by lodgepole pines, the luxurious log cabin main house sported eleven bedrooms, with a high-ceilinged great hall and a massive fieldstone fireplace. The view across the valley was like something from an American Western—clear open vistas, cattle dotting the lowlands. Lukas Rochat relished his time here.

One corner of the great hall was cluttered with satellite hookups and computer equipment intended to capture Joyce's image, encrypt it, and then broadcast it to a satellite in geosynchronous orbit—where it would then be beamed 10 million kilometers to the laser receiver atop the *Konstantin*'s solar mast.

Nearby hewn-log tables were cluttered with notes and diagrams. Aerospace and mining engineers as well as Dr. Angela Bruno were on hand to help Joyce convince the crew of the *Konstantin* to continue their mining expedition. None of them necessary, as it turned out.

Now that the matter had been settled, and Joyce had had a chance to speak—albeit on delay—with the crew and with mission controllers, he was in a triumphant mood.

Several of Lacroix's mission control managers moved about pouring champagne from incredibly rare bottles of 1841 Veuve Clicquot. Rochat enjoyed every sip because he knew just how much had depended upon this expedition *not* ending tonight.

Crisis avoided. Joyce might pull off his greatest trick yet by creating several fortunes not just out of thin air but out of the vacuum of space itself. It would be the entrepreneurial story of the millennium. Rochat imagined *SpaceNews* magazine asking for an interview about his own role in the great expedition. Rochat's eyes glazed in reverie, imagining all the people who had looked down on him now seething with envy.

Joyce finished speaking to the mission control staff and grabbed a champagne bottle from a table. He motioned for Rochat to follow him out onto the terrace, into the chill evening air.

Joyce seemed to enjoy gazing up at the heavens these days, particularly in the evening, when planets like Venus and Jupiter were bright on the horizon. The planets were, after all, no longer mere concepts to a man like Joyce; they were future markets. Perhaps for this reason, tonight there was a sizable telescope mounted on the stone deck.

Rochat exchanged satisfied grins with Joyce as they leaned against a log-and-fieldstone railing overlooking the twilit landscape.

Joyce raised his champagne flute. "We made history tonight, Lukas."

Rochat smiled.

They clinked glasses and drank deeply.

Rochat stood side by side with his idol at one of the greatest moments in space exploration. (He'd had a small role in this, surely.) He turned to face the valley as the light began to fade, stars now twinkling on the horizon.

Joyce handed the antique champagne bottle to Rochat, who gladly accepted it. He then watched as Joyce took out two Cuban cigars and a combination cutter/lighter. Joyce trimmed the end of one and then offered it to Rochat.

Rochat waved it away. "It will be wasted upon me, Nathan."

"Suit yourself." Joyce put the unclipped one away and subjected the tip of the other to a blue-hot heat from something more akin to a rocket engine than a lighter. He puffed rhythmically.

Rochat's Swiss accent was thick from drinking. "Nathan, I haf not seen you smoke before."

The cigar now lit, Joyce leaned his head back and puffed languorously. "Special occasion." He took another puff to his evident satisfaction. "If those miners can live dangerously, then who am I to play it safe?"

Rochat let out a loud laugh. "You haf hardly played it safe. We both know you haf cheated the devil himself."

Joyce smoked with relish as he beheld the world—his world, Rochat realized. At least as far as the eye could see.

"I must say—and you must forgive me, Nathan—but you are the most re-markable man I have ever known."

Joyce turned slightly. "That means a lot to me, Lukas. That really does. I don't think I could have accomplished this without your help."

Rochat held on to those words. Joyce's validation was the pinnacle. This was it. He had arrived.

"The risks you took. How did you *know* these were the right people? How did you know you could trust the crew of the *Konstantin* with such awesome responsibility, so far from Earth?"

Joyce nodded as he appreciated the cigar. Then he said, "I'll tell you, it was a calculated risk. But one I knew had to be taken for the expedition to proceed properly." He took another puff of the cigar. "Besides, you didn't think I'd be stupid enough to actually give them enough fuel to get back, did you?"

Rochat's smiled faded. He waited for Joyce to laugh—but it never came.

Instead, Joyce slapped Rochat on the back and started to walk back to the house—then he turned and said, "To send tons of extra fuel just to allow the crew to do something they must absolutely not do—well, that doesn't make sense. Instead, I provided them with extra supplies, which could very well make all the difference. And my having faith that they would make the right decision might very well save all their lives. Yes, Lukas, selecting the right people is *everything.*"

With that, humming happily, Joyce entered the house.

Rochat stood in shock, shivering in the evening air.

CHAPTER 30

Gremlins

APRIL 17, 2034

Klaxons and strobe lights jolted Tighe awake in the middle of the night. A female robotic voice said, "*Warning: bang-bang control failure. Repeat: bang-bang control failure. Ship off station.*"

Tighe was now assigned to Hab 1 with Jin, and they both sat up and put on crystals.

It was the sixth time in two days the crew had been disturbed in the middle of the night by alarms, and both stress and lack of sleep were beginning to take a toll on them all.

The Klaxons suddenly reduced in volume.

Clarke's weary voice came over the comm link. She'd lately been looking more careworn than any of them—the weight of command showing. "*Ade, these readings say the ship is 2 kilometers off station and nearly upside down.*"

Adisa's voice also sounded groggy. "*It is not possible. A half hour ago the ship was on station. The gravitational attraction of Ryugu to the* Konstantin *is only 1.9 newtons. That could only place us at most . . . 36 meters off station.*"

Tighe brought up exterior cameras and was relieved to see Ryugu, and the silhouettes of two Honey Bee mining bots, right where he expected them to be. "Nicole, CCTV cameras show everything normal outside."

Jin said, "Catalyst engineers need to fix these software problems."

Adisa said, "*Nicole, we must not mute our bang-bang alarm. It is too important.*"

Morra piped in, "*We need to be able to get some sleep, Ade.*"

Clarke sighed in irritation and opened a laser comm channel. "*Mission control, mission control. We have a station-keeping alert. This is a false alarm. Repeat: yet another goddamned false alarm. I need Gabriel Lacroix to contact me. Wake him up if you have to—it cannot wait. Over and out."*

Several minutes later the capcom on duty warned, "Konstantin, Konstantin. *We show you 2 kilometers off station and off axis. Please respond. Over."*

"It's like talking to a senile grandparent with this signal delay." Tighe placed his feet on the deck and shielded his eyes against the cabin lights.

Several minutes later the appropriate response came in, but it still wound up taking two and a half hours to get Gabriel Lacroix on the line.

Clarke unloaded on him. *"Gabriel, I'm looking at our alarm log and it's . . . 6,432 alerts long. Either we're orbiting in a burning barn or something is seriously wrong with our software. We're using up hundreds of man-hours chasing down nonexistent faults—hours that could be used trying to fix the SCADA system. And no one can get any sleep because of these false alarms. Over."*

After a several-minute delay, Lacroix's voice returned. *"We are doing everything we can, Nicole. The ship's operating system has been reuploaded several times. We cannot replicate your errors. Over."*

Chindarkar said, *"Sounds like a hardware problem."*

Clarke's voice replied to Lacroix. *"Gabriel, for the last time: give Adedayo Adisa admin rights to the* Konstantin's *OS. He's a systems expert, and unlike your engineers, he's physically here. Over."*

After the transmission delay Lacroix's voice said, *"Negative, Nicole. I cannot authorize local administrative control of the* Konstantin. *You have all the system permissions you need to perform your work. Over."*

Clarke sent her answer immediately. *"Then we need to do a hard reboot of the ship. Ade believes that one or more of the computer processors may have been physically damaged by cosmic radiation. We have spares for this very reason. It's worth a try to power down the ship, replace them, and reboot. Over."*

After transmission delay, Lacroix responded, *"Negative to a hard reboot, Nicole. The* Konstantin's *OS is a hypervisor—a collection of virtual machines that are instantiated on demand with integral failover capability. The ship was designed for continual uptime. The OS has never had a hard reboot—at least not in deep space, and there is a small chance that the* Konstantin *would not come back online if we power it down completely. In which case, we would not be able to reestablish contact with you. Over."*

Clarke opened the channel to Earth. *"Gabriel, Ade tells me we could switch the processors individually without having to reboot the ship, but he needs admin rights to do that. Over."*

After another tense delay Lacroix replied, *"Negative, Nicole. There will be no chip swap except as a last resort, and we are far from that. Over."*

Clarke responded, *"Gabriel, the ship's OS has become too unreliable. If you will not help us hot-swap the chips, then we have no choice but to do a hard reboot. Over."*

Clarke spoke to the crew over the local comm link. *"I don't know about all of you, but I don't think we can wait until they agree to this."* She paused. *"Do any of you object to our swapping out processors without approval from mission control?"*

Jin frowned and spoke over the comm link. "You propose to disobey orders?"

"This isn't the navy, Han. We're out here, and they're not. And so far they've got no answers."

Suddenly another alarm appeared, and the Klaxons blared all over again.

Tighe checked the active alarm list. "Spin-down in Central Hab."

Morra's voice quickly followed. *"That's madness! We still have gravity in the habs. There's no spin-down."*

Clarke sounded exhausted. *"This is only going to get worse. There's something wrong with the ship, and we need to act. Does anyone object to Ade performing a hard reboot of this ship?"*

No one spoke.

After a moment more Clarke said, *"All right. Everyone suit up and go on oxygen. We need to prepare for temporary loss of life support."*

As the crew prepared, Lacroix's voice came in over the *Konstantin*'s PA speakers, his French accent thicker than usual. *"Nicole, this is irresponsible and unnecessary. You are violating your contractual agreement. If you reboot the ship without authorization, there will be financial penalties. Over."*

Clarke replied, *"I have reason to believe the* Konstantin *is in imminent danger unless we take action. That is in our contract under force majeure, Gabriel. Read it. In the meantime, we're rebooting the ship. Or are you going to help us hot-swap the chips? Over."*

No reply came. Tighe assumed it was because Lacroix was busy trying to get

Nathan Joyce on the line. "Gabriel's not going to take the chance to authorize this on his own."

Adisa's voice interjected, *"We have three new critical alarms. One of them indicates Engine 4 is at full throttle."*

Clarke said, *"Let's do this, Ade."*

The entire crew traveled up the transit tunnels to gather in the microgravity of the Central Hab. They all wore their blue flight suits with the hoods pulled back and were breathing from oxygen masks.

Adisa called out to them. "Everyone, your attention, please. I have closely studied the *Konstantin*'s technical documentation. We must first spin down the ship. This will take much longer with the mass of extra radiation shielding we have piped down to the habs."

Clarke asked, "How long, Ade?"

"Almost an hour."

"Get it started."

As the radial-arm thrusters rumbled beyond the core, the rotation of the Central Hab slowed only gradually. Critical alarms of all types kept streaming in without rhyme or reason. Eventually the *Konstantin*'s radial arms came to a stop.

Adisa called out once more. "I will now begin to shut down ship functions one by one. You will see many warning messages. Are you ready?"

The crew nodded.

"Commencing shutdown . . ."

Among the hundreds of alerts that appeared in Tighe's crystal, he noticed one in particular: *Laser Comms Offline.*

The sensation of being out of contact with Earth was both frightening and—if Tighe was honest with himself—a little exhilarating, like taking a swim off a sailboat in midocean. Everything counted on getting back.

After several more minutes of alerts, Adisa looked up from his crystal. "I am about to shut down the ship's core OS. From this point, your crystal will no longer work. Once the ship is powered down, I will require five to ten minutes to install the new chips. In the meantime, Ryugu's gravity will pull us in slightly, but if we are back online within ninety minutes, we can recover."

Jin asked, "And if we aren't back online in ninety minutes?"

"We might not be able to reverse our acceleration in time to avoid impacting Ryugu's surface." He paused. "And we will all perish."

Tighe cleared his throat. "And if we leave the chips in and do nothing?"

Adisa clenched his jaw. "I am convinced the OS will become more and more unstable and eventually kill us."

Morra clapped his hands. "Right. Let's get on with it, then."

Adisa floated near the server rack, in front of one of the very few physical screens and keyboards aboard the ship. "Powering down system in three, two, one . . ." He tapped a key.

Suddenly everyone's crystal went blank. Lights around the ship blinked off in stages as the ship began an orderly shutdown. The life support and heating systems stopped. Water drained from supply lines. Ventilation fans slowed to a halt.

Tighe floated next to the other crew members, oxygen masks on but flight suit hoods pulled back. They watched intently as every system on which their lives depended extinguished itself. Before long the *Konstantin* was eerily silent—and dark.

Morra said, "Well, here's your silence, Amy."

"Not exactly what I had in mind."

Adisa called out as he monitored his terminal in the core vault. "Shutdown almost complete . . ."

The last indicator lights winked out, and except for the lights on their helmets, they were surrounded by darkness so complete it felt physically solid.

Tighe looked around. "Aren't there supposed to be emergency lights?"

Jin stared into the black. "Yes. Apparently someone screwed up."

"Great."

Adisa called out, "I am starting to swap out the processors. This will take a bit."

The sudden silence of the ship was fearsome. Tighe tried not to focus on the time elapsing. If they had difficulty rebooting the ship or couldn't reactivate the bang-bang control that kept them on station, within a few hours they would crash into the surface of Ryugu—although, as Ade mentioned, the point of no return would occur earlier than that.

After five minutes with no word from Adisa, the tension grew. The hab became cold.

Clarke called out, "You need any help, Ade?"

He replied, "There is only room for one in here. I need a few more minutes."

Five minutes later and everyone's breath stabbed out visibly in the cold air. Clarke floated over to the pressure door of the core. "Ade, we are going to pressurize our suits. How much longer?"

Adisa's voice was tense as he said, "Water don pass garri!"

Morra hissed, "Bloody hell, he's speaking pidgin. That can't be good."

"English, Ade, please."

"I am not certain how much longer. The processors, they were difficult to remove, and placing the new ones has been no easier. Whoever designed these mounts . . . ?" He muttered to himself.

The crew exchanged concerned looks, zipped up their suits, and pressurized.

They waited another few minutes before they heard Adisa's voice. "There! Restarting now. We will quickly find out if I have done this correctly."

In just a few moments the emergency lights came on—followed immediately by other systems whirring to life around them.

Their crystal displays restarted soon after, and they could finally sense the ship around them again. The first thing Tighe noticed was that most of the error codes and alarms were gone.

The crew applauded and smiled as they watched their oasis slowly being restored.

The next thing Tighe noticed was that they were slightly less than 3 kilometers from Ryugu's surface. However, the *Konstantin*'s thrusters were already slowing their descent.

Adisa's voice came through to them over the comm link. *"The chip replacement appears to have been successful."*

The crew applauded again.

Clarke, a smile in her voice, added, "Well done, Ade."

A few hours later, and after their first solid sleep in more than a week, the entire crew gathered in their habs for a videoconference call—with Chindarkar and Tsukada sitting at the galley table with Jin and Tighe in Hab 1, while Abarca, Adisa, Clarke, and Morra sat around the table in Hab 2. As always, the AR feature of their crystal glasses virtually extended the hab wall to make it seem like they were all in one big room.

The transmission delay back to Earth was now 109 seconds one way—over three and a half minutes for a reply. Nonetheless, today's discussion required a face-to-face meeting.

Joyce's video image projected onto a virtual screen in both crew habs. He was sitting in a Spartan office somewhere on Earth, waiting expectantly.

Clarke, also virtual to Tighe, seemed real enough that he could see the toll stress had taken on her. She looked haggard as she stared at Joyce. *"Nathan, we just solved a potentially catastrophic fault with the ship's systems, and now I see you've ramped up production targets to the original numbers. This is unreasonable. Over."*

After the several-minute delay, Joyce replied, "Now that you've solved the OS problems, Amy should be able to get the production plant up and running—and produce steel replacement parts for the mining robots. Now is the time to double down on our efforts."

While Joyce was talking, Morra muttered, *"Is he insane? Half the machines are busted."*

Clarke motioned for silence.

Joyce: "—have to make up for the shortfall in production. The return tug next June will have a narrow orbital window, and we need as much tonnage on that shipment as possible. Every kilo of resources it carries could spell the difference between success and failure for Catalyst Corporation. Over."

Clarke: *"We've still got a hundred preventive maintenance items on the ship that need attention. The crew is exhausted and injured. Han's still got two cracked ribs from a fall, and Dave injured an eardrum in a depressurization accident. Priya has a welding burn. We can't be expected to increase the pace of operations for a whole year just to meet some arbitrary production target. Over."*

The crew busied themselves for several minutes, awaiting a reply.

Joyce: "It won't be for a year. You're playing catch-up right now, but with a few months' hard push, you can get back to the original production goals. Over."

Clarke: *"Those goals were a complete fiction, and you know it. Nobody knew how much we could produce here—if anything. We need to slow the pace before someone gets seriously hurt. Over."*

Joyce: "This first return shipment is critical, Nicole. The real production goal is every single metric ton that can possibly be refined and sent Moonward. The maximum is the minimum for this first shipment. Over."

Clarke: *"We have proven space-based resource extraction is viable. You may have had a big up-front investment, but I've worked with petrochemical companies. They make long-term, capital-intensive investments, too. At our present pace, this expedition will produce tens of billions in profits long term, not to mention the value of the patents, and the scientific data to NASA and other space agencies. We've got the first operational spin-grav ship. I would think you'd be ecstatic about all we've accomplished."*

Tighe added, "She's right, Nathan. I don't think Neil Armstrong got shit for missing production targets."

Next to Tighe, Chindarkar leaned in toward the camera. "And whatever happened to making this expedition public? We've proven asteroid mining is possible. We've survived months in deep space. We deserve recognition back on Earth."

Jin said, "I am beginning to suspect that Catalyst has no intention of telling the world we are out here."

"That's enough of that, Han. Let the man answer." Clarke turned to the screen. *"Over."*

Joyce's face registered dismay as the message reached him. He replied, "This is not a mission of sovereign exploration; you were all sent to Ryugu to produce resources. This isn't about fame. This is a business. I was very up-front about that." He paused for a moment. "But let me be frank—"

Morra muttered, *"There's a first . . ."*

Abarca said, *"Shhh."*

"—Catalyst Corporation will not be able to publicly announce the existence of this mission until the first shipment of resources you send back actually arrives in cislunar space."

The crew howled in outrage.

Morra pounded the table in Hab 2. *"What a load of shite!"*

Clarke shouted down the others. *"We need to hear this, please!"*

The others reluctantly listened, arms crossed, as Joyce continued to talk.

"—you'll no doubt be expressing your dissatisfaction with this news when I hear from you in"—Joyce looked at his expensive watch—"218 seconds. However,

I'll use the interval to explain a few things." Joyce moved closer to the camera. "I have played fast and loose with the truth. I admit that. However, I only did so to make this expedition possible. I spared no expense to make the *Konstantin* the best way we knew how. I got the best people money could buy. Are there bugs? Were mistakes made? Yes, and yes. But look around you; does it look like I cut corners? I know that if you perish, I will be ruined. Your lives are more important to me than you can imagine."

Joyce stared at the screen for several more moments. He looked down as he said, "I have lied to investors in my other companies. I have falsified tax returns and SEC filings. I have embezzled. I have begged, borrowed, and essentially stolen the money required to make this expedition happen. An expedition that officially does not exist because no one was willing to fund something this risky. No one had faith that it could work—and they still don't. Investors gave me money to do more of the same bullshit that billions of dollars are wasted on every day here on Earth. And I took their money, and instead I did this . . ." He gestured to the screen—to them.

Joyce sat for several moments in deep contemplation. He finally looked up at the camera. "I know I'm a bastard. You no doubt hate me. But think hard on this: who did I lie to? Was it you?" He shook his head. "No, because I will publicly announce your achievement to the world. Everyone knows I love publicity—but not all publicity is good publicity. Not when publicity can get me arrested. And I'm no good to you if I'm in jail or bankrupted by lawsuits."

To Tighe's surprise, Abarca suddenly launched at the screen in Hab 2, more enraged than he'd ever seen her. "*You son of a bitch! You lied to me! You planned this from the start!*"

Clarke pulled her back. "*We need to listen to this, Isabel. Please.*"

Joyce was still talking. "—expedition will still be made public, no matter what the outcome. You will all make history. And it's precisely because there's now such a high chance of your success that we should wait. Only when I have proven resources returned from deep space will I be in a position to make the case to my investors that they'll profit more with me still at the helm of my companies. In success, all sins will be forgiven. That's how business works." He paused. "In fact, that's how life works." He paused, then said, "Over."

The crew of the *Konstantin* sat in shock—with the exception of Abarca.

She moved in front of the camera, staring hard into the lens. *"You and I have business, Nathan. You lied to me from the very beginning, and now because of me these people are here."*

Tighe, Morra, Jin, and the others looked at her in surprise.

Clarke asked, *"What do you mean by that, Isabel?"*

Abarca turned to the others. *"I'm the one who selected you all."*

Tighe narrowed his eyes. "How do you figure?"

"I told you back on Ascension, J.T.: Nathan Joyce funds my expeditions."

"Your expedition?"

"I led candidate selection. The training in Concordia." She turned and glared at Joyce—who would not hear her confession to the crew for over a minute still. *"I was the one Nathan told first when he came up with this plan. He chose me to build the team for it. And here we all are."*

Clarke sat down, agape.

Morra ran his hands over his scalp. *"I'll be goddamned . . ."*

Jin added, "Then you knew this ship existed—even back on Ascension?"

Abarca nodded. *"Which is why I made sure the people I was bringing could handle it. Did I choose wrong, Han? I don't think so."* She looked back up at Nathan Joyce—still oblivious due to the time lag. *"You and I will talk later, asshole. In the meantime, you'll accept whatever we feel like sending you next year. And you'd better hope to hell we feel generous."*

With that, Abarca disconnected the video link. Joyce's hologram disappeared.

Clarke sat in stunned silence along with the others. She finally looked to Abarca, who paced the decking in Hab 2. *"Am I still captain of this ship?"*

Abarca stopped pacing and her expression softened. *"Of course you are, Nicole. Who here would trust a liar like me to be captain?"*

It took a moment, but Morra laughed—and the rest of the crew started laughing with him.

CHAPTER 31

Alchemist

J ames Tighe opened the Fab Hab's inner pressure door and carried a duffel bag into Chindarkar's robotics lab. He depressurized his suit and unzipped his helmet, flipping it back like a hood.

At a nearby work bench Chindarkar focused on a circuit board with a soldering iron, smoke curling away. Behind her a board printer whirred and clicked. The table was littered with servo motors and electronics clutter.

She spoke without looking up. "Hey, J.T."

"Brought food supplies." He opened the bag and started stowing packages of dehydrated food in an overhead cabinet. "You guys have been spending too much time down here."

"Only way to catch up on production." She looked up. "Thanks. Did you bring me ice cream sandwiches?"

"I brought the desserts on the schedule. If you eat all your favorites first, it's gonna be a long goddamn four years."

He finished stocking the cabinet and walked to the far side of the hab's round aluminum core, crossing into Tsukada's chemistry lab, which occupied the other half.

Tsukada stood at her lab bench, crystal on and earphones in, as she interacted with an invisible UI. She was bobbing her head to inaudible music, apparently in the zone.

Tighe moved into her field of view and waved.

She gestured to turn off the music. "Hey, J.T. What's up?"

"Resupply."

"Oh, thanks. I was going to head up to the core tomorrow."

"I had to inspect Tunnel 3 anyway." He started stocking the pantry. "Dave says we can make steel machine parts now."

"Yes, the refinery finally works. Here . . ." She gestured and a holographic schematic of the *Konstantin* instantiated in midair. It had the appearance of a cartoonish color-coded subway map but was a view of the piping that ran throughout the ship. Numeric values changed here and there showing current temperature, pressure, and volume for various feeds. She tapped at one of the lines, opening a valve that led from the Central Hab down into the refinery.

Tighe studied the hologram.

"This is the UI for managing liquid and gas flows throughout the ship." She pointed to rectangles on the ship's piping diagram. "O_2 generators split water at these five locations on the ship. The excess hydrogen they produce is fed back into the CO_2 scrubbers"—she pointed to other boxes on the diagram—"to produce methane and water. The water recirculates back to the oxygen generators, but the methane we pump down to the aft fuel tanks"—her finger trailed down the ship's spine and into the refinery—"where we'll mostly use it to create methalox rocket fuel for the return tugs."

"They didn't show me this in training. What's this?" Tighe pointed.

"I'm creating plastic feedstock for the 3D printers, using carbon monoxide."

"You create plastic from a gas?"

She tapped at the diagram. "I use a nickel or cobalt catalyst under heat and pressure to cause an exothermic reaction that creates polymer strands." She looked up from the hologram. "Which can cause an explosion if not properly controlled."

"And here I've been sleeping so well lately."

She laughed. "It's fine." She tapped a virtual button and it expanded into an entire plastics production control panel. "I refine the molecules into different types of plastics. They can be fed into our 3D printers, deposed into polyamide films or into laminates to repair hab walls, or to manufacture mining containment bags, new bladder tanks, to build frameworks for the return tugs—you name it."

Tighe felt reassured. "So we're actually up and running."

She pointed. "Look, I'll show you what I'm working on. Hop onto that telepresence station and jack in to Valkyrie-5."

Tighe sat at a nearby desk and opened a UI that listed available telepresence robots. He selected V-5 and waited as his crystal went opaque. Moments later he was gazing out from the POV of a 2-meter-tall robot with stereoscopic camera eyes. It was standing in a charging bay inside the refinery reaction chamber. As he looked around, he saw the chamber walls were punctured here and there by louvers, valves, lights, cameras, exhaust ports, and a sealed pressure door. The walls were stained multiple colors from past, violent chemical reactions.

He examined his metallic arms and hands. A second up-armored, all-metal Valkyrie stood in a charging dock on the far wall. "All right, I'm here."

Tsukada's voice spoke close to him. "See the white object in the center of the reaction chamber?"

Tighe activated his VR controls and marched, as a robot, on magnetic feet toward a several-meter-long plastic object resting in the center of the reaction chamber. A wire ran from it to a plug in the ceiling. The object appeared to be two halves of a long open mold, the inside of which was a complex corkscrew pattern. "An injection mold."

"Right. A high-fidelity polymer mold of an Archimedes' screw—printed from a 3D model. Notice the wire. It powers a conduction heating element inside the mold. Do you remember our harvested metals—the nickel, iron, and cobalt—that we stored in the form of liquid carbonyls?"

"Sure."

"What I'm doing is called chemical vapor deposition—or CVD. It allows us to create high-quality metal parts for our mining machinery."

"Do I need to move back?"

"No, you're fine where you are. See that the mold is empty?"

"I do."

"Close it for me."

He moved toward the mold and closed it with his robot hands. "Done." He stood up straight.

"We need 200 atmospheres of carbon monoxide for this iron-carbonyl reaction to take place."

Tighe watched as a growing globule of orange liquid formed in microgravity at the end of a pipe. He assumed this was the iron-carbonyl liquid.

"The interior surface of the mold is being heated to a precise 175 degrees Celsius. Then I wait."

"For what?"

"In this atmosphere the carbonyl vapor from the liquid will begin to depose onto the interior of the mold as solid metal."

"The metal accumulates out of thin air?"

"Correct."

"And only inside the mold?"

"Correct."

"How?"

"Chemistry. Exposed surfaces at 175 degrees will attract metal deposition. The rest of the chamber is cooler. If we wanted openings in our mold, we simply don't heat certain spots of the mold. The metal that forms is so pure it won't rust, and much stronger than if we forged it in a furnace."

Tighe leaned his robot forward to examine the open end of the mold and noticed that a uniform metallic film was indeed beginning to coat the interior. "This is steel?"

"Cobalt steel—an alloy. The same stuff they use to make high-speed cutting tools back on Earth. Exceptionally durable and heat resistant."

"You don't need a forge?"

"Nope. I can stop the process early to create a hollow auger, or let it continue until the entire form fills solid—creating a solid machine part. I think we'll make this just a few centimeters thick to keep it light. See if that works for the Honey Bees."

Tighe studied the accumulating metal with his robotic eyes. "I had no idea this technology existed."

She laughed. "It's existed since Ludwig Mond invented it back in 1890."

"I've honestly never heard of it."

"Back on Earth it's less toxic to just use a blast furnace. Up here in space, though, CVD is going to be critical for precision manufacturing."

The metal was already getting thicker. "It's like alchemy."

"No, it's *better* than alchemy—it's science."

CHAPTER 32

Lottery

JULY 8, 2034

Despite their resentment toward Joyce, mining production at Ryugu continued to increase. The robotic systems steadily improved as Morra, Chindarkar, and Adisa kept iterating improvements to hardware and software—and Tsukada produced durable steel parts for their designs.

Tighe and Jin programmed and unloaded the Honey Bees, feeding regolith into the refinery and removing full bladder tanks of water ice, liquid nitrogen, ammonia, methane, CO_2, and metal carbonyls from the refinery bays. A growing storage yard of 7-meter- and 2-meter-diameter spherical polymer bladder tanks had begun to take shape, linked together by a printed latticework of polymer beams fashioned by Archinaut ULISSES 3D-printing robots.

The *Konstantin* mining operation was beginning to find a rhythm as the crew gained experience. To their great annoyance, Joyce turned out to be right: the workload began to ease even as their production increased.

Well rested now, Tighe spotted something unusual during one shift. An ARS robot pulled an 8-meter-diameter boulder from Ryugu's surface, trailing a minor cloud of regolith dust. The work lights of Tighe's remotely piloted mule illuminated the cloud, but something glittered in the hole the boulder left behind.

After the cloud settled, Tighe popped thrusters to bring the mule closer.

At the bottom of the hole he spotted a black boulder, perhaps 3 meters in size. The rock didn't look like anything else he'd seen on Ryugu. It wasn't ash-colored at all. It sparkled beneath the work lights.

Tighe activated the mule's lidar and did a 3D scan of the new surface. With a few taps at the AR image, he added the black boulder to the ship's topo-graphical map. The mining software dubbed it Boulder 134, and with another tap Tighe added it to the harvest queue. A few weeks from now, one of the ARS robots should pull it.

He studied its surface for several more minutes before moving on.

JULY 29, 2034

Tighe stepped off the lift and opened the Fab Hab pressure door, moving out into Chindarkar's robotics lab. She had classic hip-hop music playing while she fixed a broken inspection drone.

She looked up in surprise as he stood nearby. "Hey, J.T. What brings you to our gravity well?"

Tighe curled a finger for her to follow. Curious, Chindarkar got up to fol-low him as he walked around the hab's round metal core. En route he and Chindarkar crossed into Tsukada's chemistry lab.

Chindarkar answered Tsukada's curious expression with, "J.T.'s up to something."

"What?"

"Don't know."

They all three descended the gangway to the lower deck of the Fab Hab. Here, the level was dedicated to additive manufacturing systems—3D printers, computer-controlled milling machines, chains, hoists, overhead rails, work-tables, and storage lockers. Part of the space was occupied by Nicole Clarke's geology lab.

Clarke had a piece of carbonaceous chondrite under a microscope, but her head was on her hand, as though she were dozing. She looked up as the trio entered. "Hey, guys." Then her facial expression changed. "What's wrong?"

Tighe said, "Nothing's wrong. Well, nothing serious. The centrifugal sorter on Honey Bee 3 is damaged."

"I thought we solved those problems with the change from aluminum to cobalt steel."

Tighe waved her off. "We did. The metal is fine. It was just jammed. I couldn't fix it with a mule or a Valkyrie. So Jin and I had to EVA."

"EVA? Your cumulative radiation exposure is—"

"Everything went fine. It turned out the centrifuge was jammed—with this." He held up a clouded crystal the size of a hand grenade. Tighe handed it to her.

Clarke's eyes widened as she hefted the crystal. She grabbed a loupe from her worktable and studied it closely. "Where the hell did this come from? This isn't Ryugu regolith."

"A black rock. About 3 meters across. It was buried near Boulder 92. Looked different from the others. So I pulled it."

Clarke rotated it. "Ureilite." She looked up at Tighe. "This is older than Ryugu. It must have impacted Ryugu millions, maybe billions of years ago."

"So it's a meteorite?"

"Ureilites are a rare class of asteroid from before the formation of the planets—from when protoplanets were colliding to form the Earth, Venus, Mars, and the rest. They're rich in carbon. The early collisions created enormous pressure—over 20 gigapascals."

"So it's carbon."

She laughed and held it up to the light. "More specifically—it's a diamond."

Tsukada and Chindarkar gasped.

"Get out."

"A space diamond."

Clarke hefted it again. "Must be a few hundred carats at least. Back on Earth this would be one of the largest diamonds in the world."

Chindarkar laughed. "Really?"

"Yes. Diamonds are ridiculously common in the universe. They're just carbon subjected to immense pressure." She handed it to Tsukada.

Tsukada held it up to the light. It was coated in black. "It must be worth something."

"It'd be worth something on Earth—for now, anyway." Clarke spoke into her comm link. "Hey, Ade, I'm sending you a video feed. J.T. just found this clogging the centrifuge of Honey Bee 3." She motioned for Tsukada to hold up the crystal.

Adisa's voice came in over the link. "A diamond?"

"I knew you'd recognize it." Clarke eased the diamond out of Tsukada's hand. "I used to polish stones as a child. I even took gemology courses." She used her crystal's optics to zoom in on it. "Priya, could we use some of the robotics equipment down here to programmatically cleave the facets—if I showed you where to make the cuts?"

Chindarkar shrugged. "Sure. I could put together a diamond-cutting rig."

Clarke studied the crystal again. "This would make an impressive pear brilliant—probably 250 carats. It'd be a nice after-hours project."

Tighe looked up at the company surveillance cameras he knew were watching. "So do we send it back with the return tug next year?"

Clarke handed the diamond to Priya, as she also looked up at the nearest camera. "No, I say we hold on to it. Bring it back to Earth in person. We can hand it to Nathan Joyce once we're all back safe."

"So it *is* worth something, then."

"On Earth, probably a billion dollars."

The others laughed and whistled.

"Jesus."

"But out here . . . well, diamonds are space dirt. In fact, did you guys find any other diamonds in that black boulder?"

"A few . . ." Tighe paused. ". . . thousand. Much smaller than this, though."

"Catalog them, and we'll figure out what to do with them later. Abrasives, probably."

Over the next few weeks Clarke and Chindarkar used their personal time to cut and polish the huge diamond in the Fab Hab. In the meantime, they kept the gem under wraps, refusing to show it until they were ready.

By the early August hab rotation, Tighe, Jin, and Tsukada had been assigned to Hab 1 with Clarke, and after the now-weekly update meeting with Catalyst mission control was over and they'd signed off, Clarke placed an object wrapped in a chamois cloth on the galley table.

The other four crew members watching via AR from Hab 2 were still online to notice.

Clarke looked tired but happy.

Abarca asked, *"What's that?"*

"Priya and I have been working late."

"No wonder you look exhausted."

"Worth it. I'm really pleased with how it turned out." She unwrapped a glittering pear-shaped white diamond the size of a kiwi fruit.

Everyone in both habs leaned forward.

"Holy shit."

"That's amazing."

Clarke held it up to the company's surveillance camera. "There's your rock, Nathan. Come and get it."

Morra laughed. *"Nice work, Nicole."*

Clarke smiled. "Thanks to Priya it turned out well."

Chindarkar nodded. *"My pleasure. I've never created a robot to cut a diamond before."*

Clarke said, "It's near flawless."

Tsukada held out her hand. "May I?"

"Sure."

Tsukada lifted it up to the light. "So, a billion dollars?"

"Probably more. But I wouldn't invest in diamonds if I were you. Asteroid mining is going to make them more common than they already are."

Tighe leaned in. "Maybe we should make it a lucky charm for the ship. Something to hang from the rearview mirror."

Adisa's AR projection said, *"The largest diamonds on Earth are usually named for the places in which they were found."*

Clarke scowled. "Please, not Ryugu. That's a terrible name for a diamond."

Morra added, *"Endless Void is a worse name."*

Adisa continued. *"One of the biggest diamonds is called the Star of Africa. Your diamond could be called the 'Star'-of-something—given that it was found in space, and it glitters like a star."*

Jin looked to Tighe. "You found it, J.T. You should name it."

"I do like the 'star' idea, Ade."

Tsukada tapped the diamond. "We found it farther away from Earth than anyone has ever been. That's significant, right?"

Tighe said, "The Far Star."

The others murmured and nodded.

Clarke nodded. "I like that."

Adisa said, *"Maybe this diamond should belong to whoever has gone farthest from the Earth."*

"You mean, like a trophy?"

"Ooh, I like that." Tsukada smiled and passed the diamond around her table.

Chindarkar rubbed her chin. *"A billion-dollar trophy is overkill, isn't it?"*

Morra shrugged. *"Why not? It cost a lot more than a billion to get us out here."*

Clarke shook her head as if to stay awake.

Tighe asked, "You okay, Nicole?"

"Just exhausted. Too much time staring into loupes." She stood and headed toward her quarters. "I'm going to get some rack time."

Everyone spoke at once. "'Night."

Tighe hefted the billion-dollar diamond, holding it up to the light. "Well, at 92 million miles from home, the Far Star belongs with us . . . for now."

Within a few weeks, everyone in the crew could tell that Clarke was ill. At first it manifested as constant fatigue. However, now that the Far Star was finished, set in a cobalt mount, and floating on a chain in the Central Hab, bed rest did not seem to help her. She often failed to rise in the morning with the rest of the crew.

By the third week of August, Clarke looked gaunt as she attended the weekly meeting with obvious difficulty. Now assigned to Hab 2 with Tighe, Abarca, and Chindarkar, she eased down into a seat at the galley table. Hab 1 beamed in via AR.

Clarke spoke plainly. "Before we begin the meeting, I have . . . unfortunate news. Isabel has run tests and consulted with the flight surgeons back at mission control. They tell me that I have a fast-moving cancer—lymphoma."

Chindarkar placed a hand over her mouth. "Oh god, Nicole."

Morra sighed and shook his head and looked grimly to Adisa, who was sitting next to him in Hab 1.

Jin just stared down at the galley table.

Tighe looked to Abarca. "What's the prognosis?"

Clarke fielded the question. "It's okay, Isabel." Clarke turned to Tighe, her eyes red-rimmed. "In the absence of advanced treatment—the closest being 107 million miles away—my case is terminal. They estimate a month, maybe two."

Tsukada teared up. *"My god. Nicole, I'm so sorry."* She looked to Abarca. *"Are you certain?"*

Abarca nodded. "We sent the radiology back to Earth. Specialists there confirmed the initial diagnosis. The most likely cause is galactic cosmic radiation, but there's no way to be certain."

Jin looked pained. *"How can we best help you, Nicole?"*

"You keep going." Clarke hesitated, then said, "I don't regret coming on this journey. I'd do it again. I think about how I spent my life on Earth. If I stayed there . . ." Her eyes teared up. She gestured to the ship. "To change the future for the better . . ." She smiled slightly. "Well, that's worth dying for. Isn't it?"

Most of the crew wiped away tears. Abarca hugged Clarke close.

Clarke shook her head. "Don't feel sad. I'm luckier than almost anyone who's ever lived. What an adventure this has been."

Clarke lasted longer than the doctors predicted—all the way through September and October. She had good days and bad days, and on October 31, she was able to sit at the galley table and celebrate Jin's thirty-eighth birthday with rehydrated cheesecake. She insisted on attending, her blue jumpsuit hanging loosely on her thin frame.

By then, the biweekly crew rotation had been altered to let Clarke and Abarca remain in Hab 1, with only the other two slots changing. On November 6, Clarke called Abarca, Tighe, and Jin into the medical bay. She was sleeping in the hospital bed there now since concern about cosmic radiation was moot. Abarca had Clarke on an IV to manage her pain.

Clarke was calm and lucid as she looked up at them. "Isabel and I have discussed this with the specialists back on Earth. They tell me it gets much worse from here on out. And I refuse to use up all the ship's pain meds on a lost cause."

Jin shook his head. "None of us here want you to suffer. You must use whatever medication you need."

"That's just it, Han. I need to end it." Before he could object she held up her frail hand. "Like I said: it gets much worse. I don't want to be remembered like that. It's my decision. I need to go."

All three stood silently around the bed.

"I need your help, J.T."

"My help?" He looked at Abarca. "Is Isabel—"

"It's not that. I don't want to waste critical medication that cannot be replaced. You may need it in coming years."

The word *years* fell heavily on him. It occurred to Tighe that he and the rest of the crew would very likely be joining Clarke down the line.

He looked at her. "What do you need?"

"I've been out here almost a year, and I haven't gone on an EVA. Can you believe it? I want to see the cosmos—not through a hologram—but with my own eyes. That's where I'd like to pass—out there."

Tighe tried to keep it together.

"Can you help make it as painless as possible?"

Tighe struggled to steady his breathing. He nodded. "I . . . I can pressurize your suit." He took another breath and focused on the task. "To a full atmosphere—and then pipe in pure nitrogen. You won't sense asphyxiation, not in the absence of carbon dioxide. It will feel like going into a peaceful sleep." Tighe looked into her eyes. "I'll make certain of it."

She gripped his hand as tight as she could manage. "Thank you."

The entire crew came to the upper airlock to bid Nicole Clarke good-bye. Tighe was prebreathing pure oxygen, a step Clarke could forego since she was going to fully pressurize her flight suit. A mercy, as it allowed the other crew members to kiss her cheek and hug her tearfully just before she left the ship for the last time.

Tighe had never seen Morra cry. The ex-soldier hugged her.

While the rest of the crew said their farewells, Tighe quietly floated toward the suit airlock. As he did so, Abarca floated up behind him and looked into his eyes. "It's up to you, J.T."

Tighe took a deep breath.

"Listen to me . . ." She held his face. "You cannot tear up. Do you hear me? Not in microgravity. Not on an EVA. You need to be able to see what you're doing to get back. We can't afford to lose you."

He nodded.

"You grieve later. Right now, help ease her passage."

Tighe took deep, slow breaths to steady himself. "I understand."

Tighe entered the suit airlock, sealing it behind him. Next he removed his flight suit and oxygen mask before climbing through the hatch of his clam suit and sealing it behind him.

He pressurized, checked the diagnostics, then undocked the suit from the ship. He moved handhold by handhold down to the mule airlock. Soon he floated outside the hatch.

In a moment it opened, revealing Clarke, puffed up in her blue flight suit, pressurized at a full atmosphere by a life support pack. The flight suit wasn't meant for extended EVA operations, but today that hardly mattered.

Tighe reached in and took Clarke's gloved hand, gently pulling her into space.

He heard her gasp and worried for a moment that she was choking.

Instead, he saw the look of joy on her face and was grateful to see her smile. *"It's so beautiful. J.T. It's so beautiful."*

It took every ounce of willpower Tighe had not to tear up. Instead he turned and saw that Chindarkar had remotely guided a mule near them. Tighe carefully secured Clarke atop the cargo rack. He then clipped himself in and mounted the running board. He waved back to the ship, as he knew they were watching via cameras.

The mule's cold-gas thrusters fired, and it coasted out into space, away from the mountainous shadow of Ryugu. In a minute or so they cleared the sweep of the *Konstantin*'s three radial arms.

Clarke smiled as she looked back. *"She's a beautiful ship. And I was her captain."*

"You *are* her captain, Nicole—the first captain *ever* of a deep space commercial vessel."

"That should go on the wall." She chuckled slightly and squeezed his hand.

"It'll be written on a lot more than our wall."

Five hundred meters out, the mule's thrusters pushed them downward along the dark face of Ryugu. It was as though they were diving beneath the hull of some gigantic ocean liner.

Finally, Clarke said, *"Here, J.T."* She gasped again. *"Yes, here."*

Tighe gazed ahead at the glow. The very center of the Milky Way stood before them. He knew Clarke was seeing it with her naked eye, and so he did the same, pulling back his helmet visor so she could see his face. He smiled as he looked at the center of their home galaxy. "Isn't that something?"

"I didn't think anything could be so beautiful."

Tighe unstrapped Clarke from the mule and then righted her to "stand" alongside him as they drifted slightly away from the mule, still linked by his tether.

Clarke smiled—a look of serenity on her face as she beheld the universe. *"Do you realize how fortunate we are, J.T., to be here at all?"*

"I do." He pointed. "Look, the Large Magellanic Cloud."

"It's incredible."

He then pointed lower and to the left. "And there's Earth. The Moon on the far side."

Clarke stared, her eyes blinking in amazement. Home was just a point of white light, like a bright star.

Tighe stayed silent, he didn't know or care how long. He didn't even check his oxygen. Instead he held Clarke's hand as she absorbed the enormity of the universe and her place in it.

Finally, she nodded, whether to herself or to him, he wasn't sure. *"I'd like to go now. Just like this."* Her weak hand gripped his. *"Thank you so much for this gift. I love you all so much."*

Pangs of grief tore through him, but Tighe smiled and nodded. "And we love you." Tighe clipped a nitrogen bottle to her input feed. "I'm right here."

"I know." She smiled as she gazed into the starlight. *"I know."*

Tighe opened the nitrogen and let it flow into her suit.

It took several minutes, but slowly her eyes closed, and she descended into sleep. Tighe monitored her heartbeat in the suit's sensor, for the minutes it took to slow—and finally stop.

Tighe breathed deeply for several moments to steady himself.

He then folded Clarke's hands across her chest and then motioned for the mule to come in. He got back onto its running board and held Clarke's body as the mule's thrusters fired, sending them upward.

Chindarkar remotely piloted the mule toward a collection of polyamide columns packed with silica powder—solid waste from regolith processing. Tighe and Jin had gathered and lashed them together over the months. Each column was 10 meters long and a meter in diameter. Two dozen of them were bound together by polymer straps into an emergency radiation shelter—what would now become a cairn fashioned from Ryugu's stone.

Chindarkar guided the mule to the darkened entrance.

Tighe unstrapped Clarke's body from the mule and turned on his helmet lights as he gently guided her inside the cairn. The chamber was a barren space 5 meters on a side, formed by silica columns arranged like logs.

Tighe spoke to Clarke's now lifeless face. "We'll bring flowers. Something to brighten this up." He settled her to the floor, where he'd prepared Velcro straps. Tighe secured her body with a chest strap, and then he purged the air from her suit, leaving the valve open.

He knew that the other crew members were viewing what he saw through his helmet-cam. Now Abarca spoke, but though he would never admit it, at the time he deliberately did not listen to her words. Instead he kept his gaze on Clarke's peaceful face.

Finally, when there was silence for several moments, Tighe roused himself and left Clarke in the cairn. He said nothing over the comm link as the mule brought him back to the *Konstantin*. His limbs moved robotically as he docked his suit and returned through the airlock.

Abarca was waiting for him there, alone. She embraced Tighe, holding him close.

And Tighe finally wept.

CHAPTER 33

Company

JANUARY 1, 2035

T ighe, Adisa, and Chindarkar sat around the galley table in Hab 1. Their New Year's celebration was muted by the presence of only three people instead of four in their hab. The ship's software had scheduled Nicole Clarke in Hab 1 this rotation, and her absence was keenly felt. Midnight had come and gone. They'd watched video of the ball dropping in New York's Times Square. The old year had ended, but its consequences were still with them.

Catalyst mission control had promoted Isabel Abarca to captain after Clarke's death, but an atmosphere of consensus reigned on board. No single person was in charge.

Looking up at the AR link to Hab 2, Tighe could see Abarca, Jin, Morra, and Tsukada trying to play an AR board game. The fact that Tighe had six staples in his forearm didn't help his mood—an injury received from one of the milling machines in the Fab Hab. He was no replacement for Clarke, despite Chindarkar's attempt to train him on the equipment. However, if they were going to finish building the first return tug on time, everyone was required to pitch in. They had lost one very skilled person.

Tighe looked up at a virtual window to Catalyst Corporation mission control back on Earth. Eike Dahl and Sevastian Yakovlev celebrated among the company engineers.

The *Konstantin* had been gone nearly a year. Tighe longed to have a live conversation with Eike, but the best they'd been able to do in recent weeks was one or two video messages. Now that the *Konstantin* was 163 million miles from

Earth, it took fourteen and a half minutes for a broadcast to reach them—double that for a reply. He might as well have been writing letters for all the interactivity their conversations had. In some ways, Tighe preferred writing to her; at least then there wasn't the sadness at seeing her face, unattainable. Tighe felt like a ghost she could no longer see.

Adisa spoke. "Champagne, J.T.?"

Tighe shook his head. He couldn't help but notice that this year's bottle was only a split. Half the delta-v to get it here. When the award locker unlatched, it contained very little.

What did that mean?

Sitting across the galley table from Tighe, Chindarkar gazed through the virtual window at mission control's party back on Earth. "Looks like fun. Check out Yak and Eike. Yak's a good dancer."

Abarca spoke from Hab 2. *"You guys should at least try to enjoy yourselves. You know Nicole would have wanted us to."*

Tighe and his hab mates stared blankly at the virtual Abarca.

Abarca persisted. *"Doctor's orders. Try to move your bodies for a reason other than survival."*

In the background behind Abarca, Jin and Morra were folding up the galley table to clear space for a dance floor. A compelling guitar riff suddenly played in both habs—Phantogram's "When I'm Small."

Abarca shouted, *"Amy's DJ tonight! C'mon. Let's all dance. We're still alive."*

Behind Abarca, Tsukada, Morra, and Jin started to move.

Chindarkar laughed and got to her feet, too. She tapped at a virtual UI and turned up the music in Hab 1. "You heard her, guys—doctor's orders." She extended her hands to both Adisa and Tighe.

Adisa smiled and got up. "I do enjoy dancing."

"You haven't lived until you've danced in space."

"Technically, dancing on Earth *is* dancing in space."

"Don't ruin it, Ade. C'mon, J.T. You get up, too!"

Tighe reluctantly got to his feet. They folded the table aside and started dancing. The floor of the hab trembled with their movements. It was worrisome how flimsy the *Konstantin* felt beneath their feet.

Chindarkar didn't seem to notice. She danced with extraordinary grace and laughed at Tighe's reaction. "What? We rock climbers know how to move!"

Suddenly her expression changed, and she quickly sat down in a chair against the hab wall. "Shit. Coriolis effect . . ." She leaned forward and breathed deeply. "Thought I was going to be sick there for a second."

Adisa danced while barely moving his head. "Perhaps dancing is not a good idea on a spin-grav ship of this small radius."

Tighe tried to keep nausea at bay through sheer force of will as he danced. The effect wasn't what he'd hoped.

Jin pointed from the AR screen. "*You are a terrible dancer, J.T.*"

"I call it the Coriolis Shuffle." He moved cautiously.

The crew laughed. It was the first time in months. There hadn't been much to laugh about. The ship was already starting to show signs of wear. Tighe had no doubt the others harbored unspoken concerns about what it would look like a year from now, much less in three. They mourned for Clarke—and they also knew what her death implied.

Suddenly the music dimmed and the ship's Klaxons sounded a critical alarm. Strobes flashed. The ship's robotic voice said, "*Warning: impact alert. Repeat: impact alert.*"

The crew grabbed their crystals from a nearby charger and put them on.

"What the hell!"

Adisa muted the Klaxons and instantiated a hologram where the galley table would normally be. Everyone stared at the image. "There is an object on a collision course with us. Distance, 1 kilometer."

"What speed?"

"This cannot be correct." Adisa tapped at an invisible UI.

Tighe asked again, "How fast, Ade?"

"At low velocity. It seems to have originated from the far side of Ryugu."

Tighe watched as a radar ping moved toward them. "Could it be an old object from the Hayabusa2 mission?"

"No, the orbits of those objects are all known." Adisa brought up a virtual screen for the CCTV camera on the lower spine of the ship. He focused it on an approaching reflected light.

Tighe, Chindarkar, and the entire crew of Hab 2 stared at the screen.

Morra frowned. "*What the hell is that?*"

"It is a spacecraft."

Chindarkar said, "Not ours. And it is not slowing down."

Abarca spoke into the laser comm link. *"Mission control. Mission control. We have an unidentified spacecraft inbound. Repeat, we have an unidentified spacecraft on a collision course."*

Morra corrected her. *"It's already here."*

The mysterious craft moved under the ship as Chindarkar tried to focus cameras on it. "What the hell. Where'd it go?"

"It is changing course! Heading up the length of the ship."

"Shit!" Tighe stood. "It could impact the radial arms."

Abarca shouted, *"Everyone into the hab core! Now! Suit up!"*

The crews in both habs scrambled. Tighe and Adisa unlocked the pressure door. They all three rushed inside and sealed the door behind them. Tighe and Adisa pulled on flight suits as Chindarkar descended through the floor hatch to the lower crew quarters.

Jin called out the object's movements. *"Whatever it is, it has moved through the arc of the rotating habs. A collision could have destroyed the* Konstantin. *It is now headed up past the solar mast."*

"How big is that thing?"

"It is 4 meters in length."

Tighe looked up. "That could weigh tons."

Abarca was now calling out developments for mission control, but Earth's response was still twenty-eight minutes in the future. The crew of the *Konstantin* was on its own.

Jin said, *"Now it is heading back to the far side of Ryugu."*

Tighe took a deep breath. "Thank god."

Morra's voice came over the comm line. *"You reckon it's in orbit? It could come back around."*

Adisa shook his head. "That was no orbit. That was a controlled maneuver."

A minute later the object disappeared behind the kilometer-wide rock— gone as quickly as it had appeared.

Tighe sat on his cot and unzipped the hood of his flight suit again. "We *need* to know what that thing was. Do we have any visuals on it?"

"Yes." Adisa poked at the air in front of him, manipulating unseen virtual objects. "I am going to stitch together video from all exterior cameras...." Moments later he said, "Look..."

He tossed up a virtual layer that every crew member perceived as floating just a few feet in front of them. It was a 3D model derived from imagery taken by the *Konstantin*'s external CCTV cameras. Adisa zoomed in on an object as it passed by the fuel bladders of the refinery at the stern of the ship. A burst of thruster gas sent it upward along the *Konstantin*'s spine.

Tighe watched the footage. "Jesus, it nearly hit the methalox tanks. That would have been the last anyone ever heard from us."

"Look . . ." Adisa paused the imagery and rotated the model, expanding it into a somewhat grainy close-up. The point at which Adisa froze the image showed the craft moving between the sweep of the rotating radial arms—about 30 meters away from the spine of the *Konstantin*. The spacecraft was at least 3 meters long and cylindrical, with twin solar arrays.

"Fuck me . . ."

Morra whistled. *"Blind luck that it didn't kill us."*

Chindarkar pointed. "It's a probe."

Adisa zoomed the image out and unfroze the video. The object sailed up along the ship's z-axis, past the solar mast, and then arced back toward Ryugu. It soon disappeared over the upper horizon and the terminator line.

Abarca said, *"We can't have that thing sailing around us again."*

Adisa sat down across from Tighe, tapping at an invisible UI once more. "This makes sense."

"What makes sense?"

"Its arrival today. Apparently we were not the only ones to take advantage of that once-in-a-century delta-v window that Mr. Joyce mentioned."

"Then why is it arriving only now?"

Adisa studied invisible screens. "I am looking at various Hohmann transfers from low Earth orbit on the day we left. One of those transfer orbits—in fact, the very lowest delta-v trajectory—would have arrived here at Ryugu two days ago."

Tighe considered this. "A robotic spacecraft that—thanks to Joyce's secrecy—has no idea we're here. If that thing had struck one of the radial arms we would have collapsed like matchsticks. The whole ship would have been lost, and we would be dead."

Abarca spoke into the comm link. *"Priya."*

"Yes, Isabel."

"Take a mule out. Ade, give Priya a trajectory to follow. We need to find out where that thing went and where it's liable to go next."

"Give me a moment." Adisa started working UIs. In a few seconds he said, "There, Priya. Follow that path."

Tighe looked up to see that Adisa had opened the camera view of the mule Chindarkar was already remotely piloting. The entire crew could see through its camera eyes. Tighe changed his crystal to VR mode. Now, it was as though he *was* the mule, sailing out and away from the ship—headed toward the sunlit rim of Ryugu. The screen was almost entirely black except for the terminator line.

Abarca's voice: *"Be careful, Priya. That thing is still flying around."*

The asteroid's surface approached and then passed beneath the mule. As they crossed to the sunlit side, glare flared momentarily until the software adjusted. Now Tighe could see an ashen boulder field below.

But straight ahead—several kilometers away—was something else: an unfamiliar spacecraft. It was at least 100 meters long—its large solar array unfurled, radio antennas aimed back at Earth, and a dozen spherical tanks running along its underside. Half a dozen smaller craft moved around it.

Jin spoke first. *"A mother ship."*

Morra said, *"Looks like a whole robotic mining operation."*

Abarca's voice: *"Priya, bring us closer. We'll need detailed video. Mission control has to identify who sent this."*

Tsukada said, *"Why would they buzz us like that? It put their own equipment at risk."*

Chindarkar answered. "Because we're dealing with an AI. The distance to Earth is too great for human telepresence. That means an AI must be guiding these machines, and we don't know how dumb it is."

Chindarkar brought the mule toward the equatorial ridge on the sunlit side of Ryugu. The robotic mother ship was just over 5 kilometers away according to the mule's lidar.

Morra said, *"Looks like they've set up shop on the far side."*

Adisa studied the screen. "To keep their solar panels in constant sunlight. It makes sense. Robots can be hardened to the Sun's radiation."

Chindarkar ran a 3D scan of the ship and stored the geometry for transmission back to Earth. The mystery vessel had the word "Argo" stenciled in blue letters along its aft panel, and the star-filled logo of Celestial Robotics Corporation.

Morra asked, *"Anybody recognize the company?"*

Adisa replied again. "CRC is an asteroid-mining company that belongs to Alan Goff—the industrial robotics billionaire."

Tighe nodded. "So Joyce wasn't the only Titan with his eye on Ryugu."

"Try to get us a little closer, Priya."

The mule edged a kilometer closer to the robotic ship. It looked like the vessel was built in four cylindrical sections—as if it had been launched as multiple payloads on a Burkett or Macy heavy-lift rocket. Each of the modules had panels open to reveal complex plumbing and processing equipment, as well as racks to recharge rugged-looking cylindrical mining robots. These were studded with bug-eye-like camera lenses, robotic limbs, and thruster ports.

Abarca said, *"Mission control can contact Goff, and we'll deconflict this situation."*

"Whoa!"

The view of the mule suddenly lurched.

Chindarkar shouted, *"I've lost control!"*

Suddenly the view shifted, and one of the newly arrived mining robots was up close—its hydraulic limbs gripping one of the robotic arms at the front of the mule.

Abarca called out, *"Escape, Priya!"*

"I'm trying!"

The mule's thrusters popped, and the screen jolted around.

A blinding white light pierced the screen, and Tighe pulled off his crystal. "Damn! What the hell was that?"

"Laser. The damn thing's cutting up the mule."

Priya's voice came through on the comm link. *"Connection to Mule 3 lost."*

"Goddamnit! That's a piece of equipment we can't afford to lose."

Adisa called out, "Isabel, we have more problems. Look at the radar. A craft is approaching Honey Bee 1."

Tighe put his crystal back on and took it out of VR mode.

Adisa put up an exterior view of the rim of Ryugu. Two kilometers above the surface, Honey Bee 1 rode a terminator orbit while its optical mining reflectors slowly chewed up a bagged boulder with concentrated sunlight. The silhouette of one of Goff's mining robots closed the distance to it.

Abarca called out, *"Ade, cut that Honey Bee loose from its bag and bring it back to the* Konstantin."

Tighe interjected. "Isabel, it has 10 tons of water ice on board. It'll barely be able to move."

"J.T.'s right, Ade, jettison the slush bags. Get that Honey Bee out of there—we can't afford to lose it."

Tighe watched the video in disgust as the Honey Bee jettisoned its payload. It then fired its rocket engine, propelling the machine back toward the *Konstantin*, leaving a month's worth of work behind.

The rival mining robot quickly latched on to the bags of water ice, nitrogen, and more.

"We left behind the centrifugal sorter. The Archimedes' screw, the—"

Abarca broke in. "*We can build new ones.*"

On-screen the Honey Bee appeared to have escaped. Two more rival mining craft were now taking charge of what it left behind.

Tighe looked to Adisa. "Joyce needs to straighten this out or we are in serious trouble. We've got a storage yard containing 700 tons of mined resources that isn't leaving here for another five months. That's a whole year's worth of work. Nicole *died* for it. How long until those things tear into it?"

Abarca's voice came in over the comm link. "*Ade, send that video footage to mission control. And get Gabriel on the line—tell him it's urgent . . .*"

CHAPTER 34

Titans

L ukas Rochat found it difficult to relax during the thirty-minute heli-copter flight from Seattle's Sea-Tac Airport. The last time he'd flown in a helicopter, he'd been unceremoniously tossed out the door with a bungee cord around his ankles, and it had been done on the order of the man sitting next to him—Nathan Joyce.

However, as the black ACH145 executive chopper soared across the Strait of Juan de Fuca and over the forested San Juan archipelago between Vancou-ver and Seattle, the scenery helped ease his anxiety. In any case, Rochat was nowhere near as anxious as Joyce, who'd sat in brooding silence ever since they boarded his jet back in Colorado.

The helicopter soon descended toward an island Rochat recognized only from magazines—Allan Island, the private home of industrial robotics billion-aire Alan R. Goff, chairman and CEO of Celestial Robotics—Catalyst Cor-poration's rival and newest neighbor on Ryugu. It was here, at this secluded 292-acre retreat, where they'd scheduled a meeting far from prying eyes.

The chopper alighted on a clearly marked pad in the middle of a mani-cured lawn surrounded by pine forest. As Joyce and Rochat exited they noticed an autonomous golf cart waiting for them. An LED sign on it scrolled the mes-sage: *Welcome to Allan Island. Please climb aboard.*

Joyce grumbled, "Fucking robots . . ."

As he and Rochat climbed aboard the golf cart, the chopper pilot waved, then lifted off and away, leaving them in relative silence as the electric cart whirred along pleasant asphalt paths into an orderly forest. Birdcalls echoed from the surrounding trees.

Try as he might, Rochat never got used to the capability billionaires had to alter their surroundings. The entire island had been tended to like a giant bonsai tree—not one branch out of place. During their half-mile ride, they saw no human beings. Instead, robotic vehicles rolled past or flitted by on rotors, focused on inscrutable tasks.

In a couple of minutes, the golf cart glided to a stop in front of a postmodern mansion that was all glass walls and Tetris-like slabs of white marble suspended in cunning ways that made them appear to defy gravity. Rochat and Joyce were greeted at the front door by an actual human domestic, a young Southeast Asian woman in a simple blue dress who brought them through cavernous chambers fronted by multistory seamless windows offering an expansive view of the strait. A massive sailboat stood at the dock below, with human workers lovingly polishing its decks and railings.

From there they walked along a terrace large enough to host a rugby match, and finally entered a near-invisible opening in a glass wall.

They now found themselves in the immense corner office of Alan Goff. Two of the exterior walls were crafted of pure glass. A postmodern fireplace occupied the interior corner and somehow managed to project a chill over the room.

Goff stood behind his desk and nodded as the men entered. Standing next to Goff was a woman in her fifties, with perfect silver hair cut in a severe bob. She wore a tailored suit and did not nod in greeting. Goff's domestic departed, the glass door sealing seamlessly behind her.

Goff gestured. "Gentlemen, please have a seat." He looked to his companion. "My attorney, Karen Cano." He glanced at Rochat but spoke to Joyce. "I see you brought your son."

"Very funny." Joyce sat down in a black leather and metal chair. "This is my personal attorney, Lukas Rochat."

"No doubt a wunderkind, like yourself." Goff sat behind his desk. Cano remained standing.

After some hesitation Rochat decided to sit.

Goff peaked his hands beneath his nose for several moments before speaking. "Nathan, I used to think you were just another bullshitter. Now I realize you really are insanely irresponsible."

Joyce glared. "I didn't come here for a lecture, Alan. There are lives at risk."

"Whose fault is that?"

"You need to reprogram your mining robots to avoid—"

"It's already done."

"You've made sure there's no danger to the *Konstantin* or her crew?"

"No danger from me. I've instructed my engineers to revise the operating perimeter of our mining craft. They will remain on the sunlit side of the asteroid— for now."

Joyce visibly unclenched. "Good. Thank you."

"There wouldn't have been any danger to begin with if someone had notified us there were going to be spacecraft at Ryugu."

Joyce took several moments to answer. "Neither was paperwork submitted concerning any robotic mining missions to Ryugu."

"That's because the Grand Duchy of Luxembourg doesn't own outer space. We're operating under the US Space Act of 2015. We have a commercial space transportation license from the FAA."

Joyce scoffed. "The FAA."

"You did think to check other licensing authorities to ensure your secret— and illegal—activities wouldn't conflict with other lawful operations, I trust." Goff didn't wait for an answer. "No? That is a surprise. But then, you have the world's youngest attorney to help you keep track of things. I would think he'd have boundless energy."

Rochat burned with humiliation. He couldn't believe he had failed to monitor filings at the FAA. Could he even have done that? He didn't know, and that made him feel all the more out of his depth.

Goff continued. "It's interesting that you bring up legal filings, because my people have been unable to discover under what lawful instrument you are mining Ryugu. You've submitted detailed proposals and permit applications—which were very informative. And yet, your much-publicized mining ship, the *Konstantin*, has no legal right to exist. Not yet. Nor has it been cleared for human spaceflight—which isn't surprising, since it looks like something the Wright brothers glued together. Where did you find the poor souls unwise enough to climb aboard it, much less sail it to the far side of the Sun?"

Joyce silently clenched his jaw.

"Not only are you breaking the law, Nathan, you're putting human lives at risk. It's unethical. Immoral. It's—"

Joyce shot up out of his seat. "It's exploration! Don't you understand that?

Do we not take risks anymore?" He gestured outside. "Is everything going to be done by fucking machines from here on? Why do we even bother to exist, Alan?"

"Sit down, Nathan. I'm not one of your investors or your unfortunate asteroid miners. Your impassioned speeches won't enthrall me."

After a moment Joyce sighed and sat back down.

"You probably know that I play poker as a hobby. Professionally. I know when I have a strong hand and when my opponent has a weak one. You, Nathan, have a very weak hand."

Rochat felt a hot flash of fear spreading through his body. This was how it was going to end. His time in the limelight—over.

Goff leaned back in his office chair. "You sent humans to do a machine's job. By sending robots, we were able to take a longer, slower trajectory. We reached Ryugu with a total delta-v budget of only 4.97 kilometers per second."

"I reached it with a delta-v of just 2.6."

"Bullshit, and you know it. You left out the delta-v necessary to bring 560 metric tons of materials to a lunar DRO to assemble your ship. Your total delta-v from LEO was at least 5.9 kilometers per second."

Joyce remained silent.

"And what has it gotten you? We'll exceed your tonnage in a few months. It makes me wonder why you publicized this plan of yours in the first place—suggesting you wanted investors—when you'd already built the ship."

Joyce muttered, "I needed to design the ship. That process was impossible to keep confidential."

"Ah, so you announce it so that no one pays any attention—just another harebrained scheme by Nathan Joyce." Goff paused. "Which was convincing because Catalyst Corporation does not have anything like the resources required to construct and launch the *Konstantin*. In fact, none of your aerospace ventures do. It looks like you got some sovereign fund money—probably petro-states looking to diversify into the future, willing to bet on the visions of some tech-bro who throws a great party. But I figure that still leaves you, what—about ten or fifteen billion short?" Goff let his words sink in. "I wonder where you got the extra money."

"What do you want, Alan?"

"You misappropriated resources, Nathan. Fund managers who thought they were investing in telecom or biotech might be surprised to discover that their money has been siphoned off to other uses. I wonder how long until someone discovers your little shell game?" Goff looked at his attorney. "How long was Bernie Madoff's Ponzi scheme operating? I think it was *fifty* billion he swindled, wasn't it?"

"Okay, Alan. I get it. What do you want?"

"So why did you do it? Was it a last-chance Hail Mary pass to erase your liabilities before they swallowed you whole? Was the plan to come roaring back with one last big score? To become a legend?"

"What. Do. You. Want?"

Goff studied Joyce. "I want you to understand that what you did was not clever, or pioneering, or even original. It's the sort of reckless thing people on the verge of going bankrupt engage in. My engineers have been monitoring your crew's radio communications at Ryugu. You already have one crew member dead. Does it bother you that your little stunt got someone killed? Those foolhardy people you sent out there are still facing three more years in oblivion—no possibility of rescue even if we sent out a ship for them *today*. They are all dead. It's just a matter of time."

Joyce sat, his hands balled into fists.

"I will grant you this much: you built the first spin-gravity ship, and it appears to work. But how selfish do you have to be to send those people out there while robbing them of the glory for what they're doing? A hundred and sixty-three million miles from Earth! Farther than any human has ever been. They've accomplished more firsts than the Apollo missions, but do you allow them to become the famous pioneers they should be—even as they sacrifice their lives to save your empire of bullshit? No. You do not. Instead you conceal this historic endeavor to save your skin in the hopes you can buy your way out of bankruptcy. You're pathetic. It's not the world economy that's going to collapse, Nathan. It's your net worth. But then, I guess you are your whole world."

"Are you finished?"

Goff took a deep, satisfied breath. "I am."

"What do you want?"

Goff's attorney whispered in his ear. He listened intently, then looked up. "Forty percent of the net profits of Catalyst Corporation."

"Is that right? I might as well go bankrupt now and save myself the trouble."
Joyce looked to Rochat.

Rochat had no idea what to say.

Joyce said, "Twenty percent."

Rochat was shocked this discussion was even happening.

Goff and his attorney consulted. "Thirty-five."

"If this mission isn't going to save me, then I won't—"

"Fine. Twenty-five percent."

"Twenty-three point six percent."

Goff was taken aback. "Strangely precise. Intended to make me believe
that you anticipated this juncture and that this is the very best you can offer."
He laughed. "You might be a fair poker player after all. Okay, Nathan. Twenty-
three point six percent it is."

"Net of all expenses."

"We will agree upon what constitutes expenses—and there will be audit
rights."

Joyce nodded.

Rochat leaned in, whispering, "You are not seriously contemplating this,
Nathan?"

Joyce gripped Rochat's arm, whispering, "You have no idea how fucked I am,
Lukas. I won't just lose everything. I'll go to jail. I'll lose my reputation." Joyce
turned to Goff. "Agreed. In principle. But for that I get your nondisclosure. And I
want your signature so that if the news comes out later, you'll take the heat, too."

"Why would I reveal any of this, Nathan? It's not credible. Besides, I hope
to be making good money with you—at least, that is, until your people at Ryugu
expire. Poor, brave souls. However, I'm not the one who sent them there, am I?
And they are beyond saving in any event."

Rochat felt like he was in a conference with devils, and then he realized he
was one of those devils.

Is this what success is—gambling with other people's lives?

He couldn't recall how he'd gotten here—and how it had all become so
awful. He thought of the crew of the *Konstantin*. Their straightforward, noble
view of things. How had he ever thought Joyce was brilliant? And yet, Goff's
supposedly high-minded principles were satisfied by a cut of the action. The
man was as heartless as his machines.

Though it was morning, Rochat suddenly needed a stiff drink.

Joyce said, "Your robots mine only the sunlit side. We mine the dark side."

"That sounds appropriate, but given Ryugu's rotational rate, it's not workable. However, we can constrain our high-altitude movements to the sunlit side."

After a moment of consideration, Joyce nodded.

"Your crew appears to be readying a robotic tug for a return trajectory to Earth. I want a manifest of what's on that shipment—and its orbital elements. Realize that I have surveillance cameras that will be able to monitor your crew's activities."

"I want back the eleven thousand kilos of water your mining robots stole from me. The nitrogen and ammonia, too."

Goff considered this. "We hardly stole it. It was a misunderstanding, but I'll have your containment bags left in a terminator orbit. They might be damaged, but there's nothing I can do about that. My representatives at Ryugu aren't as adaptable as yours."

Joyce stared intently. "Alan, you need to understand how vital it is that I return as much tonnage as possible to cislunar space. If I'm going to keep my house of cards standing, I need that first shipment to be big. Seeing as you're now my partner, I expect you to not get in my people's way."

Goff put up his hands. "Perish the thought. I have nothing but sympathy for those people."

With that Joyce stood.

Rochat was about to get up when Joyce put his hand on Rochat's shoulder.

"Stay, Lukas. Work out the details with Ms. Cano, and get back to me with a written draft as soon as possible. This remains entirely confidential. No emails."

Goff nodded. He also passed a card across his desk. "Since we're now partners, Nathan, here is my public key. I suggest you give me yours as well—in case we need to discuss any news from Ryugu."

Joyce cast one more glare at Goff before grabbing the card and storming out.

Rochat felt utterly corrupted as he remained behind.

CHAPTER 35

Breakdown

MARCH 23, 2035

James Tighe stared at a holographic projection of the orbits of Ryugu and Earth floating above the galley table. Amy Tsukada and David Morra watched along with him from across the galley table as they ate breakfast.

Jin Han pointed at a trajectory between the two celestial objects. "Just over two and a half years. No matter how I calculate it."

Tighe leaned back in his seat. "You're saying our first return tug won't reach cislunar space until . . ." He observed the hologram animation complete. ". . . December 2037?"

"The math does not lie."

Morra shook his head in disgust. "Meanwhile, Goff and his robots are headline news all over Earth as the first asteroid-mining operation."

Tsukada asked Jin, "Who decided on our return tug's trajectory?"

"It is not a decision. The tug only has a delta-v of 500 meters per second. Two and a half years is the fastest transfer it can do."

"And Joyce said he wouldn't announce our existence until our first shipment arrived in cislunar space." Tighe looked up at a virtual TV screen showing an Earth news broadcast. "And he hasn't. It's like we disappeared off the face of the Earth."

Morra headed to the kitchen with his empty cereal bowl. "This Goff guy knows we're here. Why doesn't he tell the world?"

Tsukada folded her arms. "And let us steal his limelight?"

"Let *Joyce* steal his limelight, you mean. That's why I—"

Adisa's voice came in over the comm link. *"You should all see this. One of CRC's mining ships is passing near us."* He made a hologram of Ryugu visible for everyone. An ethereal *Konstantin* rotated above both hab breakfast tables—with a radar blip coming in at a slow arc a kilometer below.

Morra growled, "They're supposed to stay away from us."

Adisa said, *"Look closer,"* and the hologram zoomed in on the mining robot.

Chindarkar's voice said, *"It's tumbling."*

The several-ton mining robot was slowly turning on a couple of axes.

Tighe stared. "It looks dead."

"The solar panels are covered with regolith."

Morra said, "They'll come out and get it."

"It's on its eighth orbit already."

"Maybe their maintenance tugs are backlogged."

"I would think retrieval of a tumbling ship would take priority over ones safely in a repair dock."

Tighe looked at his shipmates across the table. "CRC wouldn't just jettison a broken-down mining rig. That thing cost a few hundred million to bring out here. Letting it drift loose would be as hazardous to them as it is to us."

Abarca spoke over the comm link. *"J.T.'s right. We need to find out what's going on."*

Sitting at his workstation on the first floor of Hab 2, Tighe used the VR capabilities of his crystal to control a Valkyrie robot as it glided just above the surface of Ryugu. The robot uncoiled several lengths of 100-meter tether cord behind it as it coasted toward the asteroid's terminator line. The cord led back to a mule, concealed beyond Ryugu's horizon. The mule had imparted forward momentum to his Valkyrie before he'd released his robotic grip on its handrail.

It always amazed Tighe how realistic the telepresence system felt. The cratered surface of the asteroid passed below in shades of green in his robotic night vision. Finally a blinding light up ahead washed out his screen, and Tighe switched to a normal camera view.

Bolts of electricity arced sporadically all along Ryugu's terminator line. They looked like flashes of gunfire in the darkness. Tighe asked no one in particular, "What is that?"

Adisa's voice came in first. *"The difference in electrical charge between the day- and nightside. The terminator is a zone of electrical instability."*

Crossing into sunlight, Tighe spotted something rising above the horizon to his left, arcing up into space. "Hang on. I see something."

In fact, he saw several things. A half dozen objects traversed the featureless blackness of sunlit space.

"We see it."

Adisa's voice: *"Whatever that is, it is in a decaying orbit."*

Tighe dialed his camera zoom, tracking glittering metallic objects in the sunlight. "Mining robots." There was also asteroid material, and what looked to be a charging station with shattered solar panels. "They look damaged."

Chindarkar's voice: *"I count three more mining rigs. Dead, apparently. There's a lot of debris."*

"A collision?"

Jin's voice: *"They all seem to have lost power."*

Tighe followed the objects with his robotic eyes. "I say we try to lay eyes on the mother ship."

There was a momentary silence, and then Abarca said, *"Okay, but keep your head on a swivel."*

"It *literally* is on a swivel." Tighe kept watch for CRC mining robots as the Valkyrie kept gliding forward. Below, Ryugu's sunlit surface was obscured by something resembling haze. "How is there fog? Ryugu has no atmosphere."

Adisa's voice again: *"Dust levitation. The solar wind gives particles a positive electrical charge on the dayside. It can create a fog-like layer. Perhaps this layer caused the failure of CRC's robots."*

The Valkyrie neared the end of its coil of tether, and Tighe squeezed his robotic hand on the line to slow to a smooth stop.

Several kilometers straight ahead a large spacecraft floated off Ryugu's equator.

"Would you look at that."

A cloud of metallic debris glittered in space above and around the mother ship, *Argo*. The ship's dozen docking bays were all empty. Closer at hand was a maintenance bot locked in an embrace with a mining rig—both of them seemingly inert. On Ryugu's surface a few hundred meters ahead, a mining bot had impacted the ground at high speed, leaving its own crater and a tangle of sparkling wreckage.

Tighe looked first one way, then another. "They're all down. I don't see a single CRC rig still in operation."

Morra's voice: *"Looks like somebody screwed up."*

Adisa said, *"Perhaps regolith got into their circuit boards—caused short circuits."*

Jin observed, *"Whatever it was, CRC failed to anticipate it."*

Tighe said, "The mother ship still has power, though. Look." He zoomed his robot eyes in on it.

Sure enough, red, green, and blue LED lights were still active in the equipment bays. The mother ship's large solar array was clear.

"But I'd say our competition is out of business."

Nathan Joyce waited in his office for the encrypted video call to go through. In a moment a hologram of Alan Goff floated before him. Lukas Rochat observed, waiting off to the side, unseen.

Goff's ghostly image grimaced. "Nathan, I prefer to restrict our contact to scheduled calls. I'm very busy."

"I imagine you are—especially with your entire Ryugu mining operation broken down."

Goff stared in silence. He then spoke to someone off-screen, waited a few moments, then loomed larger. "We are working on the problem."

Rochat could see it in Joyce's eyes—ready to twist the knife, relishing it.

"There's your tell, Alan. I have some very detailed video that indicates Ryugu chewed up your machines and spat them out."

Goff said nothing.

"A small design error, perhaps? Some forgotten detail? What was that I said about failing fast and often?"

A vein in Goff's neck visibly throbbed. "I suppose you're enjoying this."

Joyce clearly was. "I have a proposition for you, Alan. Your entire mission does not need to end in failure."

Goff stared. "Go on."

"I have people on site who may be able to help. For a price."

Concerned, Rochat snapped alert.

Goff closed his eyes and sighed. "What price?"

"Reversing our deal. You pay *me* 23.6—"

"I will merely refrain from exposing your crew's presence at Ryugu, saving you from criminal prosecution."

Joyce gave him a sideways look. "But my going to jail won't help you. And of course, then everyone will know you've failed."

"Unlike you, this setback does not ruin me. I didn't sink everything I had into this. I will be able—"

"But your mission is so very public. Do you think you'll ever get another dime from your investors? All you've done is proven your designs don't work. But think how close you were. You were outproducing us, Alan. Now I guess we'll never know if you could have succeeded."

Goff stared.

"We both know robotic asteroid mining will generate trillions in profits. Too bad you won't be participating. On the bright side, they might teach CRC as a case study—a lesson on what not to do."

Goff stared at the screen for several moments. "Five percent."

Joyce slapped his desk. "Done."

"You asshole. You just wanted to be on top, didn't you?"

"Be thankful my people can help."

CHAPTER 36

Hot Fix

APRIL 6, 2035

T here's no way in hell!" Isabel Abarca stared down a hologram of Nathan Joyce. Although their orbit had now swung back toward Earth again, they were still more than 154 million miles distant— which meant a transmission delay of nearly fourteen minutes. She may as well have been cursing at a television show.

Joyce's hologram continued. ". . . CRC engineers have sent you complete schematics to guide you through the troubleshooting and repair of their machines."

"He's insane if he thinks we're going to agree to this." Abarca started pacing like a puma in a cage.

Tighe, Morra, and Abarca were crewing Hab 1 this rotation, with Jin, Adisa, Priya, and Tsukada in Hab 2. They were all linked, as usual, via the AR portal.

Joyce continued. "No doubt you consider this request unreasonable. However, Celestial Robotics is in a position to force our hand. Unless we help them get back up and running, their CEO, Alan Goff, intends to reveal to Earth authorities the presence of the *Konstantin* at Ryugu."

Tighe shouted. "Good! It's about damn time."

". . . will result in civil and legal action against me and Catalyst Corporation. The true extent of Catalyst's liabilities will no doubt result in its liquidation to satisfy creditors. If that happens, I cannot be certain your mining contracts or your bonuses would be honored in any bankruptcy proceeding."

Morra sat up. "What did he just say?"

Joyce continued. "Only by repairing and reactivating CRC's mining equipment do we have a chance to keep the *Konstantin*'s existence confidential long enough to achieve success. The robot tug you're launching back to Earth on June 10 will be that success. Once it arrives in cislunar space loaded with mined resources, we will no longer have any reason for secrecy. However, to enjoy that success, we must first cooperate with Goff in the short term."

Chindarkar shrugged. *"Screw the mined resources. Once word gets out we're here at Ryugu, we'll be famous back on Earth. We won't need Joyce."*

Joyce pressed on. "You'll find engineering and maintenance manuals, as well as 3D-printing files and updated operating firmware for CRC's Klondike and Prospector robots in your inbox. Study these and message Gabriel when you're ready to begin technical sessions with CRC's engineering team. In the meantime, I must again emphasize how vital it is that you continue to maximize the payload on our first return shipment. For that reason, we should not begin repairs on CRC's robots until our own tug is safely en route back toward cislunar space. All our mutual hopes depend on it exceeding a thousand tons payload."

Abarca glared at the hologram.

"I hope you are all well and that you understand my reasons for this request. I promise you it will be worth it." Joyce's hologram dissolved.

Abarca shook her head. "This is the final straw. I won't—"

Proximity alarms suddenly went off. Everyone scrambled to load the perimeter display. The hologram revealed a small radar blip coming toward them from around the asteroid.

Adisa's voice said, *"More mining debris. Baseball-sized—too slow to do damage."* He silenced the alarm.

The crew watched the radar blip sail through the *Konstantin*'s rotational arc and impact the metal side of the Hab 1 airlock. The *clang* reverberated like a bell throughout Hab 1.

Tighe looked at the ceiling. "It's just luck that none of these have been large enough to cause damage."

Morra said, "Our luck may run out yet."

Chindarkar frowned. *"Repairing CRC's mining robots isn't in our contract."*

Tighe said, "I say we just clean up this orbiting debris and salvage CRC's robots for parts."

Tsukada added, *"I agree with J.T. and Priya. Screw CRC."*

Morra leaned forward. "Normally I'd agree with you, but if Goff does go public about our presence here, Joyce's goose is cooked—he'll be gone, sent to jail. Catalyst goes bankrupt. Then what happens to our contract?"

"Who gives a damn?" Tighe gestured to Chindarkar's AR image. "Like Priya says—we'll be famous back on Earth. The humans who've gone farthest and longest into deep space."

Morra turned toward Tighe. "How much is fame worth?"

Chindarkar said, *"I imagine there'd be . . . product endorsements."*

"Three countries have landed on the Moon. An international Mars mission is being prepared. Do you really think a brief flurry of media attention will replace the money we'd make from our mining bonus? How much are we sending back on this shipment, Ade?"

Adisa tapped at invisible screens. *"About 720 tons of water, 120 tons of ammonia, 140 tons of nitrogen, 40 tons of iron carbonyl, 36 tons of nickel carbonyl, and 26 tons of cobalt carbonyl. A bit over a thousand tons total."*

"A thousand tons. That's worth a hell of a lot in a lunar DRO. And that's just our first year. Remember all the problems we've solved since then. Our machines are working twenty-four/seven now. We could triple or quadruple that output in the next twelve months."

"That is optimistic, but—"

"Possible. It's possible, Ade. Our contract guarantees six million each—plus production bonuses, and at this rate, that means tens of millions per person. Maybe more. Now, I didn't go through all this just to have my daughters' inheritance erased by some bankruptcy judge back on Earth."

Tighe and the others considered Morra's argument. "What's to say Joyce will honor our agreement?"

Morra folded his arms. "I think Joyce wants to prove the other Titans wrong—above all. And he does that by making this a successful business. I say we keep our eyes on the prize and go fix Goff's robots. But I do think we demand payment for it."

Abarca stared at Morra—but she appeared to be considering his argument.

Chindarkar balked. *"You can't be serious."*

Jin also looked surprised. *"I would not have expected you to argue Joyce's case."*

"I'm not doing it for Joyce. I'm doing it for us."

Adisa flipped through the virtual technical manuals. *"Repairing these systems will be too complex for telepresence. That means several EVAs—amid orbiting debris."*

Tighe nodded. "Ade's right, and those would be long-distance EVAs—the longest we've done so far. At least 8 or 9 kilometers away from the *Konstantin.*"

Morra considered this. "We could use mules to tow the dead robots back here."

Abarca shook her head. "Oh no. We don't want those things anywhere near the *Konstantin.* Who knows what they'll do when they reactivate."

"Well, what do you propose, Isabel? If we sit here and do nothing, Goff wrecks everything we've worked for. We'll be famous back on Earth. Whoopee—a free drink in every bar. Do you really want to go back to Earth empty-handed? I don't."

Tsukada said, *"Surely we wouldn't lose everything if Joyce went bankrupt."*

"Let's not find out. Joyce may seem bad, but he's the devil we know. He built this ship, and it has kept us alive. His creditors? Who the hell knows?"

Chindarkar asked, *"What's to stop Goff from revealing us after we fix his robots?"*

Abarca shook her head. "No, Goff has to know we could easily sabotage his mining operation. We're here. He's not. He has too much to lose by betraying us."

Morra pointed. "Exactly. Which means we should do this." He looked around the table. "I volunteer. No one else has to go."

Jin shook his head. *"It is against procedure. I will go with you."*

Tighe added, "I'll go, too—in case you need rescue."

Abarca intervened. "We don't even have a plan." She looked to Adisa. "Ade, finish reviewing those CRC tech manuals. When you're ready, we'll get their engineers on the line. Let's have the minimum number of crew involved, and we turn back at the first sign of trouble."

Morra, Jin, and Tighe exchanged looks and nodded.

"In the meantime, let's make sure our first return shipment departs on schedule."

JUNE 10, 2035

Tighe floated in his EVA suit, tethered to the rim of a large metallic solar shield. The 25-meter-diameter shield was actually an inflatable polymer shell with a metallic film applied to its leading surface via chemical vapor deposition. It formed the prow of a newly built spacecraft that gleamed beneath the LED work lights of a mule hovering nearby.

Next to Tighe floated Isabel Abarca and David Morra. To the other side of Abarca floated Jin Han. It was the first time all four clam suits had been in use at once and Abarca's first EVA since the *Konstantin* arrived a year and a half earlier. Company policy stated that the ship's surgeon should remain on board the *Konstantin* unless absolutely necessary. However, today was necessarily historic.

The four of them floated alongside the words "Nicole Clarke," stenciled in meter-high gray letters. They'd named the vessel in honor of their friend and former captain.

Behind the solar shield the *Nicole Clarke* consisted of a latticework of printed polymer girders containing a ring of half a dozen 7-meter spherical bladder tanks, each filled with 180,000 liters of various resources—water ice, liquid nitrogen, or ammonia. In the gaps between the large tanks were another half a dozen small ones, each containing 14,000 liters of various carbonyls. A seventh large tank occupied the center of the ring, supplying fuel to the single methalox rocket engine mounted within a girder framework at the back of the ship.

Over the last several months Tighe, Jin, and Morra had unstepped one of the *Konstantin*'s engines and installed it on the *Nicole Clarke*. The task required hundreds of man-hours and close attention to AR-guided instructional videos, plus numerous consultations with mission control engineers back on Earth. However, the engine was eventually mounted, and with Tsukada's and Chindarkar's assistance, custom piping, valves, fuel pumps, cold-gas thrusters, solar panels, and circuitry were fashioned to complete the robotic tug based on a CAD plan transmitted by Catalyst managers. Once the tug's OS was loaded and diagnostics run, mission control declared it ready for use.

Barely 5 percent of the *Konstantin*'s length, the *Nicole Clarke* was nonetheless twice the *Konstantin*'s mass. However, since only 412 meters per second of delta-v was needed to depart Ryugu for cislunar space on this date, one lone rocket engine and a single large fuel tank would suffice to propel it homeward. Software would manage its journey.

Tighe and the others posed, arm in arm, near the tug's name, each of them making a thumbs-up gesture with their heavily padded gloves.

Chindarkar took several images with the mule's cameras.

Adisa's voice said, "*We have just received a message from mission control—it is Nathan Joyce. Gabriel would like us to play it before the launch.*"

The four miners on EVA exchanged annoyed looks.

Abarca nodded. "*All right, let's hear it, Ade.*"

Moments later Joyce's voice came in over the comm link. "*Today is an historic day—the launch of humanity's first ship returning space-mined resources back toward our home world. A ship that is itself mostly fashioned from resources mined in space. What you've achieved is the realization of a long-held dream—and proof that humanity has a future in the cosmos. Nicole Clarke would be proud to know this historic vessel bears her name.*"

Tighe muttered, "Hopefully people back on Earth learn about her someday."

Joyce continued. "*Congratulations to each and every one of you. Launch the* Nicole Clarke *whenever you are ready.*"

With that Tighe passed a snowball-sized white plastic sphere to Abarca. "Care to do the honors?"

She took the object into her hands. "*What's this?*"

"We can't christen a ship with champagne out here, so Amy put together a polymer shell filled with liquid nitrogen."

"*I throw it onto the hull?*"

"When you're ready."

Abarca wound up her pitch. "*I christen this vessel the* Nicole Clarke. *May she find her way safely home.*" With that Abarca hurled the object at the solar shield.

On impact the egg-thin shell shattered, dispersing the liquid out into space. The crew cheered.

Tighe turned to see two mules coming in to retrieve them, remotely piloted by Chindarkar and Adisa. The miners climbed aboard, two on each mule, and hooked in their tethers. In a few moments the mules retreated back toward the *Konstantin,* half a kilometer away. As they did so, Tighe watched the *Nicole Clarke.*

Adisa's voice came in over the comm link. *"T minus ten, nine, eight . . ."*

Tighe glanced across the top of his mule toward Morra. "We'll need to end this countdown custom at some point."

"I suppose you're right. Think of all the time we'll save. . . ."

They both turned to watch.

". . . three, two, one—we have ignition."

A silent cone of lavender flame sprayed out behind the *Nicole Clarke.*

Another cheer from the crew.

"C'mon, baby . . ."

Hinting at its mass, the ship at first slowly began to glide away, heading not toward the white dot of Earth but in the opposite direction—embarking on a winding two-and-a-half-year spiral that would eventually deliver it near Earth's moon just the same.

They all watched the tug pull away and gather speed.

"Well, that's a year and a half of work."

"And a human life. Let's hope it means something."

Eight days later Tighe again stood on the running board of Mule 2. Jin and Morra clung to another mule a couple hundred meters away. Both craft headed toward the sunlit side of Ryugu. Chindarkar remotely piloted Jin and Morra's mule, while Adisa piloted Tighe's.

"What's the weather look like today, Ade?"

Adisa's voice came in over the comm line. *"No solar flares predicted."*

The two mules crossed the terminator line half a klick above the surface, and suddenly they were bathed in sunlight. Tighe's helmet software instantly dampened the Sun into a white ball. Up ahead he could see CRC's robot mother ship, several kilometers off Ryugu's dayside equator.

Tighe's mule slowed to a stop as Morra and Jin continued, headed toward glittering debris. Tighe gave them the thumbs-up. "I'm close by if you need me."

Morra and Jin gave him a thumbs-up in response.

Tighe used the optics in his helmet to follow their movements.

Jin's voice came in on the radio. "*I have marked the target. It is the one clamped to that mining rig. You see it, Priya?*"

"*I see it.*"

The plan was to fix CRC's maintenance robot so that it would fix all the other robots.

The mule popped thrusters and accelerated to match the velocity and trajectory of the entwined dead robots.

Tighe observed from a growing distance. "Ade, keep me close. I don't want to be more than a hundred meters away."

"*I copy, J.T.*"

Priya's voice: "*Ten meters out. Eight meters. Five meters.*"

In Tighe's zoomed optics, he saw bits of asteroid regolith and small mechanical parts spiral away as the mule's robotic arms grabbed the tool booms of the dead maintenance rig. The three spacecraft now glided together 2 kilometers above Ryugu's surface.

Tighe felt relief. "Nice flying, Priya."

Morra and Jin pulled themselves along the running boards and toward the CRC robot. "*Looks like the maintenance bot was trying a repair. It's got the mining rig's service panel open. I'm going to clean this regolith off before we continue.*"

Jin and Morra each took out cans of delta-v and sprayed CO_2 gas to clear away asteroid dust from the surface of the machines.

After several minutes of cleaning work, Morra began climbing over the white-painted aluminum surface of the maintenance rig, while Jin hung back on the mule. "*A few dents here and there, but I think we can get it working.*"

Morra stopped at the open side panel, consulted an AR schematic, and then withdrew a custom ratchet tool from his chest harness—tools printed from 3D models supplied by CRC engineers. Morra used the ratchet to unbolt an interior access panel on the maintenance robot. In a minute or so he had it open and kicked on his helmet lights.

"*Yeah, the regolith is everywhere in here. You catching this on video?*"

Abarca's voice came over the comm link. *"I have it. I'm sending the video to CRC's engineers. It'll be thirty minutes minimum until we get a response."*

"Copy that. Well, gents, smoke 'em if you got 'em."

For the next forty-five minutes Tighe, Jin, and Morra gazed down at the surface of Ryugu and chatted idly. There wasn't even a star field to see here on the sunlit side of the asteroid. Instead, Tighe zoomed his optics in on CRC's mother ship and realized that its cameras were undoubtedly aimed straight back at them.

"How much you suppose Goff spent on that thing?"

"Five billion or so."

"Cheapskate."

Finally the CRC engineers sent word back.

Abarca's voice came in over the comm link. *"Dave, the engineers say you need to clean out the regolith and replace Control Boards 3, 5, and 6."*

"We waited for that? Bunch of geniuses, my arse . . ." Morra moved back toward the mule. *"Confirm that CRC is beaming a lockout signal from the Argo."*

Abarca replied, *"Stand by. It'll take another thirty minutes for confirmation."*

Morra gazed at CRC's distant mother ship. *"I'll get ready."* He took out a can of delta-v and started blasting CO_2 through the interior of the spacecraft—blowing away the metallic asteroid dust.

Tighe watched Jin climb toward the maintenance bot's rack of replacement parts.

Morra lowered his upper body into the service panel. *"This stuff gets everywhere. . . ."* He sprayed the interior.

What happened next occurred with inhuman speed. The maintenance robot suddenly sprang to life—its robotic limbs quickly inserting a control board into the open panel of the larger mining rig.

Tighe shouted, "Get out of there! It's active!"

Then the mining rig suddenly sprang to life as well.

"Abort!" Jin clambered to pull Morra from the service bay as the maintenance bot undocked from the mining craft, its thrusters popping. The mule was still clamped onto its hull.

Chindarkar shouted, *"Grab the mule!"*

The larger mining rig's scanners swept over the mule, and it popped thrusters to close the short distance to it. Large robotic arms seized the mule's cargo rack, and its mining laser stabbed blinding red light as it sliced through Jin's tether on its way to process the mule's metal. The maintenance bot's thrusters popped as it tried to free itself from the mule—hurtling Jin into space and down toward the surface of the asteroid.

"Han!" Tighe shouted. "Ade, go after him!"

Tighe's mule popped thrusters to pursue Jin, who was now tumbling down toward the distant surface of Ryugu. Tighe glanced back behind him.

The mining rig wrestled with Chindarkar's mule as their robotic arms intertwined. The mining robot's red laser burned at its maw. Morra, meanwhile, held on to the mule's running board.

Abarca's voice: *"Priya! Abort!"*

"I'm trying to break free! It's got the mule."

Tighe looked ahead at Jin and then back at Morra.

Morra's voice came in over the comm link. *"J.T., get Han! We've got this!"*

Tighe reluctantly turned forward again and concentrated on the tumbling orange form of Jin 100 meters ahead. Tighe's crystal display indicated they were just over 1,700 meters off the cratered, ashen surface of Ryugu now, and closing fast. "Han! I'm coming for you."

He could see Jin's SAFER harness pop thrusters, and with remarkable skill Jin managed to dampen his tumble—but before he could diminish his descent speed, the thrusters were empty. Jin's voice came in: *"J.T.! Turn back. You cannot reach me in time."*

They were now 1,300 meters above the surface.

"You know I'm bad at physics, Han. Faster, Ade!"

Adisa replied, *"J.T. He is right. The mule will not have the delta-v to pull out of this trajectory in time. We must slow our descent."*

"Listen to him, J.T.!"

Morra's voice came in over the comm link. He was panting and grunting as he spoke. *"Priya, take over J.T.'s mule! No offense, Ade, but she's a more skilled pilot."*

In moments Tighe saw Adisa log off and Chindarkar log on as the pilot of his mule. "Priya, bring me as close as you can."

"Hold on."

The asteroid surface loomed 800 meters below as they closed on Jin. He was still 50 meters away. Then 30. Then 10.

Jin shouted over the radio, *"Abort this rescue! You will lose the mule and your life!"*

"Reverse thrusters, Priya!" Tighe pushed off from the mule—which was now only a few hundred meters above Ryugu. Jin faced him, arms outstretched. Tighe hurtled downward, his tether trailing behind him. Tighe tried not to notice the surface looming behind Jin. They grabbed each other, and the moment they did, they both fumbled to hook one of Jin's carabiners onto Tighe's harness.

Jin clicked in.

Suddenly the tether snapped taut—and they both bounced like a locket at the end of a chain as the mule's thrusters buffeted them. "Climb, Priya! Climb!"

The surface of the asteroid was less than 200 meters away now.

Tighe looked up to see that Chindarkar was riding the mule's rear thrusters—accelerating them forward as well as in reverse. They were headed toward the asteroid's equatorial ridge. Now the surface closed in even faster. "What are you doing?"

Her voice came in over the comm link. *"It's the only way! We're not going to have much left in the tank if we make this."*

Tighe and Jin looked down at the ashen surface rising to meet them. Their forward velocity was increasing. They both looked ahead and could see the ridgeline approaching. They were hanging 10 meters below the mule as it raced above the surface, still pulling out of its dive.

Jin shouted, *"Climb! Climb!"*

They both clawed at the tether line, slowly rising.

Chindarkar's voice again: *"This is going to get hairy!"*

"What do you mean it's *going* to get hairy?" A glance ahead told him.

Chindarkar was bringing the mule down a narrow gap between huge boulders on the equatorial ridge. Rock walls rose around them as they soared through. A glance down showed blurred regolith racing past just beneath their feet. Jin actually kicked a rock off the peak of the ridge, sending up a dust cloud behind them.

On the far side of the equator the asteroid's surface quickly sloped away again. The mule gradually gained altitude until it was clear they were safe. Tighe and Jin still held on to each other.

Jin eased his grip. *"That was reckless."*

"This whole expedition is reckless."

Jin stared but then nodded in silent thanks.

Tighe slapped him on the shoulder. "Great flying, Priya."

"Thanks."

They both pulled themselves back onto the running board of the mule and clicked into the eyebolts.

"Dave, Jin and I are secure." Tighe turned back toward the mining rig and Morra—who was now several kilometers away.

The distant CRC robots looked motionless again.

"Dave! Dave, do you copy?"

There was no response.

Suddenly an alert popped up in Tighe's crystal display—*Morra, David, cardiac arrest.*

"What the hell . . . ?" Tighe zoomed his optics in to see Morra's burnt-orange space suit flailing alongside the inert mining rig, his exposed titanium legs shining in the sunlight. "Priya! Priya, get us over there!"

She pivoted the mule. *"We won't have enough CO_2 to get back to the Konstantin."*

"Get us over there!" Tighe brought up an AR readout of Morra's pulse and respiration. Morra was flatlining.

Jin shouted, *"Priya, bring us there now!"*

Abarca broke in. *"You don't have the propellant to get back even if you reach Dave."*

Jin said, *"There will be more propellant on Mule 1, Isabel."*

"Dave's suit has been compromised."

Tighe and Jin brought up Morra's suit readings. Morra's clam suit atmosphere was at zero pressure.

"You'll have no way of resuscitating Dave even if you reach him, and there's still an active CRC mining rig on the loose. We can't lose both of you as well."

"Priya! Move this mule or I will take manual control."

"J.T., there is no room for sentiment. Do you understand me? We're over a hundred million miles from Earth."

Tighe stared at Morra's distant form, no longer struggling—just floating. "The mining rig is not active."

"We can't be sure, and you don't have enough thruster gas."

"The mining rig isn't moving, and neither is the maintenance robot. They're not operational."

"We can't be certain of that."

Tighe zoomed in his optics and nodded at what he saw. "Yes, we can be certain."

He shared the image of Morra floating lifeless, space suit shredded at the legs—and CRC circuit boards clutched in each of his gloved hands.

On the return trajectory to the *Konstantin*, with the second, damaged mule towed behind, Tighe and Jin rode in silence. Morra's body was strapped to the equipment rack between them, Morra's EMU torn open in several places.

Later they reviewed Morra's helmet-cam video and watched the struggle—how Morra, with his suit depressurizing, suffocating and blind, nonetheless pulled himself into the service bay of the large mining robot and yanked its control boards out by the roots as his last, defiant act of life.

But here and now, Jin stared at Morra's dead face. Morra's frozen eyes stared into the deep, his transparent visor slid open.

"Don't, Han."

"This is my fault."

"No. The robot severed your line. If anyone's to blame, it's me for not acting fast enough. If I'd responded—"

"David told you to come after me. He chose my life over his own." Jin grappled with the enormity of this realization.

It was a realization Tighe had known himself. He reached across Morra's chest and gripped Jin's shoulder.

CHAPTER 37

Flameout

L ukas Rochat rode in the passenger seat of an electric Range Rover, heading out to Nathan Joyce's private airstrip. The paved road was smooth, but the Stetson-wearing driver rolled through the acreage at a sedate 40 kilometers per hour.

Rochat checked his watch—the expense of which now mocked him. Joyce's investment company, Asterisk, was months behind on paying Rochat's attorney fees. He looked to the driver. "Can we drive faster, please? This is an emergency."

The sixty-year-old ranch hand looked at him, appearing more like the proprietor of a scented candle store than an American cowboy. "Mr. Joyce has prizewinning genetic cattle in these fields. He'd take it badly if I were to strike one of them. If it's real urgent, you phone him."

Rochat had indeed phoned and texted and emailed Joyce repeatedly, to no avail. "Just please go as fast as you can."

"That's what I'm doing." He pointed to the 25-miles-per-hour sign as they passed it.

Fortunately they soon came over a slight rise and crossed a cattle grill and fence line. Rochat could now see Joyce's private airstrip, tarmac, and hangars just ahead. The AS2 hypersonic business jet was still there; however, another plane was positioned near the taxiway—Joyce's red, white, and blue star-spangled Pitts Special S-1S biplane. Joyce was walking across the tarmac in his flight suit, helmet under one arm.

Rochat pointed. "There! Please hurry."

"All right. We'll get there. Hold your horses."

The Range Rover rolled up just as Joyce reached the biplane. He turned to laugh as Rochat got out. "You really want to talk to me apparently."

"I have been trying to reach you all morning. We have a problem. A big problem."

Joyce clapped Rochat on the shoulder. "So big it can't wait an hour or two?"

"Nathan . . ." Rochat glanced toward the driver, who was still standing by in the SUV.

Joyce waved him off, and the Range Rover moved away toward the hangars. They were now alone.

"Nathan, the authorities have raided Asterisk's offices in New York. They're raiding subsidiary offices in San Francisco and London. It's only a matter of time until the FBI or the IRS issues warrants for your arrest. You need to make arrangements. I am not a criminal defense attorney. You need to start preparing for seizure of your assets."

"You came all the way down here to tell me that?"

"Then you know about the office raids?"

He nodded. "Bank accounts frozen. The board has already voted to remove me as CEO of Asterisk. The others will do the same."

Rochat was amazed at the sanguine expression on Joyce's face. "Then they know about the *Konstantin*? They know about the expedition?"

"Oh no. But they know about the embezzlement and stock fraud."

"How are you not frantic? You need to be taking steps to preserve whatever you can, not puttering around with your toys. Arrangements also need to be made to safeguard the crew of the *Konstantin* through this chaos."

Joyce rested his flying helmet against his hip as he let the sun shine on his face. "Looks like I ran out of time. Got so close, too." He looked at Rochat. "Did you ever wonder why I paid you so much money, Lukas? Quite a lot to such a young, inexperienced attorney."

Rochat felt a spike of fear shoot through him. The investors and the authorities would be coming after him, too.

"It's because I could see it in your eyes. You really understood why I did this. If I was laundering cash for narco-traffickers, then I don't think you would have helped me. I think you wanted to be here at the start of something big. Humanity's next great leap."

Rochat found himself nodding. Joyce was right.

"That's why I chose you. But like most people your age, you rationalized that it made perfect sense for you to get rich—because you're *you*, after all."

That didn't sound as complimentary.

"You don't know the half of what I've done to launch the *Konstantin*, Lukas." He straightened Lukas's tie against the breeze. "Your ignorance will be what saves you."

"They'll come after me anyway, Nathan."

"There's no evidence you knew anything."

Rochat focused on the matter at hand. "Your shell companies will be uncovered and seized. The finances will be unraveled. They'll be looking for tens of billions of dollars. They will never stop looking. They will want that money back. They will discover the *Konstantin*."

Joyce laughed. "You know, when I was your age, forty or fifty million seemed like a lot of money. I'll bet it seems like that to you now, too. Don't let them have it, Lukas."

Rochat felt a pang—and also gratitude. Joyce had made him into someone. "I hope you know how much I appreciate everything you've done for me. If you need it back—"

Joyce gripped Rochat's shoulder. "That money wouldn't begin to fill the hole I've dug for myself. Besides, you'll need it."

That sounded worrisome. "Need it . . . for what?"

"The authorities know I embezzled money, but they don't know about the existence of the *Konstantin*. If the investors find out, I don't think they'll tell the authorities either. Because if they do, then it'll probably all get seized by one government or another."

Rochat was horrified. "If the authorities don't know about the *Konstantin*, what will happen to the crew?"

"That's up to you now, Lukas." Joyce gripped Rochat's shoulder. "I've destroyed all my records."

Rochat stammered, "What . . . but I—"

"Oh, before I forget . . ." Joyce pulled a scrap of paper from his pocket and a pen. He pressed it against Rochat's shoulder and wrote something down. "If you run into trouble, call this number—from a burner, like I taught you. The person on the other end will know what to do. They've been involved from the beginning." He paused. "Since before the beginning. You might say they're the catalyst—for all of this."

In shock Rochat accepted the paper. "Nathan, I—"

"Daylight's wasting, Lukas." Joyce clapped him on the shoulder and then started strapping on his flying helmet. "One last spin before they come for me . . ." He walked toward the biplane.

"Nathan, I don't know what to do!"

"No one does, Lukas!" With that Joyce climbed up into the cockpit of the Pitts Special. A moment later, he fired up the deafening engine. Bluish smoke raced away in the prop wash.

Rochat stepped back, shielding his eyes as Joyce brought the plane rolling down the taxiway. A glance back revealed the Range Rover coming back to retrieve him. Rochat sighed and walked to meet it.

He heard the biplane's powerful engine rev, and it thundered down the runway past him—almost immediately lifting off. Rochat stopped to watch it rising, the sunlight gleaming on its polished wings. Joyce brought the plane rolling and circling back.

Rochat realized that it was headed straight for him. He ducked down as the biplane buzzed just 5 meters overhead, buffeting him with wind. He quickly got to his feet and noticed Joyce waving a gloved hand—no doubt laughing.

The plane then climbed, spiraling skillfully upward, going up, up, a thousand feet or more, before stalling, falling back on its tail, and then rolling to the side as the engine revved again.

The Range Rover came up to Rochat. He was about to turn away, but something compelled him to stay in place.

He watched the Pitts Special continue to plummet downward, twisting one way, then another, clearly still under control. Yet, it did not turn from the ground.

Instead it plowed into the concrete tarmac at the far end of the landing strip at 300 kilometers per hour, disappearing in a fiery explosion as pieces of flaming shrapnel bounded away.

Rochat stared at the wreckage in mute shock. He vaguely heard people shouting and vehicles racing across the runway, but all he could see were the flames. He felt a hand on his shoulder.

"Son, you okay?"

Rochat nodded absently. "Call the police. Tell them there's been an accident."

Erika Lisowski exited NASA headquarters and walked across E Street SW, heading for the Rise 'n Shine café to grab a coffee and a croissant. As she moved through the morning pedestrian traffic, she checked email on her phone.

Entering the café, she stood in line, still reading email, ordered, and then moved to pay. Glancing up, she noticed a flat-screen TV mounted high in the corner. On it was a scene of smoldering plane wreckage, with a chyron caption that read, *Billionaire Nathan Joyce dies in stunt plane crash . . .*

Lisowski lowered her phone and stared at the screen, shock spreading over her.

As the chyron scrolled it added, . . . *amid charges of fraud and embezzlement.*

Lisowski left the croissant and the coffee on the counter, walking out of the café and turning left, around the corner and away from NASA headquarters. She marched stone-faced for blocks, barely registering the passage of time, feeling instead an emotional detachment not unlike what she imagined someone experiencing physical trauma might feel—her system flooding with cortisol and adrenaline.

At some point she came to a small plaza with benches fronting an office building, where she calmly sat down. She felt tears come, but she simply wiped them away, betraying no emotion.

Lisowski had no idea how long she remained there, but when she was ready, she stood and walked back toward her office, stopping on the way to check her appearance in a mirrored window. Then she stopped in for coffee and a croissant.

CHAPTER 38

Silent Earth

JUNE 14, 2035

J ames Tighe, Jin Han, and Isabel Abarca guided David Morra's body, clad in a blue flight suit, to the cairn formed by cylinders of radiation shielding. They gently placed Morra alongside the remains of Nicole Clarke, her hands still folded across her chest. Her face unchanged and peaceful behind her visor.

Tighe and Jin secured Morra's body to the floor of the cairn with Velcro straps and then folded his arms over his chest, holding them in place with Velcro tabs on the sleeves.

Tighe then floated alongside Abarca and gazed down at Morra. The rest of the crew watched through the trio's helmet cams.

Jin moved close. *"I owe you my life, David. Your daughters will want for nothing as long as I live."*

Abarca spoke to Morra. *"We will see that your family receives all that you worked for, and we'll make sure they know it's from you."*

Tighe gripped Morra's gloved hand. He tried to speak but was mute with grief.

The three of them floated in silence for several minutes. None of them were religious, but the endless void surrounding them was too much to bear at the moment. Tighe clung to the idea that this journey somehow mattered. That what they were doing out here would make a difference to humanity. Yet, he began to wonder if they would be able to fulfill their promise to Morra after all. For that they would need to get back to Earth—and enforce their contracts.

Eventually Abarca lightly bumped helmets with Morra, and they turned to go, sealing the cairn behind them.

After Morra's death, Tighe expected Nathan Joyce to show his face in a condolence message, as he had done with Clarke. However, the video message that did arrive showed only Gabriel Lacroix, Eike Dahl, and Sevastian Yakovlev. Lacroix spoke in somber tones about Morra's sacrifice, while Dahl and Yakovlev stood to either side.

Then Dahl and Yak extended their own tearful condolences, as Yak placed his hand on her shoulder. Tighe felt like a bastard for not hearing her words—seeing only Yak's hand.

Life had apparently gone on without him back on Earth.

Dahl made a brave face that Tighe knew hid a thousand terrible things—things she was either unable or unwilling to say. "J.T., it's hard to get private time on the uplink now. There have been cutbacks."

Following their message, detailed mission control briefings were replaced by a slide deck showing the *Konstantin*'s orbital position around the Sun and mining production targets for the coming week. Business had resumed but even more impersonally than before—as though their close friend hadn't just been killed while carrying out a clusterfuck operation at the insistence of the company's CEO.

Thankfully, the CRC mining robots were dead, too. The robot mother ship, *Argo*, repositioned in an orbit 50 kilometers from Ryugu in the hours after Morra's death—perhaps fearing retribution.

Smart, Tighe thought.

More alarming, news and television broadcasts from Earth suddenly ceased. Catalyst mission control had, without notice, placed them in a media blackout.

Catalyst Corporation messages began to arrive on a haphazard schedule. There were fewer people in the background of each camera shot at mission control. Yak and Dahl sent occasional videos, urging the crew to keep up their morale. Yet, the miners' numerous questions went unanswered. Tighe suspected Dahl and Yak weren't receiving them.

Nearly a week after Morra's death, the crew of the *Konstantin* gathered in their respective habs to watch a communication marked "Urgent" from mission control. On-screen, Gabriel Lacroix stood in front of an otherwise empty mission control room. He was unshaven and looked haggard.

Lacroix spoke softly. "Crew of the *Konstantin*, you should be aware that . . . Nathan Joyce is dead."

Abarca sat up and paid close attention.

Tighe said, "Bullshit."

Chindarkar silenced him with a hand on his arm.

Lacroix continued. "Nathan committed suicide on his Colorado ranch. Authorities in several countries have seized his personal assets and are investigating allegations of stock fraud. Most of his companies have filed for bankruptcy. There will be a period of reorganization, and it is likely that Catalyst Corporation's assets will be acquired by another organization." Lacroix sat in silence for several moments. "We will keep you abreast of new developments. However, I must stress that in the meantime it is more important than ever that you continue to maximize production. This will help secure the best terms for the company's continued operation—and for your benefits package."

With that, Lacroix clicked off.

Immediately afterward, the newsfeed from Earth resumed. In the feed, there was no mention of Ryugu, or of Goff's mining robots failing, or about the existence of the *Konstantin*. However, there were dozens of news stories about Nathan Joyce—about his suicide by plane crash and his lavish lifestyle, financed by fraud. Lurid exposés with clickbait titles. Even in death, Joyce was generating publicity.

Despite Lacroix's message to keep working, the crew moved about listlessly. The physical deterioration of the ship and its equipment added to the general gloom. A second mule had been badly damaged in the struggle with the mining rig that killed Morra. Portions of the *Konstantin* were leaking atmosphere from worn seals. There were micrometeor punctures in two transfer tunnels and another in the wall of the Central Hab. Temporary patches were keeping up with the leaks, but more permanent repairs were needed.

However, the up-armored ARS and Honey Bee robots continued their work, harvesting and processing asteroid regolith, moving through the queue of selected boulders.

Crew morale, on the other hand, was nonexistent.

Sitting in his workstation, Tighe stared at the empty desk across from him—where Morra would normally have been sitting this rotation. He still could not believe his friend was gone. A friend whose last instinct, even as he was suffocating, was to protect his crewmates.

Tighe felt another convulsion of grief, but he knew that the only way Morra's death would mean anything was if the expedition succeeded. For this reason, Tighe eventually sat up and started taking tasks off the work queue. Losing himself in work was the only thing likely to make things better.

The rest of the crew slowly started performing their duties again as well, often sharing meals in silence. They watched movies and TV shows from the ship's library, and read or listened to books to remember that there really was an Earth—even if, for now, it was just a distant white dot.

And then the laser comm link to Earth went dead.

After prebreathing, Tighe and Adisa suited up. They undocked their clam suits at the upper airlock and moved, hand over hand, up the 100-meter solar mast toward the peak of the *Konstantin*—the aluminum ladder rungs serving as handholds for pulling forward in microgravity.

Soon they emerged from Ryugu's shadow and floated into the sunlight between hundreds of square meters of blue gallium arsenide solar panels.

Farther on, at the apex of the ship, they reached the radio tower and the laser comm array. It was here that Adisa got busy opening panels, checking voltages, and inspecting cable connections while Tighe clipped in nearby.

"That laser can really reach all the way back to Earth?"

Adisa focused on his diagnostic tests. "*It beams to one of two transmitter/ receivers—one at the Sun-Earth L5 Lagrange point, another near the Moon. Depending on whether the Sun blocks the line of sight.*"

"And it's our only outside communications link?"

Adisa glanced up. "*A laser requires the receiver on the other end to be in just the right position. So, yes.*"

"Meaning no one but Catalyst Corporation can hear us broadcasting."

Adisa nodded.

"What about all these radio antennas and dishes?"

"*They are meant for local communication—our telepresence systems and the mining robots. Star and Sun tracking. They were not designed for long-range communication."*

"So Joyce isolated us intentionally."

Adisa continued his diagnostics for another fifteen minutes. He finally put away his tools and stared silently into the starless, sun-faded space around them.

Tighe cleared his throat.

Adisa looked up. *"The laser is functioning correctly, and we still have a connection to the receiver on the other end."*

"Then why aren't they answering?"

Adisa hesitated but finally said, *"Because I do not think anyone is listening."*

The crew floated in the Central Hab—all six of them physically present. They held on to storage racks as Abarca floated near the core. The room rotated around them.

She studied their faces. "Here's the situation: we've lost contact with Earth. It's not an equipment problem but more likely a result of the insolvency of Catalyst Corporation and the seizure of most of Nathan Joyce's assets. There's probably some corporate chaos going on down there right now, but there's no reason to think this situation will persist."

The entire crew looked shell-shocked. It was difficult to absorb the reality of their situation.

Tsukada said, "What if Nathan died with the comm codes?"

"Let's not panic ourselves. This expedition is Nathan's best legacy, and I don't think he'd purposely sabotage it."

Jin said, "Even if that meant his creditors would become rich on the mission he planned and designed—but which bankrupted him?"

Tsukada added, "Over which he committed suicide?"

Abarca held up her hands. "Look, I'm not a member of the Nathan Joyce fan club. If I'd known he was going to pull this shit on us, I wouldn't have recruited you all. But as for choosing each of you—I wouldn't want to be out here with anyone else. My mistake was in trusting Joyce, but that's a mistake we all made. And it doesn't mean this expedition was a mistake."

Chindarkar said, "What about our return to Earth?"

Abarca instantiated a virtual model of the solar system and zoomed in to show Ryugu and Earth orbiting the Sun, playing leapfrog. A calendar date incremented at the bottom of the model as the planets moved.

"Our next close approach to Earth is in February 2038—a little under three years from now. A Catalyst Corporation spacecraft is supposed to arrive then, deliver a new crew, refuel, and then fly us back to Earth."

Tsukada stared at the hologram. "How do we even know they're sending a ship for us in 2038?"

The crew exchanged somber looks.

Jin said, "I cannot imagine they would abandon this investment. Even if Catalyst went bankrupt, the *Konstantin* and its cargo represent a twenty-billion-dollar asset. The resources we are now producing are incredibly valuable. Not to mention geostrategically important."

Abarca gestured. "Jin's right. So let's proceed on the assumption that we are too valuable to abandon. Someone will come for us."

Tighe stared. "Or for the ship at least."

"Either way."

Chindarkar said, "So we just continue mining Ryugu—business as usual?"

"For the next two years, the Earth will be too far away to contemplate an abort—even if we could pilot the ship, which is doubtful given our lack of admin rights. So I say we continue working until we find out what's going on."

"And if we don't hear anything?"

"Well, that's finding out, too. Isn't it?"

Three days later Tighe, Abarca, and Jin were performing maintenance on the aquaponic systems in Hab 2's lower level when Adisa slid down the gangway. He'd come all the way across two transfer tunnels—unannounced. His expression was grim.

"Everything okay in Hab 1, Ade?"

Abarca and Jin stood up, concerned.

Adisa spoke softly. "There is something you need to know, Isabel. . . ."

Abarca approached. "What?"

"I was just consolidating storage in the refinery . . . transferring fuel to the main tanks—the ones we used to reach Ryugu. They should have had a quarter million liters in them—the fuel we would have used to return to Earth on a mission abort."

Tighe confirmed, "After the go, no-go."

Adisa nodded. "Yes. But I was still able to transfer the full amount into them. I looked closer. It appears the refinery software has a hard-coded offset for Fuel Tanks 1 through 4. The system reports more fuel than the tanks contain."

The other three looked to one another.

Tighe cursed under his breath.

Jin moved close. "What are you saying?"

"I am saying that—from the very beginning—Nathan Joyce did not provide us enough fuel to get back. If we had been unable to mine Ryugu, we would never have been able to return to Earth."

Abarca stared at the wall for a moment. Her eyes fluttered, and then she lashed out, kicking the aquaponic line, scattering plastic pipe sections. "God-damn asshole!"

Abarca marched off and up the gangway to the second floor of the hab.

Tighe and Jin exchanged looks.

Adisa looked after Abarca. "I hope I am not the cause of—"

Tighe grabbed Adisa's shoulder. "Not you. It definitely isn't you."

Jin put his tools down. "Joyce was going to erase us if we failed. . . ."

In a moment, they heard Abarca's footsteps on the panels above, and then she slid down the gangway onto the first floor. In her hand she held a tool that Tighe had never seen. It looked like a metallic mountain-climbing ice ax. Where it came from, he had no idea.

He stepped toward her. "Isabel, talk to me."

"Not now, J.T."

"Where're you going with the ice ax?"

Jin: "Where did you *get* an ice ax?"

"Give me some space."

"You need to tell us what you're going to do."

She pushed into the storage room and walked up to the gift lockers—the bank of sealed containers meant to boost crew morale as the mission continued.

The others followed her.

"Stand back." She reared the ice ax back.

"Isabel, what—"

And she drove the spike end of the ax through the aluminum plating. Abarca then started prying outward, wrenching the door out of shape with a metallic shriek and finally popping the lock.

Alarm codes appeared in their crystal displays, indicating—of all things—a break-in. Abarca silenced the alarms with a gesture.

She looked inside the locker.

Tighe and the others came alongside and peered in as well.

The locker was empty.

She spoke without emotion. "Step back. . . ."

The others cleared away.

Abarca broke open locker after locker. They were all empty.

Jin leaned against the storage room wall, holding his temples. "Why?"

"The disease of short-term thinking." Tighe nodded to himself as he looked at the empty gift lockers. "The source of most of humanity's problems."

Eventually Abarca tore open a locker that contained a lone bottle of Suntory Hibiki thirty-year-old whiskey. She let the ax clatter to the deck, then tore the seal on the bottle's glass stopper. Abarca raised the whiskey. "I wish hell existed—because then Nathan Joyce would be in it." She took a deep swig and then passed it to Adisa.

"I do not drink, Isabel."

"This could be the last bottle of *anything* that we will *ever* see. So take a drink."

Adisa hesitated and then took a tentative swig—and instantly doubled over in a coughing fit.

Tighe grabbed the bottle and took a deep pull, then passed the bottle to Jin—who also took a good swig.

Tighe shook his head and laughed.

Abarca glared at him. "What the hell's so funny, J.T.?"

He gestured to the room and the torn-open lockers. "The situation. You have to admit, it's kind of absurd."

After a beat the others broke out in deranged laughter, too.

Jin passed Abarca the whiskey bottle. "Good stuff. Back in Beijing, Hibiki is forty thousand yuan a bottle."

She took another swig. "A lot cheaper than sending tons of rocket fuel." Abarca passed the bottle to Adisa.

Adisa took another sip and coughed less this time.

Half an hour later, Tighe, Abarca, Jin, and Adisa sat on the floor, inebriated, their backs against the wall.

Tighe gestured to Abarca's ax. "Your father's?"

She hefted the scuffed and weathered ax, examining it. "I didn't plan to take it. I just wanted to find him. When I did, it was like he was offering it to me."

Tighe imagined what it must have been like, high up on K2.

She lowered the ax and looked at the ceiling. "Joyce actually got me to believe his bullshit."

Tighe leaned his head back against the wall. "Bullshit is how he got this ship built."

Jin pointed a finger at Tighe. "Do not even think of defending him."

"I'm not defending him. If Joyce was here right now, I'd put that ice ax through his forehead."

Abarca shook her head. "Not before I did."

Tighe continued. "Besides, Joyce already beat us to it."

Jin ground his teeth. "Coward. He escaped punishment."

Tighe nodded. "But I don't think Joyce planned on dying. I think he was hoping this would all work out. That he would be a hero."

The others laughed bitterly.

"I know, I know. The guy stole tens of billions of dollars to build this ship and send us out here. He lied to us and to the entire world—didn't even give us enough fuel to get back—and yet, he wasn't *wrong*. We *are* mining this asteroid. If CRC hadn't shown up, Dave would still be alive."

Jin said, "Nicole would not be."

Abarca stared. "Let's just say that Nathan's a complicated figure and leave it at that." She swigged the last of the whiskey.

Adisa snickered. "This is the difference between Africans and you Westerners—"

They all turned to him. Adisa looked seriously intoxicated.

Jin said, "I am not a Westerner, Ade."

Adisa waved Jin away. "In Lagos we all *know* the e-lites are corrupt. They have always been. We expect no less from them, and so we are never disappointed."

Abarca tossed the bottle into a corner. "Well, that's just depressing, Ade."

CHAPTER 39

Goldstone

JUNE 24, 2035

Lukas Rochat moved through his days in a near trance. It was difficult to believe Nathan Joyce was actually gone, even though he'd witnessed the plane impact the tarmac. He kept expecting Joyce to phone him from some tropical locale. Then Rochat remembered he was present when they pulled Joyce's charred remains from the wreckage.

Not long after the county police, ambulances, and coroner left, US Internal Revenue Service and FBI agents arrived at Lodgepole Ranch with search warrants and began taking away computers and files.

To Rochat's surprise, the communication equipment for uplinking to the *Konstantin* was gone when he let the authorities into Joyce's study. In that corner there was now a glass case containing architectural models of a proposed condominium development in Dubai—one Rochat had never seen before.

The IRS then seized the entire ranch.

During his police interview, Rochat said only that one of Joyce's companies was his client, and that he'd come to the ranch to discuss invoices that were months overdue—which was true enough. He claimed attorney-client privilege for the rest.

The IRS agents said they'd seek a court order for access to Rochat's files, but days later he found himself alone, in a generic chain hotel outside Colorado Springs. Rochat vaguely recalled driving there in a rental car.

Government authorities in eight countries had locked everyone out of Joyce company offices. They'd confiscated encrypted computer systems. The corporate bank accounts were frozen. No one was answering phones or emails.

Lukas Rochat was on his own.

It took him a day or two to wrap his head around the enormity of the crisis, but when he did, it hit him all at once: the *Konstantin* was still out in deep space. Almost no one knew about the asteroid miners, and unless he did something, there was no guarantee the crew would receive the help they needed to survive. But how could he contact them, much less help them? He had no idea where Lacroix and the mission control team were, nor how the encrypted communications with the *Konstantin* worked.

And yet, there was a return payload from the *Konstantin* en route to cislunar space—the orbital parameters for which were probably somewhere in an encrypted message from Joyce. Was that actually true?

Rochat sat at his business suite's kitchen table and studied the crumpled piece of paper that Joyce had given him just before he climbed into the biplane. Joyce had written a phone number with the penmanship of a five-year-old. It actually made Rochat laugh.

Joyce had educated Rochat on burner phones—and how important it was to never use one's own phone on *Konstantin* business. Today definitely qualified.

Rochat held a cheap burner phone in his hand. He installed the battery and called the number on Joyce's note. The line rang three or four times until it finally picked up. His pulse raced as he listened.

No one spoke on the other end, but he could hear the sounds of traffic in the background. Someone had picked up and appeared to be waiting for him to speak first.

Rochat cleared his throat. "He told me to call this number. He said you'd know what to do." Rochat's mind raced. "The crew is still out there. The authorities seized everything. I don't know if anyone even realizes there's a ship. We need to do something."

Still no one spoke on the other end. Abruptly, the line went dead.

Rochat stared in disbelief at his device. "Shit."

But then his phone chimed to indicate an incoming text. The message contained only a series of coordinates with a day and time:

35°32'6.85"N, 117°33'31.94"W –Tuesday, 14:15 PST

Two days later Rochat stood next to his rental car at the intersection of two dirt roads in the middle of the Mojave Desert just east of China Lake, California. Studying a map, he couldn't help but notice that the nearest major facility was NASA's Goldstone Deep Space Communications Complex.

Here at the crossroads, however, there was nothing but creosote bushes and barren desert hills as far as the eye could see. It was 45 degrees Celsius—113 degrees Fahrenheit—in the shade. Just past 2:15 p.m. He was utterly alone.

Suddenly, in the distance he noticed another vehicle coming in from the south—not from the east-west direction he'd taken off Trona Road. As the vehicle approached, he could see it was an older model white Jeep Cherokee. It had no front license plate. A Caucasian woman with brown curly hair was at the wheel. The Jeep slowed as it neared the intersection. The woman scanned the horizon before coming to a stop across from Rochat's car.

She got out and stared at him across the Jeep's roof. Rochat wasn't sure what to expect, but the woman was dressed plainly and looked more like a frugal scientist than a financier or intelligence agent.

Rochat nodded to her and cautiously approached. "My name is Lukas Rochat. I was Mr. Joyce's personal attorney." He dug in his bag for a notarized document and passed it over to her.

She did not extend her hand. "I know who you are, Lukas."

Rochat lowered the document. "He said you were involved . . . from the beginning—that you'd know what to do. Who are you? Are you with the US government?"

"Never mind who I am. Have you been in contact with the crew of the *Konstantin*?"

"No! Mr. Joyce's creditors have seized all the assets of Catalyst Corporation. Nathan appears to have erased all evidence of the *Konstantin*'s existence. The mission control personnel have scattered to the four winds. Their emails no longer work, or their phones. I have no way of contacting anyone. I don't even know what country they're in or whether anyone has told the authorities about the *Konstantin*'s existence. The company bank accounts have all been frozen."

She contemplated this. "What instructions did Nathan leave you in the event of his death?"

Rochat saw no emotion, no regret as she said this. Anger rose within him. "If I knew anything, why would I be asking you? *You're* the one who has been involved from the start."

"You need to calm down."

"Was all this your idea? I hope you know that two of the ship's crew are already dead. We sent them out there without enough fuel to get back! How could you do this?"

"What do you mean 'not enough fuel to get back'?"

"Nathan said it was better that they had more tools and resources than fuel." She muttered under her breath. "Goddamnit, Nathan . . ."

"The deaths of these people are on your hands."

She walked around the hood of the Jeep.

He tensed. "I want no part in this evil!"

She came up to him and grabbed his shirt with surprising strength—her eyes boring into his. "Don't you *dare* start rationalizing away your responsibility, Lukas Rochat! You are by no means finished with this mission."

He stammered for a moment before blurting, "We have killed people!"

A frightening rage was visible in her eyes. "No one *killed* anyone. People died. This is what happens on frontiers. You want to save lives? Fund a quit-smoking campaign. But if we're going to get humanity off this rock and into the cosmos, some people will need to go into harm's way—and fortunately, there are people willing to take up that solemn responsibility. The least you can do is fulfill your responsibility to help keep them alive!" She released his shirt.

Rochat tried to collect his breath. Adrenaline coursed through him still. His hands shook. "How can I help them?"

"Do they have enough fuel now to get back?"

"Yes. Yes, they have thousands of tons—but no return ship. There was supposed to be a spacecraft sent out to retrieve them in 2038. That spacecraft isn't even built, and even if we find plans, there's no money to build it. Or time. And even if there was time, it would have to be approved for orbital flight, licensed for launch, human-rated—"

"Do you have access to Catalyst Corporation files?"

"I did. But the Feds took everything. Everything."

"The files were encrypted."

"Yes."

She stared. "Nathan would have copies in a cloud."

"I wouldn't know where or how to access it."

"Are you sure? He never sent you anything? Do you have any unpublicized email addresses that you and Nathan used to communicate privately?"

"Well . . ." Rochat thought for a second. "Yes, but I was at the tarmac with him when he took off. He couldn't send me an email from his stunt plane."

"Before the flight. Before he committed suicide. Have you checked your private email address?"

Rochat realized that in all the frenzy he'd neglected to do so—after all, the only other person who knew about that inbox was Joyce, and he was dead. Rochat nodded. "Okay. I haven't."

"The first thing we have to do is reestablish communications with the *Konstantin*. The crew may have no idea what's happened here on Earth. They need to know that someone is going to help them."

"Help them? How? Reestablishing communications will require accessing the laser transmitter at L5—which requires a sophisticated communications facility here on Earth. The only ones I knew of were at Catalyst mission control on Ascension Island and . . ." Rochat paused. ". . . Nathan's office. But the equipment was gone by the time the Feds raided the house."

"Like I said: check your email. Nathan was a lot of things. Undisciplined, irresponsible—but never stupid."

Rochat nodded to himself.

"Do you have access to funds?"

Rochat paused. "I . . . Nathan paid me rather well over the last two years. He helped me set up my space-law practice."

"It's time to repay the favor. Consider it an investment, Lukas. . . ." She got back into the Jeep and started the engine. The passenger window lowered.

Rochat leaned in.

She handed him a piece of paper. "This is my public key. Nathan taught you how to take precautions to conceal your comms?"

"Yes."

"I'm not talking about just encryption. I mean completely sanitizing metadata and your device trail. Your behavior patterns."

"Yes. Yes, he did."

"Good. Let me know when you get the laser encryption codes. In the meantime, find out where the Catalyst Corporation mission controllers have gone. You'll need them. Hire skip tracers to locate them if necessary. I have access to some resources, but only unofficially. We'll help you however we can."

"Okay." Rochat stood in the road, bewildered by the turn of events.

"Get going, Lukas. Those asteroid miners are still up there, and this expedition isn't over. Not by a long shot."

"I understand. You can count on me."

With that her Jeep pulled away, continuing northward. Rochat stared after her through a cloud of dust.

CHAPTER 40

Storm

FEBRUARY 8, 2036

Tighe lay on his bed watching a Bollywood musical in his crystal display. The improbable physics of the film notwithstanding, the joyous dance numbers with scores of colorful costumes transported him far from where he was. They were a celebration of life.

Sci-fi films were hard for him to watch these days.

The *Konstantin*'s digital library held hundreds of thousands of entertainment choices, but he was still running out of things he wanted to see. And whenever he went to read something, the newsfeed from Earth appeared on the main screen—with the same frozen headline from a year before.

Nathan Joyce dead in stunt plane crash.

It was as though civilization itself had ended with Joyce's death. No doubt that would have pleased Joyce. In any case, Earth seemed to have forgotten about the crew of the *Konstantin*.

The mining robots did not stop, however. The perfected Honey Bees were now producing hundreds of tons of mined resources per month from boulders the ARSs pulled from Ryugu's surface. Magnetic rakes harvested still more regolith. The refinery—optimized by Tsukada—was processing it all, and they were using those resources to create new bladder tanks and polymer frames in the storage yard to hold it.

Tighe couldn't help but wonder, *Who for?* It had been nine months since they'd lost contact with Earth. Or more accurately, since Earth had cut the connection.

The Bollywood dancers suddenly froze midleap as Klaxons sounded.

Emergency strobe lights fluttered, and a female robotic voice said, *"Warning: collision alert. Repeat: collision alert."*

In the adjacent cot Jin Han bolted upright and grabbed for his crystal.

Someone muted the alarms.

Tighe scanned the alarm console and did a double take. "Jesus . . . 999 radar echoes inbound?"

They raced to put on pressure suits.

Tighe spoke into the comm link. "Ade, what's going on? Is this a false alarm?"

Adisa replied, *"Everyone move to the Central Hab immediately—into the core module."*

"What's happening?"

In answer a video layer appeared in everyone's crystal display. It showed the round shadow of Ryugu, silhouetted by an aura of sunlight—and yet something resembling a sandstorm rose over its horizon, blotting out the sun.

Jin and Tighe frowned in confusion.

"What the hell is that?"

"Something massive just struck the dayside of Ryugu. The impact kicked up thousands of tons of debris. Konstantin's computer predicts the debris cloud will arc around Ryugu before falling back to the surface. However, the Konstantin is within the fallout zone."

Jin asked, "Can we move the ship?"

"We do not have sufficient system privileges—and in any event, we have added 450 tons of radiation shielding since we arrived. Our thrusters cannot move us in time. Get to the Central Hab. We have just over twenty minutes until the debris cloud strikes the ship."

Tighe raced to get suited up. "How bad are we talking?"

"The cloud will slow as it arcs, but it will still be going a couple hundred kilometers an hour when it hits us."

"What kind of debris?"

"Impossible to know—the radar data is messy. We need to take shelter in the central core."

The ship's female computer voice returned. *"Emergency spin-down commencing. Repeat: emergency spin-down commencing. Prepare for microgravity."*

Adisa said, *"I've activated the de-spin, but the storm will hit us well before our rotation has stopped."*

Jin blanched. "If one of our radial arms is damaged while we're spun up, the *Konstantin* could fly apart—especially with the habs now much heavier."

Abarca's voice broke in: *"Everyone do as Ade says; move to the central core as fast as you can."*

Tighe heard the radial thrusters kick in to decelerate the radial arm—but there was now 140 tons of water shielding the hab walls. It would take more than an hour to stop the *Konstantin*'s spin. He glanced over at Jin. "Take whatever emergency equipment you can carry."

Seven minutes later, Tighe, Jin, and Amy Tsukada—who had been in the crew quarters downstairs—floated across the Central Hab. Within ten minutes the entire crew was sealed within the aluminum-walled inner core at the heart of the ship. It was, in essence, the axle of the *Konstantin*'s radial spokes. Here, they stored replacement processors and other advanced components. The chamber was crowded.

Adisa and Chindarkar worked virtual control panels.

"Eleven minutes to impact."

Abarca took stock of emergency medical and food supplies. "What about the Honey Bee mining bots and the ARSs?"

Adisa answered, "The Honey Bees are above the debris wave. So is the burial cairn."

Chindarkar said, "I undocked both ARSs and all our mules to move them to safety as well."

Tsukada asked, "Shouldn't we be evacuating in the mules?"

Abarca shook her head. "We don't survive out here if the *Konstantin* is destroyed. We need to be here for damage control."

Tighe said, "What about the clam suits at the upper airlock?"

Adisa shook his head. "We must hope they're tough enough. There is no time for a prebreathe."

Tighe was already nodding—of course, Adisa was right.

Jin spoke as he tapped at invisible objects. "I am moving the Valkyries and vidbots inside the upper airlock."

Tsukada said, "I'm clearing supply pipes and closing all valves."

Adisa added, "Deploying laser comm shroud."

Everyone except Tighe was now tapping at virtual UIs. "What can I do?"

Adisa answered. "Fold the solar array. We need to shut down all unnecessary systems and go to battery backup power."

Tighe searched through the ship's UI for solar array controls. As more systems were shut or battened down, alert codes scrolled past in his crystal.

The *Konstantin* was hunkering down for a storm, but there was no telling what this storm would bring. "Habs 1, 2, and 3 are in hibernation mode."

Jin asked, "What about the storage yard—and the refinery? If any of those bladder tanks get hit—"

Adisa answered. "They are too massive to move in time. We just have to hope that nothing large strikes them. The tanks are flexible. They have a chance of withstanding small impacts—as do the inflatable hab units."

"But a pressure wave could send the storage yard adrift. It has barely any station-keeping thrusters. We could lose an entire year's work."

Abarca interjected, "There's nothing we can do about that now, Han. If we survive the next hour, we'll deal with it then."

Sobered by this, the entire crew continued making preparations until additional alerts sounded. Adisa quickly silenced the Klaxons and brought up an exterior view from multiplexed CCTV cameras for the entire crew to see.

"Thirty seconds 'til impact."

"Jesus . . ."

Without much to hold on to, the six crew members held on to one another, Tighe's arm around Abarca.

Abarca said, "We've done all we can. Good luck, everyone."

They all murmured in agreement and held hands tightly.

Moments later a swirling cloud like charcoal etching swept through the frame of the CCTV cameras—and then the screens went dark as the distant sound of a billion pennies being dropped onto a corrugated tin roof reached them. Vibrations began to rattle the corners and shelf units.

"Holy shit . . ."

Klaxons sounded anew as alarms scrolled by. The *Konstantin*'s computer voice said, "*Ship off station. Emergency thrusters engaged. Repeat: ship off station. Emergency thrusters engaged.*"

A sudden, sharp shock echoed through the superstructure, and several impact alerts appeared in the crystal display. A deep *thud* and an air pressure warning appeared for Tunnel 3.

The crew hugged closer.

Serious pounding sounds began to echo throughout the ship, like field-stones bouncing off the wall of an oil tank. Each impact had a different tone—some striking hard, unyielding objects, while others struck softer targets. Tighe's anxious crewmates stared up at the walls, their eyes darting in the direction of the latest unseen boom or crash.

Then an enormous impact caused the entire ship to shudder, and involuntary shouts of alarm came from all of them. They clung tighter together.

The *Konstantin*'s computer voice said, "*Pressure loss in lower airlock. Fire in Refinery Manifold 3. Communication failure, z-axis, Zone 2.*"

Tsukada tapped at an invisible UI. "I'm purging atmosphere from the lower airlock to contain the fire."

Several more violent *booms* ricocheted off the ship, and these seemed to create secondary noises.

The computer voice said, "*Structural failure, z-axis Box Truss 9. Pressure loss, Tunnel 2. Pressure loss, lower z-axis tunnel. Comm tower offline.*"

Gazing at the mostly grayed-out virtual CCTV camera displays, Tighe noticed several whirling rocks the size of watermelons whizz past the ship. Alarm codes were streaming fast now, too—broken pipelines, failed equipment, pressure warnings, proximity alarms, temperature and moisture alarms.

The computer voice continued. "*Ship off station. Repeat: ship off station. Repeat: ship off station.*"

The entire ship rumbled now, like it was riding down a waterfall.

Tsukada covered her ears and shouted, "Stop!"

Tighe and Jin exchanged dour looks.

But then the barrage stopped—as suddenly as it had begun. It was as though someone threw a switch. The CCTV camera screens cleared, and the exterior views of the *Konstantin* remained. The ship's radial arms still swept along their course. However, gases vented from several hoses, and there were broken spars and cowlings in various places.

But the *Konstantin* remained.

Shouts of relief spread as the crew hugged one another.

Adisa checked his crystal, then smiled. "The debris wave has passed. We have survived."

They all cheered and hugged again.

Tighe asked, "Is it going to come around again, Ade?"

Everyone froze.

"No. The cloud will pass far below us on its next pass. I believe we are safe." As the others started to sigh in relief, he said, "Choose some of these alarm codes. We need to prioritize and patch puncture holes in pressurized compartments."

Tsukada was already clicking through UIs. "The fire's already extinguished in the refinery. We've got leaks, though."

Abarca nodded. "We need to complete this spin-down and do exterior visual inspections. Everyone start breathing pure oxygen. Parts of the ship are depressurized."

Hours later and with the *Konstantin* finally spun down, Tighe and Jin found themselves on the running board of a mule remotely controlled by Chindarkar as they glided along the *Konstantin*'s length, shining searchlights onto girders and equipment.

It looked like a thousand maniacs had blasted the *Konstantin* with bird shot—every inch of the upper side of the ship was pockmarked, the flexible surfaces of the inflatable habs scarred by impacts. In places some of the composite box-truss girders had been splintered. Tunnel 3 was torn open, but the folded solar array was undamaged—probably because its thin edge was facing the storm. The hab airlocks were also undamaged, though dented in spots. By and large the *Konstantin* had weathered the hailstorm admirably.

Jin looked across the top of the mule to Tighe. *"This could have ended us."*

He nodded to Jin. "But it didn't." Tighe felt elated. It was the sort of euphoria he experienced whenever he cheated death. They were alive, and now he was more determined than ever that they remain so.

CHAPTER 41

Isolation

AUGUST 14, 2036

Repairs to the *Konstantin* took months—although they were able to spin up again in just over a week. The difficult work of effecting repairs allowed them to concentrate on the present, to work to exhaustion, followed by sound sleep. It gave them respite from worry over the continued lack of contact with Earth. They were alive. That was all that mattered.

Once the repairs were completed, the isolation again began to take an emotional toll on the crew.

However, the mining never stopped. The robots continued producing water, nitrogen, iron, and more.

The expanding resources in the storage yard gave the crew their new focus: constructing a much larger robot tug to return resources toward cislunar space. Tighe, Jin, Chindarkar, and Adisa had spent most of July laboring to assemble Catalyst's modular design in preparation for an October 2, 2036, shipment—now only seven weeks away. Catalyst had supplied not only the design but also the software and controllers capable of piloting robot tugs homeward on highly efficient but slow trajectories.

To propel the tug, Tighe and Jin had somberly repeated the task of cannibalizing rocket engines from the *Konstantin*, keenly feeling the absence of David Morra as they did so. Located on the "bottom" of the *Konstantin*, the delicate engines had been spared from the hail of debris kicked up by the meteor impact on Ryugu five months earlier. Because the crew no longer had technical support from Catalyst mission control they relied on Adisa's prodigious genius in comprehending the wiring and piping of the complex engines.

Due in part to its huge mass, the new robot tug required two methalox engines instead of one, and this time it consisted of twenty-four spherical tanks, with thirty-six smaller tanks in the gaps between—4,500 tons of water, ammonia, nitrogen, and iron-nickel-cobalt carbonyls in all. It was more than four times the size of the first return vessel. Additionally the return delta-v to depart for cislunar space this time around was 706 meters per second—almost double the previous tug's acceleration.

The crew's fourfold production increase over the past year would have thrilled Nathan Joyce.

But screw Joyce, Tighe thought.

Due to the vagaries of orbital mechanics, the new return tug was scheduled to arrive in cislunar space in one and a quarter years (January 2038)—sooner, in fact, than the previous shipment, which had departed more than a year earlier.

And yet, the question of *why* they were sending any shipment at all began to press in on them. Whom were they producing these resources for—investors who couldn't even be bothered to contact them? And how would those investors locate these resources? There was no one with whom to communicate their trajectory. At least not yet.

However, mining was why they'd come to Ryugu, so they continued. What else was there? With the loss of Nicole Clarke and David Morra—even accounting for the provisions lost in the fire en route—the crew had enough dehydrated food to last until the fourth quarter of 2038—roughly two more years.

Forgetting the fact that they were all sick to death of every dehydrated dish in the ship's pantry, surviving beyond then wasn't going to matter much. Ryugu's closest approach to Earth in May 2038 would only bring them within 55 million kilometers—which was ten times the distance they'd traveled to rendezvous with Ryugu outbound. That return journey would take months to cover even if they had a ship—which they did not. None of the crew knew how to operate the *Konstantin*'s engines or how to load navigational data, and Adisa was prevented from learning the system due to a lack of administrator rights to the ship's OS.

Riding one of the preprogrammed robotic tugs back to Earth wasn't an option either. The tugs followed multiyear, low-delta-v trajectories. Any humans on board would die of starvation or radiation by the time they reached cislunar space.

Despite three hot meals a day, and despite maintaining the air and warmth of the ship, it was getting increasingly difficult to ignore the fact that they were all going to die out here unless something changed.

Sitting across the galley table from Jin and Abarca one night, Tighe said, "If they're willing to abandon us, they sure as hell aren't going to honor our contracts—or Dave's and Nicole's contracts. Why send this next shipment back? I say, make them come and get it."

Jin looked up. "No one can reach us until 2038, and if we do not send shipments, they might believe we are already dead."

"Then why don't they contact us? The laser transmitter works—Ade checked it."

"Maybe the new owners . . ." Jin's voice trailed off.

"What happened to Eike and Yak? Where is everyone?"

Abarca said, "Maybe creditors just liquidated everything. Eike and Yak can't communicate with us on their own."

"So we just keep working out here until we're dead?"

Abarca looked down at the table. "It could still make a difference to humanity."

Tighe stared at her.

That night Tighe lay sleepless in his cot. Reaching for his crystal, he thought he might read, but then he noticed his personal effects pouch nearby. He decided to open it for the first time in years, dumping its contents onto his chest. He studied his US passport and the various ID cards he carried in his wallet—all the things that told him who he'd been back on Earth. They were meaningless out here—just pieces of paper.

But then he withdrew a copy of an old color photo from one corner of his wallet.

His father's young face stared back at him, handsome and smiling, photographed at the head of a forested trail, heavy pack on his back. Whitecapped mountains loomed in the background. Tighe ran his finger across the photo's surface. His father's face looked different to him now. There was a forced quality to that smile that he hadn't detected before, as if the path was not so clear to his father either.

Tighe placed the photograph on the edge of his nightstand, and soon he fell into a sound sleep.

OCTOBER 2, 2036

They named their new tug the *David Morra*, but there was no celebration this time. No speech. Tighe and Jin stood on the running board of a mule and watched from a hundred meters away as the engines they'd installed ignited. Tighe was too numb to take joy in their handiwork. The vessel was 30 meters long and 25 on a side—nearly six times the mass of the *Konstantin* the day she disembarked. This was again historic, not that anyone was watching. The resources were worth a fortune back in a lunar DRO.

So much had been sacrificed. Tighe felt powerless to fulfill his promise to Morra. Would any of that wealth reach Morra's family? From the look on Jin's face, the taikonaut was thinking much the same.

As the weeks passed and radio silence from Earth continued, Tighe went back to watching Eike Dahl's VR BASE-jumping film. To make it more real, he floated in microgravity in the Central Hab and let the beauty of Norway's fjords flow around him as she flew. But after a while he couldn't handle seeing Dahl's beautiful, smiling face on a green, healthy world, diving joyfully off a cliff, riding the razor's edge between life and death—blowing him a kiss and saying "Hi, J.T.!" as she jumped.

So he explored the other VR titles in the ship's library. There were tours of the great monuments of Earth—the pyramids, Versailles, Yosemite. The shrinks had also added a few therapy titles—the VR camera "walking" through crowded shopping plazas and dance clubs. He'd always been fond of desolate places, but the *Konstantin*'s isolation was too great.

Eventually, Tighe took to playing first-person video games, the constant feedback loop short-circuiting his introspection. He stayed up all hours, pulling an imaginary trigger.

Even Abarca began to lose her disciplined edge. As the months passed and it became increasingly apparent that no one was coming for them, the crew began to pursue their own therapies—work, reading, watching movies and

TV, exercise, sex, sleep—anything to distract them from their hopeless circumstances.

One evening, standing in the galley, cleaning up dishes, Tighe brushed against Chindarkar's arm while stowing something in a cabinet. After a lingering look, suddenly they were kissing, and then they stole away to the crew quarters to make love—both of them yearning for a human touch.

A week or so later Tighe entered the crew quarters to find Jin and Abarca lying in bed next to each other. The next week he saw Tsukada and Adisa kissing in the Central Hab. All the crew had was each other, and it was palpable that their end was slowly approaching.

The crew no longer followed the two-week hab rotation schedule. Instead, Tighe and Chindarkar took up residence in the upper compartment of Hab 2, while Abarca and Jin and Adisa and Tsukada had on-again, off-again liaisons.

Days went by where Tighe and Chindarkar saw no one else.

One day in mid-November Adisa broadcast over the ship's comm that Tsukada was missing. Her crystal had dropped off the *Konstantin*'s tracking display, and she was not responding to radio calls. She had simply disappeared.

The last place the system had logged her was the Fab Hab, and since Tighe was in the Central Hab playing VR video games, he was closest. He quickly headed for Transfer Tunnel 3.

Tighe found Tsukada at the bottom of the tunnel in a pool of blood.

He noticed the winch line was halfway down the tunnel, and in retrieving it, he found one of the cable carabiners still held a clip from Tsukada's pressure suit.

Commuting daily between her hab and the workshop, she had apparently used the same clip on her suit harness every day. It had simply worn out.

Surveillance video later showed that she was halfway to the top of the tunnel when her clip broke off. Due to the peculiarities of spin acceleration, she didn't fall—or even notice the failure at first. Instead, she continued reading in her crystal until her back bumped against the anti-spinward wall of the tunnel. Then she began to slide down it as the wall altered her trajectory, slowly at first. She couldn't grab the nearby ladder rungs with her back facing the wall, and her speed increased. Toward the end of her trajectory it was as though she'd fallen from a third-story window onto the aluminum airlock door. The impact shattered her crystal, knocking her offline.

Tighe covered Tsukada's body with a silver emergency blanket before Adisa arrived. Their reunion was hard to witness. Adisa's sobs echoed in the transfer tunnel.

Abarca later examined Tsukada's injuries in the medical bay of Hab 2 as Tighe stood by. She declared the cause of death to be a fractured skull and internal bleeding—among a dozen other broken bones.

"She died instantly."

Tighe was thankful for that much at least.

Only Chindarkar remained aboard the *Konstantin* for the funeral service. Tighe, Abarca, Jin, and Adisa carried Amy Tsukada's remains to the cairn and laid her to rest alongside Nicole Clarke and David Morra. It had been months since Tighe had beheld Morra's and Clarke's perfectly preserved faces.

Adisa hadn't gone on an EVA since his inspection of the laser comm link, but instead of being shaky or nervous, this time he stared at Tsukada's peaceful, beautiful face with fortitude. He appeared to be trying to commit her to memory. Tighe suspected that from early childhood Adisa had been no stranger to loss. The Nigerian was mature beyond his years.

Adisa placed his gloved hand on Tsukada's helmet. *"I want always to feel this pain. A part of me will always be here beside you."* He floated there for minutes in silence, eyes on her.

Tighe looked upon Tsukada as well. She had taught him miraculous things. He would miss her voice. Her smile. Her refusal to accept the hand the universe had dealt her. She had escaped the Hum for a few brief years. Now she was free of it forever.

Tighe couldn't help the feeling that they would all be joining Tsukada, Morra, and Clarke. It was just a matter of time. Eventually some minor mishap or major catastrophe would claim them all.

Yet, Tighe felt no fear. Looking upon the calm faces of his dead friends, he realized that if he died, so be it. But he wasn't going to go quietly.

As if in answer to Tighe's challenge, the mourners were barely back in the shadow of Ryugu when alarms went off. Riding on the running board of a mule, Tighe could see high-radiation alerts in his crystal display—warnings from their relay satellites. He and Jin turned to see charged particles, colorful waves of red, blue, and green light—a mini aurora borealis—rippling around the horizon of Ryugu and fading into space like a ship's wake.

It was indescribably beautiful. The great rock shielded them as it cut a path through space.

Adisa spoke over the comm link without emotion. *"Solar flare. The largest yet. A lethal dose of radiation."*

If it had occurred minutes earlier, they would have been caught in the open—and they would all be dead right now, leaving Chindarkar alone.

Tighe gripped the mule's running board, then held his other gloved hand up and extended his middle finger to the universe. "You'll have to try harder! You hear me?"

Two days later and 300 million kilometers from Earth, the communication link with Earth suddenly sputtered back to life.

CHAPTER 42

Renegotiation

Tighe and Jin had joined Adisa to live in Hab 1. They didn't want him to be alone with his grief. Abarca and Chindarkar moved to Hab 2. Now all of them sat at their respective galley tables, staring at the wall and the video message projected there.

Across the virtual table from them sat representatives of Catalyst Corporation's creditors—three men and a woman arrayed around a table adorned in gold leaf somewhere back on Earth. There was no obvious leader. All four were in their sixties. One was a Caucasian man with a heavily jowled face and an exquisite suit. Next to him sat a younger Arab man with a trimmed beard and crisp white thawb and shemagh head scarf. To his side was a Chinese businessman, also in a well-tailored suit, and finally to his right, a South Asian woman in a designer suit and jewel-encrusted broach.

The recorded message played.

The Caucasian businessman on the right was the first to address them, and while he spoke in what sounded like Russian, it was simultaneously translated into English—in a cold and clinical tone.

"Crew of the *Konstantin*, we represent the investors defrauded by Nathan Joyce. It took considerable time to unravel where our money has actually been spent. Now we want to understand the status of our investment. Immediately forward a full accounting of what's been mined from Ryugu—as well as the status of the *Konstantin* and its equipment. We await your reply."

With that the message ended.

Adisa said, "Our new oga."

Jin looked his way. "How can we be sure these people are the legal owners of the *Konstantin*?"

Adisa replied, "Who else would have access to the encryption codes and the laser relay?"

Abarca sighed. *"Let's give them what they're asking for. Ade, send the current manifest from the storage yard. Also a listing of our equipment and its condition, as well as the status of our crew and the casualties we've suffered. Survivor benefits will need to be paid."*

In a few hours the information had been collected and beamed seventeen minutes back to Earth. It took much longer for an answer.

Finally a video message arrived, and Adisa screened it.

The group of businesspeople looked even less friendly this time. The Russian businessman spoke, simultaneously translated. "The loss of nearly half the crew shows an incredible failure in leadership. Effective immediately, the new captain is Major Jin Han."

Jin looked to Abarca. "I will refuse, Isabel."

"Let's listen to the rest of the message."

The businessman continued. "This consortium has lost over fourteen billion US dollars to your illicit venture. We intend to recoup our loss. Your production numbers are woefully insufficient. You are immediately to double production, and you must not miss your next orbital window for return of Ryugu resources—orbital parameters for which you will transmit to us."

"Double our production? What the—?"

Abarca said, *"Quiet, please."*

The businessman continued. ". . . send a confirmation that you received this message, Jin Han. Given how you have disgraced your family's good name, you should be grateful for any chance at atonement."

The crew stared blankly as the message ended.

Chindarkar looked to Jin and then Abarca. *"They can't be serious."*

Tighe gestured at the screen. "Do they look like they're kidding?"

Abarca was already tapping at a virtual keyboard. *"Sons of bitches . . ."*

Adisa leaned forward. "I do not approve, Isabel, but the new owners have the right to assign a new captain. We may lose legal standing if we mutiny."

Abarca stopped typing.

Jin shook his head. "No."

Abarca sighed. *"Ade's right, Han. We have to pick our battles. Besides, it doesn't matter who's captain."*

Tighe frowned. "We can't double production. That's insane."

Jin gestured. "Ade, record me with your crystal. I want to send a reply."

Chindarkar frowned. *"We should talk about what you're going to say first, Han."*

"Let me record it. If any of you disagree, we won't send it."

The others exchanged looks and nodded.

Adisa stared at Jin. "I'm recording."

Jin took a deep breath. "This is Jin Hua Han. I would like to know the names of the people I am dealing with. Since you have taken over this enterprise from Nathan Joyce, you have not only assumed his assets but also his obligations. Among those obligations are the employment contracts we signed. Our contracts detail production guidelines as well as bonuses and incentive structures. Over the lifetime of this operation, at our present production rate, we will return many times your original investment. We have honored our commitments. And yet, the ship and its equipment need maintenance. For this we will require the guidance of Catalyst mission control—including mission control manager Gabriel Lacroix and the previous capcoms, Eike Dahl and Sevastian Yakovlev. I await your reply."

The crew nodded.

"That was good."

"Yeah, that's a good start, Han."

They uploaded the message.

The response came very close to thirty-four minutes later. This time it was the Chinese businessman speaking. "Our identities are none of your concern. We own the ship you inhabit. Nathan Joyce stole our capital to fund your operation. You owe us fourteen billion dollars—plus accrued interest. Your previous bonus structure, production numbers, and work contracts are null and void."

"Oh, screw this guy!" Tighe threw up his hands.

The others fumed.

"The entity that signed your contracts—Catalyst Corporation—has been dissolved. It has no assets. However, it does have a great many liabilities."

The businessman narrowed his eyes. "I can see why the CNSA rejected you, Jin Han. You are weak willed and unwise. You let a *guilo* trick you into becoming his manual laborer. Here is your new incentive plan: if you and your crew ever wish to see Earth again, meet your new production targets. That is all."

The message abruptly ended.

The room was dead silent for a long time.

Tighe finally stood. "Ade, record me. You all tell me if this is an appropriate response."

Jin sighed. "J.T.—"

"C'mon, record me."

Adisa sighed, then aimed his gaze at Tighe and started recording.

Tighe nodded a greeting to the camera. "Let's clear something up. Since we're out here and you're not, we can send thousands of tons of your precious resources spinning off into the Sun, and there isn't a goddamned thing you can do about it." Tighe leaned toward the camera. "So I suggest you take our contracts out of the garbage and honor your commitment to us and our dead colleagues. Because if you fuck with us, you will end up with nothing. I promise you. Now get us our goddamned mission control people—before we start cutting your inventory loose."

Adisa stopped recording.

The others exchanged looks.

Abarca said, *"That's not bad, actually."*

Jin sighed. "Amy, David, and Nicole gave their lives to mine those resources. We are not going to simply jettison it into space."

Chindarkar replied, *"The new owners need to know we're serious, Han. Our friends weren't slaves. And neither are we."*

Tighe asked, "Do you really think we can double production, Han?"

He shook his head. "Of course not."

"Then we need to establish the terms of this new relationship now. We meet our commitments, and they meet theirs. It's not negotiable."

The others nodded.

Adisa grimaced. "I have one correction, J.T. The minimum delta-v to send the resources into the Sun is almost 30 kilometers per second. The tugs cannot do that."

"Just send the message, Ade."

No immediate answer came. Tighe took this to mean the new owners were taking the demand seriously. But after a few days, the crew of the *Konstantin* began to feel concerned.

Thus, it was welcome news when Adisa informed them that a rare event was approaching: on December 6, Ryugu would have a close approach to Mars—moving within 58 million kilometers. Earth, meanwhile, was 306 million kilometers away, almost on the opposite side of the Sun. Everyone hoped this was why the new owners had been unable to contact them.

The crew decided to make a celebration out of the Mars close approach, projecting a virtual window into the habs. Mars was now the brightest planet in the celestial globe, with Mercury, Jupiter, and Venus clustered nearby. It looked like a planetary jamboree.

When the moment came, they raised cups of rehydrated juice and toasted to being the humans who'd come closest to Mars. It was another first for the crew of the *Konstantin*, and Chindarkar wrote it in black ink on the aluminum core wall next to the hundreds of other firsts for the expedition. The home-made chronicle covered most of the wall already.

Three days later Adisa awoke the ship in the middle of the night, speaking over the PA system.

"*We have a message from Earth.*"

Tighe and Jin left the crew quarters and walked out to join Adisa at the galley table. Adisa set up the AR link with Hab 1, and then he played the incoming message.

A different Chinese businessman appeared on-screen this time. He was well dressed and handsome and looked statesmanlike—but dour. He stared into the camera and spoke in Mandarin. Again, his words were simultaneously translated into English in Tighe's crystal.

"Jin Han. This is your father . . ."

Tighe and Adisa snapped a look at Jin, who looked stunned.

The recording continued. "I would not have believed it if I did not see the evidence myself. The hours and hours of surveillance footage on this . . . space-craft. The money stolen. The paperwork for the orbital launches. You were always headstrong and reckless. And now I see video of you living in filth with this mon-grel crew." He stared at the camera. "We feared you were dead! You were my son. My only son. I gave you everything, and this is how you repay your family. You disgrace us. For what? To go into space? Mining rocks as a laborer? I never thought you would come to this."

The man stared silently for several moments. "Legitimate business interests have asked that I intervene on their behalf—to try and talk some sense into you. If you have no honor, at least honor your family name. Start to repay your debt to these people. Then maybe you can begin to repair the damage you've done. If you refuse to do this, you are no son of mine." After a moment's pause, he clicked off.

Tighe and Adisa looked to Jin.

Jin stared at the tabletop.

Tighe said, "They could be threatening your father, Han. Fourteen billion is a lot of money."

Jin turned to Tighe. "No one can threaten my father. He is one of the rich-est men in the world."

Tighe and Adisa exchanged startled looks.

"Come again?"

"My grandfather founded the largest manufacturing concern in China. My father expanded it."

Adisa narrowed his eyes. "You were *already* rich?"

"*I* am nothing."

Tighe leaned back in his chair. "I'm confused."

Adisa leaned in. "Why would your father be ashamed of you? You have traveled farther in space than—"

"My father does not place value in such things. When I was accepted by the CNSA, he tolerated it, but I was expected to join the family business. He thought I wasted my life trying to be a taikonaut. I am a great disappointment to him." Jin stared at the table.

"Our parents don't own us, Han. If they did, then nothing would ever change."

Adisa added, "I, for one, am glad you are here."

"So am I."

Face taut, Jin nodded. Then he motioned to Tighe. "Record me."

"You're sure you—"

"Just do it. Please, J.T."

Tighe tapped his crystal and commenced recording.

Jin looked to Tighe and spoke in Mandarin. Fortunately Tighe's crystal simultaneously translated.

"Father, there was a time when I desired your approval . . . more than anything." Jin thought for several moments and then finally shook his head. "That time is over. You have built grandfather's business into a global enterprise, and I know I disappointed you by not continuing it. I do not know why I am the way I am—why I refuse to take the sure path."

Jin ran his fingers through his hair before staring back into the camera. "You are right—I am irresponsible. I have always been. Too reckless, perhaps, for the CNSA. But out here, I feel at home . . ." He looked to Tighe and Adisa—and through the AR screen at Abarca and Chindarkar. ". . . with those who understand me. Out here, things are clear. I would risk my life without hesitation for my crewmates. I would never betray them. Not for you. Not for anyone on Earth."

Jin stared into the lens. "I am not Nathan Joyce. I have honored all *my* commitments, and my crewmates have honored theirs. The 'legitimate business interests' you mention have not honored their commitments to us. You should feel shame in supporting them. I wish things could be different between you and me. However, the past is the past, and it is time for me to make my own way. Good-bye, Father."

Tighe stopped recording.

Adisa gripped Jin's shoulder.

Tighe asked, "You sure you don't want to sleep on that one?"

Jin shook his head. "No. I am certain. More certain than I've ever been of anything."

CHAPTER 43

Root

n the middle of the night, Tighe awoke covered in sweat, his heart racing. Something terrible was happening—he could sense it.

However, looking around, he saw that everything was peaceful. Chindarkar slept close to him in the narrow bed. He grabbed his crystal from the nightstand and put it on.

There were no alarms. The ship was stable and quiet. All systems were nominal. And yet, Tighe's heart raced. He touched Chindarkar's forehead and felt perspiration on her skin. His crystal indicated the ambient temperature was a comfortable 22 degrees Celsius.

Tighe sat up. "Priya."

No response.

"Priya!"

Her head lolled and her eyes remained half open as she slurred in response, "Smatter . . . wass iss it?"

Tighe's temples pounded. He brought up the ship's UI again and checked the atmosphere in the crew quarters.

Everything was within normal parameters. There were no alarms.

Something is wrong.

Tighe struggled to stand, and his blurred vision and frantically beating heart confirmed it. He'd felt this before—during dive emergencies.

High levels of atmospheric CO_2—very high. He was sure of it. Perhaps nearing 6 percent. No wonder Chindarkar was passed out. Soon they'd both be dead.

Tighe staggered across the aisle, collapsing as he grabbed a cabinet door. He clawed his way up to a cabinet marked "Emergency Breathing Apparatus" and yanked out a mask. He fell against the wall, pulling the whole apparatus down into his lap. Sprawled on the floor, he willed himself to pull the oxygen mask's elastic band around his face and head. The last thing he remembered was turning the O_2 valve on the emergency tank.

An unknown period later—perhaps mere seconds—Tighe awoke with a hammering headache. He pushed himself unsteadily to his knees, his clarity of mind swiftly returning.

The others are in danger.

Tighe climbed back to the emergency cabinet and grabbed another breathing mask. He moved to Chindarkar and affixed the mask to her face, activating the O_2.

He heard his own muffled voice through his emergency gas mask. "Priya! Priya, wake up!" Tighe tried to rouse her with his free hand. He called into his comm link. "Isabel! Jin! Ade! Come in! Anyone, come in! Life support failure in Hab 2!"

There was no response.

Tighe grabbed an oxygen candle from the emergency cabinet and struggled to ignite the potassium perchlorate with the striker. It was as though he'd lost all manual dexterity, but finally the stick ignited into a blinding reddish pink. It illuminated Chindarkar's unconscious form with macabre, guttering light.

He spoke over the comm link again. "Isabel! Jin! Ade! Come in!"

Chindarkar shook her head and struggled toward consciousness.

Tighe placed the oxygen candle in a wall clip designed for that purpose and knelt close to her. "Priya! Wake up!"

Her eyes finally focused on him, momentarily confused about the gas mask. She tried to sit up. "What happened? What's happening?"

"The atmosphere's fouled with CO_2."

"Why are there no alarms?"

"I don't know. We need to check on the others."

She sucked in pure oxygen as they rushed to pull on their pressure suits. Once they were suited up, they linked in life support hoses—but did not pressurize.

Chindarkar called over the comm link, "Ade! Isabel! Jin! Do you copy?"

She manipulated the ship's UI and turned to Tighe. "No alarms in Hab 1 either." Her expression showed she was confounded by the ship's readings. "How could triple-redundant life support systems fail all at once—without any alarms?"

Tighe pointed at the virtual display. "Those atmosphere numbers aren't just normal—they're perfect. They've never been so good." He looked at her. "We need to get to the others." Tighe checked his crewmates' vital signs, and those also looked perfect—identical, right down to a synchronized heart rate. "I don't know how, but somebody is making the ship's OS lie to us."

Chindarkar stared at her own crystal. "There's enough air in these habs that O_2 could be down for days before CO_2 would reach dangerous levels. But somehow CO_2 levels rose to dangerous levels in just a few hours." She looked up.

"I need to get to Hab 1." Tighe strapped on a life support pack, then pulled down the ladder to the upper hatch. He started turning the airlock pressure door handle.

"Why would the new owners try to kill us? It makes no sense!"

"We know their secrets, Priya. If they got rid of us, they could send another crew—or robots to retrieve what we've mined already."

She nodded to herself. "And they'd still have the *Konstantin.* . . ."

"Right. But without witnesses." Tighe felt his normally calm temper rising. "We don't have the fifteen minutes it will take for me to take the transfer tunnels. If Hab 1's CO_2 reaches 10 percent, then Isabel, Han, and Ade will be dead."

"It'll take over an hour to spin down the ship. And besides, you can't EVA without prebreathing."

Tighe started pressurizing his suit, adjusting its settings. "I'll go with as much pressure as possible."

She grabbed his arm. "Without prebreathing you'll get the bends, J.T. You'll die!"

"I've had the bends before. I know how much I can withstand." He pulled his arm free. "We have no choice, Priya!"

Chindarkar hesitated, then nodded and gazed past Tighe at virtual UIs as she started manipulating invisible controls.

Tighe climbed the ladder and sealed the airlock hatch behind him. Then he slammed the airlock evacuation lever. Air swirled around his suit as he opened a cabinet and pulled out a coiled length of tether equipped with carabiners at each end.

Pressure sickness ambushed him almost immediately—piercing his joints. He groaned in pain as he quickly prepared an alpine coil to strap the tether over his back. It was difficult to move about in his overpressurized suit, and yet the pressure was lower than it needed to be. Already it felt like someone was grinding knitting needles into his joints.

Holy shit. I forgot how much this hurt.

Chindarkar's voice came in over the comm link. *"J.T., I can't access any ship controls! I can't remotely control the mules either. They've taken over the* Konstantin. *They're killing us!"*

Tighe struggled toward the outer hatch. "They haven't killed us yet. We just need to reach the others."

"How? The owners have cameras everywhere."

The red light illuminated, indicating the airlock was fully evacuated. He unlatched the exterior hatch door and pulled it inward. Agony from decompression sickness intensified.

Truss girders with a spinning star field beyond greeted him through the hatchway.

"Priya, whatever we do next, Earth won't know about it for at least eighteen minutes. Which means they won't be able to send commands to the *Konstantin* in response for another eighteen minutes after that."

Chindarkar's voice sounded more resolute. *"Right. That's right."*

"So who has control of this ship for the next thirty-six minutes?"

"We do."

"Goddamn right. I'm taking the exterior maintenance plank up to the hub—then I'll traverse directly to Radial Arm 1."

"We're spun up! You'll get thrown clear of the ship."

"Not if I catch hold of the arm first." Tighe closed his eyes to settle his mind against the agony of nitrogen bubbling out of his blood. Sweat dripped into his eyes. He backed through the hatchway and poked with his booted foot for the upper rung of a ladder he knew must be there. "Secure your life support—pull out Hab 2's data links if you have to. Do you understand? Save yourself."

After a moment's silence her voice returned, resolved. *"I'm on it. J.T., I en-joyed us."*

"I did, too, Priya." With that, Tighe stepped out into the vacuum of space, staggering across the flat roof of the hab, clinging to truss girders. The stars and the shadow of Ryugu whirled all around him as centrifugal force pressed him against Hab 2's roof. Nausea assailed him—whether from motion or decompression sickness didn't much matter.

Tighe focused on the sight of Hab 1, 160 meters away at the end of the neighboring radial arm. It followed Hab 2 in its circuit around *Konstantin*'s axis. Despite the whirling star field, Tighe knew where he was, and he knew where he was going. He willed himself to override the pain and his middle ear confusion as he grabbed the ladder rungs of Radial Arm 2's spinward mainte-nance ladder.

There was no time to repeatedly clip in his tether as he climbed, so Tighe went without safeguards. He'd practiced this climb with Jin back on the ship's mock-up in Antarctica. However, here in real life, if he got disoriented and fell, he'd be hurled off into space.

Tighe closed his eyes and focused on the increasing pain in his joints as he climbed, listening to his breathing. His nausea eased, and as he rose along the ship's radial arm, the sensation of gravity began to lessen. He opened his eyes and could see the bulbous white wall of the Central Hab edge on, straight ahead. The flag of Luxembourg was printed there just beneath the word "Konstantin."

When Tighe had climbed most of the way up the arm, he released the lad-der and grabbed the truss girders surrounding the inflated transfer tunnel. Ev-erything was still pockmarked from storm damage.

He pulled himself, hand over hand, through the girders to the trailing side of the radial arm. Tighe now had an unobstructed view of Radial Arm 1 in the distance—closer now, since he was nearer the core. Nonetheless, the gap was sobering.

"I'm about to make the jump, Priya." He tried to ignore the blinding de-compression pain.

"The arm will be coming fast. Try to use the tunnel to cushion the impact."

With that Tighe let go of the girders and floated in space.

At first the box truss of Radial Arm 2 remained alongside him, but as it rotated around the Central Hab and Tighe's trajectory remained straight, it began to curve away from him.

Soon Tighe was in the void between the radial arms. He floated, hands outstretched like a skydiver, and braced himself for impact.

Since his own trajectory continued straight, he was halfway down the length of Radial Arm 1 by the time it caught up to him—approaching at 50 kilometers per hour.

He ducked under a cross brace as the white polymer wall of the inflated transfer tunnel impacted him, collapsing and tearing several stringers that held it in place. Tighe clawed at anything he could as he started to slide down the length of the tunnel's exterior, almost rolling between the girders before he managed to grab one of the Kevlar stringers.

Tighe braced his feet on the girders of the box truss and looked down at the hab 50 meters "below" him—a star field spinning beyond. He was now spinning along with Arm 1. "I made it! I'm on Arm 1!"

He didn't even hear Chindarkar's response as he looped the 100-meter tether coil to one of the box-truss girders and then tied a Munter hitch through one of his suit's carabiners. Tighe imagined Oberhaus's calm voice even now.

If you are careless and lose your belay device, you can use a Munter hitch to rappel in an emergency.

Tighe laughed, delirious with pain. "I know, I know . . ."

With a deep breath he pushed off from the spinward girder and paid out tether cord as he rappelled down the length of Arm 1. Ahead of him the universe turned in a nausea-inducing spin: the Milky Way, Ryugu, the Milky Way, Ryugu.

Tighe focused his gaze on the low curve of Hab 1 and ignored the 90 percent of his vision field above that. His joints pulsed in agony with each beat of his racing heart. His skin itched, and he felt numbness growing in his fingers and toes. He vaguely discerned a voice calling to him over the radio but did not dare break his concentration.

Soon Tighe's boots landed on the inflated roof of Hab 1. He unclipped the tether line and staggered over to the airlock hatch. He slid the lever and fell inside as the hatch opened. The pain of hitting the deck barely registered against the excruciating torture in his joints and chest. He groaned as he crawled to push and lock the exterior hatch, then slammed the pressure lever closed.

He tugged at Hab l's airlock hatch until the pressure equalized enough for him to open it. Tighe leaned through the upper hatchway, kicking on his helmet lights to see Isabel Abarca sleeping alone in one of the upper crew compartment beds.

She looked peaceful.

Tighe dropped down into her quarters, collapsing against the cabinets. He ignored the pain as he rose and pulled an oxygen candle out of his utility belt. He struck the igniter and the candle erupted with an eerie pink light. Tighe pulled up the emergency hatch leading into the crew quarters below. There he could see Jin and Adisa, also unconscious in their beds. He dropped the oxygen candle into their compartment and then pulled a breathing apparatus out of an emergency locker.

Tighe stumbled over to Abarca. She looked lifeless, but he secured the oxygen mask over her face and turned on the O_2. He began to compress her chest.

"C'mon, Isabel! Breathe! Breathe!" He glanced at her vitals in his AR display, but they were an absolute fiction of healthfulness. He kept compressing her chest as the O_2 flowed.

In a moment, her eyes fluttered. He felt her chest rising and falling. "That's it! That's it! Keep breathing. C'mon!"

She started coughing, then clutched the oxygen mask to her face. Her eyes met Tighe's and she read the urgent look in his eyes almost immediately—then gave a thumbs-up.

Tighe collapsed and crawled through the emergency hatch, dropping into the lower crew quarters. He broke open the lockers, pulling out emergency masks. He quickly secured these over Jin and Adisa's faces, opening their oxygen valves. He spoke into the comm link. "Priya, I'm in Hab l. I revived Isabel. I've got masks on Han and Ade." He groaned in agony. "Stand by." He leaned against the wall and gritted his teeth against the pain.

"J.T.! Are you all right?"

"No. Not really." The edges of his vision blurred, and he hit the purge valve to depressurize his suit. His ears popped as the higher pressure of ambient air streamed in. Then he collapsed onto the deck.

Tighe awoke in the Hab l medical bay, his joints pounding with an ache like distant thunder. He guessed he was on serious pain meds. He lay beneath a blanket with an IV running into his left arm and an oxygen mask on his face. Tighe looked up to see Abarca and Chindarkar sitting at his bedside. Jin and Adisa stood at the foot of the bed.

Abarca said, "Don't try to move. I have you on oxygen therapy."

Tighe tried to focus on her face. "How long was I out?"

"You woke up briefly an hour ago, but you've been unconscious for almost a day."

He looked around, his anxiety rising. He tried to sit up. "We can't sit here. The ship has been taken over. They—"

"Hey!" Jin and Adisa held him back. "Easy."

Chindarkar said, "Ade took care of it. The owners no longer have a remote link to the ship."

Tighe unclenched. He turned to Adisa. "How?"

"I took physical control of a mule and placed the maintenance shroud over the laser transmitter/receiver. They can send no commands to the *Konstantin* from Earth."

Tighe leaned back, sighing deeply. "They tried to kill us."

Jin nodded. "And they would have, too."

Abarca held Tighe's hand. "Thank you, J.T."

"You think I want to be out here alone?"

After a moment Chindarkar said, "We're not in the clear. The owners still have us locked out of everything. The Honey Bees, the ship's network. We can't even use the clam suits or access the ship's computers."

"Or monitor station keeping." There was a smoldering rage in Adisa's eyes—something Tighe had never seen before. "This situation must be rectified."

Over the next several days, the entire crew remained together in Hab 1, manually checking oxygen levels and temperatures. No one was certain what they'd do if the ship's systems started to malfunction. Not even their crystals worked anymore.

On the fourth day Adisa, wearing an oxygen mask, leaned into Tighe and Jin's crew quarters. "Please begin your prebreathe. I will need your assistance outside."

Two hours later Tighe, Jin, and Adisa pressurized their lightweight blue flight suits, strapped on life support packs, and exited the upper airlock. The flight suits were meant only for short, emergency EVAs, but without access to the ship's network, the clam suits' high-tech helmets were inert.

The trio climbed the *Konstantin*'s solar mast, noticing again the thousands of dings and scars from the rock storm the ship had weathered. Adisa had loaded Tighe and Jin down with packs containing computer equipment, cabling, and tools. After a few minutes' pulling along the length of the ship, they reached the sunlight and the top of the antenna mast, where the laser receiver/transmitter stood under a white polymer shroud.

Without speaking, Adisa took equipment out of the packs, securing a rad-hardened computer server and wireless router to nearby girders with zip ties.

Tighe opened his own pack. "So what is all this, Ade?"

"*The* Konstantin *communicates with Earth via a DTN system—delay/disruption tolerant networking. NASA developed it as an open-source Internet protocol intended for use throughout the solar system.*"

Jin also opened his pack to Adisa. "*Then it is different from the Earth Internet.*"

Adisa talked as he assembled equipment. "*Yes. Traditional Internet protocols require that all nodes in the transmission path be available, but here in space—due to distance—that will not always be the case. DTN supports automatic 'store and forward' data transmission; it can store partial bundles of data along a communication path until those parts can be forwarded and reassembled into the complete message. This means we will be able to gather what the owners of this vessel send us, even if we are not the final destination.*"

"You're not allowing them to connect to the *Konstantin*, I hope."

Adisa unbolted a port in the side of the laser comm tower, pulling out the bundle of wires inside. "*I have no intention of letting them connect to the* real Konstantin *ever again.*" He extended a gloved hand. "*Please hand me a wire cutter.*"

Tighe produced the cutter from his chest harness and handed it over.

Adisa severed the cables, then rewired the upstream lines to his own server. He followed by splicing the shipside wires to a separate router and then powering up a holographic projector. The first thing he instantiated was a virtual keyboard and a virtual terminal screen.

Jin said, "*We should know what you are doing, Ade.*"

Adisa didn't look up as he talked while typing with his space-gloved fingers. *"I am creating a virtual* Konstantin *from physical copies of the ship's OS discs."*

Tighe exchanged looks with Jin. "Where'd you find those?"

"In the central core's rad vault. They are intended for rebuilding the Konstantin's *OS from scratch in the event of emergency."*

Jin nodded to himself. *"So you create a virtual* Konstantin *and make them think they are connecting to the real one."*

Adisa kept typing. *"And I will monitor their connection as they transmit their log-on hash."*

Jin and Tighe exchanged looks. Tighe recalled their first conversation about Adisa back on Ascension. *The kid seems smart.*

"First deep space computer hacking—that should go on the wall, Ade."

Adisa kept typing. *"Only if it is successful."* He brought his gloved finger down onto a virtual "Enter" key, activating a script. Gold-colored holographic text scrolled through the virtual terminal to a blinking cursor. He handed the end of a cable to Jin. *"There is a maintenance jack beneath the service panel on your side. Please connect this."*

Jin did as instructed.

Adisa motioned to Tighe. *"Float clear of the laser, please."*

Tighe did so.

Adisa pulled the shroud off the optic array. He then powered up the laser transmitter/receiver. The meter-wide pearlescent optics glowed with a reddish light—although no beam was visible.

Tighe, Jin, and Adisa watched the holographic terminal display—its cursor blinking against a background of deep space.

Within moments text started scrolling across the screen.

"They've been broadcasting a connection request this whole time."

The screen halted with a long alphanumeric sequence.

Adisa's calm eyes remained focused. He pointed. *"This is the hash that they wish to pass to the* Konstantin *in order to log on."* He opened another holographic UI, this one linked to the real-world *Konstantin.* Adisa swept his glove to move the alphanumeric sequence from one holographic screen to another. Almost immediately the real *Konstantin*'s admin console appeared.

Adisa spoke without emotion. *"We now have control of our ship."*

Tighe and Jin shouted and high-fived, gripping Adisa's shoulders.

"Well done, Ade!"

Adisa remained focused. He changed the master administrator password and the other user passwords as well.

Jin watched over Adisa's shoulder. *"You are now the sysadmin of the* Konstantin."

Adisa nodded. After a few more moments of typing, Tighe's crystal display came back to life.

Judging by Jin's facial expression, his had as well.

Tighe laughed. "Outstanding."

Adisa did not smile.

"What's wrong, Ade?"

"We have admin rights to the Konstantin, *but we still have not solved the problem of communicating directly with Earth. The ship owners still control the laser relay back at L5."*

Jin contemplated the radio dishes on the mast above them. *"What about NASA's Deep Space Network? They can detect very faint radio signals."*

Adisa started packing up his equipment. *"With admin rights, I may now be able to repurpose a transmitter."*

Tighe asked, "And if it works, what do we transmit? Mayday? SOS?"

"That is something I am still working out."

CHAPTER 44

Back Channel

For nearly a month Adedayo Adisa's jury-rigged radio transmitter beamed a low-powered distress call back toward Earth—transmitting under the ship's Maritime Supervisory Authority call sign. But there was no reply.

Adisa did manage to tune in Earth radio stations, and occasionally he would play music or news throughout the habs. The news was strangely the same—war, political crisis, and celebrity. There was no word about the existence of the *Konstantin,* and it didn't sound like much progress had been made in deep space since their departure either.

Listening to radio commercials in the wee hours, Tighe was strangely comforted. But the normalcy also made him miss Earth more.

Celestial Robotics' mother ship, the *Argo,* still orbited Ryugu at a distance of 50 kilometers, and though emptied of mining craft, it was apparently functional.

Tighe sometimes watched the rival ship via a CCTV camera mounted on the *Konstantin*'s solar mast. The many digital eyes of the *Argo* seemed to be trained on the *Konstantin.*

A few days later Tighe was remotely piloting a mule, transporting a 14-ton bag of water ice back to the *Konstantin* from a Honey Bee, when Adisa's voice came through on the ship's comm link.

"I have received a message from Earth—a message sent to the virtual Konstantin. *It is a message that we all need to see."*

Half an hour later, the surviving crew of the *Konstantin* floated in the Central

Hab, watching a holographic screen that Adisa cast from his virtual server. Since it wasn't linked in to the ship's OS, they had no choice but to be physically present to watch it.

The video message opened to a face Tighe had not seen in over a year—Sevastian Yakovlev. Stunned gasps came from the assembled crew.

Yak's bushy beard and broad shoulders filled most of the frame as he smiled and laughed into the camera. "Crew of *Konstantin*! Greetings from Earth." His smile faded. "Too late it seems, for *Konstantin* reports that you are all dead." He brightened. "Good that CRC engineers tell us you are alive. They have been watching you. Perhaps you create wirtual machine to fool your new masters?" He laughed again. "Ade! Clever boy!"

Tighe felt relief flood over him. He laughed as the entire crew hugged and turned back to the screen.

"We have managed to hijack L5 laser transmitter from new owners to send this message. There are people who wish to speak with you." Yakovlev moved aside to reveal the core of Catalyst Corporation's original mission control team. At the front was Gabriel Lacroix. The engineers cheered and waved to the camera.

Yak moved back into place. "Took very long time to take over laser transmitter, and lock out new owners. After all this inconvenience, we hope you receive this message. The window for your return to Earth approaches, and we have idea how to save you." Yak grew serious. "Amy, my *kotyonok*. Even if you have fallen in love with some *vyperdysch*, I wish to see you safe." He held up his fingers in pantomime. "Call us."

With that the message ended.

Tighe unclenched from a stress he did not consciously realize he was under. Chindarkar hugged him and Jin gripped his shoulder.

"I knew they wouldn't forget us."

"Yak, you magnificent bastard."

Tighe noticed that Adisa was not smiling. The reminder about losing Tsukada appeared to have hit him hard.

Adisa asked, "Do we believe him?"

Everyone regarded Adisa with surprise.

He continued. "Yak and the others may have been kidnapped and threatened with death if they did not convince us to turn on the real transmitter."

Tighe paused. "I didn't see Eike."

Adisa nodded and said, "Her absence concerns me."

Chindarkar frowned. "We must reply." She pointed at Adisa's disconnected server. "If you don't trust them, reply through this virtual machine of yours."

Adisa brooded for a moment, then nodded.

Not long afterward, the five remaining crew of the *Konstantin* floated in front of a surveillance camera and recorded a message.

Abarca spoke first, smiling. "You have no idea how glad we are to see your faces." Her expression turned serious. She glanced to either side. "There are still five of us. Sevastian, it saddens me to tell you this, but Amy died back in November. From a fall." Abarca gripped Adisa's hand. "We placed her next to David and Nicole. Aside from radiation, meteor strikes, and assholes back on Earth trying to kill us, we are all well. But we'd like to hear more about this idea for returning us to Earth. We've done a big job out here, and it'd be nice to come home."

Just over eighteen minutes later, they received a reply from Gabriel Lacroix. He looked pleased but also emotionally restrained. Behind him the mission control staff likewise looked subdued. Lacroix leaned in to say, "We are glad to see you five. Sevastian needed a moment."

Lacroix gestured to the crude mission control room behind him—a collection of cheap desks in what appeared to be a warehouse. "Our budget has shrunk, but we have gathered most of the original mission control team. Unfortunately, we have no funds to produce or launch the ship that was originally planned to bring you home. . . ."

Tighe's hopes fell—along with those of the rest of the crew.

"However, we have another idea." Lacroix stepped aside as a hologram of a streamlined spacecraft glowed nearby. "We think you can build the return ship yourselves—from the design that Catalyst originally developed. We're sending you the CAD plans—just over 62 tons dry mass—a seamless cobalt-steel lifting body with a ceramic ablative heat shield, loosely based on NASA's canceled X-33 VentureStar."

Lacroix rotated the hologram. The ship was sleek and had no windows, with vestigial wings near the rear and twin, stubby tail fins. It had no rocket engine. It was just a glider.

"With this lifting body you can achieve Earth aerocapture. We estimate that you'll be approaching the Earth at a minimum of 18 kilometers per second. By using Earth's atmosphere to aerobrake, you won't need rockets to slow down—those would require a massive ship with systems capable of cooling hundreds of tons of liquid oxygen and methane en route. Instead, with this design you can depart Ryugu in a much smaller vessel that is far easier to build."

Abarca narrowed her eyes. "He's not seriously expecting us to build our own spaceship, is he?"

Lacroix's message continued. "This return ship was designed years ago by the same team that designed the *Konstantin*. We've got a complete parts listing, and we'll guide you. Likewise, we've written software to assist your return craft with astrogation, propulsion, life support."

Abarca threw up her hands. "Does he really think we can build a hypersonic lifting body?"

Adisa was already studying the digital plans they'd received. He nodded to himself. "We're not going to *build* it, Isabel." He looked up. "We're going to *grow* it. Just like Amy taught us."

Tighe, Adisa, and Chindarkar reviewed Amy Tsukada's tutorials on chemical vapor deposition repeatedly in the following days. The mission control engineers sent additional CAD plans, and the entire crew got busy reviewing them.

The engineers also sent a VR flight simulator so the crew could learn how to fly their theoretical return ship. The aerobraking maneuver had such tight tolerances that it would be handled entirely by flight control software. However, just getting into the vicinity of Earth was going to require a lot of skill.

Jin was already poring through the return ship's two thousand pages of technical documentation. "I flew fighter jets, and I have a hundred hours on capsule reentry simulators. I believe I can fly this."

Tighe slapped him on the back. "I think we have our pilot."

After several days reviewing CAD plans, manifests, tech manuals, and software, all five crew members sat around a worktable in the Fab Hab. A holographic blueprint floated between them of the aerobraking craft mated to a booster stage. The much larger booster consisted of a scaffolding framework holding six spherical fuel tanks in two rows of three with twin rocket engines between. Forward of these was a cylindrical crew quarters.

Chindarkar rubbed her tired eyes. "A thousand tons of fuel, turbopumps, piping, rocket motors, thrusters, crew module, life support—and it all needs to be integrated with control systems. But to tell you the truth, my biggest concern is the lifting body. I think it would be easier to remain in space and fire rocket engines to slow down. Then we could just go into orbit around Earth."

Jin shook his head. "We have less than a year to build this. Adding refrigeration systems to store fuel for a month-long journey is complex. Then there is the mass of extra fuel, extra tanks, plumbing—and what if we cannot reignite the engines? We have no ullage motors." Jin pointed at the aerobraking stage. "This way, we only need to burn once—on departure."

Adisa sighed. "I agree with Han. Aerobraking is not our biggest concern. Astrogation is."

Everyone looked his way.

"At the velocity we are proposing, our trajectory will need to be incredibly precise. If we are even a micro-arc second off course, we will miss the Earth—and be lost forever."

Jin nodded. "This all needs to be constructed, tested, and ready for departure"—he looked up at his crystal—"by February 10 of next year."

Tighe whistled. "Eleven months."

The crew exchanged grim looks.

Adisa said, "Then it is best we get started."

CHAPTER 45

Lifeboat

AUGUST 15, 2037

J ames Tighe and Jin Han floated on tethers near the *Konstantin*'s refinery in well-worn EVA suits. Bolted to the lower spine of the *Konstantin* was a polymer latticework scaffolding that contained a vessel under construction—a vessel that itself mostly resembled scaffolding.

Tighe watched a mule coast slowly past him. It held a 2-meter bladder tank in its robotic arms. Remotely piloted by Chindarkar, the mule soon popped thrusters and came to a stop near Jin. The robotic arms placed the bladder tank inside a frame, between two identical tanks.

Jin moved to secure the tank to the frame with stays, hooking them to eye-bolts on the tank's surface. *"Bring over the last hose, J.T."*

"Coming . . ." Tighe climbed from girder to girder in microgravity, pulling a polymer hose behind him. He joined it to a valve at the base of the bladder tank.

The hose floated behind Tighe, as did two others, leading to a 20-meter-long, 10-meter-wide, and 5-meter-high white polymer mold inflated within lattice-work scaffolding. Shaped vaguely like a wedge, it resembled a captive Thanksgiving Day parade balloon. The interior of the mold, Tighe knew, was far more intricate than its exterior suggested.

Chindarkar's voice came in over the comm link. *"What happens if we screw this up?"*

Tighe clipped the hose in. "Then we've got ourselves a 62-ton paperweight." He tightened the hose collar, then checked that it was secure. "Locked."

Jin gazed up at the *Konstantin*'s z-axis, rising 80 meters over them, the ship's radial arms rotating like a colossal ceiling fan. "*We're ready, Ade.*"

Adisa's voice said, "*Powering the pumps.*"

Chindarkar's voice: "*Pressure's good. Heating elements good.*"

Tighe scanned the three hose lines for leaks. The hoses, he knew, were slowly pumping 60,000 liters of cobalt-steel-carbonyl into the inflated mold.

Adisa's voice again: "*Timer set to eight hours, fourteen minutes.*"

Jin checked the voltages on the electrical wires.

The mold was a large chemical vapor deposition chamber—much bigger than the one Tsukada had used to make machine parts inside the *Konstantin*'s refinery. It would form the hull of a 20-meter-long aerodynamic lifting body all in one piece—seamlessly—out of metal so pure and heat resistant it should help withstand aerocapture through the Earth's atmosphere at 20-plus kilometers per second.

Mission control's use of the word *should* was what gave Tighe pause.

This CVD session would be the first of many. They'd depose the interior of the ship in a series of layers—structural supports, inner walls, conduits, hatches and a heat shield. Their to-do list was seemingly endless.

Adisa's voice: "*It will be hours until this completes. Come in and get some rest.*"

Chindarkar brought the mule alongside. Jin and Tighe floated wearily onto the running boards and clipped in. Holding on as they moved beyond the sweep of the radial arms, Tighe gazed out at the cosmos.

The majesty all around them no longer inspired Tighe. The universe now seemed cold, uncaring, and incomprehensibly remote. The Earth was just a white dot in an endless void. And yet it was home.

More than anything, he yearned for home.

His body aching, Tighe lay on the worn sofa in Hab 2, listening to a classic rock station out of Berlin. He found the music soothing. Jin dozed in a nearby reading chair, also exhausted from another long EVA—their eighth in six days.

Tighe gazed up at the dozens of world's firsts scrawled in black ink on the aluminum core wall, but it was their deadline written in larger, underlined characters that was impossible to ignore: *February 10, 2038.* The date loomed over every waking moment. It was the departure window for return to Earth, roughly six months from now.

For the first time in his life, Tighe fell asleep dreaming of rocket trajectories.

DECEMBER 8, 2037

Tighe, Jin, Abarca, and Adisa stood on the running boards of two mules. Only Chindarkar remained on the *Konstantin.*

The mules floated a hundred meters away from the largest robot tug they'd built yet. The name "Amy Tsukada" was emblazoned in meter-high letters on the spacecraft's solar shield. The vessel was identical in form to the previous two tugs, but longer, and composed of half a dozen rows of bladder tanks—6,000 tons of water ice, nitrogen, ammonia, and carbonyls in all—and powered by eight small rocket engines cannibalized from CRC mining robots.

The tug was already almost completed before Yakovlev and mission control contacted them with plans to build a crewed return spacecraft, and while that construction project continued, it was Abarca who insisted they complete the robot tug, too.

"It's why we came out here," she said. "If we don't return these resources, the last year will have been for nothing. And it's the biggest shipment yet."

And so Tighe and Jin worked all hours, mounting and connecting the CRC engines, working with mission control to integrate them into guidance software, even as the deadline to return to Earth loomed.

Now that the robot tug was ready to launch, everyone turned to Adisa, who stared at the 40-meter-long spacecraft.

Adisa spoke softly. *"Amy was a special human being. She taught us how to draw the building blocks of life from this dust. She kept us alive—and does still. I hope the cargo on her ship makes life possible for many more."*

With that, Adisa tapped a virtual button that ignited the 6,000-ton behemoth's eight rocket engines.

The engines all silently ignited, but the vessel did not move—at least at first. Tighe and Jin exchanged nervous looks. However, the tug finally began to move, almost imperceptibly, and then noticeably, propelling the craft away from Ryugu and into deep space.

The launch was for safekeeping. The ideal return window to cislunar space for a craft this massive would not arrive until March 17, 2039—well over a year after the crew of the *Konstantin* would have departed.

It was being moved to a position a few hundred kilometers from Ryugu, where it would lie dormant until the time was right. Then it would fire its engines, accelerating 551 meters per second to send it on a two-and-three-quarter-year trajectory back toward cislunar space—arriving near Earth's moon on December 3, 2041.

They watched the receding engine-glow for several minutes.

This was the last of three robot tugs sent toward Earth on long, low-delta-v trajectories. The human crew of the *Konstantin* would beat all but two shipments back—if they ever managed to depart Ryugu, that is.

Watching the glow of the rockets fade into the distance, Abarca said, "*No matter what happens to us now, we've fulfilled our purpose here. We've returned 11,000 tons of resources. That's more than Nathan hoped. More than enough to jump-start humanity's leap into space. Now it's time to rescue ourselves.*"

A few days later Tighe was on another EVA, moving around the scaffolding to install fuel pipes on the return ship.

He glanced down to see welding flashes emanating from within the hull of a sleek, dark-gray spacecraft, whose hatchways had not yet been installed. The vessel was seamless—with no opening for a front windscreen, only smooth cobalt steel dotted with integral housings for plenoptic camera sensors. The ship resembled a jet fighter, and Tighe had to admit it gave him confidence.

That they could build such a thing seemed miraculous. And yet, here it was. Tsukada had taught them well.

Then he noticed Adisa on an EVA, moving along the hull near the tail fins. He seemed to be applying a mask of lettering to the ship's surface with black Kapton tape.

Tighe secured his tools and floated down to the scaffolding just above Adisa. He craned his neck and read the name aloud, "James Caird."

Surprised, Adisa looked up with difficulty within the stiffness of the EVA suit. *"All ships must have a name. I elected to give ours one—in tape, should anyone have objections."*

"All right, I give up, who's James Caird?"

"He was a prosperous textile manufacturer in 1870s Scotland."

"Okay . . . I'm as big a fan of nineteenth-century textile manufacturers as the next guy, but why are we naming our return spacecraft after one?"

"Mr. Caird had another small vessel named after him—it was a lifeboat. Ernest Shackleton piloted that lifeboat across 800 miles of Antarctic sea, amid terrible storms, to find a tiny dot of land: South Georgia Island. The journey of the James Caird *was considered one of the greatest feats of small-boat navigation in all human history."*

Tighe nodded to himself. "That sounds about right, Ade. You've got my vote."

It wound up being unanimous.

CHAPTER 46

Reason

FEBRUARY 10, 2038

J ames Tighe performed CPR on Adedayo Adisa, who lay unconscious on the medical table in Hab 2.

Isabel Abarca inserted a needle into Adisa's neck. "C'mon, Ade.
Stay with me!"

Jin Han stood nearby holding up an IV bag.

Chindarkar's voice came through the comm link. "*How is he doing?*"

Jin answered, "Give us a second, Priya."

Still unconscious, Adisa vomited onto his chest, then sucked for air between coughs.

Abarca cleared Adisa's airway and then affixed an oxygen mask. The heart
monitor beeped fast but steadily. She nodded to Tighe. "He's breathing."

Jin spoke into the comm link. "He's breathing. Stabilized."

"*Thank you.*"

Tighe wiped sweat away from his face. "We can't keep using amphetamines."

The entire group looked exhausted and gaunt. Their jumpsuits were patched
and faded.

Abarca shined a light into Adisa's pupils. "Ade, can you hear me?"

Adisa's eyes focused, then glanced around the bed. "What happened?"

"You overdosed."

"I apologize, Isabel."

Abarca's eyes teared up. She wiped the tears away and studied his vital
signs. "Why would you exceed the dosage I prescribed?"

"Because I must not sleep. We need to finish the ship."

"You're not going to finish the ship if you're dead."

Adisa shielded his eyes against the light. "We were supposed to depart today. Each day we delay makes return less possible."

"We're working on it."

"We must fly, or we will die. Overdosing hardly matters."

Neither Tighe nor Jin reacted. They all knew they'd missed the ideal return orbital window. Earlier that morning Tighe had watched one of the ship's cameras aimed back at Earth. Ryugu was close enough now for him to discern the Earth and Moon as two separate disks side by side. A finger's width to the right were the Pleiades—which was 365 light-years away. The Earth might as well have been the Pleiades for how accessible it was to them.

Now each additional day of delay required more delta-v to reach Earth. Soon, they'd never be able to encounter Earth at all. Tighe didn't want to know the day of their point of no return. The knowledge would only weigh on him.

He knew—as all of them knew—that their return ship still needed days of work. The metallic hull, hatches, plumbing, and engines were all complete, but the electronics were still a mess. The mismatched, cannibalized parts from the *Konstantin* and CRC's mining robots caused difficult-to-pinpoint failures and errors. The guidance system was sketchy. And the ship was so stripped down that literally everything had to work—there were no redundancies.

Abarca prevented Adisa from sitting up. "Rest, Ade. Get some rest."

More than a week later, Tighe, Jin, and Chindarkar stared at nothing as they sat numbly around the galley table in Hab 2. They'd each lost several more kilos of weight and looked haggard from overwork. The *James Caird* was still docked near the refinery.

Every day the bright disk of the Earth drew closer. Now it was just 58 million miles away. However, because it was coming closer, it also meant they might not be able to close the gap before it passed them by.

As of today, Tighe, Jin, Chindarkar, and Abarca had done all they could to prepare the vessel. They'd even loaded their scant personal belongings and other supplies onto the *James Caird*, ready to depart the moment it was finished.

The remaining work was software based and relied entirely on Adisa and mission control engineers. The astrogation, guidance, and fuel management systems were still only partially complete due to flaws that Earth-bound engineers had not yet been able to rectify. There was nothing more that Tighe, Jin, and Chindarkar could do to help.

As tired as they looked sitting around the table, they all knew Adisa was even more exhausted—even as he used his considerable intellect to wrestle with complex software integration problems.

Adisa's voice came in over the comm link. "*J.T., Han, Priya. I need you to prebreathe for another diagnostic, please.*"

Tighe answered wearily. "Did mission control resolve the errors?"

Adisa had an edge in his voice as he replied, "*I will not know until we run through the tests.*"

They all exchanged looks and then went to retrieve oxygen masks.

Two hours later, they exited the lower airlock in their blue flight suits—all three of which had black Kapton tape sealing leaks from worn joints. They moved along the scaffolding where the *James Caird* was still moored near the *Konstantin*'s refinery. As sleek as the aerobraking vehicle was, the rest of the vessel was an ungainly gridwork of girders and piping, with twin rows of spherical tanks—all designed to withstand significant g-forces from acceleration. And yet, the ship was inert.

Jin keyed his mic. "*Almost in position.*"

"*I copy.*"

There was a standard docking hatch on the starboard side of the aerobraking craft, but it was easier to enter the ship by pulling themselves past the booster's rocket engines, hand over hand across rows of fuel pipes, between fuel tanks, and then to enter the crew module. The hatchway here was square and much larger.

Once inside, they continued through another narrow hatchway and into the aerobraking vehicle itself. Here, there was room for four rows of two seats in a narrow compartment—although only five seats were installed. The ship had originally been designed to return the entire eight-person *Konstantin* crew. Every time Tighe saw the empty slots, he felt the absence of Clarke, Morra, and Tsukada.

Soon they strapped in, Jin in the pilot seat, Chindarkar as astrogator, and

Tighe monitoring fuel systems. After tapping at a few virtual buttons, Jin instantiated a virtual windscreen. Tighe could now "see" through the steel hull of the vessel via the plenoptic cameras embedded in housings there.

Jin spoke over the comm link. *"Ready for diagnostic check, Ade."*

"You are all seated?"

Jin looked around the cabin. *"Affirmative."*

The vibration of turbopumps winding up reached Tighe's inner ear. He exchanged confused looks with Jin and Chindarkar.

Jin stabbed at virtual controls. *"We hear the fuel system pressurizing."*

Adisa said, *"That is because I've launched a countdown timer."*

"A countdown timer?"

Tighe sat up.

"I am launching the James Caird. *For real. Remain in your seats."*

Jin scowled. *"Ade, what the hell are you saying? Isabel! Ade needs help. He's suffering some sort of nervous—"*

"I am not suffering a breakdown, Han. Everything else is. The return ship will launch in four minutes whether you are on it or not."

Tighe shouted, "Why are you doing this?" He unbuckled and pulled himself out of his seat, floating back toward the crew module.

Chindarkar called to him. *"J.T.! The ship's on a countdown!"*

Tighe exited through the rear hatch.

Abarca's voice came in over the comm link. *"Listen to Ade! He isn't delirious. And this decision isn't sudden. Adedayo and I made it some time ago."*

Chindarkar shouted through the link, *"What are you talking about, Isabel?"*

Tighe glided through the crew module as fast as he could, headed back toward the *Konstantin.*

Adisa's measured, calm voice said, *"Listen, all of you: we are out of time. I have reviewed the calculations with Isabel and confirmed them with mission control. If we wait even twelve more hours, none of us will ever reach Earth."*

Tighe shouted over his radio, "Then why aren't you and Isabel on board?"

Adisa answered, *"There are too many uncontrolled variables for this ship to fly a predictable trajectory without external aid—and the minute we launch from the* Konstantin *you will lose contact with Earth. An error of a fraction of a radian at the beginning and you will miss Earth entirely."*

Tighe exited the crew module and moved between the piping and fuel tanks. For the first time he noticed the tanks were wicking off white vapor—loaded and ready to go. He called over the comm link, "We are a *crew*, Ade. A family. We decide together!"

"*J.T., there is no other reasonable choice. If we all stay here, we all die. There is not enough food. But if you three go, Isabel and I have over five years' of supplies. You can send help for us.*"

"Goddamnit! That's too dangerous. Even if you live—" Tighe reached the *Konstantin*'s lower airlock and tried to slide the lever—but it was stuck. He looked up at the glass portal.

Abarca's face stared back at him, the handle of her ice ax jamming the lever in the locked position. She shook her head, her voice coming in over the comm link. "*Get back on the ship, J.T. You have less than three minutes.*"

He pounded on the hatch. "Cancel the launch! This isn't how we say good-bye! I know you can cancel it!"

Adisa's voice: "*That is where you are wrong, J.T. I have overfilled the fuel tanks with superchilled liquid oxygen and liquid methane. It is the only way to give you the higher delta-v you will need—over 20 kilometers per second. Without the added mass of Isabel and myself, or the food and oxygen we would need, you will go even faster. However, if you do not burn this fuel in the next five to ten minutes, it will expand as it warms. It will burst the tanks and possibly explode, killing everyone and destroying the* Konstantin."

Tighe looked back at the growing white clouds wicking off the fuel tanks.

"*Jin and Chindarkar cannot fly the ship by themselves. Two people to handle the fuel-line switchover, and one to effect the course corrections I will provide by radio. You must go now, J.T. There is no stopping the launch.*"

Abarca said, "*Get on the ship, J.T. Or you're killing us all.*"

Tighe turned to look at Abarca's face through the portal. "I understand why Ade is staying, but why would you?"

"*Ade is here because of me. And I don't leave until my entire expedition is off the mountain.*"

Adisa's voice: "*Two minutes! You must board the ship, J.T. Please, I beg you!*"

Tighe moved right up to the borosilicate glass, placing his glove on it. "Let me take your place, Isabel. I once left my diving partner to die. I won't do it again."

Abarca nodded to herself and smiled at Tighe as she placed her hand against his beyond the glass. "*I think Richard Oberhaus would be proud of what you've done with his years.*" She shook her head. "*But you and Han are the most experienced on EVAs. I've barely been in a suit.*"

Adisa shouted, "*J.T. Board the ship!*"

Tighe stared at her. "We will return for you."

"*I have no doubt.*"

With one last glance, Tighe pushed off and moved across the scaffolding with practiced ease. He grabbed the piping of the *James Caird* and moved between the rows of steaming fuel tanks.

CHAPTER 47

Injection Burn

FEBRUARY 19, 2038

A s James Tighe pulled himself aboard, he turned back for one last look at the *Konstantin*. He committed to memory the image of Abarca and Adisa floating near the ship's core in their faded jumpsuits, the Far Star glittering in its perch beneath an LED light.

Tighe noticed Jin Han exit the crew module of the *James Caird*. Jin glided over the piping. He pointed urgently at the steaming tanks. *"Take position for launch."*

Tighe nodded and moved to the first of three fuel-line levers on the port row of tanks. Here, a series of eyebolts were placed for him to clip in, along with spiral steps running the length of the starboard piping. Jin clipped in at the base of a second spiral stair on the port side.

Tighe spoke over the radio. "Adedayo Adisa, Isabel Abarca, Nicole Clarke, David Morra, Amy Tsukada—it has been an honor crewing with you."

Adisa said, *"You are all my brothers and my sisters."*

Chindarkar answered, her voice cracking. *"I love you, Ade. I love you, Isabel."*

Abarca responded, *"I love you, too, but don't get too weepy just yet. For all we know, you're the ones who are about to die, not Ade and me. If you have any chance to make Earth, you will need to remain focused and follow Ade's radioed instructions closely for as long as you're in range. Emotion comes later."*

Chindarkar sniffled. *"Copy that."*

Adisa's voice came in. *"Releasing docking clamps . . ."*

Clamps at the four corners of the scaffolding released the return ship, and cold-gas thrusters vented, pushing it slowly away from the *Konstantin*.

Tighe looked up at the black shadow of the asteroid Ryugu. The Honey Bees were still at work up in the sunlight above its horizon. A line of a dozen boulders waited there in a terminator orbit. The mining would continue.

The *James Caird* was still gliding slowly away from the *Konstantin*—not quite 20 meters away now. The larger ship's radial arms swept past overhead. The lights on the girders of the *Konstantin* made it look like a refinery in the night.

Adisa said, "*Priya, I will track your position using the Ka-band transmitter and advise you. Check your display for my trajectory adjustments. As of ten minutes ago, the* James Caird *will need to achieve a delta-v of 24.4 kilometers per second to encounter the Earth in forty days. Mission control knows to listen for you on or after March 31.*"

Jin answered, "*Twenty-four point four kilometers per second? Ade, can we achieve aerocapture at that speed?*"

"*You have no choice but to try. You will have to make adjustments, Han. If any of us can do it, it is you.*"

Tighe looked at Jin's anxious expression.

"*It is time to go. . . .*" Adisa began a countdown over the comm link. "*Ten, nine, eight . . .*"

Tighe studied the familiar form of the *Konstantin*, pirouetting, now 300 meters away. It was hard to believe that after all these years, the expedition would end so suddenly. "Godspeed, *Konstantin*."

"*. . . two, one, ignition.*"

Nothing happened.

"Shit." Tighe turned to Jin.

Chindarkar's voice: "*Ade, we've popped a circuit breaker. Fuel control system. J.T., Han, there's a short somewhere. The computer's preventing engine startup.*"

"We're on it." Tighe pulled himself along the lattice framework as though climbing over monkey bars. "What subsystem?"

"*Fuel Pump 2.*"

Jin called out, "*Here.*" He motioned for Tighe to join him, and they pulled apart a section of cabling.

"Yeah, Priya, the shielding on the cabling's damaged. We'll wrap it."

"Copy that."

They started wrapping the cable bundle with Kapton tape. Tighe looked up at the fuel tanks wicking white vapor more furiously now.

Ade's voice said, *"You must hurry. The fuel is warming. We do not have much time to get the engines started!"*

Tighe knew the six bladder tanks around him contained 180,000 liters of methalox rocket fuel each—more than a million liters in total. A thousand tons of explosive energy. If there was even a small spark among the engine piping, then the explosion might actually be visible from Earth.

In a few moments, he and Jin finished wrapping the ignition cable. They returned to their stations, clicked in their tethers, and held on to steel handles, bracing for acceleration.

"Ready! Try again!"

Chindarkar's voice: *"Begin the countdown, Ade!"*

"No time for a countdown! Safe journey!"

"We—"

Suddenly the twin Starion rocket engines roared to life, their red-white exhausts forming interlocking cones. There was no sound—but the steel plumbing all around Tighe vibrated, and a bass rumble entered his middle ear.

He and Jin examined the piping for leaks. There were no telltale gas plumes.

"Good burn—both engines, Ade!" Tighe glanced back at the *Konstantin.*

They didn't appear to be moving. His view of the black shadow of Ryugu behind them wasn't changing either. Neither was he experiencing much in the way of acceleration. Yet, the *James Caird*'s engines—each capable of 430,000 foot-pounds of thrust—were at full throttle.

Jin said, *"She is heavy!"*

Tighe nodded. Ninety-five percent of the *James Caird*'s 1,200-ton weight was fuel, and they were going to burn through all of it in the next ten minutes.

Adisa's voice came to them again. *"Check your AR display. We have tank changeover in two minutes, forty-five seconds."* Tighe and Jin took up their positions across from each other at the first set of valve handles.

Although the process was ludicrously crude, Tighe and Jin would have to manually switch over the fuel tanks as they drained. The *James Caird* was a fly-by-AR vessel, piloted exclusively with virtual controls and monitored by virtual gauges. Even now a virtual row of fuel tank levels appeared in Tighe's crystal display. His crystal had transferred to the *Caird*'s wireless network, and now he was looking at this ship's telemetry readings. They were traveling at 6 meters per second and accelerating.

Each fuel tank would burn for three minutes and thirteen seconds. The valves had to be manually switched from one tank to the next before the rocket's fuel source ran dry. Once started, if the engines were not properly shut down, any sudden loss of pressure would cause the engine to explode—which would in turn cause their entire ship to explode, killing everyone.

"We can't screw this up, Han."

Jin nodded.

Tighe and Jin would do the cutover with an eight-second buffer. As each tank emptied, they would unlatch the brackets holding the empty bladder tank in place—and it would pull free from its fuel hose and fall away behind them as they accelerated away, shedding several tons of deadweight.

As the total mass of the *James Caird* dropped, g-forces from acceleration would increase. Mission control engineers estimated they would endure a maximum of 3 g's acceleration. However, with the extra fuel Ade had loaded, it was anyone's guess what the final acceleration would be.

Looking back between the exhaust plumes, Tighe could see they were now noticeably accelerating, pulling away from the *Konstantin* and from Ryugu. He never imagined that leaving the asteroid would be bittersweet.

The *James Caird* continued to pick up speed. Suddenly they moved out from the shadow of Ryugu and into the sunlight, and most of the stars and nebulae faded to invisibility.

Adisa's voice came in over their local comm link. "*You are approaching 10 kilometers' distance from us and will soon be out of voice radio range. After this, we will only be able to communicate with you through a Ka-band data channel. I am sad to say that this is, for now, good-bye.*"

Abarca's voice came in over the radio. "*Don't be sad. You will need all your focus for the challenges ahead. Ade will guide you. Reach out to us, and we will be here.*"

Tighe spoke over the comm link. "Isabel, Ade, take care of yourselves."

Moments later the radio link to the *Konstantin* disappeared in a fuzz of static.

But there was no time to mourn as the first fuel tanks emptied, and Tighe monitored his gauge and performed the cutover, then watched the rocket plume as the new fuel tank took the place of the first. To his relief it went smoothly.

He glanced over to see Jin only now starting his switchover. Tighe assumed the engines must be burning at a slightly different rate. That was probably bad, but he was too exhausted to ponder the guidance implications. He instead focused on the tasks that he had practiced so many times he could even do them in his present state of exhaustion.

Tighe braced himself against the metal framework and grabbed the fuel-tank latch. Pulling hard, he unlocked it and watched as the gate for the 7-meter-diameter fuel tank opened. The enormous tank pulled from its hose and rolled along the ship, into the exhaust wake, which sent it spinning off into the cosmos. Moments later the nearly empty fuel tank exploded in a sphere of fire, kilometers behind them.

Jin's tank soon joined it.

The two of them climbed forward on the spiral steps, against increasing acceleration.

A glance back and Tighe's crystal display showed that Ryugu was almost a hundred kilometers behind them now, about the size of a grape at arm's length. He could still make out the *Konstantin*'s silhouette to the left of it, in its shadow.

"*J.T.! Keep moving!*"

Tighe looked ahead to see that Jin was already in place at his next fuel lever. It took tremendous effort for Tighe to pull himself forward against the rapidly increasing g-forces. The ship had just shed 400 tons and the engines were starting to take command.

Tighe pulled himself into place.

"*Fifty seconds to cutover!*"

Tighe clipped his tether to the nearest eyebolt. Watching virtual gauges, he waited, and then opened the valve for Tank 3. Another glance showed the cutover was seamless—but by then, he needed to grip the metal rails with both hands to stop himself from sliding backward. Then he dropped down to kneel on a step instead. His crystal display showed he was already experiencing 2 g's of acceleration.

Jin struggled to hold on to the valve handle. His cutover had not occurred yet, and the acceleration continued to increase.

Two point two g's.

"Han! Do the cutover!"

"Not yet!"

Suddenly a plume of gas stabbed out from the piping aft of Tighe's position. He looked back to see that one of the manifolds had failed and was venting pressurized fuel.

"Shit!"

Priya's voice came over their local comm link. *"Engine 1 is losing pressure. I'm shutting it down."*

"Do it!"

Two point five g's.

At this acceleration Tighe weighed about 450 pounds.

Engine 1 stuttered, and the flame extinguished. The leaking plume of gas disappeared. Suddenly the g-forces of acceleration plummeted to 1.2.

Tighe got back to a leaning position and watched as Jin performed the cutover. Engine 2 continued burning as the ship accelerated more reasonably—at least for now.

Jin pointed. *"We need to turn the crossfeed valve—to feed your third tank to Engine 2!"*

Tighe nodded. Both he and Jin moved to the center of the pipe array, searching for a valve they knew was there.

"Hurry!"

Tighe found it and braced his feet as the g-forces built up again. Almost back to 2 g's. "Hang on!"

Jin knifed his hand. *"Now!"*

Tighe turned the valve head until it stopped. He then slammed back into the nearest piping as the ship's acceleration continued to increase.

Jin pressed his back against a vertical pipe and winced against the g-forces. *"I think it worked!"*

Tighe was unable to reply as their acceleration raced past 3 g's. After what he knew must have been three minutes, he heard Chindarkar's voice over the comm link.

"Shutting down Engine 2."

In a few moments the almost unbearable g-force eased, and Jin cut away the last fuel tank. They both watched it roll away behind them as the exhaust plume shortened, then ceased. They were again in free fall. He and Jin embraced each other in relief.

Chindarkar said, "*MECO.*"

After he recovered his breath, Tighe looked back behind them.

Ryugu was now just a glowing white dot. Tighe's crystal display indicated it was already 1,426 kilometers away, the distance increasing at a blistering 24.42 kilometers per second.

"Holy shit, we're going fast."

"*J.T., Jin, are you guys okay?*"

Jin answered, "*Yes. How is our trajectory?*"

"*Ade helped me make several corrections.*" Her voice strained with emotion. "*He says we look good. That we're on course for an Earth encounter. Would you both please come inside?*"

CHAPTER 48

Chasing Earth

nside the crew module, Tighe fell asleep almost immediately—and in free fall that was a first for him. He woke up more than six hours later and thrashed about for a moment in a panic, forgetting that he was in microgravity. The familiar sensation of stuffed sinuses had returned.

Tighe floated over to see Chindarkar and Jin staring into a holographic display of their trajectory. "How's it look?"

She turned tired eyes on him.

Jin said, "We are going very fast—which is necessary to have any chance to catch up to Earth. But I am concerned about the aerocapture maneuver."

Chindarkar pointed and said, "Han thinks we might skim straight through Earth's atmosphere without slowing down enough and then hurtle off into deep space."

Jin adjusted values in the diagram. "Earth gravity will accelerate us even more as we approach."

Tighe looked from one to the other. "Didn't mission control calculate all this?"

"They wrote the autopilot software for an 18-kilometer-per-second aerocapture—not 25. In fact, it might be higher than 25. I don't know yet. If we dive deeper into the atmosphere, we could burn up—or die from the g-forces necessary for capture." Jin stared at the diagram. "I need to calculate whether it's even possible."

The *James Caird* was designed to spin lengthwise, creating one-sixth gravity in the crew module. However, because it lacked the *Konstantin*'s spin radius, the crew had to lie on the floor to keep the Coriolis effect from sickening them.

Sleeping in low gravity, however, was much easier for Tighe than sleeping in free fall.

On the second day of the transfer, Tighe awoke to see Jin and Chindarkar eating in a reclined position.

Jin motioned for caution. "Do not sit up. And do not try standing."

Tighe rose slowly to his elbows.

Chindarkar tossed him a water pouch.

He took a long sip from it. "Forty days of crawling? Maybe space *is* like caving." He looked around at the confined cabin. "Is the ship holding up?"

Chindarkar ate rehydrated oatmeal out of the package. "Life support is sketchy. We've got overheating problems. There's almost no radiation shielding. We could all die any second."

Tighe nodded. "So the usual shit." He finished the water. "Any word from Isabel and Ade?"

Chindarkar grew somber. "They're monitoring our progress. Still giving us slight course corrections."

"When's the earliest we can return for them?"

Jin considered the question. "Not until Ryugu's next close approach in 2042."

"Twenty forty-two! That means over eight years in space for them both."

"It is a lot of rads."

Tighe crawled forward and reached for a food packet. "So let's say we survive and get Earth capture—what then?"

Jin said, "Assuming Earth capture, Ade's plan was to then swing around again to circularize into a low Earth orbit."

"How do we get back to the surface? Fly a reentry?"

Jin shook his head. "We'll have almost no delta-v to select a glide path. We'd most likely land in an ocean—and sink."

Chindarkar added, "It's 2038. There are more people in LEO now. Someone should be able to rescue us in orbit."

Two weeks into their transfer orbit, they lost the Ka-band link to the *Konstantin*. The connection did not return. They were now on their own, with no communication with either Earth or their crewmates back at Ryugu. Tighe wondered what it meant. Was it an equipment failure or had something happened to Abarca and Adisa?

With no physical windows, Tighe instantiated a virtual window in the hull using imagery from cameras on the nose of the ship. Exposed to the Sun as they were, space appeared as a featureless black void. Only the planets were bright enough to be visible in the glare.

Tighe watched as day by day, the bright white disk of the Earth continued to glide in from the left edge of the screen. It eventually resolved into two dots of light: the Earth and the Moon. The bright dot of Mars appeared just above Earth. Jupiter, dead ahead.

Tighe found it impossible to wrap his head around the enormous distances. They'd been traveling at 87,000 kilometers per hour—more than 2 million kilometers per day—for weeks, and the Earth looked the same. The only thing that changed was that it had edged rightward, moving toward the place the *James Caird* was headed.

Behind them, Ryugu had long since disappeared in the vastness of space. Thinking of their lost friends and crewmates only added to the misery of living inside the *Caird*.

By March 28 they were 6 million kilometers and three days away from Earth rendezvous. The Earth and Moon still appeared only as points of light—albeit now a thumbnail's width apart—moving ever into the path of the *James Caird*.

It wasn't until twenty-four hours before their encounter with Earth that Tighe, gazing forward through the virtual viewscreen alongside Jin and Chindarkar, finally could discern the Earth's blue, sunlit side. Chindarkar gripped Tighe's shoulder. It was no longer just a white dot. Now 2.3 million kilometers away, the Earth was finally a crescent. However, the Moon, two finger's widths to the left, was still just a point in space.

Jin used the positions of the Earth and Moon to rerun calculations on their trajectory. Since they lost contact with the *Konstantin*, they'd been using star-tracking software for astrogation. However, it was apparent that Adisa's accuracy early on had saved them. They would indeed encounter Earth.

Tighe stared unblinking as, hour by hour, his home world approached.

At 1.1 million kilometers' distance, the Earth was now a sphere, the size of a pebble held at arm's length. The Moon, still only a white light, was now a hand's width to the left. Glancing at his crystal, Tighe could see they were twelve hours from the aerocapture maneuver. After forty days in transit, it hardly seemed possible the final phase would happen so fast.

While Jin reran the aerocapture simulation in his crystal, Tighe and Chindarkar popped thrusters to halt the spin of the *James Caird* and pointed the ship forward.

Now in microgravity again, Jin looked grim as he called Tighe and Chindarkar over. He projected a virtual diagram of the Earth onto their crystal displays. It showed their trajectory, coming in at a nearly flat angle across Earth's atmosphere.

He pointed. "We are gaining more velocity due to the Earth's gravitational pull. My calculations show we will be going 26.8 kilometers per second when we attempt aerocapture."

"Jesus."

Chindarkar did some calculations of her own. "That's about 60,000 miles per hour."

"We must lose at least 14 kilometers per second to achieve Earth capture, and we will only have about 4,000 kilometers of atmosphere to do it in—roughly three minutes in deceleration that could peak at 9 g's—maybe higher. Possibly much more. I cannot say precisely. Earth's atmosphere is too variable."

"Oh my god . . ."

"If we do not burn up and we manage to achieve Earth capture, then we can orbit around and perform more aerobraking maneuvers at perigee to bring our velocity down further." His diagram showed another low swing through Earth's atmosphere. "Then we fire cold-gas thrusters to circularize our orbit." He looked up. "Right now we are 750,000 kilometers out. We should strap in to our seats at 250,000 kilometers. Do you both understand?"

They nodded.

Tighe turned to look out the virtual windows. The Moon was now visible as a tiny sphere, with a nightside and dayside. The Earth lay dead ahead, pea-sized.

In the following hours it grew.

At 500,000 kilometers from Earth, the Moon passed left beyond the edge of the forward screen. They were now six hours out.

Three hours later they pulled on their blue flight suits.

Chindarkar hugged Tighe. "Good luck, J.T."

"You, too."

She then hugged Jin. "Let's hope the *Caird* can take it."

Tighe gripped Jin's shoulder. "I know if it's possible, you can do it, Han."

Jin nodded grimly.

They then entered the aerocapture vehicle through its aft hatch, sealing it behind them. During the transfer from Ryugu, they had removed two of the five seats and remounted the remaining three to face rearward in order to help them withstand g-forces of deceleration. Tighe took a seat near the rear hatch, while Jin and Chindarkar strapped in alongside each other in middle seats and busied themselves preparing the ship.

Jin instantiated a virtual viewscreen on the stern bulkhead, creating the illusion that they were all still facing forward.

At 250,000 kilometers, the Earth was the size of a grape held in one's outstretched hand. Tighe could hardly believe the sight—a brilliant swirl of blue, white, green, and brown. He half convinced himself he was watching a training simulation.

Jin called out, "Undocking crew module and booster." After a brief pause. "Now."

There was a mild *clunk* sound as bolts disengaged. The ungainly booster stage of the ship was intended to pull away before they entered the atmosphere, and burn up on reentry.

"Let's start our prebreathe."

They all pulled on oxygen masks.

An hour and a half later they were 100,000 kilometers away from the Earth, which appeared the size of a lemon. They all marveled at the lights of Earth's cities glittering on the nightside. They'd been out in deep space for so long that the beauty of their home world brought them to tears. That, and the memory of those who would never witness this sight again.

But now it was becoming clear just how fast they were going. The Earth was visibly increasing in size as they screamed in at a flat angle across its darkened right hemisphere. "We are *really* moving."

Chindarkar said nervously, "How are we doing, Han?"

Jin worked invisible controls. "Five by five."

At 50,000 kilometers out Tighe finally recognized the continents. They were coming in from a shallow angle he hadn't expected—low above darkened

Antarctica, streaking north toward Africa—Johannesburg a recognizable cluster of lights.

Jin called out, "Pressurize your suits and stow oxygen masks."

They all did so, zipping up their helmets and going on radio comms.

"Evacuating ship atmosphere."

The air swirled around them as it vented. It was a hundred pounds less mass to decelerate and its absence would help prevent heat from radiating into the cabin.

As they closed on 25,000 kilometers, things started to happen fast. The surface of the Earth expanded beyond the edges of the viewscreen.

Jin called out, *"I will try to remain conscious for as long as possible. Due to variability in the atmosphere, I might need to make last-minute adjustments."*

Tighe said, "I wish we could help, but you're the only one of us qualified to do this, Han."

"I will do my best." Jin busied himself checking and rechecking systems.

Ten minutes later the Earth started to roll past beneath them. Their speed looked downright alarming at a distance of only 5,000 kilometers.

Jin looked up in surprise. *"The crew module—it failed to detach!"*

The *James Caird* began to yaw slightly from side to side.

Jin grabbed at virtual controls while the Earth loomed. *"The aerocapture software cannot pilot this ship with 15 tons of deadweight on our tail. We will go straight in!"*

Tighe unbuckled his straps and pulled himself toward the rear hatch.

Jin shot a look at him. *"In less than three minutes we will be in the atmosphere."*

"Then don't wait for me!"

Chindarkar looked to Tighe but was immediately forced to turn her attention to the bucking ship.

With the ship depressurized, Tighe pulled himself through the rear hatchway and back into the crew module. The whole cabin shook. The seal between the compartments shifted slightly up, then slightly right, then left. In the gap between the sections, Tighe caught glimpses of the Earth's surface. Even without atmosphere, he could feel the metal twisting and vibrating.

He grabbed a meter-long socket wrench from a bracket on the wall and then pulled himself to the upper crew module hatch. After opening the hatchway he felt something like a strong breeze whipping past the ship. They were going so fast that even the sparse molecules out here produced noticeable drag.

Tighe struggled out on top of the crew module, entering what seemed like a 30-kilometer-per-hour wind. For a moment he felt vertigo as the span of all of Earth stretched out and away below the ship—the surface closing fast. His crystal indicated they were nearing 3,000 kilometers' altitude, and he pulled himself forward toward the link between the stages. He strained against the force of a rarified slipstream.

The crew module bucked as he climbed forward and on top of the *James Caird*'s aerodynamic surface. The sleek skin of the craft was difficult to hold on to, so Tighe reached down into the gap between the sections and quickly clipped his tether into a stern eyebolt. He withdrew his gloved hand before it could be crushed by the writhing crew module—and then he spotted what was holding the sections together.

A single construction bracket.

One of the thousand punch-list items they hadn't had time to complete. The whole rear framework twisted and shook as Tighe moved to it and jammed the wrench between it and the surface of the ship. It didn't take much leverage.

As the bracket tore free, the entire aft section of the ship suddenly tumbled away, opening a cavernous view of the Earth, into which Tighe rolled as the slipstream swept him off the *James Caird*'s aerodynamic skin.

He was jerked to a stop by the tether, and the wrench fell from his hands. He yawed back and forth over a couple-thousand-kilometer drop to a swirl of ocean and clouds below. If the atmosphere hadn't been so rarified, he'd already be dead.

"That's it, J.T.!"

He twisted around to see Chindarkar braced in the rear hatchway. Tighe grabbed the tether and started climbing.

She started pulling on the tether and swiftly hauled him in. As he climbed inside and floated past her, she sealed the hatchway behind them.

The aerocapture ship had begun to vibrate again.

Jin shouted, *"Buckle up! This is going to get rough!"*

Tighe and Chindarkar both strapped in to their seats as the ship started to lurch and shudder.

Tighe looked up at the virtual windscreen again, and he caught his breath at the sight.

Jin shouted, *"We are going in!"*

At just a thousand kilometers in altitude, the Earth filled half the screen. The city lights looked beautiful but surreal as the *James Caird* soared across the surface.

Fifteen seconds later, as they streaked downward through 450 kilometers' altitude, Tighe remembered this was the orbit of the Hotel LEO. The entire ship shuddered now. The forward screen started to take on a reddish glow, and a sound like a freight train rose.

Tighe clenched his fists as they were all smashed into their seat backs.

"This is it!"

The entire viewscreen took on an orange glow as they streaked across Antarctica. The g-forces began to build. Tighe thought he was ready, but it quickly went from 2 g's to 3, and rapidly headed toward 4.

Tighe wanted to shout, but he couldn't even draw breath.

The screen glowed from orange to blue as they approached the southern coast of Africa. The lights of Johannesburg glittered ahead.

The cabin heated up. Smoke seeped in from the vents and everything jolted and thrummed.

Tighe checked their velocity. They were still going 25 kilometers per second. Within a minute they were moving across the Sahara desert. The coast of the Mediterranean loomed ahead in darkness—the lights of scores of cities below them.

The ship was now jolting in ways that would have torn any normal spacecraft apart. Tighe's body strained against the seat straps.

Seven g's now.

Studying the readout, Jin drove the ship even deeper into the atmosphere—until its nose turned white-hot.

Late in the evening Lukas Rochat stood at a bar in one of the many outdoor cafés on the Place Guillaume, a broad cobblestone square in the heart of Luxembourg City's historic center. He unbuttoned his Ermenegildo Zegna jacket and took out his encrypted phone to check messages as the buzz of nearby conversation soothed him.

He had been expecting word by now. Something. Anything.

Suddenly people around him shouted and pointed skyward. Rochat looked up to see a bright light racing toward them in the night sky. Hundreds of people in the square now oohed and pointed upward. Rochat stepped out into the open and watched the object streaking in, growing in brilliance until finally he had to shield his eyes against its white-hot light.

Then the night turned into day above the city—the entire sky blue with white clouds as an artificial sun arced over the people and streets below, trailing sonic booms that rattled windows and set off car alarms.

It was then Rochat realized, and he raised his arms and shouted, "Yes!"

Only he knew what it was—*who it was.* He smiled and ran out into the square, shouting and following the arc of the brilliant light as it traversed the heavens.

He turned to the crowd, laughing and shouting with joy. "Yes! We have done it! We have done it!"

The *James Caird* shuddered and jolted for another two solid minutes, the cabin temperature rising all the while. The cabin filled with smoke. Tighe wasn't certain whether he'd passed out. He couldn't see anything except the alarm messages streaming past in his crystal display. Computers were failing. Pumps were failing. Temperature was spiking. It was hot enough that he felt like he was sitting on the lid of a meat smoker.

Just as the cabin temperature reached 110 degrees Celsius, the vibrations slowed—and then suddenly ceased. The ship was heading out again into deep space—glowing like a hot coal.

Tighe shouted, "Jin! Did we do it?" His crystal suddenly went dead as the ship's computer systems failed. And then the power died.

The ship started to slowly tumble. Tighe felt around his seat in the blinding smoke and soon found a gloved hand—which squeezed his own. It then felt around his chest, searching for something.

Suddenly Tighe heard Chindarkar's voice in his ear.

". . . gency radio. Don't you remember anything from your training?"

Tighe embraced her. "Are you okay?"

"Yes. Jin? Are you okay?"

Jin's voice sounded exhausted. *"Have I killed us?"*

Tighe laughed and looked around. "No, but if that didn't achieve Earth capture, then I don't know what could."

Suddenly the smoke began to clear and lights came on.

Chindarkar said, *"Emergency power. I'm purging the smoke and repressurizing."*

Tighe's crystal flickered back to life. Half his screen consisted of ship alarm codes. Now that the smoke had cleared he could see his crewmates again. He and Chindarkar unbuckled and floated over toward Jin.

"Did we achieve capture?"

Jin brought up a holographic display of their projected path. It showed a glowing red line arcing past the Earth. It was clear that their aerobraking had radically warped their trajectory, curving it.

But the red line kept bending around the Earth as their position was updated moment to moment. They all watched the red line curving, curving.

"Come on, baby! Do it!"

Almost closing the loop, the red line instead hooked around the Earth and proceeded back into deep space.

Jin cursed under his breath and started stabbing at a virtual UI. *"We have very little gas."*

Thrusters popped outside, and the ship lurched. They all glided into the hull wall.

Tighe pushed off. "Hot! Hot!"

They all rotated to place their boots on the hull and watched transfixed as the holographic display showed the red line resume its bending as Jin rode the forward thrusters—slowing them ever so slightly.

"C'mon . . . c'mon, baby!"

The red line kept curving around the globe—until it finally connected into an eccentric circle whose apogee was halfway to the Moon. The word *Aerocapture* appeared in the display.

"Yes!"

In microgravity, they all exchanged high-fives and were hurled back against the cabin walls.

They then assessed the damage. The *Caird* was a tough ship, but it smelled of burnt plastics and ozone, even through their pressurized suits. Or maybe that was the suits themselves.

Chindarkar scrolled through alert codes. *"I hope you like your toast dark."* She tapped at virtual controls. *"EHD cooler back online. What's our ETA for another pass, Han?"*

Jin studied his display. *"Two days. One day to apoapsis, then another day to loop back to periapsis."*

"And then an aerobrake?"

He nodded and laughed. *"This one will be a lot more gentle. I promise. Until then, we should try to get some sleep."*

Two days later, Tighe watched as the viewscreen again glowed in a reddish light, but it was far less intense this time. So were the vibrations of the ship. He felt in capable hands with Jin at the helm. Within thirty minutes they again rose from the surface of the Earth, and the shuddering of the ship ceased. Nothing was smoking either.

Jin unclenched visibly. *"Prepare to circularize orbit."*

Chindarkar smiled. *"Roger that."*

The *James Caird* arced across the dayside of Earth. They all stared in amazement. The view was gorgeous. Their ship glided silently above Asia, headed toward the Pacific coast at an altitude of 500 kilometers.

Jin fired the thrusters to slightly accelerate them.

Tighe was gently pressed into his seat for a moment.

Chindarkar laughed and placed an affectionate hand on the ship's hull. *"Remind me that we owe the mission control design team a thank-you letter."*

Jin cut the thrusters. He smiled. *"Orbit circularized. We are now in a stable, low Earth orbit."*

The three of them gripped gloved hands and exchanged grateful—but then suddenly mournful—expressions. It took several moments to contemplate the severity of all they'd been through. The years. Their dead and stranded crewmates.

After a minute or so, Tighe activated the ship's radio. "If we're going to help Isabel and Ade, we still need to get ourselves rescued." He spoke into the emergency frequency. "Mayday, mayday. This is the crew of the mining ship *Konstantin*. Call sign KSTN. In circular orbit at an altitude of 500 kilometers, 38-degree inclination. In need of immediate rescue. Repeat. Mayday, mayday. This is the crew of the mining ship *Konstantin*..."

Tighe repeated the broadcasts for several minutes, listening after each transmission. Theoretically the 1967 UN Agreement on the Rescue of Astronauts meant that any vessel nearby would be obligated to render aid. However, the agreement had never been tested.

Finally, a clear male voice came in over the radio. "Konstantin, Konstantin, *this is Poker Flat Tracking Station. What is your transponder ID, over?*"

A palpable relief spread through them at receiving a response. Tighe smiled and keyed the mic. "Poker Flat, we have no transponder, over."

"Konstantin, *what is your hull number?*"

Tighe immediately replied. "Poker Flat, we have no hull number. You have our trajectory and altitude. Ground-tracking stations can confirm our orbit. We are disabled and in need of immediate rescue. Over."

"Konstantin *crew, you are not authorized for your current orbit. Repeat, you are not authorized for your current orbit.*"

Tighe laughed. "Well then come and arrest us! But for god's sake, send somebody."

The first voice said, *"What orbit did you descend from?"*

"From deep space. Is there any nearby craft that can render aid?"

There were several seconds of static. Finally, another voice spoke in a Chinese accent. "Konstantin *crew, this is Tiangong-4. We are 300 kilometers downrange of your present position and have you on radar. We can attempt rescue. How many are you?*"

Tighe's smile faded. He sighed as he said, "We are three. Only three."

It took more than thirty-six hours, but a Chinese-flagged space capsule gained on the *James Caird* in orbit. It looked like a newer, larger craft—but it was nowhere near the size or sleekness of the *James Caird*.

Jin handled the radio communications, and finally the capsule docked at their starboard emergency hatch.

Chindarkar said, "Guess we'll see if the dock works."

Their visitors waited for several minutes to test that they had a good dock seal and finally the vessel hatches were opened. Two taikonauts glided inside the *Caird* with puzzled expressions.

Tighe met them, smiling. He shook their hands. It was the first time he'd seen a new face in more than four years. "You have no idea how great it is to see you guys."

They wrinkled their noses as they smelled the smoke and burnt materials.

The lead one said, "You had a fire."

His partner said, "Your entire hull is scorched black."

"Yeah, we were going a bit fast."

The lead one locked eyes with Jin and the expressions on both of their faces made it clear they knew each other. The second taikonaut appeared stunned as well—as though he'd seen a ghost.

"Jin Hua Han."

Jin nodded. "Fei Liwei."

"But you . . ." The taikonauts exchanged shocked looks.

"You were lost, training in low Earth orbit."

"I wouldn't say I was lost."

"I . . . I don't understand."

The taikonauts looked warily at Tighe and now Chindarkar as she floated over to them.

The lead one looked around at the interior of the strange ship. "What is this vessel? There is no record of it."

One of them rapped the hull wall with his knuckles. It sounded solid. "Is this . . . *steel?*"

Tighe nodded. "Cobalt steel."

Chindarkar added, "No point in skimping."

A voice came in over the radio. "*Konstantin crew. Konstantin crew. This is Redu Tracking Station. We have someone on the line who says he needs to speak with you. Over.*"

Tighe answered. "This is *Konstantin* crew. Who is it? Over."

"*He says he's your lawyer.*"

CHAPTER 49

Karagandy

The Hotel LEO was the nearest vessel able to accommodate three surprise guests. It took nearly twenty-four hours, but James Tighe, Jin Han, and Priya Chindarkar were transferred to the hotel in the taikonauts' capsule.

Entering the airlock brought back bittersweet memories, and the place was now bustling with commercial astronaut trainees, working toward their orbital operations certificates. Kaspar Eld, the gregarious first manager, had since moved on, replaced by a more straitlaced corporate type. The hotel had apparently pivoted to cater exclusively to business travelers.

The presence of Chindarkar, Jin, and Tighe at the Hotel LEO—as well as their transportation there—had been paid for by a Swiss holding company. Nathan Joyce's former lawyer, Lukas Rochat, had advised the three returned crew members of the *Konstantin* not to speak with anyone—especially government officials. Given the traumatic nature of their return, this suited them fine.

There was considerable curiosity about them among the students. Catching up on Earth news, Tighe and his companions were amused at coverage of an "asteroid" that had reportedly burned up in Earth's atmosphere a few days before their arrival—lighting up the skies above Europe and North Africa. Officially, the crew of the *Konstantin still* did not seem to exist.

However, a stack of messages began to pile up for them—from the FAA, NASA, ESA, and others. They ignored these and instead took solace in one another's company, staring through the hotel's windows at the Earth rolling by below—at the indescribable beauty of life.

Finally, on the third day, an old Soyuz spacecraft arrived. It came for them alone—no doubt at a cost well above that of one of Macy's or Burkett's reusable rocket launches. It was marked by the logo of a commercial spin-off of Roscosmos—now reportedly running at a loss to maintain national prestige. The Russians must have been happy for the business. Whatever the reason, Tighe was glad to see the capsule.

Jin warned them that it would be a tight fit. And he wasn't wrong.

As they roared out of the mesosphere, the capsule bucking, Tighe looked over at Jin, who as a trained taikonaut had performed a hundred simulated Soyuz reentries and was commanding the capsule. Jin looked somber. A glance at Chindarkar showed she felt the same. Strangely, Tighe didn't experience the slightest anxiety about their descent—even though the capsule shook violently and an orange glow appeared outside the window while he was smashed into his seat by 4 g's. By the time they slowed, the windows were blackened.

The reentry was tame by comparison to the *Caird*'s aerocapture.

There was a *bang*, then a rush of air outside as the Soyuz's drogue parachute deployed—tossing the capsule around crazily against the dragline. Finally the main parachutes deployed, and the descent calmed. After minutes dropping through clear blue sky, the landing rockets fired, and suddenly the Soyuz capsule was on the ground. It rolled slowly onto its side.

Outside the blackened porthole near him, Tighe saw blades of young grass. He smiled at the sight.

The three of them unbuckled their harnesses. Tighe looked at Jin. "Let's do it . . ."

He crawled to the top of the capsule and turned the hatch lugs. With a bit of effort he pulled the hatch door inward, and a fresh breeze swept past him. Tighe laughed and heard startled shouts of joy behind him.

He crawled out on all fours, finally rolling onto flattened grass. He gazed up at a blue sky dotted with cumulonimbus clouds and breathed deeply the air of Earth. It had been years since he'd smelled so much life.

Chindarkar and Jin climbed out, rolling onto their backs in the grass next to him. They, too, gazed up at the sky.

Chindarkar laughed with delight. "It's beautiful!"

Tighe carefully stood up. He was shaky but otherwise able to stand in Earth gravity. Flat grassland spread to the horizon in all directions. They were, he knew, somewhere in the Karagandy region of Kazakhstan.

Back on Earth. Finally. After four and a half years.

The only other time he'd felt this alive was after he'd climbed out of Tian Xing. His emotions now were every bit as conflicted.

The sound of helicopters soon reached his ears. Tighe turned to see a couple of Mi-8 Hips headed their way.

Chindarkar stood shakily next to him, as did Jin.

"Well, here we go."

The three of them linked arms.

Tighe said, "You two are the most important people on Earth to me. I will never forget that."

Jin and Chindarkar nodded.

They turned as the helicopters closed the distance and alighted 20 meters away, the chopper wash flattening the grass even more.

A dozen soldiers disembarked, as did a few civilians. And then Tighe suddenly saw a face he recognized approaching—Sevastian Yakovlev.

The bearded ex-cosmonaut stormed forward, grinning as he opened his arms. "Welcome to Earth!"

Chindarkar laughed and hugged him. He kissed her on both cheeks.

"It is so good to see you alive!" He turned to Jin. "What a pilot!"

Jin struggled as he got bear-hugged and kissed on both cheeks by Yakovlev as well.

Then Yakovlev turned and gave Tighe the same treatment.

"Goddamn, it's great to see you, Yak."

Yakovlev held up a hand. "I know all is not happiness. But today is *great* day! My friends have returned to Earth."

Tighe then turned around to see Kazakh military people, male and female, examining the capsule. He looked searchingly back toward the choppers. "So, still no Eike?"

Yak grew more somber still. He gripped Tighe's shoulder. The look in the Russian's eyes said it for him. "I could not tell you. Please understand."

Tighe felt the world shift. "No." He knelt back down on the grass. He held his head in his hands. "No."

Yakovlev knelt close. "She had an accident in the Dolomites. A year and a half ago. I am sorry, J.T. They said it was instant."

Tighe wrapped his head in his hands. "No."

Chindarkar and Jin came over to Tighe and each placed a hand on his shoulder. Tighe gripped Chindarkar's hand. He couldn't help but recall Dahl's worries about the *Konstantin*. The variables were known, she had said.

Tighe felt waves of grief—but also joy at being alive—washing over him all at once. He was confounded.

Several land vehicles approached, and in a few minutes an armored car pulled almost right up to the Soyuz capsule. A Kazakh customs officer in a peaked hat got out as the side door opened. He loomed over Tighe and said in English, "Travel documents, please."

Tighe looked up. "Yes. Of course . . ." He dug into his flight suit pockets and handed over his US passport and FAA launch paperwork.

Jin and Chindarkar handed over their Chinese and Indian passports and launch paperwork as well.

The official examined the documents, stopping first at Tighe's. He frowned. "This is error. NASA officials have recorded incorrect launch and return dates."

Tighe sighed. "Yeah, about that . . ."

Yakovlev stepped in, sweet-talking the official in Russian, but they quickly started bickering. A glance at Jin's launch paperwork made things worse.

"This will need to be taken to my superiors."

Tighe unzipped his flight suit again, and after a moment he withdrew a jagged, uncut diamond the size of a throat lozenge. "Maybe we can take care of it here. Will this cover our fine?"

The official made a doubtful expression.

Tighe placed the diamond in the man's hand.

The official held it up to the sunlight, then pushed his hat back skeptically. Turning away, he swept the stone across the bulletproof side window of his armored car.

It left a deep scratch.

The official then turned to Tighe, smiled broadly, and held out his arms. "Welcome to Kazakhstan!" He then embraced Tighe and kissed him on both cheeks.

CHAPTER 50

Earthlings

JUNE 20, 2038

J in Han exited Terminal 3 of Beijing Capital International Airport and was enveloped by a beautiful spring day. Dressed in a suit jacket and open-collar shirt, recently tailored for him in Hong Kong, he relished the air and the life all around him as he crossed the wide sidewalk toward the taxi stand. Crowds of travelers moved around him. He couldn't help a smile. To be alive. To have purpose. To have limitless horizons. These were now his.

Suddenly he slowed to a stop.

Waiting there at the curb was his father's Mercedes limousine, with black SUVs ahead and behind. Jin's father stood in his path on the sidewalk in his usual pinstripe suit, a security detail around him. And yet something was different.

Jin felt no fear.

He and his father stared at each other for several moments.

Then Jin proceeded to walk past.

His father fell to his knees, hands together and head bowed. "I did not know. You must believe me."

Jin stared for a moment more and then said, "It hardly matters, Father." He continued walking, leaving his father on the sidewalk as Jin hailed a taxi.

Erika Lisowski stood alone in the oppressive heat and humidity of a Florida afternoon, the sun beating down on her. The memorial park in suburban Rockledge was not, itself, memorable—just a sweeping lawn dotted with plaques, carnations in cellophane, and the occasional tiny, faded American flag.

She knelt next to a humble granite marker set in the grass. It bore the inscription:

GERARD ZYGMUNT LISOWSKI

1942–2034

APOLLO PROGRAM ENGINEER

Tears filled her eyes, but she quickly wiped them away. She brushed aside grass clippings from the marker and placed her palm on the cool stone.

More than anything, she wanted to be a little girl again, sitting at the kitchen table, listening to this kind genius teach her about the universe. Or to be able, at this moment, to lean close to this kindred spirit and whisper in his ear, *We did it, Dziadek. We finally did it.*

James Tighe and Priya Chindarkar walked through the carpeted hallways of a luxurious hotel, past oak panels and beneath large crystal chandeliers. The hotel was an ivy-strewn redbrick landmark not far out of Sheboygan, Wisconsin—one that Tighe had known of since childhood but had never entered.

Today he wore a navy blue suit with a tie—the first he'd worn in decades. Chindarkar looked beautiful in an off-the-shoulder gray chiffon gown and heels, sans jewelry.

They entered the hotel's Grand Hall of the Great Lakes ballroom, where a sign on an easel at the entrance proclaimed: "Vinter Reception." Glancing around, Tighe saw there were easily four hundred people in the place, but few he recognized.

Chindarkar motioned for them to keep walking as they looked for their names on place settings. "I'm still not used to seeing so many people."

"I was never used to it."

Eventually Tighe found his name on a half-empty table at the very rear of the ballroom. The far side of the large round table was occupied by a portly middle-aged man in a plaid suit and two teenagers consumed with their phones.

Chindarkar picked up her name tag and read it aloud. "'James Tighe plus-one.' Don't expect me to answer to that."

"Sorry. I gave them your name."

She studied the ballroom. "Any farther back and you'd be beyond your family's gravitational influence."

"Very funny. Have a seat."

Chindarkar smiled at the middle-aged man across from her. "It was a lovely ceremony, wasn't it?"

The man smiled, shook her hand. "Did you hear about this UN treaty on genetic modification? It's all over the news."

Confused, she shook her head. "No, we've been away."

"What kind of world are we living in these days?"

"I'm sure I don't know."

Someone clanged a spoon against a glass, and others joined in.

Tighe looked toward the front of the room. There, the groom—his step-nephew Morgan Vinter—smiled as he kissed his new bride. They stood near a table, speaking with Tighe's mother. Next to her was Tighe's stepsister, Jillian Beris, looking slim and sophisticated. Older than Tighe, she was now a partner at a Milwaukee law firm. Tighe's mother laughed, clearly reveling in the event.

Tighe and Chindarkar had met the bride, Helen, for the first time after the ceremony, and he knew nothing about her—except that she was friendly and kind enough to invite Tighe to her wedding.

Chindarkar leaned in. "They make a lovely couple."

"Yes, they do."

All around, Tighe family members abounded. People shook hands, glad to see one another. Children in suits and dresses ran around.

Chindarkar studied the room.

At the table next to them two young boys, one Asian and one Caucasian, were playing with what appeared to be astronaut action figures. Chindarkar smiled and leaned toward them. "Spacemen, eh?"

The Caucasian boy held up his action figure. "We're landing on Mars."

Chindarkar nodded. "I hear that's coming up soon."

They both nodded.

The Asian boy said, "I'm going to live on Mars."

"No, I am!" the other one said.

Chindarkar looked to Tighe. "You hear that?"

Tighe chuckled. "Joyce would be turning in his grave."

He noticed one of the men at the table look toward Tighe and whisper to his wife. The woman leaned down to the two boys. "Mason, Trevor, play over here. Stop bothering those people."

Chindarkar turned back toward Tighe and raised her eyebrows.

"You want a drink?"

"Definitely. White wine, please."

"Be right back." Tighe went to the bar, moving through distant relations and other strangers. He wasn't even sure why he was here—except for the emotion he'd felt when he'd learned he'd been invited.

After a few minutes in line, Tighe returned with a scotch and a glass of Chardonnay—only to see his brother-in-law, Ted Vinter, in a tuxedo, thicker and older than he remembered, and sitting next to Chindarkar.

Vinter turned to him as Tighe handed Chindarkar her Chardonnay.

"There he is." Vinter extended his hand. "Good to finally see you again, Jim."

Tighe gestured to Vinter. "Priya, this is Ted, my brother-in-law."

"Father of the groom."

"Yes. Ted, this is Priya Chindarkar."

"A pleasure." He shook Chindarkar's hand.

"It was a lovely wedding."

"Thank you. It better have been for what it cost." Perfunctory greetings out of the way, he grimaced. "This is awkward, Jim. But your mother has asked that I speak to you."

"What about?" Tighe sat.

"This is a special day for us, and your mother wants to avoid unnecessary drama."

"Unnecessary drama."

Vinter sighed. "Right, we all know you 'went away' for five years, and suddenly you seem to have some money. The family doesn't want any part of whatever you're caught up in—especially today. Your mother wants you to stay clear of the bride and groom."

"They're the ones who invited me."

"They were raised to be polite. No one thought you would attend. Given the circumstances, it would have been better not to accept the invitation."

Chindarkar narrowed her eyes at Vinter.

Vinter held up his hands. "I just want what's best for everyone."

Chindarkar leaned in. "You have no idea—"

He side-eyed her. "No, I don't." He turned to Tighe. "So let me ask; where have you been, Jim? Have you really been crawling around in a cave for five years? Couldn't write? Couldn't call?"

Tighe said flatly, "Priya and I traveled to the far side of the Sun to mine an asteroid."

Vinter nodded. "Great. I see you haven't changed. How can we trust you when you won't be honest with us? I wish you'd finally grow up." He stood.

Tighe grabbed Vinter's sleeve. "Wait." He took an envelope out of his jacket and handed it to Vinter. "This is for Morgan—since I won't be talking to him."

Vinter took the envelope. "By the way, you still owe *me* money."

Chindarkar watched him go, her mouth open. "Oh my god. What an asshole." She turned to Tighe. "But I think I understand you a little better now."

Tighe took a sip of his scotch. "Good. Maybe you can explain me to me."

"You're the black sheep of your family." She smiled and put her arm around him. "So am I."

He laughed lightly. "You want to get some air?"

She nodded vigorously. "Please."

Tighe and Chindarkar stood on a terrace next to a vine-strewn railing in the evening air, sharing his scotch. The night was beautiful, with crickets sounding all around them.

Chindarkar took a deep breath. "This is what I missed most about Earth—living things everywhere." She turned to Tighe.

"Thanks for coming with me, Priya." Tighe put his arm around her, and they both looked up at the Moon. He couldn't help but feel a pang of guilt. They had friends out there, and it weighed on his mind.

His phone warbled.

Chindarkar looked at him.

"Only five people on Earth have this number." He pulled the phone out of his jacket and frowned. He answered on the third ring. "Lukas?"

"J.T., did I catch you at a bad time?"

"No. It's fine. Priya's here with me. Let me put you on speakerphone . . ." He tapped the screen and placed his phone on the thick stone railing. "Can you hear us?"

"Yes. I have news—about the Konstantin."

Tighe and Chindarkar leaned close.

"The new owners apparently sent a ship and a crew to retake control of the Konstantin. Their vessel arrived a few weeks after yours left."

Chindarkar grabbed Tighe's shoulder. He felt his own heart sink. "Jesus. What happened?"

"We don't know, but we do know the new crew arrived safely—and that the owners have since lost contact with them. We lost our own link to the laser transmitter, too."

"So we lost contact with Isabel and Ade?"

"Unfortunately, yes."

Tighe and Chindarkar looked at each other.

"If we are to help them, we need resources. Toward that end, I came to a preliminary deal with a new group of investors—to establish our own asteroid-mining venture. The three of you, after all, know the trajectory of thousands of tons of valuable resources high above Earth's gravity well."

"You mean the eight of us—the others get their full share."

"As you wish. I've discussed this opportunity with Han, and he's on board. All that's needed is both of your approvals to proceed."

Chindarkar asked, "What sort of deal, Lukas?"

"The outside investors would have a minority stake—while we . . . nine . . . would hold a majority share. I hope my participation is not a problem."

"We could use a good space lawyer on the team."

Chindarkar gripped Tighe's arm. "This would help Dave's daughters. And we could rescue Ade and Isabel."

Tighe nodded. "What's the plan, Lukas?"

"We would use the mined resources coming back in the next year to set up the first cislunar commodity exchange in a lunar DRO. And to invest in other startup space enterprises—for example, one capable of building you a new ship."

Tighe narrowed his eyes. "What about Joyce's creditors—aren't they going to come after us?"

"*The geostrategic nature of those materials you harvested buys a lot of forgiveness. And friends. It's like Nathan Joyce once told me: in space, possession is 99.99999 percent of the law.*"

Chindarkar said, "Lukas, what about Nicole, Dave, and Amy? The Ryugu expedition was historic. Is the world really just going to pretend this never happened?"

"*Priya, you might be surprised how many powerful people already know. And more people will know every day. In fact, your expertise will be in much demand.*"

Tighe and Chindarkar looked at each other.

"*So are we in business together? I'm telling you, asteroid mining is the future.*"

Tighe studied Chindarkar's face.

She nodded.

Tighe spoke into the phone without turning his eyes from her. "Count us in."

Further Reading

You can learn more about the science, technologies, and themes explored in *Delta-v* by visiting www.daniel-suarez.com or through the following sources:

The Age of Reconnaissance: Discovery, Exploration, and Settlement, 1450 to 1650 by J.H. Parry (University of California Press)

Asteroid Mining 101: Wealth for the New Space Economy by John S. Lewis (Deep Space Industries)

An Astronaut's Guide to Life on Earth: What Going to Space Taught Me About Ingenuity, Determination, and Being Prepared for Anything by Colonel Chris Hadfield (Little, Brown and Company)

The Darkness Beckons: The History and Development of Cave Diving by Martyn Farr (Vertebrate Publishing)

Electrostatic Phenomena on Planetary Surfaces by Carlos I. Calle (Morgan & Claypool Publishers)

Federal Aviation Regulations / Aeronautical Information Manual 2017 by FAA Aviation Supplies and Academics

The Long Space Age: The Economic Origins of Space Exploration from Colonial America to the Cold War by Alexander MacDonald (Yale University Press)

Money As Debt by Paul Grignon (www.moneyasdebt.net)

Packing for Mars: The Curious Science of Life in the Void by Mary Roach (W. W. Norton & Company)

Selected Works of Konstantin E. Tsiolkovsky by Konstantin E. Tsiolkovsky (University Press of the Pacific)

Space Chronicles: Facing the Ultimate Frontier by Neil deGrasse Tyson
    (W. W. Norton & Company)

Space Resources: Breaking the Bonds of Earth by John S. Lewis and Ruth A.
    Lewis (Columbia University Press)

Space Warfare in the 21st Century: Arming the Heavens By Joan Johnson-
    Freese (Routledge)

The asteroid mining ship *Konstantin*, spun up and en route to Ryugu. Note the four Honey Bee optical mining robots docked aft of the Central Hab. *(Ship design by Daniel Suarez. Illustration by Anthony Longman.)*

Honey Bee optical mining robot with twin 15-meter thin film parabolic reflectors. *(APIS™ and Honey Bee™ are registered trademarks of TransAstra Corporation. Image reproduced with permission of TransAstra Corporation. Illustration by Anthony Longman.)*

Orthographic view of the Mule utility spacecraft with human figure for scale. Note running boards and docking port. *(Ship design by Daniel Suarez. Illustration by Anthony Longman.)*

Robotic return tugs (from bottom to top): the Nicole Clarke, the David Morra, and the Amy Tsukada. *(Ship design by Daniel Suarez. Illustration by Anthony Longman.)*

Acknowledgments

Writing *Delta-v* has been an extraordinary journey. Along the way, innumerable people guided and assisted me—experts in many fields who shared their time and knowledge to help root this fictional narrative in reality.

My profound thanks to Alexander MacDonald, senior economic adviser at NASA headquarters, who provided key insights on the near future of spaceflight and advice on an early draft of this book. (And although he at one point had the same NASA title as my fictional character Erika Lisowski, this is entirely coincidental.)

Likewise, I'm grateful for the assistance of my good friend, NASA physicist, and part-time rock climber Eric Burt for patiently wading through the 174,000-word first draft of this book (sorry, Eric), offering comments and answering many questions, as well as writing software to confirm orbital trajectories and calculate potential Earth aerobraking maneuvers—not to mention sharing his knowledge of climbing knots and conversational French. (Best wishes on the real-world launch of Eric's own team's Deep Space Atomic Clock in 2019.)

Thanks as well to Pete Worden, former director of NASA's Ames Research Center, for clueing me in to the presence and significance of perchlorates on the surface of Mars.

My sincere thanks also to a certain real-world NewSpace titan who was gracious enough to meet with me and answer my research questions despite his hectic schedule.

Heartfelt thanks to Mark Stover, my close friend since childhood and veteran of numerous extreme caving expeditions, for helping me grok the culture and mind-set of cave explorers. I would not have been able to occupy the skin of my protagonist without those insights.

I'm grateful also to Joel Sercel, CEO and founder of asteroid mining company TransAstra, for taking the time to answer my questions and for sharing technical details of his proposed APIS™ optical asteroid mining system—components of which are already undergoing Earth-bound tests.

Arigatou gozaimashita, Dr. Makoto Yoshikawa and the entire Hayabusa2 team at the Japanese Aerospace Exploration Agency (JAXA). They *literally* brought the asteroid Ryugu into focus for the first time even as I wrote this book and also took the time to answer my questions. I look forward to the many discoveries the H2 team will make in 2019 and beyond.

Thanks as well to Julie Bellerose of NASA's Outer Planet Navigation Group at the Jet Propulsion Lab and veteran of the legendary Cassini mission team, for kindly acting as my liaison to JAXA's Hayabusa2 mission, and also providing critical insights on the electrostatic environment of airless planetary bodies, regolith densities, and more.

My gratitude to Cyrus Foster who, during his time at NASA's Ames Research Center, developed the Trajectory Browser—an online tool that helped me identify the key spacecraft trajectories used throughout this story.

My thanks as well to the many NASA engineers and scientists who conceived of and designed the canceled or unfunded projects depicted in this book, from the Asteroid Redirect Mission (which became my fictional Asteroid Retrieval System), the X-33 VentureStar, and others. Good ideas never die—they evolve.

Thanks also to the following students of the Department of Aerospace Engineering at the University of Maryland circa 2001: Matthew Ashmore, Daniel Barkmeyer, Laurie Daddino, Sarah Delorme, Dominic DePasquale, Joshua Ellithorpe, Jessica Garzon, Jacob Haddon, Emmie Helms, Raquel Jarabek, Jeffrey Jensen, Steve Keyton, Aurora Labador, Joshua Lyons, Bruce Macomber Jr., Aaron Nguyen, Larry O'Dell, Brian Ross, Cristin Sawin, Matthew Scully, Eric Simon, Kevin Stefanik, Daniel Sutermeister, and Bruce Wang, plus their faculty advisers, Dr. David Akin and Dr. Mary Bowden—whose proposal at the turn of this century for "Clarke Station: An Artificial Gravity Space Station at the Earth-Moon L1 Point" became the inspiration for the design of the *Konstantin* mining spacecraft in this book, albeit in a significantly modified and expanded form. The concept of an a-grav research station in lunar orbit is more relevant now than ever.

My sincere appreciation to Dr. John S. Lewis, author and professor emeritus of planetary science at the University of Arizona, for his scholarship on all things asteroid mining.

My thanks also to Don Donzal at the Ethical Hacker Network (www.ethical hacker.net) for helping me figure out what type of operating system a spacecraft like the *Konstantin* would need in 2033—and more importantly for teaching me how to hack into it.

Thanks as well to Seamus Blackley for demonstrating some truly mind-blowing light field technology. And thanks also to Brian Mullins for guiding me there.

I'm grateful to exceptional space-themed YouTubers Isaac Arthur, Curious Droid (Paul Shillito), and Scott Manley for hundreds of hours of informative videos on all things space, which informed this book in countless ways. May their Patreon subscriber count continue to grow.

Tremendous thanks to Vladimir Romanyuk, the brilliant creator of the universe simulator SpaceEngine, which permitted me to view the cosmos from the perspective of my asteroid miners on every single day of their expedition. Likewise, many thanks to the developers of Kerbal Space Program and its realism modders, for helping me play with rockets without paying billions.

My appreciation also to Winchell Chung, whose website, "Atomic Rockets," proved an invaluable resource for even the most esoteric details of space exploration.

I'm grateful also to Hans Zimmer and Thomas Bergersen, whose deeply evocative music inspired me at key moments in the writing of this book.

Thanks as always to my longtime literary agent, Rafe Sagalyn at ICM, and my editor at Dutton, Jessica Renheim, whose advice, patience, and hard work helped to bring this book from conception to reality.

And finally, thanks to the love of my life, Michelle Sites, for a lifetime of adventure.

About the Author

Daniel Suarez is the author of the *New York Times* bestseller *Daemon, Freedom*™, *Kill Decision, Influx,* and *Change Agent.* A former systems consultant to Fortune 1000 companies, he writes high-tech and sci-fi thrillers that focus on technology-driven change. He lives in Los Angeles, California.